Bel Kaufman

LOVE, ETC.

ALLEN LANE

ALLEN LANE
Penguin Books Ltd
536 King's Road
London SW10 0UH

First published in the U.S.A. by Prentice-Hall, Inc., 1979
First published in Great Britain by Allen Lane 1980
Copyright © Bel Kaufman, 1979

The Acknowledgments on page 6 constitute an extension
of this copyright page

ISBN 0 7139 1352 5

Printed in Great Britain by
Richard Clay (The Chaucer Press) Ltd
Bungay, Suffolk

For Sidney Joshua

ACKNOWLEDGMENTS

Grateful acknowledgment is made to the following
for permission to reprint from previously published material:

Pages 35 and 214: From 'Ash Wednesday', *Collected Poems 1901–1962*, by T. S. Eliot.
Reprinted by permission of Harcourt Brace Jovanovich, Inc., and Faber & Faber, Ltd.

Page 94: From 'As We Are So Wonderfully Done With Each Other', *The Collected Poems of
Kenneth Patchen*.
Copyright 1942, © 1968 by Kenneth Patchen.
Reprinted by permission of New Directions and Jonathan Cape Ltd.

Pages 158, 207, 244, and 440: From *The Poems of Dylan Thomas*.
Copyright 1938, 1946, © 1971 by New Directions Publishing Corporation.
Reprinted by permission of New Directions, and for the United Kingdom, by permission
of J. M. Dent & Sons Ltd, publishers and trustees for the copyrights of Dylan Thomas.

Page 214–15: From 'Trance', *Selected Poems*, by Stephen Spender.
Copyright © 1947 by Stephen Spender.
Reprinted by permission of Random House, Inc.

Page 106: From 'Her Triumph', *Collected Poems*, by William Butler Yeats.
Reprinted with permission of Macmillan.
Copyright 1933 by Macmillan Publishing Co., Inc., renewed 1961 by Bertha Georgie Yeats.

Page 176: From 'The Pity of Love', *Collected Poems*, by William Butler Yeats.
Reprinted with permission of Macmillan.
Copyright 1906 by Macmillan Publishing Co., Inc., renewed 1934 by William Butler Yeats.

From the following selections by Robert Graves, reprinted by permission of Curtis Brown Ltd:
Page 59: 'The Portrait', Doubleday & Company; © 1955 by Robert Graves.
Page 130: 'Not to Sleep', Cassell & Co. Ltd; © 1964 by Robert Graves.
Page 200: 'Despite and Still', Cassell & Co. Ltd; © 1945 by Robert Graves.
Page 207: 'Whole Love', Cassell & Co. Ltd; © 1965 by Robert Graves.
Page 236: 'In Time', Cassell & Co. Ltd; © 1964 by Robert Graves.
Page 344: 'The Sharp Ridge', Cassell & Co. Ltd; © 1961 by Robert Graves.
Page 392: 'The Winged Heart', Cassell & Co. Ltd; © 1962 by Robert Graves.
Page 403: 'Reader Over My Shoulder', Jonathan Cape Ltd; © 1943 by Robert Graves.

Contents

JESSICA'S 'BOOK'

Prologue

And they lived happily ever after. Well, not exactly. Actually, not at all. As a matter of fact, miserably. To tell the truth, their life together was sheer hell, and their struggles to free themselves from each other were disastrous.

And they lived happily ever after. At least, that is what they were supposed to do. It was promised — by the fairy tales and the ads, and by her mother. All they had to do was get married, and the rest would flow like butter, as Varya would say.

Varya does not go digging in her pocket for a Russian proverb. 'If you cut off your head,' she says, 'don't cry for your hair.' It was no comfort to Jessica, once she had cut off her head — for that's what the divorce had turned out to be: a decapitation. No use crying over spilled hair. She had become a statistic: 50 look 40, considered attractive, seeking mature, sincere Sagittarius interested in culture and permanence. The right Mr Right.

For twenty-five years Jessica had been married to the wrong Mr Right, from the timid wedding to that last day in court, when — but who would believe it? Only fiction could make it credible. Jessica would pretend she invented it. It's only a story.

Their fictional names were Isabel and Edgar, and they lived unhappily ever after. They had wandered off the safe, the beaten path. They were lost in the dark forest, at the mercy of evil creatures whom they had hired for large retainer fees.

'Oo strakha glaza veliki,' says Varya. 'Fear has big eyes.' What was Isabel afraid of? Of making demands, hurting her children, disappointing her mother, and angering her husband, the good gray doctor, the mighty lover of many women. For women patients were his

trade: One tried to commit suicide on the phone. Another threatened to tell Isabel all, and did.

But that is only a story Jessica is writing, a story about Isabel balancing on the tightrope of her marriage.

Jessica's problems are many. How to make the silent, suffering wife sympathetic, the grim, erotomaniacal husband credible? And who is to say who was right, who was wrong; who was sane, who was mad; whose truth to believe? 'On a thief the hat burns,' says Varya. He will give himself away, and justice, long delayed, will triumph.

Maybe not.

Isabel will have to overcome huge obstacles, perform impossible tasks, dare unknown terrors because she cannot ever go back to the beginning, when everything was still possible, to that first, innocent opening: Once upon a time.

LOVE, ETC.

Dear Nina —

You are my solace and my joy, and your letters never fail to delight me. I know how busy you are, being feted and applauded as the celebrated young author of *The Sad Merry-Go-Round,* autographing your book (do you autograph paperbacks too? Or only initial them, in pencil?), and technically advising (whatever that means) your film. So I doubly appreciate your letters and your encouragement of my opus, my onus, my novel of divorce. That short story I wrote about divorce, which got me this contract, was easy enough to do, but the book has become an act of exorcism. It still is difficult, even after all these years, to convert the crazy horror of those days into credible fiction. A novel must be truer than life, and more orderly. But this one is so full of unruly truths and angers bumping into each other, it's hard to mold them into *the* truth for me. And I'm too close to the pain. I can't find the affection with which I wrote my *Children and People.* What a far cry from that little book of children's verses to the bitter hatred in the scenes I am writing for this book!

Your book, dear Nina, is full of compassion for the lost and desperate youngsters you describe. That's one reason it's a best seller. I'm so proud you started it here, in my Fiction Workshop! And even though you have abandoned New York for San Francisco, I'm happy our letters still fly like shuttlecocks across the continent, carrying our news, our friendship, your compulsive puns, and my compulsive verses. With whom else can we share them?

I can understand your inability to climb back into your own skin and start writing again. You're too busy being famous, and that's a pleasant thing to be. I know how much you enjoy your lecture tours and your audiences of teenagers who adore you, and how difficult it is to sit

13

alone at the typewriter: the keys never jump up to applaud. And after the success of your first book –

It isn't easy to surpass or equal
A classic's final chapter with a sequel.
    Like Ibsen's Nora, walking through that door –
    What can you ever do for an encore?

But you still have time. For me, it has been ten long years since *Children and People*, and twelve since my divorce. It's getting later sooner. I can hear the digital clock on my desk dropping its heavy minutes one by one. Plop . . . they go – Plop – plop . . .

You don't have to write anything else, ever, if you don't want to. Your book will live on. As for me, I'm racing the clock towards my December deadline because I can't afford to return the advance. That may be the strongest motivation of all.

And stop talking about a shrink; you don't need one. My ex-Charles was a shrink – the healer turned destroyer – and look what he did to his wife and children! I'm making of Edgar, his prototype in my book, a specialist in the opposite area of the body: a gynecologist.

Shrinks are last straws, but me, I clutch at straws. I see one occasionally about resolving my problems with my book. The other day I called him, only to get an electronic: 'I am presently not in office, but . . .' Seems he was taping a David Susskind show on 'The Writer in the Nuclear Age.' That's me. I guess I'm in good hands.

Do you remember how clear it seemed, in my Fiction Workshop, when I talked about character revealed under stress? Conflicts and alternative choices. Illumination of the human condition. Fictional truth: the fallacy of 'But that's how it really happened.' All my fine words. Easier said than done – and yet, you've done it! The pupil outstripping the teacher. My pride in you is greater than my envy. I loved *The Sad Merry-Go-Round*, as who didn't? And I love you – as who doesn't?

Dear Nina – tell me about all the exciting things happening to you. I keep a scrapbook of your triumphs, did you know? 'Miss Moore's Dizzying Ride' . . . 'Moore in a Merry Whirl' . . . 'Nina Catches the Gold Ring' . . . Compared to yours, mine was a modest success, my small book of verses for children, but I still on occasion meet a child who skips rope to 'A Nickname Is a Quickname,' and that makes me happy. For a while I, too, 'skyrocked,' as one of your young fans put it, but not so high, and briefly, like a somewhat defective firecracker spluttering out before it ignites.

But you can't skip rope to the pain of divorce.

Yours was more recent than mine; you are much younger; for you there were options and freedoms and supportive organizations for singles that were not available in my day. Yet, even in a so-called civilized divorce, the amputation hurts. Tell me if I'm right. And tell me – am I describing, in the story of my fictional Isabel Webb and Edgar Webb, personal pathology of two people caught in the mangler of divorce, or a universal truth? Is it only a matter of degree? Does everyone go through a kind of craziness?

These questions are academic. Most of the people I know in the process of divorce today are the same walking crazies I describe in my book; they must pass through a similar lunacy. I have a friend who has been divorced for three years now, but who calls me periodically with fresh complaints:

> 'What do you think of a man who sends the alimony check three and a half weeks late?'

> 'What do you think of a man who gives his child ptomaine poisoning in a restaurant?'

> 'What do you think of a man who takes his ten-year-old son to his girl friend's apartment, a cheap nightclub singer, and she asks him if he'd like her to be his mother, and the boy bursts into tears?'

15

Another friend is going through all the vacillations and ambivalences I know so well, the obsession with trivia and possessions and money. She was reporting to me something her lawyer mentioned about child support, when I interrupted: 'But you have no children.' – 'I know,' she said, 'but still . . .' After weeks of outrage at her husband's behavior, she called one morning to say tearfully: 'Listen, why are we doing this? I *love* him!'

The men are no saner. One found a cockroach in the kitchen and wrote his wife a formal letter of complaint about it. I think I'll use that in my book. Another changed all the locks in their apartment while his wife was at the A&P shopping for food for their dinner. Another burned his wife's clothes in the incinerator.

A male friend called the other night: 'Would you believe, while I was out of town she sold all our furniture and sat waiting for me in the middle of the living room on two telephone books?'

I know I must try to convert anger into art, but the bitterness creeps in sideways, when I'm not looking.

I think what I need now is a great big wonderful sweeping romantic love affair with some spectacular man who probably doesn't exist outside of my fantasy. Like the Faceless Knight of my adolescent daydreams, the face to be filled in later – by Leslie Howard, by Rupert Brooke, by my high school French teacher. The Champion who would fight my battles. The Prince from a far country. The romantic hero of all those nineteenth-century novels I fed on, who would woo me with exquisite words. Someone like my handsome young father, forever dead, who exists only on a cracked sepia photograph, his left arm protectively embracing his little daughter. If you know anyone who answers that description, send him to me. Must appreciate Poetry, Finer Things of Life, and me.

> Mine has been a life that's cloistered,
> Unacclaimed, unknown, unlovered;

> All my peerless pearls are oystered –
> I've been sadly undiscovered!

It's true. Twenty-five years of marriage, mostly loveless, mostly sexless, mostly wordless. You once called Charles my 'silent partner'! Well, I was silent too. A silent giver, never a receiver. That's what I'm making my Isabel, except that – for dramatic purposes – she's older than I, had been married for twenty-nine years, and was fifty, a rounder number, a more frightening age, when she finally got her divorce in 1966. What does a woman like that do? How does she survive?

There has been a spate of books on divorce in recent years; I read them, but they go in one eye and out the other! (I'm beginning to sound like Varya.) They're either glib or inspirational: shed your husband and find yourself. All that joy and liberation from marriage seems contrived to me. There is no liberation from pain. And severance is pain. Varya, of course, has a Russian proverb. Did I tell you about Varya, the ebullient Russian lady who lives in the building I recently moved to? Remind me to describe her to you. She says: '*Zloba shto lyod* . . . "Malice, like ice, lives until warm." My book and I are waiting to be melted.

But I'm still scared – I mean, scarred – from battles long ago, and too vulnerable to trust any man. So don't bother sending him. Send me instead more glimpses of your life. More samples of 'Dear Miss Moore' letters and more lines from your schizophrenic correspondent.

This has turned out to be a long letter. It's a diversionary tactic, I know; anything to keep me from working on my novel.

> Rhymes are easy, time is shorte,
> Prose has never been my forte . . .

Passion for real poetry is a lonely passion; light verse, which seems to mock it, can be shared. I think if my novel

17

were written in verse, I would have no problem, except –
what rhymes with 'masochist?' – Don't tell me!

Love,
Jess

WEDNESDAY FEBRUARY 1, 1978

What happened to January? Nothing but blank pages, then a sudden entry: 'Nothing new,' followed by more blank pages. What possessed me to write 'Nothing new' in the middle of the empty month? And why do I begin now? Because I was promised a man? Haven't I learned that each time a friend invites me to a dinner party to meet someone 'not so tall, but a widower,' it turns out to be a disappointment, sometimes an affront? I'm expected to be grateful for a man I wouldn't spend five minutes with when I was alive . . . I mean married. Yet when Grace said: 'He's very special: we met him in Florence last month – a fascinating man,' I believed her.

Do I still believe in miracles? Years after mother's death, I hear the echo of her promises, seconded by God. But what did He do for me during the purgatory of my divorce? Where was He that last day in court?

'What was *was*,' says Varya; 'what is *is*.' She's right, as always. What *is* holds no promise of miracles. Unless my book is written by little industrious elves at night while I'm asleep. I should be working on it right now, making Notes to Myself, breathing life into my Isabel, polishing scene at the lawyer's, bedroom scene, courtroom scene. If I don't meet deadline – trouble. $9,600 – all that's left in savings: advance on new book, jingles residuals, Fiction Workshop. Still, head above water. And perhaps my book will be a best seller, like Nina's? No – too much bitterness toward Charles. How I romanticized him, in the beginning! His profession seemed to me the ultimate in caring. How very wrong I was!

Does anyone ever find it – what the poets and the movies describe? Did mother, in the brief years of marriage to my father, too soon dead? Those mustard-colored Russian postcards he used to send her, with his love poems in white ink in his minute handwriting . . .

I was always fascinated by the story of his wooing (lovely, old-fashioned word!) among the moonlit tombstones in the romantic cemetery in Kiev.

(Was I, perhaps, conceived over a grave?)

Dearest Jess,

I'm answering your letter at once. What do you expect, when you tempt me with a word like 'shuttlecock'? But I won't. That kind of pun is not for a lady's ears. Eyes.

About my divorce. It wasn't all that civilized. My husband just picked up and left. Said it was 'middle-life crisis,' though he was only thirty-seven. It wasn't even another woman. Or man. Or so he said. Who ever knows the truth? My theory is – he couldn't take my sudden success. I believe that because he talked a lot about equality of the sexes. (Can you make me a four-line verse on that subject?)

I did say yours was the silent partner in the marriage. The damage he did you was not in words. Mine was *verbal*. Countless taxi drivers, elevator operators, and waiters throughout the city were privy to our quarrels.

The men I date now – I don't know. When I invite them to my home for that little dinner for two, they expect a package deal. As the French say: '*tout compris*': drinks, dinner, bed. If I were vulgar, I'd say they want everything from soup to nuts.

You called it 'amputation' – Right on! Whether you chop off an arm or a toe, it's painful. Mine was a toe. I wasn't married as long as you. Mine didn't screw a patient like you Charles. He went a little crazy about money, that's true. I gave him some bonds – my guilt-edged securities – to pacify him.

The times *are* different. From where I sit, divorce laws in the early sixties seem barbarous. Only ten years between your divorce and mine, yet the very word 'adultery' has become quaintly old-fashioned. Like Hester Prynne's 'A.' That the amount of money allotted by court should be predicated on the degree of sexual faithfulness, that a woman could be left without any means of subsistence if she was 'guilty' of adultery seems absurd today. 'Matrimonial' is another one of those old unhappy words. Only once did I hear it in a pleasurable context: on vacation in Italy, my former husband asked the chambermaid to put two single beds together into a double bed. 'Ah, si, matrimoniale!' she exclaimed, beaming. But in our language, it stands for matrimonial disputes, matrimonial lawyers. They had – you know – a matrimonial. He was – you know – mental.

Of course it's easier now for a single woman to be independent. There are lots of organizations, singles resorts, singles apartments, singles everything. More humane divorce laws. Still – a toe is a toe. When it goes, it hurts. For a while, anyhow.

You say you're racing the clock toward your deadline. But December is miles away. Besides, the clock always wins, hands down. (That was unconscious, which rather alarms me. Unconscious doth make cowards of us all.)

I, too, must get to work on my second book. That's the hard one. The encore problem, which you so neatly summed up in your verse. Guilt. How can anyone be worth all that money? I've become a hot property. Vested interest. The goose that laid the golden egg. They're following me with a basket, hoping I will lay another one. And I don't want to lay an egg. You mention the crazy paranoia of divorce. Success carries its own paranoia on its back. Everyone warns me: 'Read the fine print' . . . 'Wait for a better offer.' At the same time, they expect me to produce another *The Sad Merry*, only bigger and better.

And then, the people. Some of my old friends who have stood by me during my lean years have disappeared, reluctant to seem opportunistic. Foul weather friends, they. I'm surrounded by people I never knew: Lawyers, agents, accountants, brokers, money managers, publicity people, lecture bureau heads, movie scouts, rival publishers. And just people who want to be near me, to touch me, as if success were a fairy powder that rubs off. They like to mention they know me. Several, I hear, claim that I

22

wrote my book in their homes, or with their collaboration. Former acquaintances suddenly write long chummy letters that begin: 'It's been years since . . .'

There are also beautiful letters from good friends and good strangers, and I treasure their words: 'You have given a voice to every cheated youngster . . .' 'Your book is an army with banners . . .' And from the kids themselves. 'Sometimes I feel like throwing myself out, but your book kept me on a even kiel.'

Even with you, dearest Jess, I find myself uneasy repeating these phrases. It's as though I were an impostor who got away with it, but now must show my true colors. I suspect my own success. I suspect my talent. I suspect I'm in trouble. That's why I asked about a shrink. Write me about yours – in prose or verse.

I understand how difficult it is for you, especially after your sunny, tender *Children and People*, to write about your divorce, but I know you can do it. You write funny and you write sad – that's why I think you'll write a good book.

Much love,
Nina

[DIARY]

Midnight.

Tonight – small dinner party at Grace and Henry's. Met the man they produced for me: a Maxwell Marler or Moller. Quite attractive – tall, with a shock of gray hair and a smile that's too brilliant: only the lips smile. Theatrical voice; his accent – British or affected. But amusing; delightful raconteur and mimic.

I think he tried to impress me with his philanthropies, his mysterious past, his travels all over the world on secret, dangerous missions. Speaks several languages, including Russian. Was divorced a couple of years ago after a brief marriage. Had been married once before, as student in Paris, to young girl who ran a pharmacy to support him and who died under tragic circumstances. Can't figure out what he does. Grace and Henry not sure either. Art dealer? Interior designer? Importer?

Grace asked if he had read my *Children and People*. He only nodded.

He kept staring at me, studying me, as if trying to decode a message. His eyes made me uneasy. At one point, he quoted Horace Walpole: 'This world is a comedy to those that think, a tragedy to those that feel.' His way of saying what a feeling man he is? Yet he made a few sharp, caustic comments about people: 'How can an intelligent God believe in man?'

When dessert was served, ice-cream cake, I quoted: 'The only Emperor . . .' and he finished the line: 'is the Emperor of ice-cream.' How rare – a man who knows Wallace Stevens.

When he took me home, I hesitated, as always, in front of my apartment house. Twelve years after my divorce, I am still a middle-aged adolescent, unsure of protocol. Are you supposed to invite a man for a nightcap after he drives you home from a party? (Are you supposed to let a boy kiss you after he buys you a malted on the way home from school?) But he made it easy for me. He brushed my hand with his lips, said he had to go out of town for ten days, and asked if he may call on his return.

Why not?

I wonder if he really has to go out of town. There is something in him that is – that makes me wary. Or is it in me?

SUNDAY FEBRUARY 5

Restless night. Dreamed of Charles, my exed-out ex. I was standing outside our old brownstone, looking up. Charles was at our bedroom window; his face was angry, and I awoke in terror. Wonder why.

Must get to work on my book. Must write to Nina. Going with my brother and Marni this evening to Shakespeare symposium at the EGG. Dryasdust dull, but I promised.

Why should I have a nightmare about Charles after all these years?

NOTES TO MYSELF

Scene in his lawyer's office: point of no return. Then – flashback to 'When Did the End Begin?' First or third person? Try third:

SO IT HAS COME TO THIS!

They met in his lawyer's office. It was status for his side (the bride's side or the groom's?) that she come to the enemy camp. There they were, sitting next to each other, almost touching, sworn enemies who had once been friends and lovers. The two who had promised to love and cherish each other; who had paced the hospital floor when their son lay bleeding after his tonsillectomy; who had run laughing along the beach to see the sun rise over the ocean; who had carefully chosen the bedroom set, the hall lamp, the drapery fabric; who had lived together for a quarter of a century – and who now, in this sleek, impersonal office of his lawyer, sat so close to each other that she could see his pale scalp showing where his hair grew thin, where she had once rubbed in a special ointment. She steeled herself: how inappropriate to be touched by his balding head. They stared straight ahead while the two lawyers, old friends, old golf buddies, talked as if their clients were not there:

'Will she take four thou a year for herself and the children?'

'Come on, Bill,' her lawyer chuckled mirthlessly, 'you know no one can live on that – '

Something not quite right. Edgar? Have him wear a shirt she had once bought him? – No.

Try first person: more urgent.

SO IT HAS COME TO THIS!

We met in his lawyer's office – a tactical disadvantage for me. This tight-lipped, tight-eyed stranger sitting next to me, avoiding my eyes, while my lawyer and his exchange meaningful smirks, this mortal enemy was once the boy I wanted desperately to marry. Once he was my young husband, the father of my children. I suddenly remembered the day Gregory was born, when the nurse said to him: 'You may go in to see your baby now, Dr Webb,' how with a quick, nervous gesture he adjusted his tie before facing his son.

Inside him, does he carry the track of his history? Is there anything left of the Edgar I once knew? Is there anything in me of the Isabel he once loved, if he ever did, as I sit here, containing my nausea, waiting for the verdict from our two champions, now openly contemptuous of this neurotic couple caught on their hook? Perhaps (I wouldn't put it past him) he had paid them off, both of them. Possibly the lawyers themselves had prearranged the terms and were here just going through the motions. Perhaps I was doomed, whatever I said.

Now they are whispering to each other in the corner of the large book-lined room, while he, my almost-ex, my young husband, my old lecher, sits cracking his white knuckles and staring grimly at the wall.

When did it start to go bad, when did the end begin? In the secret fumbling, when we were new to each other and to ourselves, mistaking anxiety for love, curiosity for passion, the pattern of future destruction already there?

The abortion, the City Hall wedding, the ferryboat honeymoon voyage. The first bookcase in the first one-room apartment. The first mattress. The first easy chair, turned to face the corner of the room so that he could study for his exams undistracted. My first job in Macy's to help him open his first office. The first baby, the money struggles, the second baby. And then? When did it start? Was it when the marriage was announced, no longer a surreptitious titillation for him? Was it the first time he went off to ski while I stayed home with the children? Was it when he met what's her name? Or the other one? Is it too late now, while the two gladiators are standing there, examining each other's weapons, sharpening their own? Too late to do what? Undo the years? Touch hands? Say to each other: 'Look, can't we . . .' No. No and no. Never.

Now the lawyers are back in their seats; I try to read their faces. His looks smug, mine – indifferent. My husband, my killer, is sitting there with his knuckles, scared shitless he might have to give up another dollar, another chair or blanket to the wife he wishes dead. *If she would only disappear*, he is thinking. No, that's what I am thinking. If he would only cease to be. If he would go away and leave me, just as I am, with my apartment, my telephone, my furniture, my children – how good that would be. But we have to sit here and wait to hear what has been decided for us by the two grown-ups, who are smacking their lips over the kill.

'Look, Doc,' his lawyer begins, 'why don't you offer her five thou a year and promise to educate the kids. The boy, anyhow; the girl doesn't need college. The wife can live in a couple of rooms on that, she's able-bodied and . . .'

'I don't *have* five thousand. I just don't have it. I'm driving a rented car, I'm behind in my rent, I had to let my insurance lapse. I just don't have enough for two households. We can't afford a divorce.'

'Come off it, Doc,' my own gladiator says. 'You're a professional man, you see twenty-thirty patients a day, you've got a seven-room office, don't give us that.'

'Well, I'm a lousy businessman,' my young love says. 'I don't have the kind of money she thinks I have. Ask anyone – my nurse – anyone. I carry my patients mostly for nothing.'

'The wife says you've got the letter C written down next to your patients,' my lawyer continues. 'That's for CASH, isn't it?'

'No, no,' Edgar's voice rises in agitation – 'Not cash, I don't get paid in cash! The C is for – the C is . . .' he cracks his knuckles again – 'the C. That's not cash – that stands for *Course of treatment*. Not cash.'

The lawyers exchange glances.

'We want ten grand a year, tax-free, and four each for the children until their majority,' my lawyer says. Ten? Since when did it become ten, when he had assured me: 'We've got him over the barrel; we'll take him to the cleaner's. We'll get you half his income, his real income, not what he declares, and we'll make him educate his children, college, graduate school, the works.'

'Maybe five and a half taxable a year,' says his lawyer. 'Maybe you can see your way to five and a half, tax-free to you, Doc? Isn't it worth it to get rid of her, this sick woman who needs a psychiatrist?'

'I can't – I just don't have it. I can manage four and a half, and that's rock bottom.'

Once in Mexico we had gone to the market, he and I, and he warned me in advance: 'You've got to bargain with these people, they expect it. Whatever price they mention, you must offer half. Then you raise it a little – not much – they're all out to cheat the rich Americans!' I had learned a word: *'Quanto?'* 'How much?' – then – 'Too much!' What was that: *'Troppo'*? How do you say: 'Not enough'?

'Nine thousand,' my lawyer is nodding, 'and educate the boy.' But these were human lives that were being bargained off, not pottery, not rebozos. This is 1963 – there are no slave marts: 'What am I offered for this woman, college graduate, all her teeth – '

I looked at my lawyer – no help there, nor any from his, nor from my husband, with that expression on his face he always gets when he talks about money, and I knew there was no other way but that terrifying one: 'litigate.'

'Then we'll just have to litigate,' my lawyer announces. His nods. Is that what they had decided even before we met? Is it more profitable for them to drag it through court, to drag us through mud? 'Court would be suicide for him,' one of the lawyers I had consulted told me. 'You can't litigate; you're too thin-skinned,' another said. 'Avoid court at all costs for the sake of the children; it will be carnage!' said the third one, what was his name? I must remember his name, it's very important, it's the way to hold on to sanity. I must think of something, anything outside this room; then go home and scrub myself in a hot shower. Let them do what they will, all three of them, there was no hope from them. Let them finish their bloody work and let me go, let me out of here, quick . . .

'Well,' says my lawyer, getting up and stretching, 'I think we can sew this up in another session. Another meeting, and we'll come to a decision. If it's no go, then we'll litigate, after the summer, when I return to the city. How does that sit with you, Doc?'

My husband shrugs. His lawyer gets up too, extends his hand to me, the sick, neurotic woman who insists on a divorce. 'Good to meet you. Thanks for coming.'

Somehow, all four of us are crowding at the door. Nothing resolved, then? A whole summer to suffer through, sleeping on the mattress on the living room floor? I can no longer endure it.

My lawyer and I are walking side by side now, out of the elevator, out of the building. (But I forgot to say goodbye to my husband, flashes through my mind –)

'We can get seven and a half, I think,' my lawyer is saying, 'and you can manage on that, if you go to work, get a job. The kids will get along, scholarships, and so on. But if we go to court, I can promise you at least twice that much. Maybe more. Any judge will . . . It will cost, you know, it will cost – my time and court costs, but it may be worth it to you. After all, you've got the rest of your life to think of, and we've got hubby where we want him, we've got the goods on him. Think about it, let me know. My advice is – litigate. We'll try to get you on the court calendar early fall, maybe October. In the meantime, don't discuss money with him. I've got to run now.'

He disappears, my gladiator, into a passing taxi. I walk like an automaton down to the subway station.

Then it doesn't end?

Feb. 6, 1978

Dear Nina —
Here I am again, waving you as an excuse to avoid
writing my book. I do try, but 'a man cannot jump higher
than his head,' as Varya says. Nor woman, either. The
Russians have a proverb for everything. Yes, I know I
promised to tell you about her, and I will, perhaps in my
next letter.

In the meantime, my friends are still trotting out men for
me. I met a rather attractive one the other night at a
dinner party — amusing, cultivated, rich, with silver hair
and smoke-colored eyes. Not one of my usual lame
ducks, but a weird duck. A bit of a poseur, I think: he
speaks too many languages and smiles with too many
teeth. I was on my guard with him, burnt child that I am.
It looks as if he has skipped town. I doubt that I'll see him
again.

Instead, fate brought me Professor Sumner Simms. Besides bearing a euphonious name, he's very strong on
masculinity: tweedy, with carefully tailored leather
patches on his elbows, and a proper pipe between his
teeth. He's a friend of my brother's, who has thrust him
upon me a few times in the hope that it would take. How
can it, when the man wears on a gold chain on his vest the
largest size Phi Beta Kappa key that is made? I almost felt
I should wear my own in self-defense, but —

> I'm afraid that seeing *my* key
> Might upset his macho psyche!

Anyhow, he called for me last night to escort me to the
EGG. You may well ask. The EGG stands for the
English Graduate Group — an august society of pedants of
which my brother Victor is an honored member.

The EGG was holding its annual Shakespeare Symposium. That's why Professor Simms was at my door.

31

'Please call me Sumner,' he said winningly.

'But Professor Simms seems less formal, somehow.' We compromised. He called me Jessica; I called him: 'By the way.' Not too sure of my Shakespeare, I said: 'By the way, I'm going to take notes, so that I will look intelligent.'

'You already,' he said gallantly, 'look intelligent.'

That was the beginning of what proved to be a strange evening's entertainment. In the hallowed halls of the Pen & Quill Club, surrounded by books permanently embedded in oak-paneled walls and by huge oil portraits of scholars and founders, some thirty eminent Shakespearean scholars were assembled to discuss Shakespeare. Unfortunately, most of the evening was spent in the chairman's iambic attempt to collect dues. They all had to speak in Shakespeare's words, presumably recognizing the playful references. This delayed the meeting considerably. In fact, it took up the entire meeting. In order to appear scholarly, I took serious notes, some of which I will decipher here for you:

CHAIRMAN: As Mr Shakespeare, the Bard of Avon, so aptly put it: *Be pleasèd, then, to pay that duty which you truly owe.* Some members, alas, have been delinquent. You might reply: *There lies no penalty in delay*; but *by my penny of observation,* methinks that we should do *what custom wills.* So please pay up!

SCHOLAR 1: *Out of my lean and low ability,* I paid last week.

SCHOLAR 2: *My poverty, but not my will consents.*

SCHOLAR 3: You mean *refuses.*

SCHOLAR 2: *I am not bound to please thee with answers.*

32

SCHOLAR 4: *Nothing will come of nothing.*

SCHOLAR 5: I have been waiting . . .

SCHOLAR 6: *Like patience on a monument.*

SCHOLAR 5: For the matter of this meeting.

SCHOLAR 7: *More matter with less art.*

CHAIRMAN: *I am no orator as Brutus is.* Was.

SCHOLAR 8: *My noble friend, chew upon this:* I will not pay this tariff.

And so it went, on and on. But before we exeunted, my Simms, my Sumner, delivered himself – with much embarrassed harrumphing – of a story he thought terribly risqué to tell a lady. Nevertheless, here it is: Seems a friend of his, an eminently eminent scholar in Oxford, was asked to attend an all-female performance of *A Midsummer Night's Dream* at a girls' school. At the end of the play, he was asked to say a few words. He got up, thought for a moment, and said: 'This is the first time in my life that I was privileged to see a female Bottom!'

To my credit let it be said I had the decency to blush.

I hope that is the end of Sumner Simms – and don't you dare make a pun of his name; it's already a pun.

You speak about my book. What I need is distance, objectivity, to be able to describe my Isabel, and her divorce. Perhaps I can even find some humor in the madness; for madness it is, a kind of temporary insanity. A friend going through a divorce called me the other day to tell me that her estranged husband has suddenly fallen in love with their sheets. 'How many sheets do we have?' he keeps asking her. And who would believe the story of my own divorce, and that final day in court?

I've changed it, of course, in my novel. I've toned down, exaggerated, camouflaged reality. I've smudged the line

33

between fact and fiction in describing the grotesque horrors, true and invented: the tapped phones, the photostats, the hamburger her friend sneaked into Isabel's bedroom, where she had barricaded herself, while Edgar stood guard outside. The doorknob she wore on a rope around her neck for days. The detective climbing the wooden ladder in the middle of the night into a stranger's window while she sat huddled in terror in his car.

I keep coming back to the same pain in the same circle: like your *Sad Merry-Go-Round*, it does not stop.

That pain may be my book. Not that I expect the fantastic success of yours – or maybe I do? So much I can do with the money: a trust fund for Jeremy and Jill . . . Oops! There I go again, as self-sacrificing as my mother, who lived for gratitude and died without it. I am *not* my mother! I have to say that to myself a lot.

Dear Nina – I know: I must stop writing these long letters and get down to work.

Let's change the subject. I see that you're the 'technical consultant' for your film, but what does that mean? Do you select actors? Examine carousels? Tell them what your book 'really means'? Caught you doing that on TV last Friday – you were great! As for your latest interview in *Time*, I disagree with you; I thought it was fine. You look beautiful in your photo, even if you *are* holding your book, title outward, perched on a merry-go-round horse! It's obvious they love you. Me too—

Yours,
Jess

P.S. I suddenly began making entries in my empty 1978 diary. I wonder why.

WEDNESDAY FEBRUARY 8

Ash Wednesday. Sudden call from Maxwell. How come he's back so soon? He said he likes surprises. He read me T. S. Eliot's 'Ash Wednesday' on the phone in his actor's voice:

> Because I do not hope to turn again
> Because I do not hope
>
> . . .
> (Why should the aged eagle stretch its wings?)

At least he knows poetry – that's in his favor.

Made date for dinner and ballet this Sunday. Learned his name is Maxwell Mahler. Tried to look it up in phone book – but he's unlisted.

Dearest Jess,

Loved your description of the EGG! Now I'm waiting to hear about Varya: what she looks like, how you met, the works. And about that new man – Maxwell What? The way you describe him – silver and smoke – he sounds like a cigarette holder or a fancy car. Rich – I like that in a man. It's a quality I admire. Get rid of Sumner, hang on to Maxwell, throw digital clock out!

I'm writing this in bed, first thing in the morning, so that I can mail it on my way out. From pillow to post. Where am I going this early? To a commencement. Not mine – I have to address a graduating class of psychiatric residents. I'll use the same talk I give teenagers, parents, teachers, and sociologists; I only change the title and vocabulary.

I seem to do a lot of moving around these days. I serve on panels, sit on daises (decorated in a merry-go-round motif) at luncheons and banquets, the prescribed fruit cup before me (served in a plastic carousel). I am posed by photographers on the merry-go-rounds of the nation, book in hand, title outward, as you've observed. I am presented with awards, plaques, honors, and affidavits. I am a 'Human Resource of the United States,' and have a certificate to prove it! But my prize and my pride, the one I have framed and hung over my desk, is a hand-drawn GOOD HUMER AWARD, each letter a different color crayon, 'FOR CHUCKELS! TRUTH!' – from Mr Weinberger's class in Mesa, Arizona. I think that's where it's at: chuckles and truth.

More truth than chuckles in the kids' letters, the Dear Miss Moore letters you ask for. Now that the book is out in paperback and the kids can afford to buy it, my publishers forward to me dozens each day. My biggest thrill was a letter which was addressed simply to:

and it got to me!

They come from all over the country, from small towns and big cities. They're written on ruled composition paper, on fancy stationery with floral designs, on scraps torn from notebooks, in pencil, in green ink, in ball-point, scrawled, printed, typed. I answer all of them. I'll keep sending you a sentence or two from each, as they come in. They say so much more than they seem to. And who will understand them better than you?

> Your book is one of the kinds of books that are meant to stick to you the rest of your life. The rest of my life have not been so wonderful to me, being Black and all, but if my mother didn't have a abortion of me, why should I complaint?

> What you wrote about has happened of course but not on paper!

> I am 17, tho not for long. I never went out of the house from 8½ to 16 except for schools and the store because of nerviousness. My father had sex with my sister but not all the way when she was 12½ but not me and my mother is helpless and has no drivers lincense, so my one pleasure is reading books like *The Sad Merry-Go-Round* and I want to thank you very much for writing it. It divides my loneliness.

> Thank you for being so kind as to read this letter. I have no one else to write to so I hope your there.

Dearest Jess – I hope your there. The last one, who thanks me for reading the letter, wrote nothing else but those two sentences. Yet I think I can understand the whole eloquent letter which was not committed to paper. And of course you can too.

More next time. And more of my schizophrenic correspondent's weird missives next time too. To complete the circle, I'm off to address the psychiatrists.

Now go back to your novel. I want to read about Isabel someday.

Much love,
Nina

[DIARY]

Out with Maxwell this evening. Really *saw* him this time: more attractive than I recalled, with silver hair like a halo over his thin, ascetic face. Shaggy dark eyebrows, and eyes that change from soft gray to steel. Hard to tell, behind his glasses. Peculiar smile. Uneasy man; keeps peering around suspiciously before entering restaurant or theater lobby; looks over his shoulder as if to spot an enemy.

I enjoyed the evening, though I feel – I don't know – leery. He spent more on our dinner than I do in a month. Is generous, thoughtful, makes me realize how deprived I've been. So different from men I've known, the clobber-ers, like Charles, that he's almost unreal to me.

He seemed to know what I was thinking – uncanny! And he knows my *Children and People* by heart! Or did he read it after we met? I wore my pink blouse: 'Pink is red that's very shy,' he quoted – and recited the whole poem. 'Only children and poets,' he said, 'and writers of fairy tales tell the truth.'

At the ballet he held my hand gently. When he took me home, he saw me to the elevator again, touched my cheek with the tips of his fingers, and said: 'You are very lovely.' Then he left, fled almost. What is he afraid of? At the restaurant he told me of a young girl he had taken out a few times. 'What do you want to be when you grow up?' he had asked her. 'Your wife,' she replied. He said he was so angry that he never saw her again.

I must tread softly with this strange man.

WHEN DID THE END BEGIN?

When did the end begin? Isabel was still asking herself on the way home from his lawyer's . What magic words could she say to him now to make the miracle happen, so that he would give her the apartment, enough money to live on, educate the children, stop hating her? Best to say nothing.

As a small child, she had made a vow to herself never to talk back to mother, with Jesus listening inside the pages of her mother's tattered New Testament, held together with a rubber band, which she always carried in her pocketbook. Silence was the only way to survive. Silence and acquiescence. Her mother had a nightly ritual: each time she tucked her into bed, she would say: 'My Saintly Babe,' and Isabel had to reply: 'My Saintly Madonna.'

With Edgar, too, she practiced acquiescence. She soon learned she dare not talk about his 'problem.' 'Sit tight on the lid,' he used to warn her. Perhaps he was right; he knew what was inside that Pandora's box.

His 'problem' was a euphemism for his impotence. Why had she accepted it all those years? Men used to find her attractive: one night as they were leaving a party a man had exclaimed: 'To go home with you – what a lucky stiff your husband is!' – the unfelicitous word emphasizing the irony.

It began the year they had announced their marriage, a marriage forced by her pregnancy and staged by her mother. Before that what used to excite him was the risk of discovery when he would steal surreptitiously into her room.

After a while she stopped wanting him to want her: she managed to lose her own desire for him. But she wanted children. When they were married ten years, she threatened, half-jokingly (only half): 'I'll grow together' – and he managed. That was Gregory. When she became pregnant with Wendy, under special circumstances, people in the next room, he said, half in jest (only half): 'I'm glad I don't have to try again.' And he didn't.

Even in those days she must have known that being deprived of what was called 'conjugal rights' was grounds for divorce. The thing was – she believed him. She believed he would perish if she left him. She believed it was her fault: she was not patient enough, beautiful enough; she had disappointed this tired, hardworking man.

There was evidence, long before she began to gather it into her two valises: a condom in its wrapper on his bureau; a woman's voice telling his Service on the phone: 'He knows my number by heart.' But she denied her eyes and she denied her ears. It was nothing but her sick jealousy, he told her. He was incapable of lying. 'If I thought you *could*, with anyone else,' she would say, in the early days (oh, she was a sly one!) – 'then there would be hope for me.' But no, he kept telling her over and over that he couldn't 'function' (that was his word for it) with anyone else, and if she would only not keep bringing it up, he was confident that, and so on.

She believed him. That's why it was such a shock, that first time, the summer she was in the cottage with the babies. She had called him in the city one evening from the telephone in the firehouse next door, but he wasn't in. She called again, late enough for him to have returned – no answer. In a panic, in bare feet, a shirt over her nightgown, she ran to that phone in the firehouse every half hour, all night long. Not until late morning did she find him in. He sounded annoyed. He had been with a very sick patient all night, trying to get the patient into the hospital. But for the first time she was unable to make herself believe him.

A few days later, when he came for the weekend, they had their long confessional in his car. He told her about the girl he was with that night, and about the others, all the others who had preceded her. They spent hours talking, first in the car, then in the room, then in bed. They talked all night and the following morning and the following day and night. The floodgates had opened; he was telling her everything. And she – the forgiving

41

mother-confessor, the tearful, patient wife – kept saying: 'I understand, I really do.' He had been afraid to tell her before, he said, because she would have over-reacted. His 'unfaithfulness' had to do only with his need. He felt unloved by her; he sensed her contempt, that was why he sought others, who made him feel like a man. He said he could 'function' with them, though minimally. Whatever that meant. 'They respect me,' he said. 'They look up to me.' He realized the danger to his profession, to his marriage. But now that he saw how wise and understanding she was, he had no need to, ever again. 'I can't imagine being married to anyone else,' he had said. 'I want to be happy with *you*!'

She believed him. When he promised that things would be different, she believed him. Through the long hours of that long weekend she kept asking him for more, for specific details. The one in the office. How did she look – her breasts, her thighs? And what was the other one like? How did it begin? What was said – done – sighed – cried out in the secret bed?

He told her: all was now known. This absolved her, gave her the luxury of forgiving him. She was the good one, the Saintly Madonna, the Cordelia of her childhood fantasy, whose father never knew she loved him. At last she and Edgar were close, they could talk. He wept in her arms, shriven.

It did not last long. Rage overwhelmed her: How dared he? No wonder he had given her nothing all those years; he had nothing left for her! And all this time she, the imbecile wife, wasted her youth, stamped out her own needs . . . It was too much to bear. She lusted for vengeance.

That was when she had her first affair, with Gideon. Giddy Gideon, who had pursued her, the chaste wife, with his burning eyes and dilating nostrils and such diligence that it finally happened. But it was an anticlimax. *Just like with Edgar*, she thought, *same equipment, same movements*. She had never known any other man, so she had expected something – different. But at least Gideon was a functioner.

Some dim honor had been vindicated; she was avenged. Not really; actually, she felt worse, for now she was guilty too, and could no longer take pride in her martyrdom. Gideon was no

42

solution, nor was her second lover, nor her third. Her sexual needs were satisfied by occasional lovers, but the warm feeling of being desired and desirable evaporated as soon as she was alone. All that was left were a few entries in her Compliments Box: 'How beautiful you are . . . Your smile, your legs . . .' That remained, was recorded.

There were no more confessions. Edgar's lips grew tight; he hardly spoke to her. When he did, he lied.

On the surface, the marriage existed. People came and went, tradesmen, friends. Children grew. Minimal conversation at dinner, served by Katie. Occasional parties, a movie now and then, a gala once in a while. On the weekends when he was away skiing or skin-diving she would stretch in the big bed, read a book to divide her loneliness, watch TV – try to sleep. When he was home, she suffered from insomnia. And hives. She had raised welts all over her body from scratching her skin most of the night. The retching was bad, too. Nothing wrong with her stomach: she had gone to a gastroenterologist, and though she did not stay for all the tests, she knew that was not it. Most frightening was the gasping for breath. She would open her mouth wide, but no air entered her lungs. She was suffocating with terror and lack of oxygen. 'It's all right,' Edgar would say in his diagonistic voice; 'no one ever died of not breathing.'

Every once in a while, she would mention a separation or divorce. 'I can't afford it,' he would say, leaving for the weekend, not slamming the door.

The end began long ago, and lasted too long, until this final humiliation at his lawyer's, bargaining with dollars for her life. The only help now was in her two valises hidden in her closet. When the time came, she would be redeemed by all that was in them; the accumulated history of her cause: photostats of ledgers, bills, check stubs, and letters from his women, scornfully referring to Madam, his crazy wife: 'To love you is as easy as breathing, but then, some women's can't even manage that . . .'

He had betrayed that, too! The Achilles' heel, she thought – only the mate is privy to its exact location. That's why, when

43

loyalties go, two who are married are each other's most dangerous enemies.

Always she had protected him, put up a front. Even her intimate friends who encouraged her to leave him did not know all.

'But why your *patients*?' she had once cried out.

'Where else would I meet women?' he said.

Not only patients. Secretaries, clerks, servants, friends, nurses, relatives. That was the most devastating: her own brother's wife, Molly, who emulated Isabel right into Edgar's bed. It was the ultimate humiliation that had sent Isabel to a lawyer. But of course for her brother's sake, she couldn't let her lawyer use it.

She saw herself as doomed as Sleeping Beauty, unable all those years to use her gifts of laughter and of love, and no Prince in sight to release her.

'Why *now*?' everyone asked her, 'why now, after so many years? What happened? What caused it?'

There was no day, no hour, no word that caused it to happen. The end began at the beginning.

NOTES TO MYSELF

Delete ‘to divide her loneliness.’ Borrowed phrases don’t graft well.

Explain to reader why Edgar confesses??

Cunning. Charles: When I learned about his Laura, how kindly Charles drove me to R, presumably for my weekly Italian lesson. How patiently he waited downstairs to drive me home, while up at R’s, of course, unable to make love – then or ever again. Diabolical! Months later, Charles said he had known about my affair with R all along, felt it only fair to give me ‘equal time’! Kept in reserve to use against me. How well he knew me – yet he never thought I’d go through with divorce!

Edgar knows Isabel; plays on her weaknesses. Show how he fed her guilt and fed on her guilt.

Why married Edgar? Pregnancy, abortion? His slender fingers with tufts of dark hair on them? His rejection: ‘Say you love me,’ she used to plead, in early days. He wouldn’t. Years later, in bed: ‘Turn to me, talk to me.’ He: ‘I have a hysterectomy in the morning; I must get some sleep.’

Yet give him something: intelligence, a quiet charm, excellent manners. Man who rose when woman entered room – rare even in those days.

Make recognizable. Nina’s fan: ‘It happened, but not on paper.’

Dear Nina —

> A gentleman, a scholar,
> A man who does not holler —
> His name is Maxwell Mahler.

He's bright, learned, youthful, divorced, involved in some kind of humanitarian cause, is art expert and importer, knows poetry, knows my book practically by heart, even seems to know what I'm thinking. He's funny, too, and can sum up a person in a phrase: 'A theologian who wears blue suede shoes.' Things like that. Yet there's something about him I don't quite trust.

Next question: about a shrink. As you know, my own ex was one, ironically — a specialist in marriage counseling — one of the early sex therapists. He should have gone to see himself about his problems. Nevertheless, though it was awkward to talk about Charles to his colleagues, I've been to four in my time: Wellerman, Burr, Tressler, and Schrank. Sounds like a Wall Street firm. But publishing my children's verses did more for me than any of them. I remember telling a friend I met on the street right after the book came out that I was feeling happy. 'Who do you see?' she asked.

The problem of whom to see is so weighty that it can only be explained in light verse. Let the title be:

WITH A GOYA IN HIS FOYER HE CAN TACKLE PARANOIA

(This should be sung, of course, with apologies to Gilbert and Sullivan.)

> He is the very model of a modern psychoanalyst,
> When David Susskind calls him, he agrees to be a
> panelist.
> He treats with objectivity and disciplined sobriety

All past and future traumas in our nuclear society.

At your initial consultation, you might observe his books, his paintings, and test his couch:

> His couch should be of rubber foam, encased in fabric durable;
> Whoever lies upon it should be comfortable and curable.

I was about to rhyme analysis with phalluses – but never mind. I'm no expert on the subject, but in working on my book I've been looking through the catalog of pain in my old diaries of divorce, reliving unresolved angers and rereading my notes about my shrinks. The first, Dr Burr, whom I saw after some fifteen years of marriage, when I realized it was hopeless, told me I was behaving magnificently and that Charles needed me. Dr Burr was so proud of me that he sent me right back to my husband. I was in love with that doctor; I dreamed transparent dreams for him, I had Freudian insights for him, I wrote him love letters I never gave him, and I stayed on with Charles in order not to disappoint Dr Burr. Years later I heard he had committed suicide by jumping out of the narrowest window in his bathroom. He had to stand on the toilet seat and squeeze himself out, to drop to the courtyard below. With his usual thoughtfulness, he avoided the street. There's something immediate and irreversible in that: there can be no going back, like in those films where the diver soars back in slow motion from the splashing water to the diving board. Unlike sleeping pills or poisons, it's a step – literally – that is final. So much for Dr Burr, who made me lose an additional ten years of my life inside a doomed marriage.

When I complained about this to my second shrink, he said: 'Are you going to his grave to scold him?' This one told me I lacked confidence and feared the future. He told me I should make more demands on life. He told me self-assertion meant aggression to me and was therefore followed by panic. He told me my anger was turned inward. He told me I had a sick dependence on my husband. As Varya would say: 'Good morning!' I saw him only once.

The third was a strict Freudian. In my book I call him Dr Kellerman (Killerman, get it?). I had finally found a shrink who was as silent, as rigid and rejecting as Charles. I felt quite at home with him. He sat behind me grunting occasionally as I lay on the couch, spilling my guts out. I kept trying to interpret his grunts. On the one occasion when he spoke, he said I put myself into situations where I *had* to be victimized. And once, when I called him in deep desperation, he said he couldn't see me because he had eight people coming to dinner. He wouldn't let me go to another, more sympathetic therapist; his technique depended on frustrating the patient, I forget why. One day I saw a note scotch-taped to his entrance door: not available today – or ever. He had died of a coronary the night before.

It looks as if I have outlived two shrinks; that's survival! I mourned for him – another loss, another abandonment, another disappointment: by dying, he reneged on his promise to tell Charles that I needed more therapy.

Then I found my present Dr Shrink. Dr Schrank. Not a doctor – a psychologist. Sensible, pleasant, easy. I sit in a chair across the room from him once a week and we chat. He's good for me: his objectivity and sense of humor help me see some of the absurdity I need to recognize. I call him 'Doctor'; he corrects me: 'Mister.' I believe because of this 'Mister' he's frowned upon by his professional brethren, who have MD licenses instead of lay.

But I'm still having difficulty with my novel. Only ten months left before deadline. 'Man is not mushroom,' Varya says, 'does not grow in one day.' I'm sure a book is not a mushroom. Mine may have been growing all this time. But I've been writing of anguish with anguish – precisely what I tell my Fiction Workshop students *not* to do. I need to understand my own divorce before I can understand Isabel's.

Dear Nina, tell me how you managed to touch that common nerve ending in *The Sad Merry*. My interest is more than idle; after all, you did begin to work on it in my class! I could use more students; how would it be if I advertised: 'Former Teacher to Nina Moore?' You know, like 'Bootmaker to Her Majesty.'

Currently I have no star pupils in my Fiction Workshop. One or two are talented; all are earnest, and hang on my every word. ('Wasn't Nina Moore in your class?') I really want to help them, but all I can do, as you know, is offer some shortcuts, some standards, and some way to develop self-critical judgment. My comments on their papers tend to be glum:

> Man who castrates himself should be handled more delicately. What is his motive?

> Is your story finished, or is a page missing?

> Story of man selling watch and woman selling hair for gifts for each other has already been done.

Who was it who was supposed to have entered a creative writing class, looked at his students sitting hopefully, pens poised, said: 'I understand you all want to write. Go ahead.' – and left, never to return?

Varya puts it this way: 'Dostoevski sit in class, learn how write? – For chickens to laugh!'

You ask me about her, as well you might. I had assumed she was *known*, like an ineluctable law of nature. It would take more than a letter to present her to you, so I'll do it in installments.

Though I understand some Russian, she addresses me in

English. I wish I could translate on paper her marvelous accent and all those rolling 'r's'!

I found her in an elevator. Shortly after I moved into this apartment, we shared an elevator and discovered we lived on the same floor. 'Is meerracle!' she cried, 'One – two – thrree, *ffft!* We frriends. Need sugar, need chai – is herre!'

'You're Russian?' I asked as she drew me into the dim hall.

'Rrawshian?' she cried, incredulous. 'How you know?' She extended a pudgy hand studded with rings. 'My name,' she said, and there was a clicking of heels and a clanking of sabers in her voice, 'my name – Varvarra Alexandrrovna Rrogova.' She smiled, and added, ingenuous as a child: 'Everrybody call me Varrya. Is small name.' She saw me staring at her: a squat, middle-aged woman encased in iridescent taffeta, a purple velvet band around her raven-dyed hair, long earrings of red glass dangling to her shoulders. 'I see you like earrrings,' she said, tearing them off and thrusting them at me. 'Is for you!'

I tried to protest, but she was insistent: 'You yawng, beautiful, mawst, mawst, mawst!'

That's how the red earrings came to rest in my underwear drawer; that's how Varya had become my friend. She feeds me Russian proverbs and *kissel* (it's a kind of dessert made with something called *klyookva*), she encourages me to write, assuring me that a horse, even with four legs, stumbles, and she passes judgment on all my gentlemen callers. She decided Sumner Simms was a *zoodnik* – one so boring he makes you itch. When I defended his erudition, she gave me a proverb: 'Smart head, but on a fool.'

I've been writing this letter a long time; I'm tired. But I must fill an order: you asked for a four-line verse on equality. Would a five-line limerick do?

> Said a man to his wife: 'It is true
> That equality must be your due;
>   Provided you know
>   The status stays quo –
> For I am more equal than you!'

I wonder how Charles feels about today's women's movement. Like your husband, he had to be the important one in a marriage; he needed to be looked up to, catered to, given to. I suppose he got this kind of adoration from Laura, though his affair with a patient – even an ex-patient – would today, too, be tantamount to excommunication from the stern New York Psychoanalytical Society. He himself found it difficult to *give*. Hiding behind his 'professional confidentiality,' he wouldn't even give me the time of day. Literally. He would have to be asked more than once, then reluctantly, look at his watch, sigh, and slowly, unwillingly, divulge the information. As a psychiatrist, he was God to his patients; it was hard for him to step out of the role outside of his office. You don't ask God for the time.

He liked my dependence, and frowned on my 'pecking' at my typewriter to write my 'silly rhymes and childish verses.' He especially resented my signing my published articles and poems with *my* name: Jessica Proot, instead of his: Galen. But he graciously accepted and deposited all my checks in his private bank account. I used to hand them over without a word; I thought it was my duty. That's why poor Isabel in my novel is in all that mess about money. As you will see when you read the book I should be writing. At least, I understand her. Edgar is more of a problem.

Yet somehow I feel it will come out all right. I haven't felt this good about myself, this hopeful, for a long time. Tomorrow is St Valentine's Day. Dear Nina – have a happy one.

Love,
Jess

TUESDAY FEBRUARY 14

Today is St Valentine's Day. This morning Maxwell called. I invited him here for drinks. I knew Varya would stop in also; I wanted them to meet. Actually, I was uneasy about being alone with him.

Before he came, twelve yellow roses with a single daisy in the middle arrived with his card, and on it – this verse by Paul Verlaine:

> *C'est Saint-Valentin!*
> *Je dois et je n'ose*
> *Lui dire au matin*
> *La terrible chose*
> *Que Saint-Valentin!*

When he walked in, his smile brilliant, I asked: 'Will you be my Valentine?' 'What do I have to do?' he said with mock fear.

He looked at my books, my records, approvingly, I think, and he rearranged his flowers in my vase.

'Thirteen of them! Are you superstitious?' I asked.

He shook his head.

'Twelve good fairies,' I said, 'brought Sleeping Beauty their marvelous gifts; but the thirteenth' – I pointed to the daisy – 'made them all useless.'

'The prince awoke her with a kiss,' he said.

'It took a long time,' I said. 'One hundred years.'

Varya bustled in, dressed in cerise satin, on her way to a horror movie. 'Not Tolstoi,' she said, 'but what can do?' She and Maxwell began to talk in rapid Russian, then switched to English for my sake. Her proverbs flew like wild darts in the air. At one point, Maxwell asked her: 'Do you know this proverb: "*Verblyoodom v tserkov nye poyedesh*"?' He translated it for me: 'You can't ride into church on a camel.' Varya was nonplussed. 'Where you find this?' she asked suspiciously.

'I just made it up,' he said.

'The tongue,' Varya said darkly, 'will take you all the way to Kiev.'

It was a lively hour. Maxwell was describing his recent visit to the U.S.S.R., where he had to go on some mysterious mission. He said he had almost lost his life in a Moscow taxi, which suddenly veered sharply, made a frantic U-turn, and sped in the opposite direction. 'What happened?' he asked the driver. 'Black cat!' the driver said.

'Where did you learn your English?' Maxwell had asked him.

'I spent my younghood in your country,' the driver answered, 'where I was shortly alive as external student.'

'Akh,' sighed Varya, 'English very hard tongue. I in America thirty-two years, can't speak good.'

I assured her she made herself very well understood; she was, in fact, eloquent.

'From your mouth honey to drink,' she said – and left us for her movie.

Maxwell looked at me silently for a long time. Then he arose, lifted my left hand, and kissed my fingers, one by one. At the door he said: '*Ma belle au bois dormant* . . . Patience. The hundred years are almost over.'

And he left.

I'm confused. He's after something. I don't know what. Or is the problem mine?

NOTES TO MYSELF

Trapped by old loyalties, seduced by guilt and pity, Isabel on pendulum of indecision – most painful period, before wheels are set irreversibly in motion. A kind word from Edgar – and her resolution melts: *What am I doing? Why?*

Her compulsion to talk about it to friends. No place does law of diminishing returns operate as ruthlessly as in sympathy.

For courage to take action, she hoards grievances, large and small. Can't stand tufts of hair on his fingers. Winces each time he goes from room to room turning out electric lights with: 'I pay a fortune for electricity.' The worst – abrasive sound of his clipping his toenails; for some reason this drives her up the wall.

His own complaints: soap melting in sink, her doodles on margins of newspapers.

He keeps advising: drop divorce; doesn't have the money for two establishments.

They live 'separate and apart' in their duplex. He refuses yield bedroom, so she sleeps on mattress on living room floor. (Had tried couch, but kept falling off.) Yet – on Mother's Day, when he returns from weekend away with his girl, he brings Isabel chocolates. Or – if it's winter, when he's on holiday in Nassau with someone else, have him call her to wish her Happy New Year.

Show: what appeared as simple amputation is far more difficult. They're Siamese twins attached at breast: monstrous, deformed creatures who must be severed, yet who are bound by bone, cartilage, muscle, intertwining veins, blood . . .

Telescope four years during which Isabel is trying to free herself from Edgar (1962–66) in series of brief vignettes of gradual, inexorable hacking away –

VAGUE SYMPTOMS

Things were ungluing at once, at all the seams – the sure things, the familiar things, and now – crime in the streets, arson in the schools, a holdup in the corner bank, mugging in the elevator, riots on the TV news, and the apartment next door looted. The superintendent's little boy's bicycle was stolen, the bath faucet had fallen off. Major and minor disasters – all were jumbled together, just as they were in her list of grievances against him, just as they were in her lousy life.

Now Isabel sat timidly in the doctor's office, holding her pocketbook on her lap, like anyone else, like any normal lady, in his impressive consultation room. The glass-topped desk spread like a placid pool between them; the doctor's eyeglasses gleamed with encouragement.

'You say a feeling of pressure and nausea?' he asked, nodding as if to draw the reluctant words from her and match them neatly to the corresponding diagnosis.

Like anyone else, she thought again. There was no reason for her to feel apologetic, she told herself. It was no defection to speak of symptoms here where illness was the norm and pain the currency that gained admittance into this office. The rows of framed diplomas on the wall, the high bookshelves filled with thick volumes in faded maroon and somber green were added assurance. Perhaps her very symptoms were labeled and described in one of those volumes. Perhaps her symptoms had nothing to do with – with anything else.

'Not exactly nausea,' she said, 'but more a feeling of – sea sickness.' She hesitated, searching in her scant vocabulary of anguish for the precise word that would convey this – what? The inchoate distress, the sudden panic, the alien sense of something gone terribly wrong. 'A kind of queasy feeling,' she added, 'and no appetite, and each time after I eat, my stomach seems sort of upset.'

The words said aloud embarrassed her by their shabbiness. She felt like an impostor, taking up the time of this busy man with her poor handful of vague symptoms. Almost she was sorry she had come.

'What do you think it is, Doctor?' she asked, hoping for a specific answer that would circumscribe her within the safety of a known disease.

'We do a thorough work-up, yes?' the doctor said. 'We look for spastic colon, cholecystitis, hepatitis . . .'

She wished he would go on listing the solid medical terms, as if to postpone some imminent and terrifying moment of revelation. She knew what was ailing her, but she was afraid to name it. How could she say to her husband's colleague: 'See, it's like this, Doctor – my husband is a bastard, he is killing me.' No, that wasn't it. 'What it is, Doctor, is that I want a divorce; at least, I thought I did; at least, I think I do, but I just can't – I mean, the way he treats me – and then, the children . . .' No. Better stay within the safety of the doctor's words: 'Sedimentation rate,' he was saying. 'Sigmoidoscopy.'

Perhaps he might really find something medically very wrong with her. She might have to be hospitalized – no problems to face, no decisions to make, just to lie there and let others take care of her – what a relief, what a luxury that would be! Perhaps the doctor (colleagues confide in each other) would tell her husband she was fatally ill. Perhaps even – but her mind stopped short in its tracks, with a squealing of brakes. No, not even then would he pity her suffering, beg her forgiveness, bring the children to her bedside and tell them how wrong he had been, how he had wronged her.

She smiled at the doctor. 'I really must go now. I mean, I didn't expect a big work-up today, I just thought I'd stop in to find out, to make an appointment. My children and my husband are waiting for me. I'll come in another time to do all that. I really feel better already, just talking to you.'

She was saying too much; the doctor was looking at her peculiarly. She was going insane right here in his office, with all those diplomas on the wall observing her. This was what they meant by 'crack-up'; having no control over your words, hearing yourself say crazy things. I'm going crazy, she thought – and that is good because then it will be out of my hands, they will have to do everything for me, even he . . .

56

She walked out into the street, head high, the wife of a colleague. She was not asked to pay for the visit: professional courtesy. She was somebody: she was Mrs Webb, wife of Dr Webb. So, far she was still safe. So far.

She stepped carefully on the wobbly sidewalk, the ground lifting slightly to meet her shoes. Sounds, traffic, voices, receded and echoed faintly in the far, far distance. Everyone was a stranger. She felt dizzy and leaned for a moment against the wall of a building. She was on the edge of the black terror, the overwhelming panic. 'It's only because I haven't eaten,' she thought. 'The thing is – I've got to get home and have something to eat and then – ' She was in the grip of nausea, and swallowed hard, to avoid retching on the street.

NOTES TO MYSELF

No. I stopped as soon as I saw I had typed 'wretching' for retching. That wasn't it, that wasn't it at all.

The feeling wasn't there; it was too 'written,' too self-conscious. Besides, would she bother going to see a doctor, no matter how eager she was to rationalize, to avoid the truth? Especially one who knew her husband? And would she bolt out of his office like that? Yes, she would, because she did. I mean, I did. But I always point out to my Fiction Workshop students that the fact that 'it happened' doesn't make credible fiction. What is needed is fictional truth – a lie made credible. I must stop remembering and begin inventing. Who would believe that – as I leaned against that wall, sick and dizzy and gasping for air, just then, at that crazy moment, some madwoman, small and shriveled, in a dirty gray hat, passing by, spat at me. Just like that – spat, with careful aim, and casually walked by, saying nothing, just walked away? The fact that 'it happened' doesn't matter; the fact that it was the last, the ultimate horror will not do. Sounds too contrived. Erase it, delete it . . . Forget it.

[DIARY]

WEDNESDAY FEBRUARY 15

Max dropped in for a while, carrying armload of books: *Winnie ille Pu* in Latin, *Le Hibou et la Poussiquette* in French, Chinese love lyrics, Ronsard's *Les Amours*, and a beautifully illustrated edition of *The Hours of Jeanne D'Evreux*. Says he wants to mingle our books together on my shelves; wants to read me his favorite poems.

'Timeo Danaos,' I said jokingly. He took me seriously. His eyes (gray, definitely steel gray) narrowed. But after a while he relaxed, told me some amusing stories about studying art in Italy, hinted at an important revelation he was about to make that would help me understand him, and once more, at the door, brushed my hand lightly with his lips. 'Have you ever held a butterfly in the palm of your hand?' he said. He smiled his radiant smile and the door closed behind him.

What butterfly, why butterfly? I feel – I don't know – I don't know.

58

THURSDAY FEBRUARY 16

Last night, when I was in bed, he called. We were on the phone from midnight to one-thirty. In his magnificent voice he read me love poems by Stephen Spender and by Robert Graves, and I wallowed in them, like a luxurious cat in catnip. I can recall only a few lines from Graves:

> She is wild and innocent, pledged to love
> Through all disaster . . .

It was a kind of lovemaking, in a way, more intense than anything physical. I couldn't fall asleep till morning. I think this is the beginning of something that will change my life, that is already making my world different.

Or did I conjure him up out of my own need?

['BOOK']

NOTES TO MYSELF

Obscene phone call; telephone masturbator; Isabel's terror? She's alone, exposed to cranks and perverts.

Street incongruities: Small boy berating a cop.
Girl in tight jeans and dirty sneakers, smelling vehemently of wild gardenias.

For future use:
arthritic tree
coin flipped in the dark
cat's eyes: pupils not round, but elongated – virgate? oblate? (Look up word)

Dorian's calls to Edgar. Isabel listens in on extension: 'Did your crazy wife call me?' The weekend he was away with someone else, Dorian's frantic calls to his Service – about her house on fire.

A life that's an open book, written in an
alien tongue.

Dialogue to conceal, rather than reveal?

I don't necessarily follow my own suggestions.

Dearest Jess,

What a delicious letter, yours of the 13th! Chuckled and chortled at all your verses.

Did I remember to thank you for cutting out and sending that article about me? You're turning out to be the best friendly transcontinental clipping service any author could have. But of all the literary criticisms of my book, this is the one I like best:

> 'With her red hair' (mine is auburn), 'green eyes' (anyone can see mine are hazel), 'flawless complexion' (flaws plainly visible in my bathroom magnifying mirror), 'and streamlined figure' (there they're on the right *track* . . .) 'she could be mistaken for a young Greer Garson rather than an authoress.'

I wince at the word 'authoress,' but on the whole, that's what I call a splendid review!

And this morning came an offer from *Men of Achievement*, inviting me to be listed in their latest volume because they were so impressed by my valuable contributions. They addressed me as *Mr Nine More*. Seems like a lot, doesn't it?

Your Maxwell sounds too good to be true. I hope he isn't invented. I mean, I hope you didn't invent him for your book. We know about you writers! If he does exist, send more details. Did he ask you to be his Valentine? Has he fallen madly in love with you? You say he knows what you're thinking – that's not so good.

You ask for more samples of my fan mail. Are you compiling a study? Turning into a voyeur? Voyeuse? I'll be sending them to you a few at a time, as they come in, fair exchange for *your* excerpts:

> I know your book is made up, but what happen to the junkie in jail?

I love your book and will never stop reading it. Are you any relative of Millie Moore?

You don't have to burn some one else house just because it look prettier than yours. Still in all if you act soft they call you a chicken.

Dear Miss Moore — Please forgive me if I have incorrectly betitled you and you are a Mrs I myself am a Minority, so can appreciate your book. I keep thinking about the people in it 10 years later, whom will they be?

Not all of my fan mail is as touching as the kids' letters. I have a whole thick file in my cabinets under N: for Nuts. These are the only letters I don't answer. I have no idea why I keep them. Maybe for the likes of you? One invites me to ghost-write her book on the American Indian for her. Another sent me a bulging manuscript asking me to publish it under my name and offering to split fifty-fifty. All I need is to be sued for plagiarism! I told you I was getting paranoid. A woman asks me to join a select sex group called Mix'n'Mingle. A man accused of raping a twelve-year-old boy asks me to testify for him in court.

But the one who is really crazy, the schizophrenic young man in the mental institution who writes me those one and two-line sentences, scraps and fragments of his mind, makes eerie sense to me. As apparently, he does to you too. Here are his latest:

I know something about something. The vertical angle is distress on the window pane. Diagonal lines are normal, supernormal, infranormal.

The rubber heel will heal. Watch for the rubber eye with the mammalian pupil. Daylight Saving will do it by subtraction because the time is never the same and it can never be the same again. That is why I understand everything in your book.

J is the 10th letter, parallel to periphery and center; birth equals death. Cross out the word not wanted.

If birth equals death, as it certainly seems to, which is the word you would cross out? Maybe he'll tell me, with his own clashing of symbols, in the next batch of his scraps, which I'll mail to you.

I've also embarked on a correspondence with a prisoner in North Carolina. I have only his Rt. # and Box #, but he receives my replies. He has recently been transferred from Death Row to Life. For what crime I don't know. He first wrote to ask for my photo. He read my book in the prison library but was afraid he'd get into trouble if he tore my picture out from the book jacket. He said my book made him feel he could talk to me. I sent him a photograph which, surprisingly, he received. He sounds like a young man, probably black, whose family, if he had any, has totally abandoned him. Then he asked for some batteries for his wristwatch, which has numbers that light up. In his next letter he says he is in solitary, and can now see his watch to know what time it is. He says he will always look at my picture. He's a lifer. Or did I already say that? I had written to him I am trying to write another book, but find it hard. Here is his reply:

Dear Nina, I hope this finds you in the best Condition of Life. I have enough faith in you to believe you can write another Book so don't let me down!

Things here are not picking up any so I'm just hoping something come my way then maybe I can see the light again. This place is far behind time. They refuse to let me write but I will find a way. Each day I look at your picture you are the only company I have.

I have to wait until I can get a stamp I hope I can so I can write more.

Be good now and write when you can.

Some letters are so full of pain! Some are sad. Some are

63

funny-sad. On my desk is one from a girl who wants to appear in my movie:

> I am 16, just the right age for me to be. With brown eyes and Titan hair. I can be sexy or not as the roll requires.

Unfortunately, I have nothing to do with casting. If it were up to me, I'd surely grab the girl with Titan hair for the roll. What I am is technical consultant. To answer your question, this means that they pay me a lot of money, let me hang around, and don't listen to a word I say.

We're filming in a huge studio painstakingly transformed into a Settlement House. Why — when any number of real Settlement Houses are available? A mystery. Everything inside is accurately reproduced, to the minutest graffiti on the wall. I find it all terribly exciting. Just think — all these people — cameramen, carpenters, electricians, prop men, script girls, wardrobe people, actors, stand-ins, makeup people, director, producer, assistants — all bustling and scuttling around just because one day I happened to put a blank piece of paper into my typewriter!

Most of the youngsters in the cast are nonprofessional kids, selected from drug centers, reform schools, halfway houses, orphanages, schoolrooms, settlement houses, city slums. More than a thousand were interviewed when the film was announced. Some stood in line all night until the studio opened in the morning. It was one of our coldest days out here. Many were cold but few were frozen . . . Sorry. Puns are my way of coping. Like your funny rhymes. I keep them out of my work, so you must bear the brunt.

These kids — they have their one moment of glory on the screen, and then what? *Whom* will they be? And how will they go back to their hopeless lives?

One Puerto Rican boy with a wonderful face disappeared for two days of shooting. Scouts were dispatched

to find him. They did – hiding out in someone's base-
ment, with a black eye and a broken jaw. The makeup
man did his best.

And a fourteen-year-old girl who had a featured role
had to miss a whole week because of complications
following her abortion.

The mother of one of the boys, who came to warn him
not to come home that night because his stepfather was
back, said to me wistfully: 'Please, Miss Moore, write
another book so my boy can be in it!'

Another mystery: Why, on one of the warmest days in
Los Angeles, were they shooting an outdoor winter scene
taking place during a snowstorm? Artificial snow sifting
from above, huge blowers of artificial gales, actors dressed
in winter clothes, perspiring under their mufflers,
makeup girls following them with tissues to blot the
sweat from their faces. The scene had to be done over and
over again. One of the actresses, during a break, rushed
up to me and said desperately: 'Who do you have to fuck
not to be in it?'

I wish I knew. Would come in handy.

I'll keep you posted on the progress of the film.

Since this letter has been only about me, I want to
know all about you. An I for an I. Tell me about Maxwell
and your book. In that order.

> *Much love,*
> NINE MORE – and then some!

P.S. I give up – what does rhyme with 'masochist'?

SUNDAY FEBRUARY 19

Tonight had dinner at his place. His apartment —
spacious, high-ceilinged, full of art treasures from all over
the world. He seemed nervous, eager to please. Wielding
a big wooden spoon, a maestro flourishing his baton,
tasting, seasoning: 'Not enough salt!'

Learned a little more about him: His father (Viennese)
died when Max was very little; here we have something in
common. His mother (French) lives alone in Cap d'Antibes. 'She lives well,' he said coldly, 'I see to that.' He has
his office downtown, but he travels a lot for his business.
Is also involved in some dangerous underground activity
— dissidents, countries in trouble: Chile, Mideast,
U.S.S.R. — not clear about that. What is clear is that he's a
generous soul, incapable of petty thought or banal feeling. And he's delightful to be with!

I asked him to tell me more about the U.S.S.R. I
explained that I left Kiev when I was five and don't
remember much. 'The Black Sea is black,' he said.
'Ukranian women are dimpled. And when the Russians
are totally puzzled about something, they say: "*Vsyo
yasno*": "Everything is clear." You can tell a lot about a
country,' he said, 'by the way they speak on the telephone. The Russians say humbly: "It is Ivan Ivanovich
who is bothering you." The French, hysterically: "Do not
quit!" The Spaniards plead: "Talk to me!" And here —
here we say "Hello!"'

But he wanted to speak about me. He said I was very
trusting, very vulnerable. Wants to do things for me, be
my 'coper.' He says he loves my *Children and People*. I
suppose I should believe him, for he quoted from it again:

> You can almost always tell
> A giraffe from a gazelle,
> But you can't tell people apart!

'They all look alike to the animals in the zoo,' I finished, and we laughed. We laugh well together.

He asked about my divorce. I mentioned briefly some of the painful incidents: told him what was done to me. 'Can you understand that?' I asked. He nodded, said softly: 'The born victim strikes again . . .'

Strange, the things he sometimes says.

'My shrink . . .' I began –

'You don't need a shrink,' he said.

'Don't you believe in them?'

'They're specialists in incurable diseases,' he said.

After dinner he read me some of his translations from the Aramaic, which he is studying. Then he just sat and looked at me for a long time in silence. 'I can look at your face forever,' he said, 'and not get tired of looking.' He said: 'With you I am calm.' His eyes (soft gray now) were sad. He said something about innocence in a depraved world. 'I'm a romantic adolescent,' he said, 'and I will take you home.'

Before we left, he took me in his arms and he kissed me. My knees went weak – it was all I had imagined in my fantasies. At my elevator he gently stroked my hair, tucked a lock behind my ear, and said: 'Things grow slowly. Call me in the morning.'

Now, as I'm writing this, I can't wait until I hear his voice in the morning.

NOTES TO MYSELF

On weekends, when Edgar is away, what does Isabel do? Choose one such evening.

AN EVENING TO HERSELF

Now that she was free of his punitive presence, now that she was luxuriously alone for the whole weekend, with access to the bed, she could do whatever she wanted. She was her own master. Mistress. The grown-ups were gone; she could play house, eat or drink anything she wished, use the telephone, there was nothing she couldn't do. She had this gift of a long evening stretching before her, and her choices were limitless.

Accustomed to draw up lists, she began almost automatically to write down all the things she might do for herself. She might take a long hot bath – she still had the bath oil someplace, then pop into bed (clean sheets, that held no trace of him) and turn on the TV and watch whatever junk she pleased, as long as she pleased, as loud as she pleased. Were there any soap operas at night? Or a funny skit, or a domestic drama? Domestic? Suddenly the prospect of lying alone in bed was frightening.

There was still time to call one of the 'girls,' one of the also-alone women on whose company she had begun to rely. A cheerful voice on the phone, a carefree laugh – these gained her acceptance into the lives of others. She might suggest a movie, or dinner in a little restaurant – no, that was out; her stomach was too queasy for her to eat in public. Or she could – what? Take down from the shelves a book she had been meaning to read – no, that required too much concentration. How about just stretching out on that big empty bed and . . . No, she had already decided against that. Couldn't she go to the movies alone, perhaps in the neighborhood? There were so many things to do in a city like New York; one had so many options: theaters, museums, and so on. At least, that's what she always used to say when defending this city. What about all those options now? All the theaters and museums?

She could wash and set her hair, maybe rinse it with that new lotion. Do her toenails. Read a – no. Why couldn't she, like other women alone, extract some pleasure from her life? Why not invite a man for that little dinner for two in her own apartment? She could whip up something simple, set the table with the yellow tablecloth, light the two candles left over from last spring, put on soft music, wear her blue robe, eye shadow, provocative lace, and then, in dim light, with wine and music and her charm – she was, after all, still a young, attractive woman – the man would, that is, might want to spend the night. In the morning he would know he was in love. 'I have waited so long for you,' he would say. They would arrange to see each other again that night, and again, and again, because even when her husband returned – it would work out. The man was unmarried, widowed, divorced. He had a little apartment – not far – she wouldn't even have to take the subway.

Yes, but in the morning, after she offered him breakfast in her kitchen – the frozen brioche, the unopened jar of grape marmalade; when – dressed and smelling of after-shave lotion (where would he get it? Her husband always took his along with him) . . .

Well, anyway, in the morning, when he had to leave to go to work (architect? engineer? doctor? – No, never doctor, never lawyer!! – just a nice person, retired, had been art dealer, importer, something like that), so in love, now that he knew her, he offered her escape from everything. He also happened to have a place – small but quite lovely, at the beach, in Cannes or Cap d'Antibes, which would be theirs, hers too. Above all, he valued her, recognized her quality. In just one night, look how her life could change! They would arrange to be together while her husband – Her what? Well, for a moment her husband was obliterated by this new man. In the morning they would stand in the foyer, clasped in each other's arms. How tenderly he would stroke her hair away from her cheek, and tuck a lock behind

69

her ear. How softly he would whisper that last night was like nothing he had ever known, and that from now on . . .

Yes, but what would the doorman think? The morning doorman was on duty by then, he would see him leaving the building; the night elevator man was sure to tell that he had taken this man to her apartment and that the man had not come down again.

All this was nonsense, of course. She wasn't that gone as to believe her own fantasies, spun out of loneliness. One day, perhaps, when she was ready for it – 'the readiness is all' (the man would know the quotation; he would even finish her thoughts). They would talk deep into the night, share all their feelings, make love, take trips around the world. He was rich; at least, he had enough to take her wherever she wanted to go, enough to buy her anything she needed, enough to bury her. What was she thinking?

The thing is – (by now it was too late to call any of the girls for that movie) – the thing is – to take one step at a time, to live through this evening somehow, somehow.

Dear Nina –
My scrapbook of *The Sad Merry* grows, bursting with superlatives. And this morning I heard you on the radio, in a taped interview; you were concise, forthright, and direct:

> 'How does it feel to be famous?'
> 'Good.'
> 'How does it feel to be rich?'
> 'Good.'

Brava! I am especially proud of you because I was with you at the very beginning, when you were struggling to give shape to all you were thinking and feeling. And I know the years of hard work that went into a book that seems as effortless as yours.

Each writer has to work out his/her (look how they have intimidated me!) salvation. My own method is long and messy. First, I must spill it all out on the typewriter because the keys are almost as fast as my thoughts. Then I revise in pen, never in pencil: a pen is much more strict. I use red and green and blue ink; I make asterisks, double asterisks, arrows; I underline and encircle; I cut, paste, cross out, insert, cross out again. When the pages are so bedoodled that no one except me can decipher them, I retype. Then again: mess up, type up, mess up, type up – until the sentences get shorter, the pages get fewer, the meaning gets clearer. After that I retype the whole thing.

I know some writers, and I marvel at them, who can sit down in the morning, after their leisurely coffee, and start pounding away sentence by sentence, into neat paragraphs, polishing their prose as they go along. I know others who spend days or weeks chewing on one paragraph. I know writers (like me) for whom the act of writing is anguish. They will do anything to avoid it:

71

make telephone calls, clean closets, go shopping, watch TV, do crossword puzzles, revise address books, and write long letters to friends in San Francisco. (I am speaking only of prose; verses seem to write themselves.)

I know writers who claim they love writing, who say they can't wait to get to their desks. I suspect they lie through their teeth – but that may be only envy. I know others who can simply sit down and dictate their words into a machine. I find that difficult to understand; for me writing has to do with fingers and silence. The spoken word is totally different from the written one, as you must know from transcripts made from your talks.

I know one writer who uses three-by-five cards of different colors: blue for characters, pink for plot, yellow for scenes. He spreads them all out on his floor and shuffles them around until he gets the combination he likes. What's interesting to me is why he chooses the colors he does.

Another writer, a very successful one, depends on his stream of consciousness – or so he says. It's a kind of automatic writing which needs only a bit of editing on his part, and gives him his distinctive, nervous, very modern style.

Once in a while, as you well know, if you have lived with your characters long enough, they begin to be real to you; they tell you where they want to go. They pull you away from your careful outline and lead you to quite another place: their own. This has already begun to happen to one of my characters: Varya's counterpart in my book. She is running away with me. I tried to hush her by putting her in a separate story of her own to star in, a story that doesn't even belong in my book. Perhaps now she'll settle down to play the part I've assigned to her.

I guess that's what they mean when they speak of the joy of creation. It comes rarely, but it's unmistakable. It happens when your characters ignite, take on a life of their own. It happens when you come close to what you are trying to express. It happens when quite suddenly an unbidden insight swims up from some place within you in a phrase that is so right it seems to tie everything together.

It's almost awesome to create something that wasn't there: a book. You have only the white paper, and twenty-six letters of the alphabet (Varya claims the Russian thirty-three!), which must be put in a certain order. It's their order that counts. If all those letters are in the right place, you have a good book, a book that people will want to read, a book like your *The Sad Merry* —

> A book that has a well-worn cover,
> A book to borrow and to lend;
> A book that — like a practiced lover
> Knows how to start and when to end.

Which brings me, by a neat transition, to Maxwell. What can I say about him, once I have said he is unique, *sui generis*; there is no one like him? At last a giving man, a man who doesn't clobber women. I'm tired of love that suffers. We laugh at the same things, we respond to the same music and poetry. Last night I had dinner in his splendid apartment; he's a gourmet cook. He goes out of his way to please me. He even knows poetry! Or did I mention that already? I think I fell into a bed of roses. Literally — for he showers me with flowers. And he knows Russian! I can understand it when he speaks it; Varya's whizzes by too fast for my ear to catch. I introduced him to her the other day, and the two of them threw Russian proverbs at each other like so many Ping-Pong balls.

I'm not sure she approves of him.

Now I've got to get back to work on my book, but I feel too — I don't know — exhilarated. Everything is suddenly possible. I've even agreed to go over my brother Victor's manuscript pages of the first few chapters of his Poetic

73

Plagiarisms. He has been involved in a lifetime scholarly project he calls 'Unconscious (?) Poetic Plagiarisms,' the cynical question mark canceling out the charitable 'unconscious.' In his dogged pursuit of similarities in English and American poems, he has gathered a formidable collection. For example:

WILLIAM WORDSWORTH: 'Or hear old Triton blow his wreathèd horn.'

OLIVER WENDELL HOLMES: 'Than ever Triton blew from wreathèd horn.'

WILLIAM BLAKE: 'He showed me lilies for my hair And blushing roses for my brow.'

JOHN KEATS: 'I see a lily on thy brow, And on thy cheek a fading rose.'

JOHN MILTON: '. . . warble his native woodnotes wild'

RALPH WALDO EMERSON: 'Whose native warble-wild . . .'

There are hundreds of these, surrounded by long footnotes, exegeses, and ibids. The introduction alone is ninety-two pages long. I don't know what help I can possibly give him, except to ask: 'Why?'

In my book he becomes Dr Q. Vincent Barshak (it took two days to come up with that name!), an eighteenth-century scholar. His wife Marni – the one who imitates my voice, my dress, my handwriting – becomes Molly, who gets involved with . . . . Never mind. I don't know why I keep referring to it as my book, when all I have are some scattered scenes not even in chronological order, which one day, I hope, will form the novel. I'm giving the reader credit for being able to see the whole in its parts.

It has just occurred to me: I wrote about little children; you wrote about adolescents; and now I am writing

about grownups. It is much harder to understand them!
Much!

Love,
Jess

MONDAY FEBRUARY 20

This morning, when I called him, his voice sounded strange. 'Did I awaken you?' I asked. His voice immediately changed. 'You awoke me last night.'

Pure white roses arrived this afternoon, and tucked into the petals, a card with this quotation from Pindar, copied in his small, calligraphic hand in Greek, and under it, his translation: 'What shall I do to be dear unto thee, and dear unto the Muses?'

Saw Varya; asked her what she thought of him.

'To think — think, but to say — what I can say, Lapochka?'

'You keep calling me Lapochka. Why?'

'Too hard say "Jessicachka." '

'But what does it mean?'

'Means hands of cat.'

'Of cat?'

'Of cat.'

'Does he speak Russian well?'

'To speak speaks,' she said, 'but with big accent.'

'Did you like him?'

She shook her head. 'Transatlantic type.'

'What do you mean?'

'Very smart. Tongue with no bones.'

'You mean, he's a smooth talker? But doesn't he have a wonderful face?'

'Is Russian saying: "From face cannot drink water." '

In spite of her doubts, I think she'll come around.

All day, all evening I waited for his call. 'Patience,' he had said — a familiar word to me! I have postponed my life away with patience.

Must get back to my book. Must write Nina. Must stop waiting for the phone to ring.

Only let me not spoil it. Let me make no false move —

Dearest Jess,

I'm writing without waiting for a reply to my last because I suddenly have a couple of unstructured hours. 'Free time,' we used to call it in camp. Shooting on the film has stopped for a while because of the rains. You can't make snow when it rains. (Sounds like one of your Varya's Russian proverbs.) All the indoor scenes have been shot, so we have to wait for the weather.

In the meantime, I got a whole new batch from my schizoid correspondent. (How his images keep recurring!)—

Horizontal is fact; vertical is fiction.

The green line of divorce is on the odd floor. Women weep on even-numbered floors.

Hoodwinked by chicanery and witchcraft, my mind was synchronized with the Government Laboratory during the afternoon entertainment in the theater.

Unknown execution in the Bureau Drawer, the upper third from Quarantine, followed by artificial cremation.

X Y Z is the last confidence. Who is your checkmate?

Can you use any of these for your divorce book? How is 'Checkmate' for a title? But do be careful – there's a certain danger in stepping into another's unconscious.

I'm glad you liked me on that TV show – when was it? Time blurs for me. Also cities, people. On my lecture tours I find myself in places I never heard of: Bemidji, Minnesota. Minot, North Dakota. Cape Gerardeau, Missouri. You can make a lovely poem of these ringing names. I've become an authority on hotels and motels: The dry swimming pools. The Coke machines in lobbies. The hermetically sealed windows and the TV sets with orange-colored faces. Sometimes I'm in a Celebrity Suite, with flowers from my publishers, fruit from the hotel manager, and a delegation of reporters with tape recorders, cameras, and microphones in the 'Conference Room.' Sometimes I am in the one motel in town, with a coffee shop off the lobby, live entertainment in the bar, and a bed that vibrates to a quarter. Wherever I am, I've learned to insist that I be taken directly to my quarters, much as I would love to go via the scenic route they propose, to see their new Insurance Building and the cannon in the town square. I explain I get deaf from the jet and require a rest before facing my audience. To add credence, I keep saying loudly: *'What? What?'*

I've also learned that no matter how carefully I plan for these trips, something invariably goes wrong. The plane is grounded. The train isn't there. (The welcoming committee never the train shall meet.) Did I tell you about the Incident of the Shoes? I will in another letter. I'll throw in my other lecture mishaps in exchange for more news of Maxwell.

Just remembered. That must have been the *Loose Talk* show. Or was it *The Author Speaks?* Except that the author seldom does. Usually, on TV talk shows, I find myself with strange bedfellows. On one – in Cleveland, I think, I was on the same program with a talking dog, a diet doctor, a girl vocalist (that's their name for a singer), and two acrobats. In the dressing room the makeup man said to me: 'And what do *you* do, dearie?' I shrugged. 'I wrote a book.' 'I'm not much of a reader,' he began. – 'Your wife is the reader?' I offered. – 'Yeah, she's the reader of the family. Open your lips.'

Back in the waiting room ('Green Room,' in the trade), more people. Heads popping in and out. Rumors fly: 'He's here' . . . 'Not here yet' . . . Waiting for the Great Man himself. Instead, a young woman with long, lank hair wearing patched jeans and a satin blouse brings tepid coffee in styrofoam cups and passes them around.

'You the one wrote the book?' she asks me. 'Sign here.'

'What am I signing away?' I ask with a gay little laugh.
'So you don't sue. It's standard.' She disappears.

Popping of heads more frantic now. More rumors: 'You go on right after the vocalist . . .' 'No, first the talking dog . . .' 'You'll go on in pairs: you and the diet doctor first . .' 'You'll be on right after the commercial . . .' 'You'll be on six minutes . . .' 'Four minutes . . .' 'You're on the whole time, only make sure the chairs . . .'

For a breathless moment I think there wouldn't be enough chairs and I'd have to go home. No such luck. My stomach churns: borborygmus. Beautiful, onomatopoetic word. I wonder if the cameras in the studio are sensitive enough to pick up the sound. *Just remember to mention the title of the book*, I say to myself, standing in the wings. Here another assistant – a very young man in jeans and a silk shirt gives me all his teeth and says, flashing encouragement: 'We're after a spontaneous effect here, nothing rehearsed.' I nod obediently. 'Now, the first question he is going to ask is – "Where do you get your inspiration from?"' I nod again. Someone says: *Go!* and I am pushed off, knees buckling, toward the bright lights and the desk at which He is sitting, pancaked and charming. I shake a firm hand and am waved to a chair next to a plunging gold lamé evening gown – the girl vocalist, who had just finished her number. I don't know which camera is on me, in my pink blouse ('Don't wear white!') and newly penciled eyebrows, so I look at Him. He is hurriedly glancing at some notes on his desk.

'I'm sorry I haven't had a chance to read your wonderful book,' he says (I'm proud to tell you I did *not* say: 'Your wife is the reader'!) – 'but I've always admired you writers. Where do you get all your ideas from?'

Millions of viewers out there, watching, listening, 'Well, I – '

'That great imagination of yours, to give pleasure to so many people, and without any pornography in it.' He shoots me a sudden, sly smile: 'Or is it – just between you and I – a bit – ?'

'Actually, my book is – '

'Tell me,' he cuts in, 'has your success changed you, personality-wise?'

For whichever camera might catch it, I shake my head modestly: 'Well, I haven't really … I'm the same, only now they listen.' (At last, a whole sentence!)

'I understand' – he is consulting his notes again – 'that you sold it to the movies for five big ones. Are you writing the screen treatment?'

'No.'

'That's a fun title!' he says, holding up my book. (That's good, that's the reason I am here.) 'The sad merry-go-round! When I was a kid – and there's a kid in all of us, I used to love to steal rides on the merry-go-round at this big playground we had down the street. But tell me' – a boyish, disarming grin – 'we're almost out of time – what is your book about?'

So much to say about all the sad children, whirling around and around, ending up in the same place where they started, going up and down and around and around on those shabby, paint-peeling horses and lions, getting no place, ever; spinning, senselessly spinning to the sleazy, tinkly music, with no destination, thinking they are having *fun* … So much to say, and my time running out: 'Well, you see, it's really a metaphor – '

'Sorry,' he interrupts, 'our time is up. I have to sell something. But I sure loved those rides as a kid, and I'm sure everyone listening in will, too.'

Only once was I proud of myself on TV. Only once did I have the presence of mind to speak up, fast. This was with a woman interviewer on a local station in the Midwest. I was there to plug my book. I was on with a man who had recently had a sex-change operation, and the interviewer spent the first ten minutes, her back to me, concentrating on him. Finally she turned to me, picked up my book, glanced at the book jacket, and said: 'That's a good picture of you, Miss Moore.'

Quick as a flash, I replied: 'But you should see the

80

original!' The cameraman made an approving circle with his thumb and forefinger and nodded.

See what happens when you just *mention* that you saw me on TV? As a matter of fact, that was a fairly good program. By this time I've learned that animation is the thing: you must talk, talk, talk, not to let the tiniest leak of silence bubble on the air. It doesn't matter what you say as long as you fill up that silence. But I'm more concerned, I'm afraid, with how I look; the words take care of themselves. And on that last show I must have looked pretty good, because shortly after that I received my one and only telephone proposal of marriage.

A man called me at home (I'm *very* listed), introduced himself as a retired textile manufacturer, said he had just seen me on TV and that I reminded him of his wife, who died many years ago.

'Are you married?' he asked.

I hesitated a moment, and said: 'Yes.'

'Then I'm too late?' he asked sadly.

'I'm afraid you are.'

'Well,' he sighed, 'Good luck anyhow,' and hung up.

No other proposals to report. But what about your new romance? And how is the book going? The two aren't mutually exclusive, you know.

Much love,
Nina

NOTES TO MYSELF

Flashback: their wedding day. Isabel's eagerness to marry him. Her guilt that it was forced by abortion she faced following day. Mother's role in this.

Make a point: how indifferent she was to money then; how she scoffed at those who even talked of it!

Show fantasy and reality mingled: her romanticism.

Use present tense for immediacy.

Look up: Cost of marriage license in 1937
         Cost of sterling ring in 1937

Call it:

HAPPY THE BRIDE

It began with the initial lie, and

No – start again:

The morning of her wedding day she

No – make clear it was mistake from the beginning.

HAPPY THE BRIDE

It was a fantasy that they were ever in love. Even in the beginning, they were already sick with the disease that had flowered in their marriage. Dis-ease. Lack of ease, lack of comfort together.

She *had* to get married, because her mother had insisted on it. And she had to do it fast, just before the scheduled abortion, because if she should die unmarried under the doctor's knife, it would be too great a disgrace. How much better it would look to bury her with a wedding ring on her legalized dead finger.

Her mother had gone to plead with him to marry her damaged, deflowered, devirginized daughter. He was a perfect gentleman, her mother said. He agreed to marry her. Happy the bride.

They arrange to meet outside the subway at City Hall station. Her dress – something old, something new. Contracting her stomach muscles, she makes the old bargain: 'If it happens, I will always. . . Just let it happen, and I will never . . .'

She meets him, the pale bridegroom, the dearly beloved, and they smile wanly at each other, like convalescents, as they walk hand in hand to the five-and-dime store for a wedding ring. This one is real sterling for ten cents – look – it says sterling – and it fits. To wear forever, till flesh of finger rots under it in the grave.

Inside City Hall they are lost in the maze of corridors. Where is the Little Church Around the Corner, the red carpet, the aisle of white flowers? They ask the guard, embarrassed by the words: Marriage Bureau, and they go up in the elevator. They get off at the wrong floor, walk up a flight of broad public steps. She stops on the landing for her one moment of nobility: 'It's not too late. If you want, I mean . . .'

He: 'Don't be silly.'

'But if you don't really want to – '

He: 'Sure, I want to; you know I do.'

'I only thought . . .' They go up. They fill out a license (church bells ringing, the villagers assembled in the square below). She forgot her pen; she picks up the public pen, dips it into the drying inkwell, and uses a pulpy blotter. What clues that blotter holds in its inky splotches; what names and what commitments? Father's name, mother's name, born, year, please print. Four dollars. He pays the clerk – a bargain, even in this year of our Lord 1937. There you are – it's all yours. Joke – she remembers a joke – something about a hunting lodge: 'Mister, if you ain't done it yet, don't do it; this ain't the license fer it!' Now it's legal. Now there is no need to hide in hallways, to tiptoe to her room and sneak out at dawn. For this small sum – a lifetime of joy: sex, companionship, children (a twinge in her stomach: what if it comes now? The ultimate irony. Stop this farce? Or tell him later, when it's all over, sealed and delivered . . . Delivered of a boy, congratulations, you have a bouncing . . .)

They are instructed to go to Chapel – a room like the others. Two clerks for witnesses, one chewing gum. The Justice – pink face, mumbling lips, mouthing the immemorial words monotonously, like an elevator man calling floors: '. . . in sickness and in health, till death do us part . . .' Edgar's tight, embarrassed kiss. The judge: 'Here is your diploma.' Mirthless smile at the little joke repeated how many times? My diploma. I have studied hard, done my homework; I have paid my tuition.

They walk quickly – as if after some shameful deed – out of the room.

People waiting their turn: the girl in lilac organdy with her family around her; the thin one in a white dress with a corsage at her shoulder. 'I didn't get you flowers,' he said apologetically. 'It was too early.' They walk out into the morning sun, in her hand the diploma that entitles her to all the rights and privileges of – the abortion tomorrow.

'Let's see,' he said, 'we're down near the . . . You hungry?'

'Not very.'

'Well, look – how about a bite? I didn't have any breakfast yet. Here's a drugstore – '

The wedding breakfast. They sat primly on their drugstore stools. Tuna-fish sandwich and chocolate malted. Not too sweet.

On white, hold the mayo.

Do I look any different? Does my diploma show? Mrs Webb, a married woman.

'How's your malted?'–

'Pretty good. Not too sweet. How's your sandwich?'–

'Fine.'

She forced herself to eat, contracting her stomach muscles, as she had been doing for days. If it should happen now? Grim joke.

They are near the ferry. 'I still have a couple of hours before class,' he says. 'Want to take a ride to Staten Island? It's a nice morning.' (Their wedding journey – an ocean voyage. She leans over the rail, his arm around her, the moonlight shimmering on the water as he whispers . . .)

'Not too chilly?'

'No, I'm fine.'

The ferry was full of working people, commuters. They sat in silence on the wooden bench until the Staten Island shore came into view, opening on the foam of perilous seas on faery lands forlorn . . . This silent stranger beside me, who is he and why am I with him? You, my beloved. Or was it something she had read someplace?

The backward voyage.

'Excuse me a moment.' She rushed to the ladies' room to see if – no. No escape. Trapped by her organs, made to bear strong-limbed sons and grave-eyed daughters.

He was holding a newspaper he was too polite to read. 'I'll just make my class if we hurry.'

They part at the subway entrance, he to take one train, she another. For a few moments they stand on opposite platforms, the subway tracks between them. She feels that something is required of her. I'm a stranger here myself. She lifts her hand and waves to him weakly. He waves back, as his train rushes in and obliterates him, thundering away. Whither thou goest. She looks into the dim narrow mirror of the vending machine at her stranger's face of wife, mother . . . contracts her stomach muscles and steps into her train.

MONDAY FEBRUARY 27

No entries all week; it has been full of Max. I think I'm afraid, I don't know why. Varya says: 'Afraid of wolf, don't go in forest.' But I'm deep in it. I may not find my way back. And why should I want to? Max says he too is afraid to stir up feelings dead for many years. 'Let's play it by ear,' he says.

His gifts today – azalea plant, with a card. But two words on it: '*Sans paroles.*' A royal Copenhagen kitten, exquisitely made, with a note: '*O, Poussiquette, comme tu es rare!*' A record of T. S. Eliot reading his own poetry.

The way he takes a firm stand – it's really admirable. Like the beggar on the street who asked him for a quarter for a cup of coffee. Max took him by the elbow, and holding on to my arm with his other hand he led us to a corner luncheonette, ordered coffee and buttered roll for the man, waited till he finished eating, and handed him a subway token to get home. The man asked him for a dollar, but Max smiled and said: 'No, you will just drink it up.'

He said to me later: 'You've got to know whom *not* to trust.' He's uneasy in crowds, reluctant to go to parties. Yet when he went with me to dinner at Lance and Teresca's, he enchanted most of my friends there. 'Such a civilized man,' they told me later; 'so attractive, so amusing! At last, a man worthy of you.' He was relieved they liked him, as if they might not.

'All my life I've been a mute in the country of the deaf,' he told me. But I hear him, loud and clear.

Some things puzzle me. Sudden outbursts of anger, mysterious missions. Hatred of homosexuals and over-painted women. How he rushed me out of that movie lobby when he saw display of sexy posters: 'Not for your eyes,' he said.

We look at each other, we touch each other, but that's all. 'My dove, my undefiled,' he quotes the *Song of Songs*.

'I'm fifty-six years old, Max,' I said. 'I'm not all that undefiled.' Strange, how angry that made him. He started for the door, but I managed to appease him.

Only one other time we talked of age. 'You're fifty-two; four whole years between us,' I pointed out.

'What kind of accountant are you?' he said. 'Together we are fifty-four!' And he quoted from Auden: 'We are all contemporaries; there is only a difference in our memories.'

He said we had come late to each other, with our separate histories, but he wants us to make our own memories.

'You are my salvation,' he said. 'You lift me from the mire.'

'What mire?'

'I have clay feet up to here' – he pointed to his chin.

I think I love him.

Dear Nina –
The words of your schizophrenic correspondent haunt
me. Yes, they do apply to my divorce: was it normal,
abnormal, infranormal? I would say infranormal, which
is why it has been so difficult for me to write about it.
Others may have gone through what I did, but not to
such a shattering degree. And I've bequeathed it to Isabel.

Horizontal *is* fact: the brownstone we lived in, one door
leading to Charles' office ('Enter without ringing'), the
adjacent door to our living quarters. Vertical *is* fiction:
the duplex I invented, with Edgar's office directly below
the bedroom.

I understand the 'green line of divorce'; the GO sign, the
permission to proceed. For Isabel, the lights kept changing; she was torn by ambivalence. 'Women weep on
even-numbered floors.' Yes, my Isabel did weep on an
even-numbered floor, on the second floor of the duplex,
right above her husband's odd-numbered office. His odd
office, where her pacing footsteps from above served as
an aphrodisiac to his screwing. She, too, found her
'Unknown Execution' in the Bureau Drawer – only it was
his desk drawer, when she was going through the letters
from all his women for evidence. She, too, was 'hoodwinked by chicanery and witchcraft' – or rather, bitch-
craft. 'Who is your checkmate?' he asks. I know well who
he is. Was. The mate of the checkbook. The man she
checked out. The stale mate.

Perhaps your schizoid correspondent would be the best
one to write my book: a madman to describe the madness
of divorce.

The kids who write to you have the same eloquence. It's a
kind of shorthand: a straight line from them to the
reader. 'The writer sees like a child or a lunatic,' Arnold

Bennett said – and in your letters, you embrace both.

You ask about Max. All I know is that I've stepped smack into a fairy tale. I'm being wooed with flowers and poetry, which he reads to me in his marvelous voice. He goes to such lengths to please me, it leaves me shaken; I am not accustomed. I agree with you – it's too good to be true. Or – I don't remember – did you say 'too *old* to be true?' But if it's a fantasy, I may as well go the whole hog and say: he is not only brilliant, handsome, cultivated, witty, rich, and unattached, but he is also attracted to me. No, we haven't been to bed yet (I did say *yet?*); there's something troubling him, but he asks me to be patient. And I am.

Last night I took him to a dinner party at Lance and Teresca's. Do you remember Teresca Kent (no one remembers Lance) from the days when you lived in New York? To watch her at the table is an experience: she doesn't *eat*, she *feeds* herself. She opens her mouth wide as a fledgling's and tenderly pops choice tidbits into it with long, blood-red talons. She speaks of herself in diminutives and euphemisms, as if to show how little space she occupies, how few demands she makes. She nibbles or tastes or treats herself to a teeny-weeny goody: 'I'll just have a sip of this' . . . 'I'll just have a bite of that.' I caught a glimpse of her washing her hands; she was not so much washing them as having each hand lovingly lave the other. She *touches up* her hair, *slips into* her dress, *tucks* herself in. She doesn't *read* a book, she *glances through it* – a less aggressive act. She doesn't quite complete a thought, but wafts it towards you in a half hearted sentence which, bravely begun, fades wearily away before reaching its destination: 'I was riding in a taxi, it was so completely.' 'I'd love to drop in, but after all.'

She covets everything. Last night she was magnificently attired, as always. She wears costumes rather than clothes, and jewelry which looks as if it should be under glass in a museum. On her finger she wore an enormous emerald ring. Yet when she noticed an inexpensive little costume ring I had picked up someplace, she admired it so insistently, she yearned for it so achingly, that I offered it to her. She quickly accepted it, though I'm sure she will never wear it.

But Lance appears to be totally bemused by her. I've been observing marriages because of my book, marveling at the way men and women accommodate to each other. Charles wouldn't have been able to tolerate her for a moment; Lance seems to dote on her little-girl lispings. I've learned to say 'seems,' for I realize how little one can ever know of what goes on between two people behind their private door, and I never (almost never) allow myself the question: 'What does he see in her?' Or she in him, for that matter. I wish I could put Teresca into my book, but in what connection? Perhaps as a contrast to the self-sacrificing Isabel, who cancels herself out to please others?

Max charmed her, as he does everyone. I think for a moment she was about to ask me for him.

Who else? Hank and Carrie Hollander were there — surely you remember them? Carrie the Good, Carrie the Earth Mother, Carrie who saved my life once or twice, during the worst of the divorce days. And Grace and Henry Loring, through whom I met Max. And Gilda, inundating Max with parlor psychology and English literature. My brother with his Marni, who has gone and dyed her brown hair blonde, the exact shade of mine. And Marge. Remember her? Blue jeans, fuzzy hair, no-nonsense Marge, hip and hep and with it. She was the only one who wasn't impressed by Max. 'He must be kidding,' she said. But the others thought he was the most interesting, the most attractive man I had ever been with. And they were right.

I wish you could meet him. You, Nine More, my ex-pupil, closest friend, confidante, correspondent, celebrity, punster – you would fall in love with him at once.

Have you made a start toward your second book? I haven't come near mine for days. Shall we make a pact: to write to each other only after completing a certain number of pages? Or once a week, say, for half an hour only? How many pages of a book would a half hour of weekly letters make? My problem is that when I receive one of your letters, the temptation to respond is much stronger than the reproachful glances my manuscript gives me. Besides, where else would I send my verses?

> A waste of time
> To write in rhyme:
> The dough's
> In prose.

Your
Jess

THE HOLLOW WOMEN

No wonder she had been retching all morning. *We are the hollow men.* Women. Soon to be made more hollow. The small waiting room – like any other. Two women and a man: the thin, pale girl holding a magazine and a young man staring at his shoes, nothing to say to each other. The fat middle-aged woman applying lipstick with her pinkie, wiping it off, applying it again.

Her mother, whispering to herself, touching the token feather in her purse. My Saintly Madonna, look how I failed you, the fruit of your womb. Perhaps even now, if she strained hard enough? Would she have to pay anyhow? Took up the doctor's chair in his waiting room. Her mother, mumbling louder now, suddenly stood up and began to walk up and down the room. Conspicuous. But then, weren't they all?

The nurse looked in, called the fat woman; they were quickly lost behind the white door. Soundproofed? Or will we hear the scream? *Come with acorn cup and thorne.* Sisters under the skin. Perhaps even now? Go to the bathroom and see? Too late. *Draine my hearte's blood away.* Where do they leave from? Side door? Secret exit? A hearse waiting around the corner? Oh, mother, do sit down. Like a tonsillectomy. But they don't give you much ether. Some don't give you any. Unless you do it in a hospital; there it's legal, if another doctor signs that there is something wrong with you. Something very, very wrong. And you, my child, my unborn, never-to-be-born son/daughter, why are you not stirring, tossing, crying to be heard? Only a speck, a seed. *For harvest time and mowing.* Swinburne, I think. Everything I am saying inside my head seems so . . .

And now – the nurse again, thin-lipped, with a mole on her chin, how can I notice it at a time like this? – beckons. To me? Sit down, Mother, for God's sake. Ask your God for a miracle now. There is still time. A split second. Just get up and walk out – *out* – not toward that white door, but out into the sun. A morning's shopping, perhaps, or a movie, why not, a daytime movie? as weak-kneed, she followed the nurse. Without a backward glance, she knew the sign of the cross her mother was making with her pigeon feather over her retreating back. Pretend this is a routine examination, a hundred a day. Do it all the time, clerks, society people. But the nauseating smell – some chemical? Sick on the nice white sheet? The operation was successful, but the patient puked. Suddenly, a piercing pain, sharp as a blade in her entrails. A moan, another moan. Help me bear it! Bear? She has borne nothing, a zero. The ether cone on her face for a moment, and the nurse's dim voice from far away: 'All morons today.'

Later (too late?) rest for a half hour in a room – where? Must be behind the other. Out of the window – gray roofs. Tears wetting the hard pillow, sterile pillow, sterile, saline tears. Nothing left but the pain, incredible pain. Must be like childbirth. Both doing well: flowers, visitors. Boy or girl? Color eyes, hair? The baby's soft mouth nursing at her breast, the faint smell of talcum and diapers, happy faces all around – look how well she has done, how brave to have suffered such pain to have moaned only once or twice. See the beautiful baby who made it all worthwhile. She could not stop her tears. Nothing to take home in a taxi, nothing to put in a bassinet decorated with lace and ribbons, no one to grow up and talk with, no one to love. All morons today. The pain continued. Will always continue. No matter what else might happen in her life, this one and only first and uniquely her own child will never be. An hour ago there was still time; now, with the blood trickling down through the napkin they placed there, it was too late. She will never know the face she erased.

FRIDAY MARCH 3

A miracle! He loves me, he loves me too! I was beginning to wonder — But what a fantastic, incredible night we had, and what a *man* he is! It's almost unreal, almost frightening.

'You see how it is with us?' he kept saying. 'You see why we waited?'

We're exquisitely attuned to each other; we feel each other's strings. We made love many times in the night; we made love in the morning. Our fantasies and our skins melted into each other, our bodies stopped at nothing, nothing was withheld. Never before was there such closeness. He clutched me to his heart: 'Thank you, God,' he whispered.

There were tears in my eyes. He kissed my cheek, he tasted my tears, he shook his head: 'Not enough salt,' he said.

I never knew one could laugh from sheer happiness while making love. 'You are magic,' he said. 'You are beautiful.'

I am beautiful for him.

He took my face in his two hands and said: 'It seems I love you, Goldenhair.'

Today — a dozen red roses, and this, by Kenneth Patchen:

Oh, my lady, my fairest dear, my sweetest, loveliest one
Your lips have splashed my dull house with the speech
    of flowers
My hands are hallowed where they touched over your
    soft curving.

It is good to be weary from that brilliant work
It is being God to feel your breathing under me.

I am not used to such joy.

Dearest Jess,

Just received yours of the 28th. So it's Max now, instead of Maxwell? Very well, then — Max sounds like the kind of man I wouldn't mind falling in love with, though I would prefer to fall in love *in* bed rather than out. My sex life has been sublimated right out of me by my frantic activities. I do get an occasional proposition, but it's all a lot of unsolicited male. (There are times when even in the most intimate moments, the Pun Also Rises.)

Enjoyed your description of Teresca. I do remember her — a big woman with a breathless voice, who wore eccentric clothes and knew how to put one foot in front of the other. All I recall of Lance is his eloquent silences and elegant cravats. After all, except for a couple of brief visits, it's been six years since I left New York: the first four writing my book begun in your class; the last two getting a divorce and becoming Rich and Famous.

The actual work on the book is just the beginning. My method of work is not much different from yours, but then come several stages. First, the total involvement, when you get up early in the morning, sit down to work in your nightgown, and when you look up — the windows are dark. You walk on the street with glazed eyes and move your lips in the cable car. In the middle of the night you jump out of bed to jot down a phrase before it escapes. In the morning it may sound like gibberish. Or it may not.

When you can no longer tell if your manuscript is marvelous or awful, when you spend hours trying to decide between 'despite' and 'in spite of,' it's time to give it to your editor. Then you spend a few sleepless nights. The number of nights depends on how fast a reader he (or she) is.

The third stage is reading the galleys. It's a strange feeling: when you pick them up, they could be anything —

a pizza, a bundle of laundry. You do not recognize them. Still you make the corrections. No matter how carefully you search for typos, no matter how many commas you change to semicolons – there are invariably overlooked errors, glaring errors that change the meaning: *swept* for *slept*; *hat* for *that*. Things like hat.

Stage four is Sudden Panic. How can you send the galleys back when the book is so obviously worthless? It must be rewritten from scratch. To think that typesetters took the trouble to set one letter after another – and for what? For *this*? It's cold sweat time, and there's nothing you can do about it.

The fifth stage is the physical book. The book exists. There it is, in the store window. People can stop and look at it. They can walk into the store and buy it. They can even read it. When they pick it up, it's as if they were touching your skin. At first you sneak by bookshops, glancing to see if it's there. Why is it stuck in the corner? Why only two copies in the window? Why does the jacket look so weird? Your name, in large letters, looks weird too. Is that how you spell it? After a while pride leads you into one bookstore, then another. You are welcomed. You are asked to autograph as many books as you can. Should you sign only your name? It seems cold and unfriendly, when people are paying all that money for it. 'Sincerely'? Too formal. 'Best wishes'? 'Here's luck to you!'?

The next is a frightening stage. You see how exposed you are. Strangers, friends, former classmates, former lovers, tradespeople, neighbors, everyone can note your every thought, every emotion, magnify every infelicitous word. It's too late; it's out of your hands. But at the same time, you experience a huge pride. You want to stand in front of the window where the book is displayed and shout: 'Hey, that's me!' You want to nudge your neighbor on the bus who is reading it and whisper: '*I* wrote that!'

Then comes the best part. The part that makes it all

worthwhile: the sleepless nights, the struggles to rewrite, the fears and the panics. Now come the reviews. How beautiful, how intelligent the reviewers are! They understood. And fan mail from all over the country. How beautiful, how intelligent readers are! And with the paperback publication – letters from kids. The 'Dear Miss Moore' letters, some of which I've been quoting to you. They say more to me than all the plaques and certificates and awards. To you too; I know how you feel about kids big and small.

Now the book assumes a life of its own. It's launched. It's off. Like the countdown at Cape Canaveral, 10-9-8-7 on the best-seller lists, until it reaches 1.

The book is reprinted, quoted. It's translated into twenty-one languages with titles such as: *Alas, the Carousel*, or *The Melancholy Merriment*, or *Circling*. The book lives: in libraries. In schools and colleges. In people's homes. In distant countries. And soon it will become a movie. One day maybe a musical (you will, of course, write the lyrics for it!).

It has given me a new identity: 'Author of *The Sad Merry-Go-Round*.' It has given me an entree into the world of other authors. It has made me an Authority on everything, like that wonderful comedian, what's his name, who billed himself as 'the world's greatest authority.'

In a way, all this has blossomed from you and your Workshops.

Your strength lies in knowing what is good, and why. That's why I'm sure you will write a good book, even about the nightmare of your divorce. Of course it's difficult for you to feel compassion for those who have damaged you. Yet the love will come. I know because I'm your friend.

And I know your feeling for kids. Here are their latest:

I'm beginning to think I'm a lesbian. Do you have any suggestions? I'm not signing my name for safety reasons.

You have a way with your words. Your book is so realistic to life, but you don't even blame us. Not many people or parents would do that.

If it's a true story, who were you?

Who was I? Hard to remember now. I was part of a couple, one of the 'young marrieds,' very poor and struggling. You knew me then. Agents and publishers on whose doors I knocked with my short stories who wouldn't see me come to me now. The vice-president of the bank that refused us a loan invites me to lunch. The high school where I flunked math is giving a Creative Writing Prize in my name, and the college that refused me a scholarship so that I had to drop out has just bestowed upon me an honorary Doctor of Letters degree! Henceforth, you will please address me as Dr Nine More.

I know, I know. What you're really interested in are my mishaps on my lecture tours. In my very next letter, I'll start with that.

All I ask is that if you have finally made it to bed with Max, you indicate it by an asterisk. Like this *

Much love,
Dr Nina

NOTES TO MYSELF

Writer's objectivity: *I* into *She*

Reader's identification: *She* into *Me*

A sharing between writer and reader.

Recollected in tranquillity? Despair recollected in anger.

Why people divorce. Overheard: 'We couldn't give any comfort to each other.'

Story: They started playing poker, while the wife stayed home. The other woman was 'one of the boys.' She seduced him, and now he's living with her in New Mexico. The wife? – She never learned to play cards.

Children of divorce. Small child complains: 'I almost had a heart attack! I won't live forever!'

Falling out of love – same stages as falling in love, but in reverse.

In marriage – vulnerability to mate's contempt. No place to hide.

Dear Dr Nine More –

In response to your query, *. Also ***. Not to mention !!!. He's incredible, everything I have ever fantasized, and he loves me, and he quotes biblical poetry – the Old Testament, not my mother's New Testament, and I can hardly believe it. I can't say more, even to you. Only know I'm happy, and be happy for me.

Let's talk of other things.

Cat is leaning with all her weight against my leg: a reminder that it's her dinnertime. I call her Cat because that's what she is, and because I'm too busy assigning names to my fictitious characters. How does Lila Noon strike you? Me too.

I've already turned Charles (no one ever called him Charlie) Galen into Edgar (never Eddie) Webb. My once husband, inappropriately enough, bears a noble and honourable name of Galen, the early Greek physician and writer on medicine. I would never have assigned him this name in fiction! But Edgar – that's Anglo-Saxon for 'protector of property' – is fitting; how he did protect it! And Webb – well, obviously, it's the web he spun around his prey, that wily spider.

I've made Jill and Jeremy into Wendy and Gregory, though Isabel's children are quite different from mine; Carrie into Martha; and Marni into Molly, who models herself on Isabel – until she goes too far. My brother Victor – did I tell you? is Dr Q. Vincent Barshak. I don't know why. Would you believe that yesterday he asked my opinion of this:

> SIR JOHN SUCKLING: 'O, so fickle, O, so vain, O, so false is she!'
> BEN JONSON: 'O, so white, O, so soft, O, so sweet is she!'

I said they didn't really sound so alike to me. In my novel, he'll be an eighteenth-century scholar, author of the monumental two-volume *Grub Street*, dealing with all the literary hacks, pamphleteers, garreteers, plagiarists, freaks, and frauds who surrounded giants like Samuel Johnson; the hireling scriveners who wrote biographies of people who never lived, last wills and testaments of people who never died, and faithful eyewitness accounts of adventures that never occurred. It should be right up his alley.

Who else? My friend Gilda, the parlor analyst, will be Gertrude (means 'spear maiden'). Who will ever want to flirt/With a girl whose name is Gert?

Marge will be Midge

And Varya will become Nadya, short for Nadezhda, which means hope. She's the positive Russian pole (no puns, please), contrasted to Isabel's mother, who is the negative one. I discarded Ludmilla (too elegant), Tamara (too romantic), and Xenia (too hard for a non-Russian to pronounce, in case the reader wishes to read the passage aloud). But even after I gave her a story of her own, she refuses to stay put in my book.

These characters are all composites of course, with much that is invented. But then, that's true of real people as well.

No, my dear friend, you are not in my book. I'm keeping you to myself.

I speak as if the book is taking shape; actually I haven't been near it for days. I'm too full of Max to re-enter the world of my former self and all that unhealed suffering. The other day I happened to be on the East Side and passed by the brownstone where I used to live with Charles. I glanced up at our bedroom window, and I saw myself standing behind it, looking out, tears rolling down my cheeks — twelve, thirteen years ago. Your young man wrote: 'Distress on the window pane.' Pain. Yes.

If only I didn't feel guilty about the advance I accepted from my publishers and the deadline approaching, I could be perfectly happy.

The minutes mock my writing block. I want to bid each ticking clock to stop the ticking and to tock!

You may ask, if you note, why the lines I just wrote are not broken by rhyme into rows. It's because I don't dare; like the man in Molière, I might find out what everyone knows: That (what can be worse?) in spite of my verse, all along I've been writing in prose!

Your
Jess

P.S. About the rhyme for 'masochist' — I've given it much serious thought. All I can come up with is a rather labored structure, but it might work. It's an opera, see, and there's this basso who has a love scene with the soprano. She can't stand him — his bristly beard, his sweat, his big belly, but she has to submit to his impassioned kiss after her aria,

> feeling like a masochist
> who is by the *basso* kissed.

If I think of a better one, I'll let you know.

J

Dearest Jess,

Any asterisks yet?

Our letters must be crossing each other some place in the sky at this very moment. But a promise is a promise, so I'll get around to the subject of my lecture mishaps.

But first I want to tell you I'm back on the movie set. I'm not actually *on* the set as much as all over it, for I'm fascinated by everything. The meticulous attention to detail. The perfection of the technical mechanics. The disregard for the written word. The kids — those that show up — are great. They're so alive to everything they're doing. They improvise on the spur of the moment and give the director some of his best shots.

As for my lectures, they're not so much lectures as talks. They're not so much talks as performances. I've become a real pro, and I've learned to handle all kinds of unforeseen emergencies. For example: Just before alighting at an airport where I was to be met by a delegation who were to escort me to my hotel, I discovered that the shoe of my left foot, which I had slipped off during flight, would not, could not go back on my foot. Whether my foot had become swollen or the shoe had shrunk was not the point. The point was — how to get off the plane with dignity? I tried to get my shoe on. The stewardess tried. The man in the seat next to me tried. But they could no longer keep me in the plane, so I removed my other shoe, threw my cape dramatically over my shoulder (you *know* I can look dramatic when I want to!) and — holding both shoes aloft — I descended the ramp, waving my booty (forgive the pun) in the air with a triumphant smile. Whether they thought it was some kind of prearranged signal so that they would recognize me, or a new way of traveling that sophisticated cosmopolites were the first to know about, or a symbol of something they should have known from their reading of great literature, the question never came up. They graciously escorted me, on my stockinged tiptoes, to the waiting car, and chatted animatedly all the way to my hotel. That evening, when I arrived to deliver my talk, a couple of them did glance down at my feet, properly shod, but nothing was ever said.

I feel apologetic that I no longer look quite as glamorous as I do on my book jacket and publicity photos. For one thing, I'm two and a half years older. It may not seem like much, but thirty-seven is *very* much older than a mere thirty-four and a half. Also, I've gained five pounds. It's all those martinis at lunch with my business retinue. I look at myself in the mirror: Was this the face that lunched a thousand sips?

And you — are you still as slim and pretty as you were when I last saw you? Do you still buy your clothes in teenage departments? I remember how hard your very large sister-in-law Marni has always tried to look like you. Has she succeeded? Is your brother Victor still chasing his poetic plagiarists? Please note: I've asked not a single question about Max. I'm only waiting for that asterisk.

Back to my lecture tours. I don't mind the long flights, the strange beds, the preparations for my talks; what I find tiring is the smiling. And it's exhausting to have to sit through a long program or an endless banquet, no matter how many papier-mâché merry-go-rounds decorate the room. I want to stand up, say what I have to, and go home. This isn't easy to come by, even though I've been trying to set up some Grande Dame rules of my own.

They all insist I appear at least an hour before my scheduled talk. Sheer nervousness. I spend that time in someone's office or in the washroom, jotting down some notes I seldom refer to, since I'm what's known as a 'text deviate.' Sounds better when I say it out loud. I also make sure I have lots of tissues for sudden sneezing fits which attack me, depending on the kind of corsage they pin under my nose. If I should arrive only a half hour early, I find them standing outside in the weather, looking up and down the street for me.

Sometimes I have to sit through a two-hour program: salute to the flag, the national anthem, the local choral group, the financial report by the treasurer, various committee reports, a list of names of people I don't know who are recipients of awards and who, in turn, give lengthy speeches of thanks. But what I mind most is when the person who is about to introduce me says badly the things I had planned to say well.

When, at last, my time comes, I do the best I can, because afterward comes my personal reward: a kind of love. People rush up to me to shake my hand, to touch me, kids, grown-ups, and they tell me what I need so much to hear. They ask me to autograph scraps of paper, programs, paper napkins. A boy handed me a dog-eared copy of my book in paperback: 'This is the first book I ever bought,' he said. 'For money.'

So you see why I do this.

Since I don't keep copies of my letters, I don't remember – did I tell you I am now a Doctor? I know that word doesn't sit well with you, but I'm not *that* kind of doctor. I received an Honorary Doctor of Letters degree for delivering the commencement address at Marden College, from which I dropped out in my youth for lack of funds. I find my new title useful only when my phone goes out of order. I call the repair service to advise them sternly: 'This is Dr Moore speaking. My phone isn't working.' Convinced that lives are at stake, they say: 'Yes, Doctor. Immediately, Doctor,' and within a half hour my phone is fixed.

I eagerly await your letter. I want to hear about Varya. And about you-know-who. Whom.

Much love,
Nina

MONDAY MARCH 13

This is *real*. After all the desolate years, this is my great love come to me. I can't believe it. He, too, says he never knew it was possible. He says I give him peace he has never known. He clasps me to him as if I might disappear. 'Goldenhair!' he calls me, his fairy princess.

Friday, Saturday, Sunday – for three days and nights we were together here. 'This is our richest love,' he says; 'it took a lifetime to arrive at.' His smile is radiant, though beneath it I think I see pain. I know so little about his past, except that he has been alone and unhappy.

He brought me a present: a table cigarette lighter in the shape of a bronze dragon spitting fire when pressed. Attached to it – this poem by Yeats:

> I did the dragon's will until you came
> . . .
> And then you stood among the dragon-rings.
> I mocked, being crazy, but you mastered it
> And broke the chain, and set my ankles free –
> Saint George or else a pagan Perseus;
> And now we stare astonished at the sea,
> And a miraculous strange bird shrieks at us.

Dearest Jess,

Our letters of the 8th did cross. I admit to an unseemly carnal curiosity, so I appreciate the asterisks and exclamation points. Just keep your eyes open and stay happy – not an easy thing to do. You are much too trusting – but what can one expect of your generation, which admired a ventriloquist on the *radio*?

I remember our talks about your mother and her very personal Christ. If the Old Testament, quoted by your lover, does it for you, stay with it. You can't serve both God and mama.

Which reminds me that you're not the only Freudian slipper in this correspondence. I was invited to spend a week visiting friends in Grenada. They urged me to get away from all the tensions of the film, the second book, and so on. I replied on the phone that I was too busy, although I would have loved to relax in their garden, breathe some fresh air, and listen to the critics chirping ...

It's true I don't have the time necessary to write a book. I feel like that Queen in *Alice in Wonderland* (the Red or the White? – you're the literary one) who had to run very fast in order to remain in the same place.

All this week I've been pursued by tapes and cameras of the National Television Educational Company, for their *Writers at Work* series. I was photographed at the Settlement House (where I got my 'inspiration'), at the Public Library (where I did my 'research'), and at my typewriter (where I 'created' my book). Also, of course, on a merry-go-round.

But it's more than a problem of time. My rise has been so swift, the contrast to my previous life so extreme, that I begin to doubt myself. This, of course, isn't new. Some writers whose first works were hugely successful have even committed suicide. No, that isn't my style. But I did consult a couple of shrinks out here. I gave each only forty minutes of my time (are your analysts still on the forty-five-minute hour back east? When do you switch to doctor-saving time?). One told me that success equals a big penis, safety — a small penis. I didn't quite get that. The second assured me it was either repressed parent-child conflict or repressed sibling conflict that was causing my block. Since I have no sibling and recall no conflict with my parents, I couldn't buy that either. Not at sixty bucks an hour. (We're more expensive out here because of the climate and all.) A third was nice. He smiled a lot and told me I had too harsh a superego. He also told me of some recent statistics about women's fear of success. A Dr (wait, let me check my notes) — a Dr Martina Horner, president of Radcliffe College, found that 64 percent of women associate women's success with depression, illness, death — while 90 percent of the men associate men's success with happiness. What do you think of that?

The last shrink was practical. He shook my hand warmly and advised me to starve. That is, to go back to the way I lived before *The Sad Merry*. The stresses of poverty and loud matrimonial quarrels may have been conducive to creativity, but frankly, I'd rather stay where I am. Being the nation's #1 best seller was never my fantasy (all I wanted was a nice, quiet husband who would love me), but I took to it at once! Remember how I cried when I had to step down from #1 to #2?

In the long run, maybe all this frantic activity around me will turn out to be ersatz, like the foamy synthetic whipped cream that squirts from a can and leaves nothing on the palate. But I like it.

The best advice, of course, came from one of my young fans: 'I'd rather read you than TV. Please sit down and write more about life for my friends and I.'

I would, if I had the time. There are all those calls, requests, lectures . . . That's where I came in. That's where I got on this old gray and gilt horse (or is it a lion?) on this creaky old carousel.

But there's no excuse for you. I know the subject of

divorce is grim, but so was the subject of the underworld of teenagers. Your book should be meaningful to anyone who has ever been married or divorced or separated or just scared of losing someone. I think you're describing the human condition, not just Isabel and Edgar, and that anyone would rather read it than TV. You're not really writing about yourself and Charles; you're writing fiction. What you lived was life. There's a big difference. Fiction is truer than life. You're the one who taught me that.

Much love,
Nina

NOTES TO MYSELF

From personal to universal.

Chapter on lonely women, finding cold comfort in each other.

Look up: sparrows, wrens. Which lonelier, sadder image?

Different ways of coping with divorce. The damage. The regret.

How it was in early sixties, before women's movement had gathered momentum. The need for man – any man.

Have Edgar take Isabel to Point Lake (They're still able to communicate), for weekend of 'rest,' while he goes off to ski elsewhere.

THE SAD BROWN WRENS

Isabel saw them as sad brown wrens huddled together on the telegraph wire, the lonely women gathered in places such as this. The bitter ones, still fighting old battles never won; the vindictive, dreaming of revenge; the losers, the failures, the shrews; the weak and the wronged, who had given up every-thing only to find late in life the struggle unequal and the night full of terrors.

Some clung to the ex-husband, not yet emotionally divorced, though it's been three years, five, six, and the man remarried, with children of his own. Some kept jumping desperately from bed to bed, seeking in many men the answer they had never found in one. They perched on chairs arranged in rows at meetings and lectures and gatherings. They perched on bar-stools in taverns, nervously ruffling their feathers. They perched here, in the lobby of Point Lake, the legion of lonely women, huddled together against the weather.

Would she be one of them?

She would have to unlearn marriage and learn what she had ignored within its safety: how to be amusing, attentive, attractive to a man, no matter how swollen the feet, how heavy the heart. These women knew this. They would never again meet a man who had married them when they were young and pretty. No man had to hold their elbow crossing streets, make love to them, take them to the hospital when they were sick. At forty, fifty, sometimes later they had to begin all over again the whole business they had gone through at eighteen: flirtation, seduction – but this time it was harder. They were less flexible, less trusting. They were tired.

Besides, there were now fewer men to choose from. Instead of hundreds of young boys everywhere – on college campuses, at summer beaches – there were only the rigid bachelors, weary widowers, homosexuals, or ex-husbands of other women, damaged by divorce.

It was not even a question of sex (love did not enter into it except as occasional fantasy); just a man. A man who might, if she earned it by undemanding affection, call her up, take her to dinner, send her flowers. These were to be wrested and won from the others competing for that flower, that phone call.

The women swooped down upon her with the chirped chorus of: 'Join the club!' They twittered and chattered and wondered about that handsome man in the ski suit who had deposited her there and gone off. 'You're leaving *him*?' they asked, incredulous. A single man was precious, to be flattered, cultivated, wooed – as her husband was being right now. The very word 'unattached' was magic.

The thing about marriage, Isabel thought, is that two people had no need anymore to prove anything, to make the effort. The attrition of the years went unnoticed. But now she, too, would have to compete with the others, the young ones. 'You have so much to offer,' her friends said. The point was – to whom?

The women huddled closer, exchanging confidences, disappointments, comparing notes. 'Did yours say he'll quit working and you can go to hell?' – 'Did yours say you can't squeeze blood from a stone?' –

But the terrible, the incomprehensible thing, they said, was that he forgot the children. Completely lost interest. Didn't show on visitation day. Never sent a penny. Or else – and this was a graver injury – he bought them expensive presents, while at home there was no money for food, or he exposed them to that whore he was living with. The ex-wives, the wrens, the shrews, and the martyrs marveled: How could a father who had once diapered the children, taken them to the playground, applauded at the graduation play, divorce himself from them or turn them against their mother?

No matter how dismal or destructive a marriage, Isabel saw that there was – at least at first – regret. And envy – for the safe ones who had managed to hold on. Or for those who had remarried, who had a man to protect them from loneliness, to be a 'substitute father' to the children, to say *'Gesundheit'* when they sneezed. A living man, breathing in the house.

'Such a good-looking man,' they twittered around Isabel. But she was not quite one of them – not yet. There was still time to – what? There was still a chance to – why? She would spend the next two days and nights here, then Edgar would return to pick her up and drive her home to her mattress on the living room floor. That was more than the sad little wrens had. That was something to hang on to. Until she was strong enough to do what had to be done.

[DIARY]

TUESDAY MARCH 14

Today he was strange on the phone. He was tired, he said; had a bad night. He was afraid he had lost me: he had called me, and when he couldn't reach me, he thought I stopped loving him. He wondered if someone had talked to me about him. My poor Max! How can he think so little of himself? The other day, when I touched him and withdrew my hand, he thought I was repelled by him!

He said he needs time to think. Think what?

I feel limp, dizzy, as if I've been swinging on a pendulum.

A couple of hours ago, flowers arrived from him by messenger: one white rose, one red. The thorns had not been removed; as I was putting them into a vase, I pricked my finger. It's still bleeding, through the band-aid. Surprising, how much it hurts . . .

IF I WERE YOU

There had been endless telephone conversations, meetings for coffee, bursts of intimate confidences with Isabel's married women friends. They were supportive and very sure: 'For once in your life, *live*!'—'It will be better for the children in the long run' – 'I have a wonderful man I want to introduce you to' . . .

She needed their certainty. She was vacillating in an agony of ambivalence; she was propelled by straws. Once in a store she spent a paralyzing half hour in a panic of indecision about the color of a spool of thread. She swung, she veered, she changed hourly.

She tried to pin her feelings down by making lists: Pro and Con, Credits and Debits. Grievances: He lied to her, was unfaithful, left the toilet seat up after urinating. Once she had found it endearing evidence of a man in the house; now she felt it as another of many humiliations: he ignored her presence in the apartment. She used to be comforted by the cozy sound of his snoring; now it was another proof of his lack of consideration for her, it kept her awake. The way his jaws worked when he chewed – but no, she was losing sight of the larger issues. Which were – what?

'I can't, I just can't go on like this anymore,' she said to her friends. 'I don't know what to do.'

And they told her. 'If I were you, I wouldn't spend another day with that man! When a marriage is on the rocks – '

Their advice was based on the fallacy of 'If I were you.' Besides, her marriage was not on the rocks; it was on quicksands. Edgar and she were pulling each other down, deeper and deeper, toward their destruction. And yet – 'He's the father of my children,' she would say. 'How can I risk their security?'

'What is security?' her friends scoffed. 'You can get run over by a car tomorrow. You can drop dead doing the dishes.'

She sought advice from the others, from the bitter women who had been through it. 'They had to feed me with a spoon.' – 'I slashed my wrists.' – 'You need a bastard for a lawyer,' they said. 'I gave him everything, to avoid court, to protect the children, and now there's no money for orthodontics, and the kids won't talk to me anyhow.'

Her mother was no help. She translated for Isabel what God had told her in dreams, and offered Isabel her life. 'I would die for you,' she said, Christ on the cross, to redeem her daughter's marriage. Her brother had his own problems with Molly, she guessed, although they never spoke of them.

There was no one who could help her.

Edgar could not understand: 'Why can't you adjust, like me, and have outside interests too?'

'You mean lovers?' she asked bitterly.

He shrugged. He could not see why she was pacing the floor, gasping for breath, and tearing her skin nights instead of finding her own amusements while he was away on his weekend trips. He saw nothing wrong with himself; Isabel's unhappiness had to do with her nature. When she brought up the subject of divorce or separation, he refused to discuss it. He repeated he could not afford two establishments, he valued their social life, he saw no reason for divorce.

Her psychiatrist, Dr K., was a non-talker. He offered no advice, though she pleaded with him to tell her what to do. He did say once that she must make greater demands on life, and that she seemed to be afraid of her husband. That was absurd: what was there to fear from that weak, ineffectual man who clung to her as to a life raft?

The children? They lived behind their closed doors, emerging only for meals, eaten in silence, for all her effort at cheerfulness. She had tried to hide her unhappiness. She would come to the dinner table in sunglasses, to hide her eyes, red from weeping, while he sat across the table, his face in his hands. But the children must have known for a long time. She remembered the card Wendy had drawn when she was six: a dark, windowless building, and under it, in black letters: 'HAPPY ANERVERSERRY, HA-HA!'

Now that they were older, now was the time to do it. Although it would be easier to wait until they were out of the house, their dark, gloomy house, and away in college. And until she herself had more therapy, so that she could find the strength to do this to him. Until she accumulated more evidence against him. Saved some money. Trained for a job. Found a man.

'You're entitled to a little happiness,' said her married friends. 'Give yourself a chance to meet a man who would appreciate you!'

'They had to feed me with a spoon,' said the others.

NOTES TO MYSELF

The children? Of course, they see through their mother. Their brief, harsh judgment of both parents: 'Phony, the two of you are phonies!' Or maybe they don't care that much. Own lives, own interests.

That can't be true.

Why am I doing this? I didn't hurt my own children that much with divorce.

Edgar mentions their social life. Certainly, marriage not all grim. Isabel can't see this; must find only pain.

Should Edgar rationalize his affairs, the way Charles did, when he told me Laura kept our marriage together?

But Edgar is not Charles. My divorce is not Isabel's. Only climax in court was the same.

Dear Nina –

It's no fantasy. Max and I have been together almost constantly. He's the most fascinating, exciting, and beautiful man I've ever known, and with him I, too, feel fascinating, exciting, and beautiful! He's like Falstaff – no, no, not fat; he's tall and lean – but Shakespeare describes Falstaff as one who is 'not only witty in himself, but the cause that wit is in other men.' I am at my best with him; that makes me love him even more. I try to make myself into everything he has ever wanted in a woman. Fortunately, he likes small, slim blondes; otherwise I'm sure I would grow a few inches taller.

Thank you for your encouraging words about my writing. I'm much too involved with Max to work on my book, though Varya keeps reminding me that time doesn't take a nap and that hunger is not an auntie.

Max and I have been staying here alone most of the time, discovering each other over and over. He doesn't like parties, so I've been refusing all invitations that have been pouring in ever since my friends met him at the Kents. I'm beginning to run out of excuses.

> I so regret to miss your party,
>   I can't express my heartfelt sorrow;
> I have a previous engagement
>   Which I shall make first thing tomorrow.

Besides, I don't have a title for my book yet, and how can one write a book without a title? *Diary of Divorce* is too stark and documentary, though it has a certain gossip value. Your title, *The Sad Merry-Go-Round*, sounds inevitable. (Do you know, I almost typed '*Marry-Go-Round*' by mistake? How would that be for mine?)

The reason for all these typos is that my old typewriter is on its last legs. Some of the keys refuse to budge.

Just got two of them unstuck, to say that you and I seem to be living our lives in reverse: you soared from married poverty into affluence; I plummeted from married affluence into poverty. Not really – I'm managing nicely. I even have a savings account; most of it – advance on my book, which I don't have to return if I finish it by December. March – April – May – that's nine whole months away. In nine months, who knows what can get born?

I was interested to learn that you sometimes have to sit through the salute to the flag and the national anthem on your lecture tours. I thought both were obsolete. Here in New York, in most schools, the salute and the assemblies have been abolished because of emphasis on individualism and danger of riots. But I remember (that's one advantage of being almost twenty years older than you), in my elementary school days, the impressive ritual of the Color Guard and the mandatory Pledge of Allegiance. I pictured legions in a public square and a flag on an invisible witches' stand. No one bothered to explain the words of the national anthem to us, either. What pearls in the night? Why was gallant Lee screaming?

This was in the dawn's early light, before war was declared between our children and our schools, in those days of innocence when stepping out of line in the communal march to pee and chewing gum in class were serious infractions. And this was before God was banished from our public schools. Do you remember the Bible reading, or was it already outlawed in your day? More often than not, the passage was the Twenty-third Psalm: 'The Lord is my Shepherd, I shall not want.' Want what? I supplied my own guilty wishes for the inaccessible and the undeserved: the too expensive skates, the long black hair, the A in gym.

Something like tribal safety lay in the communal prayer as we sat, heads bowed, silently atoning for past misdeeds and buying amnesty for future ones. For the risks were many: our treacherous lapses of memory on a test, the crooked ovals in the Palmer handwriting exercises, the uninvited blot on the composition paper, the arithmetic sum that did not coincide with the answer in the back of the book, and the dreaded spelling bee. I saw the menacing bee literally buzzing over our heads, unable to decide upon whom to alight, until swiftly, viciously, it swooped down to sting one of us and fell the victim to the ignominious seat, felling the whole row, letting down the whole team.

I know, I know, this wave of nostalgia is but another diversionary tactic. I've been talking about assemblies and spelling bees because it's difficult for me to talk about Max to you or to anyone — except in my diary.

Wish me — wish me that all should go well with us. And write me about your movie, your travels, your fan mail. *With a little tail*, as Varya would say. That means: And a little more.

Love,
Jess

NOTES TO MYSELF

Flesh out characters. Isabel's mother: combination Varya and my mother. Both: 'If God wants'; both: miracles. But totally different voices. Isabel's mother — ear to disaster. Guilt about her husband's untimely death from 'double-pneumonia-before-penicillin' (said as single word). Feels she killed him. 'You gave him pneumonia?' Isabel asks. 'Yes,' her mother says. Didn't heed God's warning. Selfishly made him go out in heavy rain with bad cold to friend's wedding. Didn't go back for umbrella: afraid to be late. Just punishment. Atoning ever since.

Her superstitions — different from Varya's. (How shocked Varya was when saw my manuscript on couch: bad luck! She picked it up as if paper on fire, and placed it gingerly on desk. Or when I dropped page on floor, she wouldn't let me pick it up until I first sat on it! Wonder where they originate. Funny.)

Her mother's superstitions — not funny to Isabel. Mother trying to direct her daughter's life by God's omens. Isabel annoyed: 'I don't believe in this nonsense!' (Plant this for later scene.)

With Edgar — still undisconnected neurons. Myth of family. Isabel gives him birthday present — how can she not?

Yet she can't hide contempt for him. Once, long ago, he told her how he was caught playing 'dirty doctor' with little girl next door. *Grown man, still playing dirty doctor,* Isabel thinks scornfully.

My own contempt for Charles. 'Why can't you adjust to reality?' he kept saying. What reality? Laura?

Reality of my 'extravagance'? — Reflection of his miserliness. All that talk, during our divorce negotiations, about 'moral obligation vs. legal obligation' to educate children! Refused put in writing: 'I will not be dictated to!'

Reality of Charles's women patients, their frantic phone calls, threats of suicide? For psychiatrist, par for course.

Icy man, incapable of love, indifferent to his children, holding on desperately to our marriage. Frightened: Defrocked by Psychoanalytic Society? Dethroned as sex and marriage expert? Or deeper fear of something I suspected?—From window, when I used to see his 'regulars' enter next door (without ringing) – always that handsome twice-a-week young man would stop before going in, take out comb and pocket mirror, and carefully comb his hair. Charles's silent denial; yet it could have been a serious threat in those days, before closet door swung wide open on gay movement. No proof – only a clue.

Isabel. For her the clues accumulate. Perhaps she finds a number, a combination to a lock or strongbox where Edgar keeps what? Where?

Dearest Jess,

You're right. Your school reminiscences and your funny rhymes are tactics to keep you from the book! I know that trick well. I'm using it now.

You notice how delicately I have refrained from asking you about Max so far in this letter?

Now then. To business. But before I answer your questions, let's get something straight. The difference in our ages is *not* twenty years but a mere nineteen. If I'm thirty-seven and you're fifty-six, figure it out yourself. But you're the youngest fifty-six I've ever known. When I saw you last you looked like a college soph, not even a senior. Love must have demoted you into a freshman. You look much too young to be the mother of grown children. How *are* Jill and Jeremy, and what are they up to?

As for my film — they have finished the shooting, that's why I'm back in San Francisco, in my newly decorated apartment. (I wrote you about the splendid view of the Golden Gate Bridge I bought myself last December.) The decorator, who charged me a fortune ('You can afford it!'), put *artificial* flowers *inside* my woodburning fireplace.

'Why?' I asked.

'Can't use fresh ones,' he said.

'But why in the fireplace?'

'Where else?'

The happy problems of the rich. More serious is the impression I give some of my friends whose marriages are shaky. They seem to think that as soon as they shed their mate and take up painting or ceramics again, they will win fame and fortune. Well, it *is* true that a lot of energy goes into making a bad marriage work. Energy that might do better elsewhere. But it doesn't follow.

I was saying — my film. They are now doing something

elsewhere with the music and the cutting. I'm all for cutting. Your Fiction Workshop taught me to say too little rather than too much. (Letters are an exception.) I've learned to trust the reader; to say it by implication. Perhaps this doesn't work in films, where everything is visual and must be *shown*. Frankly, I rather dread seeing the final version. The whole film seems to have been made of scrambled fragments, disparate little scenes. I wonder how they will ever glue it all together.

Next question: travels. I may go abroad in April. For just a few days, on business. In the meantime, I'm back on the road. I hope to get to New York again one of these days, to see you and to meet Max — before his silver hair turns gray!

I've had my small triumphs on my lecture tours, as well as mishaps. In Seattle I drew a good crowd, in spite of competition with the Vice-President of the United States. And in Houston, I had a heady experience. My plane was late, so I was met at the airport by a motorcycle police escort! If you've never had motorcycles with their shrill sirens *in front* of your car rather than behind it, you don't know what power is! There was no talking to me for days after. Spoiled rotten, that's what I am. I've even begun prefacing letters of complaint to delinquent department stores with: 'My name may not be unfamiliar to you — .' That's why I need your funny verses, to give me back my balance and put me on 'a even kiel.'

Another fan writes: 'Nina, remember the book you wrote, the Sad Merry-Go-Round? I appear on p. 209, only I'm more on the stout side. The way you wrote about me, you must be something else.'

I often feel I must be something, or someone else. I remember how afraid I was, shortly before my book was published, that I would be fired from that Settlement House where I worked. My co-workers comforted me: 'Don't worry. Who will review it? Who will know you wrote it?'

I think that covers all of your questions, except for Varya's strange phrase: 'A little tail.' Frankly, in the last few weeks, I haven't even had . . . Never mind.

I think I deserve a long letter from you, all about the Max factor, and more comments on your Fiction Workshop. I wish I were back in your class . . .

Much love,
Nina

NOTES TO MYSELF

Divorce as parallel of war?
Strategies, briefing, spying, and counterspying. Ammunition (all's fair). Offensive, defensive. Surprise attack. Ignorant armies, clash by night. Carnage. The shell-shocked. The amputees. The innocent victims . . . No – too contrived. *Imply* only.

Vignettes not in sequence. For my own reference:
1962 – Marcus. Children. Detectives. Mattress.
1963 – At his lawyer's. Samuels. The Other Woman.
1964 – Gregory's college. $7.98.
1965 – Adams & Gross. Raid. Locksmith. Doorknob.
1966 – Dept. stores. Alimony! Dorian. Court.

How does Isabel find courage in the first place to hire lawyer? Go back in time – to 1962.

YOU'RE THE INJURED PARTY

Everyone in the subway must know where she was going, Isabel thought, and what she was planning to do behind her unsuspecting husband's back.

She couldn't hold on any longer. Edgar absolutely refused to hear of a divorce, even after she had learned about Molly. 'Divorce is for the rich, I can't afford it,' he kept saying. 'I won't be able to pay for the children's education.' She couldn't use Molly, of course, but she had plenty of other evidence. Besides, she was going only for information.

Rose had recommended Mr Marcus as a very competent divorce lawyer. She herself had used him several years ago. Rose should know: she was on her fifth lawyer, still suing her husband for additional alimony, even though he got himself a Mexican divorce and had married someone else. 'Just put yourself in his hands,' Rose had said, 'and do exactly as he says.'

She was going only for information, Isabel kept assuring herself. She was planning no action; she just needed to know her rights. It would help her resolve her ambivalence, her despair. Each day she said to herself that she couldn't go on any longer; each day she went on. She was losing weight, gasping for breath nights, tearing at the hives on her skin. She needed only to know what her legal rights were, that was all. She could decide later what to do.

Mr Marcus was sensible and businesslike. 'It's an open and shut case,' he told her. 'I'm ready when you are. Don't delay: it will only get worse.' They had hubby over the barrel, he said; they would take him to the cleaners. She would get speedy action and the best settlement any lawyer could win for her. He advised her to take the bull by the horns; he would be her gladiator. 'After all,' he said, 'you're the injured party.'

His retainer was reasonable: $600. He explained that the only grounds in a contested divorce in New York had to be adultery. He would hire detectives, tail hubby on one of his weekend trips, and nab him.

Nab him? The man whose shirts were in her closet, whose ties, whose socks, whose coffee cup . . . She felt faint, she was trembling, but there was something almost fatherly in Mr Marcus' assurances. He would fight her battles for her; he would take care of everything.

He patted her on the shoulder and repeated: 'Ready when you are.'

SUNDAY MARCH 26

Easter Sunday – Mother's most important holiday, more meaningful than Christmas; for her, Christ's resurrection was a greater miracle than His birth.

My own miracle is Max – these last ten days incredible, a dream come true. He came a week ago on Thursday – totally committed: brought his shaving things, toothbrush, everything new. He even bought himself new bathrobe and slippers, 'uncontaminated' (his word) by memories. He did not go to his office all week. Tonight for the first time he went to sleep in 'the other place'; that's what he calls his apartment. Here is *home*.

This is the first chance I've had to write in this diary.

Ten days and nights of such loving I never knew existed. We step in and out of each other. I've put myself inside his fantasies: when he is in his biblical mood, I am Shulamite, his Princess of the *Song of Songs*. When he is Oriental – oh, we improvise, we play, and afterward, we lie content as cats, gently scratching each other and purring. I don't know where my skin ends and his begins. We hear each other's thinking.

'I am aware of everything about you,' he says; 'your stance, the way you move.' His memory is uncanny. He can recall every word I ever said to him, my every gesture, every cry.

He loves surprises. He brought me this group of little animals in a glass case, marvelously executed replicas of the illustrations of my poem 'Please Don't Tease the People in the Zoo.' He said he had them specially commissioned.

He's afraid he may run out of surprises. He drives to a certain spot to offer me a splendid sunset over the river, or to Little Italy for a special cheese, or to a deli on the Lower East Side, or to an intimate French restaurant. I like best when he cooks for just the two of us, sometimes in his place, usually here. 'The cook is in love!' he laughs, waving his wooden spoon, if he overseasons something.

He knows unusual side streets and mews in the city, where we walk holding hands. The other day we were caught in a sudden shower, and we kissed in a narrow alley, our faces wet with rain.

He is gradually filling my apartment with beautiful things from his own: a Moorish hassock, Japanese prints, rare books. He stocks my refrigerator with exotic foods: imported tall jars of huge white asparagus, Iranian caviar, French champagne, hothouse grapes. He makes a feast of ordinary days. This small apartment has become home: open books and half-eaten apples on the table, flowers everywhere, records — It is *he* who has splashed *my* dull house with flowers. I am no longer alone. He promises I will never again be alone.

He fixes things: he had my lights put on dimmers, rearranged my files, my bookshelves, he even had the telephone company send a man to extend the cord so that I can talk to him when I'm at my typewriter without getting up! He said something about checking out possible bugging at the same time.

'What bugging?'

'You're an innocent,' he said.

He protects me, lifts the collar of my coat to shield me from the wind, throws out his right arm in his car to cushion me from a sudden jolt.

He is my good genie. He brought me an antique oil lamp he found someplace, shaped like Aladdin's.

'Rub it and make three wishes,' he said.

'Only three?'

'Only three.'

'What happens if I make a fourth?'

'The genie will not appear.'

'Ever?'

'To be faithful to the story,' he says, 'there are two genii who appear to Aladdin.'

'Does the second undo the wish of the first, like the Bad Fairy in *Sleeping Beauty*?'

He laughs.

'Are you the first genie, the good one?'

'I am both,' he says.

'What happened to Aladdin?'

'He amassed untold wealth and married the sultan's daughter.'

'Who was she?'

'Her name was *Badroulboudour*!'

'You made that up.'

'Not I.'

(I looked it up later: he was right!)

I feel I myself am inside a fairy tale, and it scares me a little. He says this sudden change in his life frightens him too. He gets moody at times, overfatigued. Little wonder – ! Then he likes me to use what he calls 'hot words'; he gets excited when I say them. Poetry and pornography – what a combination!

'I never knew it could be like this,' he keeps saying. Neither did I.

Each time we make love it's different and new.

'I love you more deeply each day,' he says. 'In a year it will be best.'

I: 'Shall we meet right here in a year and see?'

He: 'Yes. Let's synchronize our watches.'

I: 'Will we recognize each other?'

He: 'That may be a problem.' And we laugh.

'If we can laugh while making love,' he says, 'we have it made!'

He says before he met me he was solitary and morose. Hard to believe. Though it's true he seems to have no friends. His wife, whom he divorced two years ago, was a psychotic, a paranoid, who had alienated everyone from him by telling ugly lies about him. He speaks of her with compassion. His mother lives abroad. He has one brother, he told me, whom he hasn't been in touch with for twenty-two years.

Again he said I lift him from the mire, but I see only the most noble and loving of men.

'We two, each other's best,' he quoted from Donne.

We're completely submerged in each other. He doesn't like to go to parties: 'Full of ear-nibblers,' he says with mock suspicion, referring to the time some man had bent to whisper something in my ear; yet when we do, my friends are captivated by him. Except Marge. 'What's with you?' she says. 'You look all fucked out.'

Sometimes he clutches me to him as if afraid I might disappear. 'You're my woman,' he says, 'and don't you forget it!'

As if I ever could.

Some things I still don't understand. Yesterday, when my Saturday cleaning woman came, he sat on the couch with me in his bathrobe and whispered something so urgently, in rapid French – so that the cleaning woman might not understand – squeezing my arm until it hurt, that I missed most of what he said. Something about his first wife, the French girl who died. How she had an abortion without his knowledge so as not to disturb his studying, how she had disappeared one night – '*disparu*,' I think he said – and something about the pharmacy . . . I saw he was distressed, so I kept nodding, until his grip on my arm relaxed, and he kissed me sweetly, softly, on my wrist.

Last night we made love all night long, and in the morning on my pillow I found a quote in his minuscule hand, from Robert Graves:

Not to sleep all the night long for pure joy,

. . .

This is given to few, but at last to me.

I've been writing for a long time; my arm is tired. Later tonight, when I'm in bed, he will call, and he will read to me, and I will fall asleep with his voice in my ears.

'Tonight I must sleep at the other place,' he told me. 'It is necessary.' Why? What? He put his forefinger up in front of his mouth and moved it from side to side – his way of indicating a taboo. 'I am tired – weary with two thousand years of suffering,' he said. 'Sleep well, my Goldenhair, my love.'

Yes, I am his love.

I don't know what I'm afraid of in this giving, caring, beautiful human being who is everything I have ever dreamed of, but I am.

What two thousand years?

THE MIRACLE

Not to sleep all night for misery was nothing new to Isabel, but now she was tossing in bed in pure panic.

If I could pray, she thought, *I'd ask God what to do.*

But she did not believe in God. When she was very little, He had failed her. Not Jesus, whom her mother had preempted, but the good God behind the ceiling. One evening she had overheard the adults around her speak of someone who lay dying in the hospital. She did not know the man, but somehow she had felt responsible. So she tested God that sleepless night. Once the line of communication with Him was established, she would be able to ask Him for a few things for herself, but that night until norning, she kept straining her muscles and concentrating on one spot on the ceiling, praying for the unknown man who lay dying, died long ago.

'What does it cost you, God?' Then, as now, she offered him bribes: 'If You do this for me, I will always . . . I will never . . .' If, in the morning, she learned that the man would live, she would know it was because of her.

Then, as now, she rationalized: perhaps the man was better off dead? Or possibly she didn't pray hard enough, had dropped off to sleep for a few moments? Did not suffer enough, did not offer enough in return?

God had more important things on His mind; she was too little, too insignificant. Still, she made concessions: let the man die next week, next month. Only let the miracle happen in the morning; let Him answer her so that she would always know that He heard her, that He existed.

Maybe I should have knelt? she thought. *Maybe it's because of that dime I stole from mother's purse?* Now, a lifetime away, the same questions, bargains, pleas, rationalizations – except that this time she knew they were useless.

That long-ago morning – no one knew what she had gone

through – pale from lack of sleep, she had asked about the man. What man? Oh, that one – well, too bad; he had died during the night, but that was expected. No one had expected him to live. She knew then that God had betrayed her. True, He had made no promises, but He had let her down. Then as now.

So there would be no miracle. Besides, it was too late: she had sicced the dogs on him, hired the detectives, given the information to her lawyer. At nine in the morning the detectives would follow him and nab him – wherever he was going, with whomever he was going. They would do whatever was necessary – hotel register, flashbulb cameras. If she could only stop retching, fall asleep, become unconscious until it was all over.

In the meantime, she had the bed: tonight he slept downstairs on the couch in his office. She was on top now, literally as well. After months of vacillation she had taken action. It was the only way to save herself and the children. Then why was she praying for a miracle still?

'If God wants,' her mother always said. Her mother helped Him along by pacing the floor a certain number of steps, blessing the right pigeon feather fallen from one of His doves, touching her New Testament for a sign, the torn pages held together with scotch tape and rubber bands. Her God demanded total obedience. By appeasing Him with her rituals, she averted daily disasters, saved her loved ones from heart attacks, car accidents, robberies, fires, perils lying in wait. But she could not ward off all of God's punishment because her faith was not strong enough. Or because she had misread His directives, misunderstood His omens. Or because she was – she said – a grave sinner. He made her suffer and suffer. As a child Isabel had a fantasy: She would steal out of her bed, wrap a white sheet around herself, and appear at her mother's bedroom door as an angel, His emissary, to make the sign of the cross and tell her mother, half awake in the dark room, in a deep and godlike voice: 'You are forgiven! Don't be unhappy anymore!' But she had never dared to do this.

When she first told her mother about the impending divorce, in the shabby furnished room in which her mother lived – the same room that awaited Isabel in her old and lonely age, unless Edgar were forced to support her – her mother clasped her hands and cried: 'Why did God punish me?'

'It's not you He punished, Mother.' But it was no use. Her mother always took the credit.

'God will send a miracle; there will be no divorce!' her mother promised. She opened her Bible, put her finger on a page, and said: 'God tells me . . .'

'You're always doing this!' Isabel flared up. 'Always trying to direct my life by what your God tells you! It's hard enough, what I have to do –'

'You know I would do anything for you,' her mother said, tears in her eyes. 'Must I stop praying for him, then?' she asked.

No, Mother, you need not stop praying for him, that sadist who is slowly killing me. But, of course, you don't know this because I have always protected him, as I do now.

'No, Mother, you can pray for him all you want.'

Now, looking at the empty ceiling as she lay in bed, the tears trickling into her ears, Isabel knew that God would never hear her. And even if He did, what would she ask? To go back to the time before it had gone bad? But when was that? To go farther back, farther than her adolescence, daydreaming on the stoop in the lonely spring evenings, back to her childhood, lying in bed and praying for the life of a stranger?

She had set the wheels in motion. Tomorrow morning it would be over. She had been strong, so far. To stop trembling, she got out of bed and began pacing the floor.

Suddenly she heard his footsteps on the marble staircase. Edgar had come upstairs for his pajama tops.

She could have gone back to bed, pretended to sleep, but he saw her pacing up and down the bedroom, and he did something remarkable. He walked up to her, took her in his arms, and she felt such a surge of tenderness for him, such a familiar feeling of being protected, she clung to him.

He said: 'We have grown so far apart.' And with tears choking her words, she said: 'Yes, we've become enemies. How did we become enemies?' And she thought: *Maybe this is the miracle; maybe this is the time we can just talk to each other; maybe I can call off the dogs?*

He sat on the chair in his worn pajamas, top button missing, and she on the edge of the bed, and for the first time in months, they talked. They talked with compassion for each other. He said he had been miserable too. She pleaded for a separation. 'Let me stay here in the apartment with the children,' she begged him; 'be our friend. For our remaining years, let's be kind to each other.' He nodded, he said money was a problem. He added up what she and the children would need – rent, food, and so on: at least fourteen thousand a year. He didn't have it, he said; he would borrow it for them. He talked of Dorian. He sat there with the goo on his hair he put on at night and with tears in his eyes, and he told her he was in love for the first time in his life – he emphasized that – for the first time. He said he had been too immature when he married; he had been forced into marriage, but now he knew what love was; he functioned fully as a man with her, he was his best with her. Miraculously, she loved him too. She was very young, he said, in her early twenties, very attractive; to be with her was his greatest joy, yet there were problems. And Isabel, the mother-confessor, all forgiving and all giving, stroked his greasy, thinning hair and said, with pity for this human being who had, like her, sought love, who was, like her, unhappy: 'How lucky you are to have found love, to be able to give and receive love. With her you are undamaged.'

He agreed to everything. He said there was no need for any legal documents since he had never yet gone back on his word, but Isabel felt it should be arranged by attorneys. The important thing to him was to be able to take his girl out in public. 'Will I have to give up our reading group?' he asked wistfully.

As soon as he went downstairs, Isabel phoned Mr Marcus, her lawyer: 'We talked it over and he is amenable to everything. We don't need the detectives; we can work it out together.' Her lawyer thought she was making a great mistake. 'No, no,' she assured him – 'we'll do it clean! Make sure to call off the detectives.' – 'Big mistake,' he repeated. 'You must think of yourself and your children, not of him. We may still have to use the detectives one day.' But when she hung up the phone, her relief was as deep as her panic had been. The miracle had occurred.

She began to imagine how it would be: *He'll come to dinner, he'll be a better father to the children, he will like me better.* Now that she knew he loved the girl, how awful it would have been to have the detectives burst in while they were in bed . . . But why was she mourning, as for the dead? She remembered the times he had been kind to her, when she had the flu, when he gave her a whole sheet of stamps, when the parakeet died. She had thrown him into the girl's arms, handed him over, it was all her fault. In the name of the Miracle Mother and the Holy Ghost, she had absolved him, assumed the blame. All night she was torn by her feelings. In the morning, when he was leaving for his weekend, he came upstairs to say goodbye. He kissed her forehead, and she almost said (she caught herself in time): 'Have a good time, dear.' He said he would call her that evening.

The responsibility for action was his now. Dorian was her doorway to freedom. It almost rhymed. She had failed again to manipulate her life; once more she had arranged for it to be done to her. She was left here, aging and lonely, while he was parading around with a beautiful young girl. She was back on the crazy pendulum: Was he a lecherous villain, or just a good man in need of love? Was it her sickness or her health that wanted him out of her life? She called her lawyer; he wasn't in. Or perhaps he wasn't answering the phone because he had been unable to stop the detectives? The miracle had happened, but she had spoiled it?

Too panicky to be alone, she called Rose. Within fifteen minutes Rose was with her. 'When it comes to divorce, they're all alike,' Rose said. 'I know, I've been there. When it comes to money, forget it!'

'We talked like civilized adults,' Isabel said. 'We can still be friends.'

'Don't be naive,' Rose said. 'When the time comes, you'll need those detectives.'

At eleven-fifteen at night the phone rang: it was Edgar.

'What took you so long?' she asked. 'I was worried sick.'

'It took us all this time to get settled,' he said. And then, so that she need not worry, he gave her the name of the hotel and the room number where he and Dorian were spending the night. 'If you need me,' he said, 'you know where I am.'

For a moment, the irony did strike her: this was the hotel in Boston, the very room into which the detectives would have broken with their cameras. What would her lawyer say now? Was it too late to catch him with Dorian?

'Good night, dear,' Edgar said, and she fell asleep like a baby at peace. She knew where he was; she was safe.

All weekend she rode on alternate waves of panic and relief. He had said 'Good night, dear' – or did he say 'dear' before 'good night?' She remembered, before they were married, how she would plead with him on the phone to say 'dear,' to say he loved her, and how coldly he refused. All weekend she kept worrying about an accident: she saw him on the highway, car overturned, both of them killed. She kept gasping for breath; she couldn't keep any food down. She would be well as soon as he returned.

Monday morning she heard him downstairs, but he didn't come up. He had left his pajamas on the banister; she pressed them to her face, and shocked, she heard herself say: 'I can't live without him!' She knew she was going insane.

Mr Marcus called: 'Get hubby to move out first,' he said, 'then we could discuss money.'

'But if he won't go?' –

'Then get a locksmith and lock him out.'

That was too terrifying. She thought she might find a nice place for Edgar, a suite someplace, or a small apartment she might furnish for him. 'The important thing,' said the lawyer, 'is to prove you're living separate and apart, though in the same apartment. That you haven't been cohabiting together.' *No cohabitation without representation*, she thought. Yes, definitely insane.

And how did it end, her miracle in the night? As it was bound to. They were right, of course, her lawyer and Rose. When Edgar came upstairs Monday night, he was completely changed. His face was grim; he spoke in legal phrases; he reneged on everything he had promised. He refused to move out – that would be 'abandonment,' he said, especially since he was involved with a young girl. If Isabel insisted on divorce, *she* was to move – find a room, get a job, live in Mexico, where it was cheaper. He had no money for the children's colleges: they could work, as he had, and pay their own tuition. As for the fourteen thousand dollars, that was absolutely unrealistic, he never mentioned such a sum, he didn't have it. He could not afford it. 'Then I would have nothing to offer her,' he said.

'Is she interested only in your money?' Isabel dared to ask.

He was furious; he stormed out of the room, threatening her: 'I happen to know a few things about you. By the time I'm through, you'll be sorry you ever started this.'

So there she sat, with her empty miracle in her lap. He had obviously consulted a lawyer. How could she have been so weak, so stupid? By this time it would have been over; they would have nabbed him with the goods on, they would have taken him to the cleaners. Once again she had abdicated at the last minute, at the eleventh hour. After all the weeks and months of preparation, discussion, advice, evidence, photostats; after all the puking and pacing – she was again a victim. She had been offered a miracle, the miracle of his handing her the hotel and room number on a platter – no, that wasn't the miracle, something else was . . . She had muffed it, missed her chance, missed the train, missed the boat – and now she was even worse off than before, with an embittered husband determined to fight her, and all her weapons gone.

Dear Nina —

I was thinking of names. How ironic that you, an American, are called Nina, while I, a Russian, should be named Jessica! My name is the result of my mother's literary romanticism: when she was pregnant with me, in Kiev, she was reading *The Merchant of Venice*. So – while her Russian friends gave their little girls ordinary names like Tamara, Natascha, Zinaida, she named me Jessica, and everyone said: 'How exotic! How different!' – until we came to this country, and I became lil' old Jess . . .

You can tell a lot about names: women named April or Raven. And you can tell a lot about men married to women named Muffy or Bunny. Or Marni.

As you can surmise, I've been working on names for my characters. Of course, my own name would never do for fiction. Jessica Proot doesn't sound right. But Judge Seth ('appointed') Greene rings true. Judge Karp, Judge Goldleaf (can't you *see* them?). Samson Samuels (attorney). Timothy Hall (sounds like a dorm!). I keep changing their names in the book, as they reveal themselves. I decided to change Varya not into Nadya but into Daria. It's closer to the original, and it has the rolling Slavic 'r' that goes with her full name: 'Daria Alexandrovna.' As for my brother, he refuses to be made fun of. He keeps pulling me away from the role I assigned him, and is turning into a sympathetic character. Very puzzling. Perhaps he couldn't help being married to Marni – as I couldn't help being married to Charles.

Why do so many good, kind, loving women throw away their lives on men unable to love? How hard I tried to marry Charles! How hard I tried to unmarry him! And when I finally did, he managed it so that I would be practically penniless. If only I had been better in arithmetic!

There goes my guilt again! It's been a free-floating guilt, attaching itself indiscriminately to everything in sight. I would always look at the *right* side of the menu and order the least expensive dish, even if I didn't like it. I would feel guilty if it rained. I would feel guilty when my phone rang and it was the wrong number. Once, when I was having an innocent drink with a man in a cocktail lounge, the siren of an ambulance rushing by filled me, for a moment, with the terrified conviction that it was on its way to my suddenly stricken babies!

With Max, I think I've lost my guilt, or most of it. I feel entitled to him; I've earned him. Which, of course, is a fallacy; justice is a man-made concept. Never mind the philosophy; I am so ridiculously happy, I can think of nothing and no one else but Max.

I as much as said this to Prof. Simms. You remember Sumner Simms, of the EGG? He called me the other day to invite me to a symposium on 'Life as Metaphor for Literature.' I told him I was seeing one man and was not going out with anyone else. I could almost see his gallant bow at the other end of the wire. Then came his letter. If there is such a thing as a formal love letter, he wrote it. It was a source of deep regret to him, for he had felt more than regard for me, and had he but known that I was ready for an involvement of an amatory nature, and so on. He sincerely trusted I would find fulfillment with the man of my choice, and he signed: 'Most Truly Yours, Prof. Sumner E. Simms.'

Sic transit.

Have you noticed how differently men and women sign their letters?

> In letter-writing can be found
>   The difference between the sexes:
> Men sign: 'So long, see you around,'
>   While women sign: 'With love and x's.'

To answer your unasked questions about Max, at last I

have a healthy relationship. In contrast to my life with the ungiving, unloving Charles, Max overwhelms me with his generosity. The gifts he brings me are chosen with such care, such eagerness to please, such delight in *surprising* me, that it seems sometimes like a dream from which I will awaken.

For instance: He brought me a glass case in which he had arranged painted porcelain figures of all the little animals from my 'Zoo' poem in *Children and People*. They look exactly like the illustrations in my book! Beneath each animal he had written a line from my poem in his own calligraphic hand. Under the giraffe:

His neck is half
Of the giraffe.

I'm living in a fairy tale, which I hope will never end.

I remember, when Jeremy was very little, I read him a fairy tale with a sad ending that made him cry. 'It's only a story,' he said, trying to comfort himself, tears trembling on his lashes. 'It's only a story. It didn't really happen.'

You ask about the children. Today Jeremy works on the *Chicago Magazine*, researching stories that *did* happen. And Jill, as you know, is a successful textile designer in Los Angeles. They're both well-adjusted young people, who seem to be happy in spite of our divorce; quite different from Isabel's traumatized children. I wish I could see them more often. I understand they keep in touch with Charles, who – if you remember – had moved to Denver after the divorce, where he runs a marriage counseling clinic.

In your last letter you say you're going abroad in April. Where, why, for how long? Will you write to me, from wherever you are? I've come to depend on your letters; I'm easily addicted.

When will your film be finished? When it comes to New York, I'll be the first in line. I'll even sell tickets!

Do you remember the party at the Kents I wrote you about? Well, someone there had taken some snapshots of us, and Teresca has just mailed me one of her and me standing in the doorway. Would you believe it, she apparently didn't like the way she looked on it, so she fixed her face on the snapshot – with a ball-point pen!

I, too, wish you were in my Fiction Workshop class. Do you know what subjects engage today's students of writing? They're reflected in my comments on their papers:

> Are homosexual lovers you describe male or female? Hard to tell.

> If planet earth has been totally destroyed, who is writing this story?

> I'm unfamiliar with some of these words. Are they all a synonym for penis?

I myself am not writing much these days, except for a few scenes. I believe I was most creative when I was most miserable, right after my divorce, when I sat alone over my typewriter, crumpling page after page spoiled by the bubbles on the paper – from my tears – falling on the happy verses for children I was writing.

There is a moral, if you can find it / Inside that sentence, or behind it!

Perhaps the reason you're unable to start your second book is that you're having too good a time, enjoying your success? Or that you have removed yourself from your sources? Or that you spend all your time writing letters to me?

You say nothing about the asterisks in your own life. Surely, there's an occasional one here and there?

Dear Nina – I want you to be as happy as I am!

Love and x's,
Jess

['BOOK']

NOTES TO MYSELF

Establish Isabel's guilt. From mother to daughter. One scene. Skip four years ahead to 1966, when children in college, just before final step to divorce. She is still living in Park Avenue duplex, Edgar away for long Christmas weekend; no one home. It's first time she has date with man: Irv, a successful songwriter.

SLEEP-OVER DATE

After dinner at a quiet restaurant, they taxied to his apartment, which was six blocks away from her own. When she saw the soft taupe carpets, the brown suede sofas, the geometric leather chairs (a man lives here alone, they proclaimed, but a woman has decorated it), she felt more than a little flattered.

They had a drink, he played one of his records for her, then he led her casually to the bedroom, and they made love. Just like that, immediately and pleasantly. She extended herself to please him, to repay him for the dinner and the taupe carpet.

He fell asleep at once, snoring slightly and elegantly. She heard from a distance the sound of a fire engine coming closer, closer, passing below the windows, and stopping apparently a few blocks away. Then another fire engine, then a siren (police car?) – they all stopped – let's see – five, six blocks below. Why, that's where *she* lived; that's just about where her apartment house was. It was *her* apartment that was on fire. At this very moment, the door of her apartment was being broken, windows smashed, clothes sopping from the hose . . . She saw the rubble, she heard the shattering of glass, smelled the charred, curling edges of her drapes. Her children – her children, home for the holidays . . . She was gripped by panic. How long the engines stayed there! What a big fire, out of control! Who would warn the children?

143

She nudged Irv gently on the shoulder. 'There's a fire,' she whispered urgently. 'A fire a few blocks away.'

He mumbled that yes, he had heard the engines, did they wake her?

'It's around my house – it's where I live,' she said, more desperate now. 'Perhaps I'd better get dressed and go see –'

'Don't be silly,' he said. 'Go back to sleep.'

But she knew with awful certitude that the fire was in her house. Perhaps not in her apartment, but the smoke, seeping into the children's rooms ... She shook violently:

'You don't think it's there? Those engines – '

'Poor baby, they woke you. Here – turn around and go to sleep. The traffic noises are a nuisance up here on the third floor.'

Of course he was right. It was one chance in a hundred? a thousand? that it was her house, and the best thing to do was to go to sleep, and then, in the morning, calmly walk home on the familiar street, approach her house standing intact, unscarred, uncharred, and see for herself that her children were safe.

But of course her children were not home. They were not expected until Saturday. This was Thursday. No one was home; Edgar was away for five days with one of his women, leaving no word where he might be reached. That morning the hospital had called: a patient of his had died and they needed his signature on the death certificate. 'We can't keep a cadaver here indefinitely,' the impatient voice had said.

Had she expected the children to come home, she never would have gone out. Yes, but something told her they might come two days earlier. She had a feeling they would suddenly decide, or maybe just Gregory, no, Wendy, probably Wendy, sleeping in the little room where the fire raged ...

She began to tremble again. There was the sound of the fire engine once more, the siren, softer now, appeased. It was over, then? All gone, burned, dead? Too late now for her to rush home – only six blocks, she could have made it in minutes – too late to warn, to protect them. It was her punishment, the worst kind, like her mother's, whose vengeful God punished her through her children.

Perhaps it was not too late? Could she, maybe, get up now,

dress quietly, and slip out (was the elevator man there at this hour, 4 a.m.?).

Irv stirred. 'Up again?' he asked. 'You're a light sleeper.'

'That fire,' she said, keeping her tone amused. 'It was too close for comfort.'

'You're safe here in my arms,' he murmured, ready again to make love. Well, this was an added punishment: submitting to a strange man's lovemaking in his strange bed in his apartment just six blocks from her own, where disaster had struck, was striking at this very moment.

'I really must,' she began, but he was snoring lightly, musically again. Her skin was clammy. Where did she leave her clothes – on a chair here or in the bathroom? She would leave him a note. Her whole body was shaking uncontrollably.

He was up again: 'What's the matter, you sick?' There was concern in his voice. 'A nightmare?'

The fire engines,' she began, but her throat constricted with unsaid words, her eyes were filling with tears.

'Want something to drink? A brandy? A pill for your nerves?'

She shook her head. She was behaving stupidly, irrationally, she realized that. He would see she was a crazy lady and never again go to bed with her. She had muffed this too, as always.

'Just relax – it's only five-thirty. Let's try to get some sleep,' he said.

'It was right on the block where I live.'

'What was?'

'The fire.'

He sat up in bed, lit a cigarette. 'What do you want to do? Want me to take you home? Now, at five-thirty in the morning?'

'No, of course not' – she snuggled into him, pretending to be sleepy, pretending she was normal, sane, sexy, like other women, hoping he would forget this – aberration.

She made herself stay in his bed until his alarm went off. Then she jumped out, dressed quickly (her clothes *were* on the chair), gave him a hurried kiss on his chin, and – saying something about an early appointment – left. (The elevator man, the doorman, they knew, of course, seeing her in her dinner dress and high heels.)

It was only when she saw the familiar gray facade of her own

145

building that she felt reassured. The fire had not been in her house. Her children had not come home early. She was saved.

She remembered Wendy's first sleep-over date, when Wendy was four. It was on an evening when Edgar had stalked out after one of their futile talks about their marriage. Wendy had packed her little suitcase (pajamas, toothbrush, panda) and went off to sleep at her little friend's two floors above. When she returned in the morning, she reported triumphantly to her mother that she and her friends were up all night, talking.

'Talking about what?'

'About divorce.'

'What about divorce?'

'Mustn't tell,' Wendy said.

'Why not?'

'Too scary.'

The sins of the mothers, Isabel thought dully.

As for Irv, she never saw him again. Which, considering everything, was just as well.

WEDNESDAY MARCH 29

Max in a strange mood – tired, tense. Says it's because
of me. 'You're walking on eggs,' he says. 'What are you
afraid of?'

Last night I *was* frightened. There's a violence in him I
don't understand. I happened to say: 'You're such a
perfectionist; you're not an easy man, you know.' His
eyes grew ice-gray; he said with a tight smile: 'You are
making me *very* angry.' Later, he said: 'I have lived with
anger all my life. I am plagued by the world's ills.'

I must not make the same mistakes I made in marriage:
trying to buy love with suffering. I'm not Isabel; I am
Jessica, worthy to be loved. But I don't quite believe it.

I know so little about his past. Two days ago we were
walking on Madison Avenue when a beautifully dressed
woman coming toward us obviously recognized him. He
grabbed my arm, wheeled me around, and swiftly pulled
me across the street to avoid her. I angered him by asking
who she was. 'Stop hounding me,' he snapped; then,
more gently: 'Hell hath no fury . . .' Whoever the woman
scorned was, I felt sorry for her. I am the one Max loves
now.

Today he was tender and sad. He brought me a gift:
eighteenth-century vase, exquisitely wrought, dazzling
white. 'Blanc de Chine,' he called it. His word for it:
'immaculate.' At first I didn't notice, but in a certain light,
I saw it had a crack that had been skillfully mended. He
explained that ordinarily it was almost impossible to tell
where an antique vase was mended, but that this was
visible only because its surface was so pure, so shining
white. 'Here,' he said. 'At this angle the crack is invisible.'
He smiled his radiant smile, his sad and radiant smile:
'Only you and I know it is there,' he said.

Within the vase was a card; on it he had copied in his minute handwriting this verse from Virgil:

> For if thou didst not smile,
> And if thy parents did not smile on thee,
> No god can ask thee to his table –
> No goddess to her bed.

I can't bear it when he's unhappy.

MUSIC AND LAUGHTER

Telling the children that she and their father were separating was the most difficult thing Isabel had ever done. She felt like Taras Bulba: 'I birthed you; I'll kill you.' It was her job to kill her children. Edgar had abdicated; as always, he fled for the weekend. 'What shall I say to them?' she had asked him. 'Tell them anything you like,' he said, bolting out. Anything she *liked*. Dear children, the end of the world has come, and I have done this to you.

It was time; she had delayed too long. 'They'll understand,' her lawyer had said. 'They're entitled to be told.'

She had chosen to tell them at dinner, after taking them to an off-Broadway Saturday matinee. She could not bring herself to tell them the previous night, when Edgar had stalked off, shrugging away all responsibility; She wanted them to have a peaceful night's sleep (their last?). She had prepared their favorite food: steak and french fries.

Innocents to the slaughter. After all the vitamin drops, the inoculations, the approved toys and educational games and nonallergic paints, the recommended picture books and tested records and dolls guaranteed to cry . . . After the art lessons, the orthondontics, the carefully selected camps – she had to face her children and kill them with words:

'Daddy and I haven't been very happy together for a long time – you must have sensed it.' They nod, their food untouched to their plates. 'Daddy loves you very much and I do too. We decided to live apart for a while, for a *little* while only, just to see how it works out, for a while. We'll all be happier. Daddy is happier without mè, I am happier without him, we are both happy with you . . .' (Too many *happy's* there, but this was the line to take, so that they might feel no guilts of their own.) 'You'll see how happy we will all be. Your life will be undisturbed. You'll go to the same school, have the same friends, live in the same place, and Daddy will come often to see you, and he'll be able to spend more time with you than he does now. We'll both be happier, better people, free of tensions. You'll see, there will be music and laughter in this house. You know how mournful it has been.' They nod. 'Well, we'll have fun, we'll have parties and music and laughter . . .' She was repeating herself out of desperation, and the children were pretending to eat, Wendy with tears welling in her eyes, swallowing hard; Gregory stolid, staring down at his plate.

She thought she was handling it well by shielding them from the knowledge of what their father was doing to them. Whatever he had told them about her, she would not add to their conflict by presenting *her* side.

'Well, what do you think?' she asked, her stomach sinking, waiting for their absolution.

'I don't care,' Gregory mumbled, not looking at her. She suddenly remembered taking him for his first pair of shoes: the clerk's careful measurement of the chubby little foot, the tiny white shoes with their tiny laces, the painstaking fitting, the clerk's solicitous advice: 'These are the most important shoes your child will ever have,' and the orange lollipop offered by the cashier as reward 'for that beautiful little boy, so well behaved.'

'Of course, you care,' she said. 'You care a lot, but it can't be helped. It will be better, we'll all be happier, you'll see,' she said.

When Gregory was little, when he had asked the long-expected, inevitable question: 'Where do babies come from?' she had explained it carefully, showing him with diagrams on paper where and how. Always logical, interested in the way things worked, he listened, fascinated at the way nature had arranged all this so neatly. When she was through, he said, eyes shining: 'Does Daddy know?' Now he sat staring at his untouched plate, silent, his face reddening with allergic rash.

She turned to her daughter: 'What do you think, Wendy?'

Her friend Rose had once told her that when she had explained to her little daughter about the divorce, the child asked wistfully: 'Will I still be his daughter?' Wendy was too old to say this. She said only, swallowing hard, a tear rolling down her cheek: 'I think it's great. It's about time you stopped making each other miserable. It's just – great.'

Well, she had done it, told them. It was a step in the right direction.

NOTES TO MYSELF

How old are the children here? According to chronology of novel, this scene is back in 1962, so they are fourteen and sixteen. But they appear to be much younger. More poignant this way – but how make it credible?

Dearest Jess,

Greater love hath no friend: I'm answering your letter of March 27 the very day it arrived. Never fear. I'll continue to write even from Europe; I'll jot down for you any adventures or misadventures that might amuse you. I'm leaving day after tomorrow. The trip has to do with foreign publishers, revised translations of my book, a possible play in London. I'll be hopping from city to city: Paris – Geneva – Rome – side trip to visit friends at Forte Dei Marmi, then London and home. Four countries in nine days – 2¼ days to a country. Seems fair.

I'm happy for you that all is going so well with Max. When I called you the other evening and he answered the phone, his velvety voice seduced me on the spot.

No wonder, when you read him a fairy tale, little Jeremy cried. Fairy tales are far from happy. Children need the reassurance that it didn't really happen, that it's only a story. So do adults.

You speak of the inevitability of a title. Balderdash! (I like that word: it's what Yul Brynner has!) If a book is successful, the title *appears* inevitable. If it's not, the title looks all wrong. How would *Hamlet* strike a publisher? Did you know I had to fight for my title with everyone from my editor to the booksellers? They wanted to call my book, *Teen Daze*, but I was adamant. Advice: If you ever finish your book, don't let them call it *Divorce Daze*.

The 'inevitability' can be read into the title later, after the book is published. When those kids, dizzily spinning around and around, do catch the ring, it's a brass one. They are 'taken for a ride.' They are given 'the run-around.'

I didn't think of any of that – the reviewers did.

Just finish your book, and the title will arise from it like Venus on the half-shell. But I'll try to think of a good one for you – give me a few moments.

How about *Strange Bedfellows*?

How about *O Careless Love*?

Maybe we can borrow one from the young man who writes me from that mental institution. All I got from him recently is but one sentence: 'The Utility Pencil does not erase.' Think about that.

My own book lies unborn, but we need not labor the image.

Your description of the assembly in your elementary school brought memories of my own school days. They are vivid, but few. They have nothing to do with pledging allegiance or any of my subjects or even teachers. They all have to do with Busty Lusty. Betty Lustig, that is, who was in my class in junior high. She was the bane of my existence. All the boys panted for Busty Lusty, with good reason. I had very few panters at that time; I was a late bloomer.

Which brings me to your question about my asterisks. Don't be vulgar. The word is *dates*. And the word for the man, no matter what his age, is 'boyfriend.' I've had a few, though none as serious as the man who proposed to me on the telephone after my TV appearance. A man I rather like tells me he is not 'ready for a commitment.' He makes it sound like incarceration in an insane asylum. I met a very handsome young man on one of my tours. He is smitten, but there's a problem: he's a young thing and cannot leave his mother. Most men I'm attracted to seem to be cowed by my success. Wherever we go, the rumor spreads: 'There's a celebrity in our midst!' It would take a special man, mature, secure (and I thought I couldn't rhyme to save my life!), to feel comfortable with me.

But it isn't all wasted. I have a friend, a single woman growing desperate, who said to me: 'Give me your discards!' (Sounds like the inscription on the Statue of Liberty, doesn't it?) Out of the goodness of my heart I send them to her.

You ask about my movie. My underground informs me there are to be some more retakes, but that the final version should be ready soon. Soon can mean a month, three months, six months. You need not sell tickets; I believe they have arranged to have ticket sellers in every theater. But I do have qualms about the finished movie. All I saw was a bit here and a bit there, tiny scenes that had nothing to do with each other, a disorderly mess. I hope they know what they're doing.

I had a curious offer this week. My own five-minute TV program once a week, in which I would probe 'in depth' the problems of teenagers, most of them professional actors selected by the producers. I would 'solve' the weekly problem in the last thirty seconds, right after the commercial. 'Think of the exposure!' they said to me. I thought of the exposure and politely declined. 'I'm afraid there isn't quite enough time,' I muttered. 'But it's *prime* time,' they said.

How about *Oliver Twist*?

How about *Divorce Daze*?

In the meantime, just sit down and write it. And it's got to come out all right because, you see, you are you.

Much love,
Nina

THE OTHER WOMAN

Since she would not hire detectives, her lawyer advised her to collect all possible evidence against him. Saturdays, when Edgar was away – her knees weak with dread and excitement – she stole down the marble stairs to his office, unlocked the door with the duplicate key she had secretly made, and began to search for any scrap of evidence to be photostated and put away in one of the two valises that contained all the documents she had accumulated.

Although the duplex was deserted, she tiptoed, stealthy as a cat, to his desk, to his files, careful not to dislodge anything or fall into the traps he might have set for her: a sliver of paper, a hair between envelopes. She had to remember exactly where to replace everything after her trip downtown – each time to a different photostat place – returning through the back door, to avoid the elevator man her husband might question. It was fraught with danger, but almost every Saturday yielded a new bit of evidence, a new name in his appointment book (*C* before it, for Cash?), an entry in his ledger, a note, a card, an occasional snapshot of a young girl in a bikini, a smiling woman in a ski suit. Those spanned the seasons, and came out on the photostats in reverse: black teeth on gray face.

Upstairs, in her bedroom, she arranged in alphabetical order the names of all the women she suspected, the names left with his telephone service, the names she overheard on the extension, before he had cut it off. The act of alphabetizing was soothing, like adding columns of figures: expenses, budgets, standards of living; like making long lists of possessions, grievances, needs. Her mind, anchored to specific names or numbers was, for the moment, becalmed.

Some signed only their initials, or obvious pseudonyms. One signed merely 'Me'; she felt most threatened by her. Before each name on her list she put an asterisk or two, denoting their recurrence and importance. She kept the list current, never crossing anyone out: the names remained there until the day when – together with all the other material in her two valises – she would produce in court her alphabetized, asterisked proof.

She wondered what his attraction was to all those yearning women. How did this gray, middle-aged, impotent, humorless man manage to arouse all those Aprils and Vidas? And the women: what were they like? She tried to visualize them through their names, from Anderson, Becky, to Weiss, Zarathustra. *Also sprach*, she thought wryly. Some she knew only by the first name: Thelma or Selma, Sue, Dasha – or by initial: R.N. (Registered Nurse? Rotten News?).

She jotted down fast all conversations she overheard on the extension. Sometimes she was unable to decipher her own hurried notes: 'W.C.' – Water closet? Will call? 'Drg mt std 9 brf is yr crzy wif lsting in?'

His crazy ladies calling me crazy, she thought; and why not? Didn't Dr K. tell her Edgar was capable of relating only to neurotic women?

'Like me?' she had asked.

'Like you.'

And didn't she know that her husband had been spreading the word in his hospital that his wife was insane? And wasn't that why he was still paying for her psychiatrist? It was to be *his* proof in court!

She overheard one woman tell him on the phone that she had confessed everything to her husband, and what should she do now? Another accused him of killing her unborn baby 'by malicious manipulation' while he was examining her. One – a name she couldn't get, mumbled by a woman who had apparently just swallowed some pills – told his Service that she would be dead in a few minutes, unless he came right away. 'He's out of town,' Service replied in a professional voice, 'but I'll give him the message as soon as he comes in.'

On this particular Saturday, Isabel came across her most important find: a long typewritten letter, a love letter, impassioned and adoring. It was so full of tenderness, sensual allusions, references to their closeness, deep longing for him, willingness to wait for him no matter how long it might take; it

156

was so loving, that she herself was moved by it. Here was the proof her lawyers had assigned her to find: adultery, the only grounds. She read it avidly, absorbed, fascinated by the feeling he was able to excite ... Suddenly her breath stopped in her throat. She realized it was her own letter, written to him – how long ago? Before they were married. And he had kept it all this time!

Then the other woman was – she?

THURSDAY MARCH 30

Tonight he prepared our dinner at 'the other place' – his apartment. Festive, as only he can make an occasion. We made special toasts to our future. He showed me how to break the crystal goblets against the wall, the Russian way, to fix the toast forever – 'so that no other lips can touch our glasses and undo it.' Extravagant gesture, but impressive. Then he led me to his 'Treasure Room,' repository of treasures gathered on his travels. He opened a trunk, and showed me some exquisite pieces, among them a silver belt, ornately hammered and set with semiprecious stones. He clasped it around my waist.

'Do you like it?'

'I love it!'

He unclasped it, rewrapped it in its tissue paper, put it back in the trunk, and said, smiling: 'He giveth and He taketh away.' I suppose he's saving it to give me on some special occasion: birthday? wedding?

He lifted a coral necklace from its velvet box and held it against my throat.

'Lovely,' he said – and put it back in the box.

He took me home early and went back to his place to sleep. He had worked so hard on our dinner, he said, he was overfatigued. He didn't call to read to me or to tell me he loved me; I've become addicted to both. I phoned him – but his voice was cold and far away. I quoted Dylan Thomas: 'Love me and lift your mask.'

He became agitated, he shouted: 'That's an idiotic thing to say! You don't know what you're doing!'

My hand is shaking as I write this. I've become so dependent on his smile, his frown. Sometimes it's as if he is another man: when he takes off his eyeglasses, his face looks so different, it's scary. I know I sound irrational, and I feel I'm betraying him by writing this down even here, but I don't understand.

All I know is that I love him. And a miraculous strange bird shrieks at us . . .

[‘BOOK’]

EXHIBIT A

With a mixture of indignation and incredulity, Isabel avidly read the letters of women in his office, in his active file, his active women, to be photostated and added to the evidence in her valises. The letters fascinated and repelled her. They revealed not only how these women saw him but what he was telling them about his wife. Apparently he also confided his affairs to them, seeking their understanding, sympathy, love, and offering nothing in return.

Someone named Vida complained that in three years of intimacy he had never even bought her a hot dog or given her taxi fare home after they made love in his office. She wrote:

> Whatever it takes for a man to husband a woman, you were born without it. The next time you boast to a woman: 'I have had countless affairs, but none of them has meant as much to me as ours,' I shall be there, one of the uncounted, giving a great big Bronx cheer. You would pity me, if you had any pity in you and not punish me by withdrawing in silent disdain.

R.N. analyzed him in mixed metaphors:

> You're a cautious cookie, you want your hand free for the next bird that lands in the bush to add to your stable. And all this time while you were sleeping around, you kept me warming the bench.

One who signed A. Lincoln spoke of the fun she had with him (*fun?* with *him?*) and of his attractiveness and sensitivity. Was that how he had once appeared to her too? Isabel wondered. Another, unsigned, wrote:

> Now that you've dropped Dorian and I no longer have to listen to what a hell-on-wheels she was, maybe you can manage to give *me* a little of your time? Or is your bitch of a wife still keeping you in chains?

160

Someone who signed 'Omega' had a sense of humor:

> Come on, Doc! What kind of amalgam goes into your reasoning? You forget I'm a metallurgist!

'Me' wrote how good he was to her children, how generous, how much they loved him. If only his crazy wife would give him a divorce . . .

Zarathustra's letter was so full of clichés, Isabel was almost embarrassed for him:

> My dearlingest,
> It tugs at my heartstrings to see you so miserable the way she treats you while you're keeping your nose to the grindstone for her. She is only interested in the almighty dollar. You're too good to take this punishment from her. I know I'm not the only one in your life, I love you anyhow to the bitter end. So keep a stiff upper lip and don't be a stranger.

And Janet's letter was a miracle, handed to Isabel on a glittering platter, to be presented to any future judge:

> How stupid Madam must be not to appreciate a husband who is the best lover in town! I will be willing to swear in any court of law how good it was to be in bed with you.

All those letters, Isabel marveled, from women who could just as easily see him or speak to him on the telephone! They were like a sign, like one of her mother's omens. They offered the written words as incontrovertible proof, her Exhibit A.

[NOTES TO MYSELF]

No. It's close, but not quite it. Letters should be more revealing of *him* than of *them*. Besides, too satirical. These are real women, with genuine feelings for him. Isabel should react emotionally: a touch of sympathy for Vida, a stab of anger at Janet.

Remember how it felt when I found Laura's letter in Charles's pocket! . . .

THURSDAY APRIL 6

A week of such closeness again! He gives me everything I've dreamed of. 'You've got yourself a man!' he says with pride, and it's true.

I wish I could help him fight his dragons, but I don't know what they are. I do know he is a man of such compassion, such generosity of spirit, that I will not look upon his like again. – Now, why did I write this, as if composing a valediction?

I wish I knew how to ease his pain.

The other night I sat alone, thinking of him, when he suddenly appeared. 'You called me, and I came,' he said. It was uncanny.

He had my *Children and People* bound in maroon leather, and he brought it as a present. On the flyleaf, his inscription, from Dylan Thomas: 'Children of darkness got no wings.'

On Tuesday we celebrated our anniversary: two months since we met. He says he can't imagine a life before me. Neither can I. We're making tentative plans (the gods are jealous gods) for our future. He wants to take me abroad in August, show me Florence, where he studied art, Paris, the city of his youth, the Greek islands, 'where burning Sappho loved and sung.'

We speak of marriage. We've even looked at a couple of apartments.

At night he clutches me to his left shoulder. 'I'm almost home,' he murmurs. We've been making such fantastic love, it's no wonder that at times he gets suddenly tired, withdrawn. He disappears for a day, and I get panicky until he returns to say: 'It is six o'clock, and did I remember to tell you I love you?'

His deepest concentration is in sex. He mumbles something strange; I echo his words, find a door to his fantasy. I speak his language – high poetry or hot words. I am totally his.

He holds me as if I might disappear. We can't bear to be apart, or go for more than two hours without calling each other. In a restaurant, he must sit not across but next to me, so that our shoulders and thighs touch. In bed he misses me when I go to the bathroom. When I return, he makes a cozy tent out of the blanket, where I curl into him, sucked into his flesh.

In the morning we awaken with joy, braided into each other. He sings bawdy French songs in the shower, and he likes me to sit in the bathroom and watch him shave. He says he likes my morning face. 'Nothing better is possible – or necessary,' he says.

We're staying more and more by ourselves. He doesn't like my friends, is suspicious of strangers. He almost punched a man in the restaurant for looking at me in a certain way. 'All ear-nibblers,' he said bitterly; he made it sound like ruthless cannibalism.

He keeps coming up with new surprises. When it rained and he couldn't drive me to my Fiction Workshop as he usually does, he sent a limousine to take me there and to bring me back!

Yesterday, in the Public Library, where I had been invited to read my verses to the children, I suddenly saw him in the audience, in the back of the room, his silver hair above the upturned children's faces. I had forgotten I had even mentioned this engagement to him.

And he has changed the color of his new car – a Cadillac he rents each year – four times in as many days, to match more exactly the color of my eyes! 'Who does anything like this?' I said, astonished.

He: 'The lunatic, the lover, and the poet.'
I: 'Which one are you?'
He: 'All three.'
He asks: 'Was ever woman in this fashion wooed?'
No, never.

163

Dearest Jess,

Did you ever read in high school French a book called
Le Voyage de M. Perrichon, in which M. Perrichon
travels on the continent with a notebook into which he
enters on one side: '*Les Impressions*,' and on the other,
'*Les Dépenses*'? In but two days in Paris I already have
lots of impressions and expenses, though they don't
necessarily balance. You know French – I need you here.
I'm suffering from a peculiar corruption of the English
language because I seem to be obsessed by a literal
translation from the French.

But hold, my little cabbage. This morning, ready for
breakfast and uneasy about room service (the sign over
my bed, translated into English with exactitude, advised:
FOR IMMEDIATE CONSUMMATION CALL THE
CONCIERGE), I decided to go to the little café across the
street. When it makes good weather, I like well to eat in
full air.

I sat myself, me, at a charming little café table. I told
the grandfatherly garçon that one wished to command
the coffee, since one had already commanded the eggs.
Then, after paying the tariff on the alimentation, I
returned to my hotel to wait for the people who were to
drive me to the publisher's office. They were to come at
ten o'clock less fifteen, but though I attended and
attended them, they did not come.

I asked the concierge the directions. 'If by hazard you
decide to walk at foot,' he told me, 'it must be that you
walk straight right until you fall into the street.' Needless
to say, I got thoroughly lost. Happily, I saw a traffic
gendarme a few meters away. I approached him and, in
my transatlantic confusion, I asked him: '*Parlez-vous
français?*' He did. 'The street you seek finds itself straight
right,' he assured me. 'Mercy,' I said. 'I pray you of it,' he
replied.

On the crowded boulevard I had an adventure — of sorts. I felt a sudden, unmistakable goose — direct to its target, swift as a hummingbird. I wheeled around to see a nattily dressed Frenchman immediately behind me. He bowed slightly and said: '*Pardon, madame.*' I pardoned him and continued to walk at foot until I found the offices of the publisher. All the world was desolate at the misunderstanding that had caused me to make my own way there, but our affairs were negotiated with satisfaction.

The misunderstandings are many. I've just discovered why, whenever I telephoned anyone, I was told they were out. I thought they were saying '*Ils sont parti,*' but what they were actually saying was: '*De la part de qui?*' — 'On the part of whom are you speaking?' In other words, who are you?

Another misunderstanding passed itself last night, at a soirée for a young sculptor, in his atelier — how you say — studio. I was impressed by his sculptures, and said to him, in French, of course: 'But you are so talented, isn't it time you exhibited yourself?' He had the politeness, him, to explain to me the difference between '*exhibition*' and '*exposition.*'

Tomorrow I fly to Geneva for the conference, stay overnight, proceed to Rome to discuss the film, then to Forte dei Marmi to visit friends who have a villa on the Tyrrhenian Sea, then to London, where there is a possibility of a play based on my book, then back home, over the North Pole. Four countries in nine days! Look what a merry-go-round can do!

I will continue this letter when I have time, and keep you au courant on my impressions, if not expenses. I embrace you and Max — and send you both much love.

Forte dei Marmi, Italy
April 8, 1978

Dearest Jess,
Except for two days here in this lovely villa, the pace

has been as hectic as back home. In Geneva, where I spent a day and a night, I stopped at a watch shop for a little present for you, so that you need no longer listen to your digital clock dropping those heavy minutes. I bought you a tiny little alarm wristwatch. The clerk was very solicitous: 'If you wish to be alarmed at six o'clock,' he showed me, 'you go thus.' I will send it to you with a friend who will be going to New York shortly after I return. Do not be alarmed; use your watch, and when it buzzes, that will be her signal to go.

Next stop – Rome, for only two days. But I made my mark there. In an elegant cocktail lounge, I opened my pocketbook to see too late a roll of American toilet tissue I had been mistakenly warned to take along spin crazily down the floor, under the feet of the curious.

The following morning an enterprising Italian journalist appeared in my hotel room for an interview. He would conduct it in English, if Signorina Moore didn't mind. He took off his jacket, folded it many times into a tight bundle, and sat on it on the chair. When I offered him a drink, he said no, he preferred water. 'Maybe there's a faucet?' he asked. There was. He then asked me with the same wistful modesty if I happened to have any published interviews with me, which he could copy to save us time. When I said it didn't seem fair, he kissed my hand with admiration and told me I had a man's head on my shoulders. I will never know what he wrote about me.

My entrance to my friends' villa here in Forte was not without its drama. I seem to have created a problem for the husband of their cook. Picture this: twilight. I have just emerged from a luxurious bath in a huge marble bathtub, and – wrapped in my robe – I'm standing in front of the open window to catch the last of the light, holding a pocket mirror in one hand, applying lipstick with another, before going downstairs for drinks and dinner. My lipstick slips out of my hand, rolls down the sloping windowsill, and falls into the flower bed one floor below. I'm not going to give up my one good American lipstick, so I quickly run, barefoot, down the flight of stairs, and begin to burrow in the flowers, looking for it. Suddenly I hear breathing behind me. Heavy. I turn around and see the man, the husband of the cook, who had been washing a car, standing with his sponge frozen in midair, staring at me. I feel I owe him an explanation: Why is the guest digging in the flowers in bare feet and robe? So I make up for my lack of vocabulary by excessively eloquent gestures. Clutching the robe to my chest with one hand, I point with the other first to my lips, then to the window above, and say meaningfully: 'My room. *Mia camera!*'

'Ah,' he replies. '*Si, signora.*'

Not sure he understand me, I outline my lips with my finger, point once more to my room, and repeat: '*Mia camera.*'

He nods. Then, slowly, he winks.

There was nothing I could do to undo it. I just kept averting my eyes when he or his wife, the cook, was around. Fortunately, I leave tomorrow for London.

To be continued —

London, England
April 10, 1978

Dearest Jess,

I'm all packed and ready to be driven to the airport. In a few hours I'll be home. But I thought it more sporting to mail this serial-letter from London than from San Francisco.

There is great interest here in *The Sad Merry.* I had a long session with the British publishers and with two producers interested in doing a play. But I did not escape without another embarrassment.

Yesterday morning I awoke here in this hotel too late for breakfast in the dining room; all I could get was a cup of coffee in the lounge. Another unhappy latecomer, a distinguished-looking Englishman, commiserated with me as we ruefully sipped our coffee. Last night, as I was holding a dinner press conference in the crowded hotel dining room, the Englishman entered, and as he passed my table, said: 'Tomorrow morning let's get up a bit earlier, eh?'

The cab is here – I'm on my way – will call you when I arrive to see how things have been going with you. By 'things' you know whom I mean.

Much love,
Nina

[DIARY]

I wish I could help him, but he says we must not speak of his problems. He clams up, the way Charles used to. With Charles it was 'professional confidentiality,' or unwillingness to part with a word, but with Max it's something dark and ominous. A business betrayal? He keeps saying there is something important he will divulge to me – but I must be patient.

Who has caused him so much suffering? His ex-wife? He speaks of her with compassion I wish I could summon for Charles.

Ran into someone who knew Max's ex-wife during the brief time they were married. It seems she was a beautiful young woman from very rich family. There were ugly rumors at the time – either he threw her out, or she deserted him. Threats of lawsuits, some scandal about inheritance, something that cruel people have distorted in the telling. I know how vicious people can be about divorce. When I asked Max about this, he shook his head. 'She was so very sick, poor girl.'

He left suddenly; wouldn't sleep with me that night.

I can't anticipate his moods. Sometimes he comes with caviar and champagne and makes a feast in my little apartment. Sometimes he sits in silence, absently lighting the bronze dragon he gave me, watching the flames spurt. He says he needs time to understand what he feels. He calls me his life-giver, his salvation. I can't understand why. Sometimes he pushes me away. He says he's afraid I might stop loving him. I can't understand that either.

What gives him greatest pleasure is to 'pleasure' me (a word he likes) – to surprise me with an unexpected treat. All I have to do, he tells me, is to rub Aladdin's lamp and voice my wish.

'I wish – I wish that you may have all that you wish,' I say.

This agitates him. He jumps up and moves his forefinger sideways in warning: 'That's all wrong,' he says. 'That's not the way it goes.'

'But I need nothing for myself,' I say, 'as long as I have my good genie.'

'And *do* you?'

'Of course! Am I not his mate, Badroulboudour?' He laughs: 'You have a good memory for names.'

He takes me in his arms and we cling to each other.

'Only as I am can I love you as you are,' he says.

In bed we are safe. His left hand is beneath me and his right hand doth embrace me . . .

MONDAY APRIL 10

He left early this evening. Complained of pain in left
shoulder. Doesn't know why so out of sorts. Business
clients hostile, people hate him, world is corrupt. When I
tried to remind him how much he was admired by my
friends, he demolished each with a phrase:

Teresca? – 'Narcissus drowning in her own reflection,
without getting her hair wet.'

Lance? – 'Wears a monocle which isn't there.'

Grace? – 'Never read a book; afraid it might influence
her thinking.'

Victor? – 'Trips on his own sesquipedalian words.'

Marni? – 'Pale carbon copy of you; needs reinking.'

Gilda? – 'Siren in bifocals.'

Varya? – 'Professional Russian.'

He said he had a dream about me – but wouldn't tell
me what. Strange feeling – playing a role I don't know in
another's psyche.

Also strange: He told me a bitter story – about a girl he
had once taken out, who had expressed doubt about his
masculinity because when he took her home he made no
sexual advances to her. He said he then proceeded to neck
with her, till he had aroused her to foaming frenzy, at
which point he showed her his splendid erection – and
left.

An ugly story. I don't know why he told it to me.

I'm afraid.

I'm afraid for us.

NOTES TO MYSELF

Isabel's mounting fears. Suspicions about Marcus. Is he in cahoots with Engle? Why did he say gleefully, when Edgar's first lawyer quit, 'I can work better with Engle'? Why is he now suggesting that she accept less money? Her punishment for calling off detectives? For not letting him use Molly as evidence?

She can't bear to see her mother shower blessings and prayers on Molly. Fights impulse to tell mother? No. Just show she avoids being in same room with her sister-in-law.

In panic, Isabel runs from lawyer to lawyer, looking for *the* one who would extricate her from her miserable situation. The champion to fight her battles. The law is the same, they tell her, but approaches are different:

'Get a separation first, then you'll have another bite at the apple.'

'Get a divorce, and be through with it!'

'Mexico, Alabama — not worth the paper it's written on.'

'Don't be precipitous.'

'Do it now!'

'It's which judge you know.'

'You're getting the short end of the stick, but it's worth it, to get rid of him.'

Isabel is frightenened at their suggestions: Call the cops. Lock him out. Hire detectives. Litigate.

She had tried once to use detectives, but she couldn't.

She was incapable of locking him out.

She could never, if she lived to be a hundred, call the cops.

There had to be another way.

172

Dear Nina –
The alarm watch you bought me in Geneva arrived today, via your friend, and it is beautiful. Now I'll be able to be alarmed at six o'clock, which is just about the proper hour for alarm. I really love it, but I'm not sure I deserve it. My old problem.

Your friend, the gift-bearer, turned out to be very pleasant. I was determined to like her, if only because she was your friend. I as much as told her:

> I'll speak just like an uncle (Dutch)
>   To let thee know for sure:
> I could not love thee, dear, so much,
>   Loved I not Nina Moore!

We talked about you, mostly, and how gorgeous and talented you are. None can dispute that.

Thank you for your letter from London, describing your whirlwind trip and all your adventures. You seem to draw them – adventures, that is, wherever you go. Are you sure you didn't make them up? You once accused *me* of this because I'm a writer. Seems to me you wrote something too.

I did notice one odd thing in that letter: not one pun in any of the cities you visited! It seems to strike you only on American soil.

I would be envious of your travels in all those places I've only read and heard about, but Max is planning to take me abroad for a five-week holiday this August! We will be together in the most romantic spots for thirty-five days; it's like a fairy tale come true. I keep propitiating whatever evil gods lurk about, waiting to spoil it for us: I look at the ceiling and shrug: 'Who wants to go to Europe?'

Max needs a vacation even more than I; he has been very tired lately, and at times he gets a bit moody. He has suffered greatly in his life. I'm not sure what troubles him so deeply, but I think I can help him. And he's so very wonderful, so special, so full of surprises. Did you ever hear of a man who changes the color of his car to match his love's eyes?

Varya gave me a Russian proverb once, when she first met him: 'From his face you can't drink water.' But from his face I've been drinking wine. I'm addicted to him; I'm hooked on the poetry he reads; I can't go through a day without hearing his voice.

What other news? My brother Victor is still hot in pursuit of his plagiarists. Teresca keeps calling to invite Max (I guess me too) to their parties, but we prefer being alone together. Max can be quite caustic when he dislikes someone. He has demolished in a few words most of the people I know. Varya calls it 'washing out their bones.' Even Cat didn't escape; he calls her a dental cripple because she refuses to eat anything but strained baby food. He says she wouldn't know what to do with a bird if one flew right into her mouth.

My friend who was vacillating about her divorce has up and done it. She left her husband, got a new job and a new lover – all in two weeks. I resent her for it: how dare she! Why should she get off that easy? But then, today's divorcee is a new breed. Marge says: 'Why suffer? Split!'

Did I tell you Varya is planning a big *vecherinka* – a party – on the 15th of this month? She has been decorating her apartment with streamers and balloons and steaming all her velvets in the bathroom. I'll describe it to you, if we go.

In the meantime, I've been going over a fresh batch of Fiction Workshop papers. My comments reveal my discouragement:

Rape from POV of bedroom slipper original but strained.

I suggest you do not end every story you write with: 'Somewhere a dog barked.'

Your typing is very neat.

All right, you want to know how my own work is going. I haven't been doing much except some scenes and notes to myself. But I have time until the end of December. And I have your lovely alarm watch to remind me of it. Varya fell in love with it too: 'It goes like butter,' she says, whatever that means. I've been setting it and listening to it and delighting in it all day. It deserves a little poem: I thank you for this lovely present which

> So politely and so nicely
>   Buzzes warning just to me —
> When the egg has cooked precisely,
>   When it's time to write *fini*.

Yours,
Jess

FRIDAY APRIL 14

'We must guard what we have; we must nourish it and help it grow,' he says, aware of dangers everywhere.

He read me Yeats last night before going to bed. It has become a ritual, an aphrodisiac. I don't remember all the words – I'll look it up:

> A pity beyond all telling
> Is hid in the heart of love.
> The folk who are buying and selling,
> The clouds on their journey above,
> The cold wet winds ever blowing,
> And the shadowy hazel grove
> Where mouse-grey waters are flowing
> Threaten the head that I love.

He, too, is afraid. He, too, is tired of pain. We were very tender with each other, very loving.

This morning he woke me with a kiss: 'It's 9 a.m., Friday, and did I remember to tell you I love you?'

– 'You remembered,' I said.

Tomorrow we're invited to Varya's; she's giving a party. It should be a lively evening.

THE TWO GLADIATORS

The red chair – that was the last straw. The soft red leather chair that always stood to the left of the couch in the living room was gone. When she asked him about it, Edgar said breezily: 'I need it downstairs in my office.' How dared he remove it – practically right from under her – and put it where his women could sit in it! The chair they had selected so carefully when they were furnishing the apartment – what right had he to do this? Was he dismantling the apartment, gradually, in preparation for the divorce? Was it another trap he was setting for her, like letting his practice drop so that he could prove less income, not paying her bills, scheming against her with Engle?

Her own lawyer, Marcus, was doing nothing to protect her. She suspected he might have made an arrangement with Edgar. She had to find someone else, someone whom she could trust, someone who would fight for her, understand what was being done to her, champion her cause.

She had seen many divorce lawyers; the one she chose was Samson Samuels. She liked the strength of his name, his soothing voice, his low-key pleasant manner. 'I see' – he nodded sympathetically – 'I understand. Can you and your husband still talk to each other?' he asked.

She shook her head. Neither she nor Edgar was capable, if their lives depended on it – and they did – to say the word, to make the gesture that might still save them. Not by any superhuman effort was it now possible.

'Legally, the way it's set up,' Mr. Samuels said, 'is who can get the goods on whom. If we can prove your husband guilty of lewd and lascivious conduct, then the court – '

'No,' Isabel said, 'no litigation, we must do it without litigation.'

'Of course,' Mr Samuels said gently. 'Of course.'

This was a man she could really talk to. She explained about her husband's weekends, his women, his refusal to educate the children, the bills, the red chair, the daily humiliations, the impossible situation she was in. The lawyer kept nodding and agreeing that it was indeed a most painful situation. She explained about Mr Marcus: she couldn't offend him by firing him; would Mr Samuels be willing to work together with him? He agreed; he knew Marcus, there was no problem. And for her not to worry about the fee; they would both collect from her husband.

'We'll think of something,' he assured her as she was leaving 'You're not quite ready yet. But in the meantime – please avoid any work where you might earn money. We must prove need. And one more thing,' he added, warmly shaking her hand: 'No sexual congress – with your husband or anyone else.'

She was so relieved, she was almost able to smile. *Sexual congress!* It sounded vaguely political. She felt she was in good hands. Now she had two gladiators: Marcus and Samuels.

[DIARY]

He just left, to sleep in 'the other place,' fatigued after Varya's party. He was upset by the crowd, concerned about his income taxes, irritable, not himself.

I must describe the party to Nina: Streamers and balloons. Toasts in paper cups of vodka. Assorted relatives. The food, the songs, the sad Russian songs, most of which I knew. Mr Rogov insisted on translating them for me. The one I liked especially, Max called decadent: 'Your blouse is whitening on the chair . . .'

I needed to have Max stay with me tonight. I found myself *pleading* with him not to go (have I learned nothing, then?) but he left.

Now I'm alone, can't sleep. His pajamas are whitening on my bathroom hook.

Dearest Jess,

Yrs of the 13th at hand and duly noted. Glad you like the alarm watch. My friend has returned in a glow, totally charmed by you.

So you'll be gallivanting with Max in Europe this summer! I hope it's all you wish it to be. In my experience, 'romantic spots' seem to be located mostly on picture postcards. And you don't need to look at the ceiling to avert disappointment; it lurks elsewhere. My dearest friend, you're the last of the romantics, and that's one reason I love you. One of many.

You say Max has demolished your friends with a few caustic words. I hope I escape demolition after he meets me!

And to answer your question quite honestly, I never met a man who changes the color of his car to match *anyone's* eyes. As for your addiction to his poetry – the only addicts I've dealt with are the kids I describe in my book. They're not doing too well.

Enough of that.

What I want from you now is a detailed description of Varya's party. Who, what, how, and so on. It may help me cope with my own parties. So far, my entertainment has been purely reciprocal: large cocktail parties for people to whom I owe. My formula is simple: lots of booze, more people than chairs, and scatter the bores. I would prefer a little cozy dinner for two, but seldom find an eating partner worth inviting.

My own trip to Europe I've already described to you. I seem to be wired for mishaps. They no longer surprise me. What does surprise me is that people don't laugh at obvious absurdities. For example: On my nonstop flight from Paris to Geneva, man got on the plane, looked around, caught sight of a friend strapped to his seat, and exclaimed: 'Joe! What are *you* doing here?' No one laughed.

On my return, I found a small mountain of accumulated letters on my desk. Some from the kids:

> My father left for good and he's living with that girl and I don't care anymore but my mother does. Please don't forget me if possible.

> I read all your books & their great! What did you teach me about Human Nature? Answer right away, please. Report due next Mon. Your Best Reader.

> I want desparately to do something, to find someone or something, to love, etc. Can I come live with you? Please write back.

What can I ever write back to any of them who need love, etc.? But the one who asks me for nothing is my schizoid correspondent. He simply *tells* me. There was but one sentence from him:

> An incision should have a conscience, but a scar has no heart.

I feel like writing 'How true, how true!' in the margin, the way I used to when I was in high school – but I don't exactly know why.

Did I tell you my film is almost finished? It's in the can, which sounds as if it has been ignominiously flushed away, but all it means is that it's completed. They're getting ready to show me the final product, a few days before the official release, and I'm running scared. How can they make a whole movie out of those jumbled, fragmented scenes? I'm already rehearsing the casual shrug and the carefree chuckle: 'But *I* had nothing to do with it! It's no longer my baby!' Strangely enough, it is. It has remained my baby, although it has grown out of its diapers and flown the coop, to mix a metaphor. All I have here is the physical book: proof that it's mine and no one else's. Am I making any sense?

They've used only one of my suggestions: that the girl raped by her father didn't need freckles painted on her nose. For this they paid me a whopping sum. It's strange about money: first I didn't have it, now I have it. Money stops having a familiar face. Astronomic sums exist only on paper. How casually I was able to say to my agent: 'Let's take a hundred thousand less, and stay with *this* director.' *I* said that, who only two years before hesitated between a pair of pantyhose for $1.10 and $1.35. Do you remember the party I gave to celebrate the signing of the movie deal? I think I wrote you I had invited about a hundred guests to the Fairmont ballroom: drinks, food, orchestra, the works. Without blinking an eye, I had made out a check for $8,500, then stopped at the stationer's for the invitations. I was shocked to discover the ones I liked were 35¢ each. I bought the ones that were 25¢ each, in *real* money.

You know, I just realized you are right: not a single pun from abroad, nor in this letter either. Perhaps it takes time for them to gather momentum on their native soil. Or do you suppose I'm dried out, depunned? What will I do instead?

Nervously yours,
Nina

Dear Nina —

This has been a long Sunday. Max is tired after last night's party at Varya's and is spending the day at his place, and I'm too impatient with Isabel's meek acceptance of Edgar's cruelties to work on my book, so what better time to write to you?

I wish you could have been at that party! The occasion was some kind of 'yoobilei,' though what the nature of the jubilee was I couldn't make out. Not that Varya needs any other reason for a party than 'people to see, self to show.' She had been preparing for this for days, cooking and baking all her exotic specialities, decorating her apartment with paper streamers and balloons, washing her hair blue-black 'in three waters,' and steaming her velvet gown in the bathroom. I was privy to all this because she kept summoning me in for consultation: 'You wrriter — so is balloon okay on lamp? Is velvet gorrgeous?'

Max agreed to come, though he has been very tired lately. Varya's small apartment, riotous with noise and color, rang with toasts made in raised paper cups of vodka: a toast for each guest, then another toast for each guest, and another, with a little tail. All the relatives were there full force: her husband, Mr Rogov, in a frock coat and pince-nez, looking like a visiting dignitary; her daughter, Nancy-Anastasia, a mousey little woman in her thirties, in a faded skirt, with a red rubber band around her ponytail; Poor Walter, glancing over his shoulder as if to catch his destiny with the goods on. Even the nervous Second Cousin Lisa had overcome her fear of dying to arrive swathed in a fringed shawl. The literary Aunt Maroussia was executing an intricate dance step that involved standing on one spot and shaking her shoulders. The melancholy Uncle Andrei, stamping his foot in time, was downing quantities of vodka. Assorted Russian guests were all talking at once. Strange thing – many of them have been in this country for forty or fifty years, yet they all speak English with the same rich accent and rolling *r*.

Varya was in her element! Resplendent in wine velvet, a rhinestone tiara bought at auction askew on her head, a Japanese fan clutched in her hand, she kept rushing about, glazed with excitement, urging everyone to drink. 'Drrink! Why you don't drrink? Health to Rrogov! Health to Natasha! Health to Lapochka! In Rrawshia,' she said to me, looking ruefully at her paper cup, 'we drrink, then *ffft!* brreak glass on wall!'

The highlight of the party for her was the picture taking. Waving her instamatic, she marshaled everyone into place, shouting orders like a distraught general: 'Rrogov – head! Maxvil – put foot! Lishochka – more teeth!' If any of the photos come out, I'll send you one. You'll have no trouble identifying me: I'm the only woman in basic black.

But I must describe for you the *zakooski*, the marvelous food: herring in oil and vinegar, calf's foot jelly with horseradish, pickled mushrooms, *pirozhki* (kind of meat pies), *kulebiaka* (kind of fish pie), *blini* with red caviar (kind of pancakes), cherry *varenye* (kind of preserves). 'Make everrything self,' Varya proudly announced; 'no bawtlerr!'

Suddenly she clapped her hands for silence. 'Song,' she announced in English, for my benefit. A hush fell over the room as a mournful guitarist with heavy-lidded eyes began to sing. Varya sat next to me and Max, her hands pressed together in torment and ecstasy, her lips moving silently with the words. 'Akh, how beautiful, Lapochka – listen: *Yamshchik, ne gonee loshadei!* Means: *izvozchik*, chase not horses!' Mr Rogov offered a literal translation: 'Coachman, do not hurry the horses; I have no place anymore to which to hasten; I have nobody left whom to love.' He sighed sagely. During the rest of the singing he remained at my side to make sure I understood each song:

> '*Your fingers smell of incense* – a lover sings to the corpse of his dead sweetheart.'

> '*Do not weep, do not weep, my little wife:* song of hope and encouragement in marriage.'

> '*Madame, the leaves are falling already:* she promised to come in the spring, but he is still waiting.'

> '*Volga, Volga, native mother, here is a present for you:* a cossack throws the princess he had abducted overboard because he is ashamed in front of his men.'

> '*Your blouse is whitening on the chair and your parrot Flaubert weeps in French:* she left him and he is sorry.'

'That's Vertinsky,' Max whispered to me, 'known for his decadence.' But Varya clutched my arm: 'Your soul melt, yes?'

'They – they're all so sad,' I said limply.

'Is beautiful sad! In Amerrica you sing only' – she paused, searching for the one illustration, the one American song that had remained with her through the years – 'sing only' – she shuddered – 'Mairrzy Doats!'

Max was tired (I seem to be repeating that word), so we left early, stepping over Uncle Andrei, who had quietly passed out in the hall. Varya saw us to the door, nudging me with her elbow, beaming: 'Well? How? *This* is parrty! On Amerrican parrty what you do? – sit on sofa and blink with eyes!'

You know, I've decided not to use Varya in my book, not as Nadya, not as Darya, not as anyone. It isn't the name that's the problem. She's impossible to capture on paper: her accent, her proverbs, her *aliveness*. Besides, my anguished Isabel, trained in guilt and regret, would be incapable of heeding Varya's wisdom, even in retrospect.

Varya lights the path before us –
A relentless Russian chorus!
   Should her dazzling proverbs blind us,
   She can light the path behind us.

I'm combining a bit of Varya with a bit of my mother to create Isabel's mother. Strange that I should want to do that when the two are so different. I wish you had known mother. An impressive figure, with a careful pompadour and slight Russian accent, she worked as a saleslady in Saks lingerie department, squeezing women who were strangers into tight corsets. She once told me about a customer whose husband had cut off her credit in the store; I may use it in my book.

Like Varya, mother believed in God and miracles, but unlike Varya, she did a lot of suffering. Not because God may have been wrong, but because she was. She spent her life making mistakes and atoning for them. And He, her God, spent His looking for ways to punish her through those she loved. By giving me a cold, for example, or making Jill flunk math.

Varya's God is also a highly personal one, but He keeps busy making her happy. He makes her left palm itch ('means mawney'), arranges for white cats to cross her path ('lawcky'), provides her with frequent dreams ('something good will be'), and works daily miracles for her alone. She is convinced that He has something special up His sleeve for her. 'One day you will see how will be: *ne zhizn a maleena*; means: not life but rezzberry; means: everrybody rrich!'

Dear Nina – I've been writing for a long time now; there's so much I want to share with you! Except for your phone call when you returned from Europe, I haven't had a letter since London. But I have a feeling that at this very moment *you* are writing to me!

Love,
Jess

MONDAY APRIL 17

Too awful – ugly – I feel defiled. The most terrible – A rape. Physically, emotionally, intellectually – I was raped.

Yesterday – was it yesterday? – yes, Sunday – I called him. His voice was peculiar. He didn't want to see me. 'There's something going on in my head,' he said. But he promised to come tonight.

He came after dinner, cool, controlled, and immediately proceeded to rip me apart. Dispassionately, ruthlessly, with acute psychological perception, under guise of love, presumably to help me, he pointed out all my character flaws, analyzed all my imperfections, pulled off, layer by layer, all my protective skins. He criticized everything, from my sloppy desk to my failure as a wife and mother. He said I'm undiscriminating about my friends. He said I'm undisciplined as a writer. He told me all that was wrong with me, and it was all true.

I feel I have failed him; I'm not the woman he thought I was. I sat before him, silent, crushed. I let him clobber me, and I let him take me to bed.

He made love swiftly, harshly. No poetry, no tenderness, no words but an angry breathing. It was a cruel bedding. Almost a rape.

No, he's not for me. I am no longer the Jessica of twelve years ago. I am not Isabel. I will not allow the suffering. I will not allow it.

He didn't call tonight.

My stomach hurts, my head throbs. I'll take a sleeping pill, and soon it will be tomorrow. What is it Varya says: '*Ootro vechera moodreney*': 'Morning is wiser than evening.'

Maybe.

TUESDAY APRIL 18

This morning is no wiser than last night. He didn't call.

But instead of sitting here, licking my wounds, I should help him. He needs me – as much as I need him.

I dared not call today, but I sent him, with special messenger, a book I knew he'd like: Edmund Wilson's *Letters*, with a loving inscription on the flyleaf.

Surely, now he'll call –

WEDNESDAY APRIL 19

This morning is also unwise.

Messenger delivered to me a book: duplicate of the Edmund Wilson I sent him, inscribed: 'Compliments of Maxwell M. Mahler.'

How angry he must be; he can't accept a simple gift from me.

But all may be resolved tomorrow: he's coming here for dinner. I have his favorite food ready – and we'll talk. Tomorrow –

UNCERTAIN SOUND

If he would only move out, Isabel thought, just disappear, remove himself and his oppressive silence, how good that would be. Once, when she sat reading on a park bench, a little girl tricycled over to her, studied her for a long minute, said emphatically: 'Dont *be* here!' and pedaled away. If he would only not *be* there!

But he had no intention of budging. The apartment was part of the office, he said, and he was paying the rent, and he wasn't about to move to some hole-in-the-wall. She imagined him literally crawling into a hole, dark and jagged, in a brick wall.

Clara rubbed against her legs, back arched, asking for food. It occurred to Isabel that Clara was totally dependent on her for survival. She was a petted princess of a cat, who knew nothing of her ancestral struggles, of foraging for food, of seeking shelter, of danger and violence and bloodshed. She had never been out of the apartment except for brief annual visits to the vet, when her carrier was carefully wrapped in a blanket. She had never set her delicate paws on earth or grass or stone. If Isabel was late with her dinner, Clara would meow piteously, as she was doing now. She was helpless: she could not open her own can of food or fill her bowl with water. *If not for me*, Isabel thought, *this cat would die*. It was frightening.

Isabel herself had never learned to fight. Nothing in her experience had taught her to strike back. Edgar had now stopped her allowance and was giving Katie less and less money for groceries; often, on weekends when he was away, there was no food in the house. 'We can't negotiate with that man,' Marcus and Samuels kept saying, 'we must litigate,' but Isabel was immobilized by terror. She didn't know where to turn. Her friends, involved in their own lives, were no longer as interested in hers. Her brother was buried in his studies; on the few occasions when they met, they looked at each other with much that was unspoken between them. Martha, as always, was supportive, but she could not tell Isabel what to do.

Isabel went to see her mother. They talked desultorily – of her mother's tumor, which was growing visibly, but which her mother was certain was benign. She said she had no need to see a doctor, but at her daughter's insistence, she promised she would. She told Isabel how pretty Molly was and how hard Vincent was working on his research.

Finally, Isabel blurted out sheepishly: 'Well, then, what does God say? What does he tell you about me?'

Her mother opened her tattered, dog-eared New Testament, put her finger on a page, and read: 'If the trumpet give an uncertain sound, who shall prepare himself for battle?'

Isabel got up to go. 'Pray for me,' she said.

'I'll pray for you both,' her mother said.

THURSDAY APRIL 20

I'm in shock. I don't know what's happening – I'm trying to write it down, to understand it. I'm trying to be calm.

When he came this evening, his face was grim. I had prepared everything he likes: champagne on ice, beluga with chopped onions, candles – a steak ready to cook, but he said: 'You *know* I'm not allowed this food – it's bad for me' – and sank into a chair and said – he said – we can't see each other anymore. He's too tired to fight his dragons. Those goddamn dragons again! He said he is plagued by problems he can't share with me, money problems and others. Again he said something about his 'two thousand years of conflict.' He said he isn't 'allowed' to love me.

'I'm no good,' he said; 'I'm protecting you from myself.' I think he cried: his shoulders shook, he buried his face in his hands.

I tried to fight for us. I'm not a fighter, but for the first time in my life I fought with everything: with anger, with love. I pleaded for us, begged him not to commit this senseless, monstrous abortion. I showed him his money problems were nonsense; he admitted it.

What is he keeping from me, his Jessica, who would do anything for him? He once said he had been a mute among the deaf and found his voice with me. Then how can he do this to us?

After such overwhelming giving, to take it all away is inhuman, I said. I reminded him of – everything. 'How can you be so cruel?' he cried. 'Don't you think I know what I'm losing?' He hurried out, unable to look at me, saying something about needing time to think it over.

I ran after him, I caught up with him at the elevator. By this time he had composed himself. His face was calm. He

191

looked at me strangely, bowed stiffly, and said: '*Guten abend*.' Then he stepped into the elevator, and was gone.

Is he mad? Or am I? My earth, my rock, has suddenly, crazily, changed to shifting sand. The future, where everything was possible, has evaporated.

It's almost dawn. 'A dream cannot last longer than the night.'

I must survive this.

SPECIALIST IN INCURABLE DISEASES

Isabel speaks of dying, but her psychiatrist, Dr Kellerman, her silent Dr Kellerman, is trying to keep her alive, at least, she suspects, until the end of the month, while Edgar was still paying for her sessions.

'My ex-daughter,' she said the other day. She is quick to catch the slips of her errant tongue. 'My ex-daughter has never . . .' the rest was drowned in tears. Two sessions = $60 worth of tears. Tears on tap flow in Dr K.'s office.

Another time she said: 'It's impossible for us to go on like this for the rest of our lies.' Her unconscious is devious, but close to the surface. 'It's a millstone,' she said, instead of 'milestone,' speaking of their anniversary. Once, copying down from Edgar's appointment book the names of his women patients, she had spelled 'woemen' instead, and did not bother to correct it, aware of all the sorry woemen and their pain. So many, crying: 'I, too! I, too!' And in her diary, her treacherous hand wrote 'analust' for analyst. Yet she did not find him attractive.

She remembered a cartoon: a woman lying on her analyst's couch, saying: 'But why am I telling you all this?' Why, indeed? Week after week she goes to Dr K. to try to stamp out her neuroses, while Edgar's bloom and prosper.

Edgar, the good gray doctor (gray hair, gray suit, gray soul), dispensing wisdom and contraceptives to his troubled women patients, was unalterably opposed to psychotherapy for himself. 'You want me to be a selfish, back-slapping extrovert? Risk a breakdown?'

This was before she had moved to the living room. Edgar kept saying he was making all the effort to improve their marriage, while all Isabel wanted was to be 'strong and happy.' He said those two words as if they were the ultimate in degeneracy. He worked so hard, while Isabel did nothing but indulge herself in idle chatter with her doctor. Did he really believe this?

To the world Isabel puts on her loyal face. Only to her doctor is she allowed to say: *J'accuse*: 'I accuse my husband of lies and humiliations, of coldness, rejection, and repeated wounds to my self-esteem. I accuse him of blackmailing me with his threats of poverty and coronary and suicide. I accuse him of this final, despicable thing he is doing to me and my children. Our children, whom he has turned into my enemies!' Dr K. says nothing. And Isabel is suffused with immediate guilt: how dared she? And immediate terror.

There were times when she was grateful to Dr K.: he had given her the ultimate push. There were times when she was furious with him: he was letting her drown.

Sometimes, after a session, she would make entries in her diary, and if the pain was too great to be borne, she made up little stories and fables. It helped her, when she wrote the fables.

FABLES LONG AFTER FREUD

Once upon a time there was a man who was neurotic. He met a woman who was neurotic, so they were married. They lived together for a long time, making each other miserable. One day, the wife went to see the Wise Analyst, who told her to lie on the couch and tell him whatever came into her head. Whatever came into her head was how she hated her husband and how miserable she was with him. After many years of lying on the couch, she began to grow healthier and healthier, until she grew so healthy that she no longer wished to be miserable. She asked her husband to see the Wise Analyst, but he refused, saying there was nothing wrong with *him*. So the wife divorced her husband. At first, he was angry, but almost immediately he found another woman who was neurotic. After that he found another one and another one, for there were many neurotics in the land. And so he lived and prospered. As for the wife, she was ready for a happy marriage, but every man she met was already married or neurotic or both. She grew older and lonelier, but having been analyzed, she understood *why* she was lonely. So she got herself a cat and parakeet and spent her nights in front of her TV set. She was pleased that – at last – she was healthy.

MORAL: If you want something badly enough, you will get it.

· ·

She can't go on like this. Can't eat, can't sleep, lies gasping for breath all night. Edgar is annoyed. Now he says he will not continue her 'so-called therapy.' She has already cost him 'a small fortune,' and he sees no improvement, only that she is getting worse. Himself – blameless. Isabel pleads: 'It's the only way I'll be able to survive!' But he is writing Dr Kellerman a letter, apprising him of the fact. 'Just a few more months,' Isabel begs, 'Just a few more weeks, until I'm strong enough to – ' – what? 'To get just a little stronger.' Edgar refuses. 'That may take forever; those quacks want only to milk me of all my money.' Crazy picture inside Isabel's head: Dr K. and other shrinks milking her husband, as he is crouching naked on all fours in the middle of the rug.

'I think I'm going insane,' she tells Dr K. She is talking about killing herself. His only comment: 'It's rather final, isn't it? Whom do you *really* want to kill?'

FABLE AFTER FREUD

Once upon a time there was a woman who kept trying to kill herself. She tried to jump out of windows, and she tried to put her head into the oven, and she tried to swallow sleeping pills, and she tried to slit her wrists, and she tried to drink poison, and she tried to smother and hang and shoot herself, but she was unsuccessful. Her husband sent her to the Wise Analyst, who explained to her that her wish to kill herself was really a wish to kill her husband. He made her see that her wish to kill her husband was so frightening to her that she turned it into a wish to kill herself. This made very good sense to her. So she went home and killed her husband. The policemen came and arrested her, and she was tried and sentenced to die. She was killed in the electric chair.

MORAL: If you want something badly enough, you will get it.

FRIDAY APRIL 21

Panic, Bewilderment. Was it something I said? Did? I keep starting letters to him I will never finish, quoting from his poetry books scattered around my rooms.

I wait for the phone to ring, for the flowers, the notes. I wait for his key at my door. Don't know what to do.

This morning went to see my shrink, my Schrank. He said the man is obviously too disturbed to sustain a relationship, and that he himself must know it. He said he must be full of hate, so he overloves, to compensate. 'He was really trying to protect you from himself,' he said. 'I think I understand him, but it's harder to understand you: how come you pick only sadists?' No – oh no! Max – the kindest, most generous, most sensitive of men? Who cried in my arms: 'Thank you, God!'?

Yet – I remember everything. Perhaps I'm beginning to see the clues: his 'psychotic' wife, his lack of friends, the woman he avoided on the street, the people he was afraid of meeting in public places, his secret missions abroad.

Even the poems he read to me – were they screaming out a warning, a plea?

I must not be angry. One cannot mourn a dream, or blame oneself for waking.

'Only as I am can I love you as you are,' he said to me, and I did love him as he was, with all his conflicts, with all his flaws.

The thing is – I love him still. And if he *is* sick, he needs me more than ever.

Varya only shakes her head sadly and says: '*Lyubov ne kartoshka.* Love is not potato: can't throw out of window.'

Dearest Jess,

Our letters of the 16th must have crossed someplace over Wichita, Kansas. I enjoyed your description of Varya's party so much, I wonder – did you ever think of becoming a writer? What a pity Max was tired and you had to leave early! It sounds like the kind of party from which the wildest horses couldn't drag me away.

I'm sorry you won't have her in your book. Am I the only one, then, to read about her? In that case, tell me more. And please describe her relatives, whom you mention so tantalizingly.

Yesterday I saw my movie. After several sporadic attempts to change the title to something more sexy, they decided to call it *The Sad Merry-Go-Round.* There may be some minor changes before it's shown to the public, but all I felt as I sat in that little dark projection room with some dozen others was a combination of embarrassment and awe – a combination not easy to come by. I suppose it's always difficult to translate from one medium to another. Everything that was *implied* in the book was made *explicit* on the screen. I winced at some of it, yet I was enormously impressed. Somehow, in the secret mazes of the cutting and splicing room, it all came together. The tiny bits of scenes I had watched on the set had become a whole, with a beginning, a middle, and an end. The snowstorm scene (remember, I wrote you about the blizzard in the sun?) came out absolutely authentic: a freezing, blowy, snowy, day, no question about it. The boy with the broken jaw looked fine. Though they sentimentalized some of it, and even invented a gratuitous love scene they must have sneaked in while I stepped out for a cup of coffee, on the whole, it wasn't bad. It should have been better, but it could have been worse. The camera has its own immediate eloquence, and those kids were as unselfconscious and as true as the ones I had known in 'real life.'

The director kept glancing at my face, eager for my approval, as if to say: 'I have been faithful to thee, Cinema, in my fashion.' (Look at that! It came back, the Gift!!!) They were all pleased that I was pleased and that I threw no tantrum. Afterward they gave a party for the cast and everyone involved in the film. They presented me with a little gold charm: yes, how did you guess? A miniature merry-go-round. I'm rather proud of it.

The film should open around the middle of July in all major cities. I don't know about the minor ones. Do send me an unbiased report. You know how much I value your opinion.

By now most of the kids have dispersed, gone back to their slums and tenements. I wonder what their brief spurt of glory will do for them? A couple of them are hanging around, waiting to be discovered by the big Hollywood people with the big Hollywood contracts. One sent me this note:

> Having seen my preformance in your riot scene I hope you will put in a good word for my future carreer which I intent to persue to my utmost ability depending on you.

Perhaps being in the film has done them no service. There is so much more I want to say to them and about them than could be contained in the book or the movie. So much more than anyone can say.

I feel a bit down. Must be postpartum depression. Do send me a few cheery rhymes!

Much love,
Nina

MONDAY APRIL 24

Dear Max —

It's eleven-thirty at night, and you did not remember to tell me you love me.

All weekend I've been writing this letter that will never be mailed in this diary which will never be seen — and crossing it out.

Four nights since I saw you; only four nights ago I could still stretch out my hand and touch you.

Today I found this underlined in your volume of Robert Graves, and I heard your voice. I heard you read to me:

> We have been such as draw
> The losing straw
> You of your gentleness,
> I of my rashness,
> Both of despair.
> Yet still might share
> This happy will:
> To love despite and still.

I was ready to love you, Max, despite and still.

I fought for us. I argued, pleaded, even prayed, not sure to whom, no longer sure for what.

It was miraculous that we should have found each other at this time in our lives. There was no one like us, ever.

There is only one Max in the world, and one Jessica. No — there are two Maxes, and the terror is: I don't know which one you are. The loving Max, warm, giving, happy, full of laughter and surprises, or the angry Max, cruel, tormented, who gives with his right hand and takes away with his left.

You have made me totally yours, and then unmade me.

All your great gifts were useless. It was not I who was Sleeping Beauty.

Dear Max – I loved loving you. What am I to do now?

Soon the night will be over. Surely, you will call? But if you do – I'm frightened –

NOTES TO MYSELF

Isabel more and more frightened. Edgar more brazen each day: money and children his weapons. Scene: Gregory's graduation from high school. His father refuses to pay for college 'because your mother insists on divorce and I can't afford it.' Also refuses to pay $7.98 for his son's graduation photo. (Is this likely? Yes, to punish Isabel. Eventually, he knows children's needs will be met; must make everyone suffer first.)

That $7.98 and red chair he removed from living room – two injuries which obsess Isabel. Minor grievances help obliterate major ones.

Wendy? Has won prize in art school, but Edgar threatens stop payment: because of Isabel, says has no incentive to work. Practice dropped off. No money. Wendy quits art school, though had been dedicated to art all her young life.

Tie in: Isabel's memories of her own adolescence. Her mother's imprecations about sex. Strictly defined geography of the body: above waist – acceptable; below waist – no-man's-land. Edgar – first boy to cross border stealthily at night. It explains pregnancy and subsequent marriage.

And her mother? At first, can't accept evidence of tumor. (Don't make parallel with Isabel too obvious.) Later, is forced to face it, but refuses hospital. 'If God wants – ' She's grateful for $15 a month (a month? Yes!) which Edgar gives her. Claims her as tax deduction. Mother subsists on small insurance and support from Q. Vincent. Her cheap, cluttered furnished room – for Isabel symbol of her own future. Her idiosyncrasies. Isabel's surprise when someone mentions how interesting her mother is. 'She *is*?'

Or concentrate on Dorian, who will play important role in book. After Edgar drops her, she begins to call Isabel: 'This is your husband's ex-girlfriend,' but Isabel hangs up.

Show Isabel's growing anxiety about her lawyers. Is sure Marcus and Samuels were bribed by Edgar. Convinced all she needs is right lawyer to save her. Gathers courage to fire them and hire new lawyers. Whom does she pick this time? Adams and Gross. They — divorce specialists: spout legal jargon. Charge her $1,500 retainer and promise speedy action and biggest settlement. How gets money for them? Goes to 46th Street Diamond Exchange (Scene?) — sells engagement ring Edgar's aunt had given her, also two gold bracelets and silver heirloom decanter. Borrows rest from brother and friends.

Adams and Gross tell her: only one way — hire detectives and tail him. She winces at word 'tail,' but knows she must steel herself to do it. In meantime they have applied to court for temporary alimony. She waits for court decision and strength for raid.

All this information — mostly for me. Whether I use it or not, I must know more about my characters than I need to tell reader.

But I still can't come to terms with character of Edgar. 'Why can't you be nicer to me?' he says to Isabel once, before it's too late.

Or did Charles say it to me?

Dear Nina —

Interesting, about your film: how all the disconnected snips and miniscenes 'skleyelis' (Varya's word for 'glued themselves together'), and became a unified whole. Do you suppose this might happen to my book?

You ask me to cheer you with a rhyme, but none occurs. I, too, feel a bit down. As a matter of fact, more than a bit. Max and I have split. Ugly word. In stationery stores, displayed on the racks of cards for all occasions (Relatives, Anniversaries, Humorous Birthdays), I see the cutesy-pie 'Splittsville' announcements, with funny pictures of pants ripped at the seams.

Varya follows me around with *gogl-mogl* — a nauseating drink composed of hot milk, raw eggs, and honey — to fatten me up. She advises me to 'write book with one hand, wave good-bye Max with other.' If I could concentrate on my book, it might push Max out of my mind; I think it's a law of physics.

I feel sad about those kids in your film and their storybook fantasies and fan-magazine expectations. After their dazzling hour of glory on the screen, how much harder it must be for them to accept their dismal lives.

Dear Nina — I'm hurting. Even Cat is depressed; she walked away from her favorite food after making a disdainful gesture, an atavistic scraping of her paw against the floor, as if burying shit.

I've been thinking about points of no return in a relationship. Was there one with Max? And was there a moment when Charles and I could have communicated, could still have touched each other, a split second before it was too late? Maybe when our silly little canary died. But in any event, the moment was not seized, and was gone, forever. It looks as if *I* need some cheering from *you*.

Love,
Jess

LUCKY

With an ironic lack of prescience, they named him Lucky. He was a small, lime-colored parakeet, frisky at first, mischievous even. They enjoyed watching him push crumbs off the table playfully with his beak. They applauded as he flew to to the top of the bookshelf and perched, like a small yellow raven, on the dusty bust of Hippocrates. They liked to see him flutter on their shoulders, pecking at an ear.

He explored the universe, took adventurous flights, some beyond reach; eagerly communicated with them by means of eloquent chirps; grew old, tired, disillusioned (there was no way, he finally discovered, of getting out of the window or through the mirror, or beyond the highest bookshelf), so he chose to stay in the security of his cage. After a while he did not venture out at all. He got crotchety, chirped hoarsely in anger; at the same time, the world lost interest in him (children's homework, and so on), and one day Lucky just expired on the floor of his cage, having solved nothing, accomplished nothing, added up to nothing. Such was his life and death.

But what Isabel remembered now, with a stab of such sharp anguish that she reeled a little, as if from a blow, was Edgar's face as he greeted her at the door and said simply, softly: 'Lucky is dead.' There was compassion in his face; he really grieved for the little parakeet, and she felt a surge of pity and affection for this man who was sad because a bird had died and who told her about it so simply, looking sad and a bit sheepish: 'Lucky is dead.'

She recalled it with the old, sinking regret. Why had she not, at that moment when they were open to feeling, when it was not yet too late, when there was still time, both of them grieving for the little bird who died meaninglessly after a meaningless life, why had she not followed her impulse, walked straight into his arms and said – what?

But the one human moment had passed, was gone, forever. Only the two enemies remained.

[DIARY]

Like a dream – unexpected, yet familiar: his call yesterday. His flowers, his telegram, pleading with me to see him. My custard heart trembles, but I refuse. I feel a gut panic: an animal stalked in a dark forest. Yet I'm longing to see him.

He explained last Thursday night as an 'irrational moment.' He was overfatigued, we weren't communicating, I misunderstood him. He says he loves me.

He says he has been studying compulsively – ancient Greek and Armenian, translating from Aramaic, wandering through the city. If only I would see him, he says, he can make me understand what happened.

I cannot fight shadows. I cannot trust him again. I must not see him. Yet I lure him with my voice on the phone.

The shrink doubts he's capable of love, but I know better. He gave himself to me. He runs in all my veins.

I told him I love him dearly, but we can't ever be together again. He replied with this telegram: a poem by Robert Graves. It was garbled in transmission, but I understood it well:

Then love me more than dearly, love me wholly,
Love me with no weighing of circumstance,
As I am pledged in honor to love you:
With no weakness, with no speculation
On what might happen should you and I prove less
Than bringers-to-be of our own certainty.
Neither was born by hazard; each foreknew
The extreme possession we are grown into.

Again, he reached me where no one ever has. I'm so torn. I sense my danger, but I will see him; I owe him that.

I know I can never marry him, but I can't deny us the chance to talk. He'll come this Friday evening.

I need not be afraid. 'After the first death there is no other.'

Isabel tearing her skin all night; broken out in giant hives. Asked Dr K. to give her something for it. He said only: 'What are you repressing?'

FABLE AFTER FREUD

Once upon a time there was a girl who was very lovable and popular. She was invited everywhere by her many friends because she was also so thoughtful and pleasant to everyone. There was only one thing that troubled her: she suffered from Giant Hives. She went to many Doctors and Dermatologists and she tried many salves and ointments, but nothing helped. Finally she went to the Wise Analyst, who helped her see that the Giant Hives were caused by her Hostility, which was repressed. After many years of Analysis, she learned to express her Hostility. When people saw how she hated them, they hated her back. Invitations grew fewer and fewer, until she had no friends left in the world. She lived all alone, expressing her Hostility to the four walls and the ceiling and the grocery delivery boy. The Wise Analyst had been right: she was never again bothered by Giant Hives.

MORAL: If you want something badly enough, you will get it.

THURSDAY APRIL 27

Tomorrow he'll come. Tomorrow I'll see him. I must be strong.

I'm watching Cat on window seat, immobilized between curiosity and terror. She sees something outside that frightens and attracts her: she crouches, motionless and wary, only her tail twitches eloquently.

NOTES TO MYSELF

Writer's function: 'to reveal weakness without condemning character.' Not easy.

Re-examine: Do I need a Teresca? Varya already out. Keep prototype of Marge – Midge. I like her.

Q. Vincent becoming more and more sympathetic. Though grubbing in Grub Street would have been fun to write, I can't make him look foolish. I was seduced by Grubs' own titles: *The Nun in Her Smock, Antidote Against Lust, Memoirs of a Woman of Pleasure* – still selling briskly as *Fanny Hill*. But wrong motive for writing him.

Keep cast of characters small; story of divorce – Isabel's own.

Edgar revealed through Isabel, Dorian, letters from his women. But can't get him into focus. To play his role in book, he must be a defective human being, like Charles. Hard to make such people credible. Even to me. I used to be so bored by Charles, my teeth ached. Yet I accepted his coldness, rigidity, rejection of me. Like mother, I would turn the other cheek and make sure the slap mark showed. Permanently.

But Edgar is trying to say something to me. What? – 'Who will do my laundry? Will I still see our friends?' Sounds right: he's desperate to hold on to marriage. Only within it can function sexually in surreptitious affairs. Perhaps really frightened of poverty; afraid she will drain him. Isabel doesn't see this, but reader should.

Edgar's paranoia – parallel to Isabel's. His projection: she spreads rumors about him and his girl, spends his money extravagantly, enjoys many lovers, is determined to ruin him professionally. Really believes this?

Deterioration of both: inexorable. Contrast: before lawyers chewed up their feelings, and after. Isabel's best qualities crushed now. Can't use her sense of humor. Can't offer anyone love. True: in panic, one can see no alternatives. In despair, one cannot imagine hope.

Good question from Nina's young fan: 'What did you teach me about Human Nature?'

Reader to identify with characters. But for reader to sympathize with Isabel, let her fight back at least once.

THE WORM TURNS . . . TURNS RIGHT BACK

Isabel kept waiting for something to happen she would not have to do. She kept hoping for someone to do it for her. It would be easier for her, she thought, if Edgar would throw her out and bar the door so that she could never return; then it wouldn't be her fault, would it? How dare she, who had never said 'Boo!' to anyone, beginning with her mother, upset the universe?

Recurrent nightmares plagued her, half-forgotten childhood terrors. She was on strange streets in alien cities, on winding roads leading nowhere, in some endless corridor, looking for a room where she was expected, if she could only find it before it was too late. She would be awakened by a strange animal moan, and realize it had come from her, because she heard herself make it again.

Her anger lay in wait. She could not face it, for just beneath it there was the black and terrifying edge of panic.

How could this have happened to her? She, who had held all the weapons, she, the forgiving mother, the martyr-wife, the enemy-friend, was spending her nights on the living room floor, gasping for air, while he, the guilty one, had the bedroom all to himself. He had turned the children against her, pauperized her, flaunted his affairs, and she took it, pleading only for crumbs.

'Tell him to give you the bedroom,' Midge told her. 'What's stopping you? Here – I'll coach you: "Out, you rotten Park Avenue Casanova!" – Come on, say it after me – no – louder! Like this: "Get the hell out of the bedroom, you sadistic bastard!"'

Isabel repeated the words.

'Louder! Angrier!'

Isabel tried again.

'Come up close to him and shake your fist in his face. No – like this, like you mean it. "You son of a bitch, I've been covering for you for the sake of the kids, but now I'm through, I'll expose you to the whole world, you filthy, lousy lecher!"'

Isabel repeated it. They went over it several times, until Isabel had memorized it, word for word.

That night, when Edgar came upstairs she faced him with courage she never knew she had, and she shouted the words Midge had taught her.

She shook her fist, the words came out, and she saw him cringe, she heard him mutter: 'Bitch,' but he picked up his pillow and he went downstairs and she had won, she had triumphed! That was the way to talk to him; there was nothing to be afraid of. It had worked!

The following night she was back on the living room floor, retching and gasping for breath, tearing at her skin, trembling on the brink of the abyss.

FRIDAY APRIL 28

He was here, and we talked. We talked long into the night. He has just left. He brought two roses: one white, one red: 'Rose of memory/Rose of forgetfulness,' he quoted Eliot.

He said he was not himself that Thursday night. He had been overworked, fatigued, depressed. He said I had misinterpreted his mood. 'I love you and I need you,' he kept saying.

He was careful not to touch me.

A proud man, pleading for his life. As I was for mine. I reminded him of what he said soon after we met: 'We will love each other if it kills us.' And it almost did.

He said it had been too precipitous, too overwhelming. We wanted so desperately to be in love, we *made* it happen, he said. But this, now is *real*, he said.

I'm afraid. I'm so afraid of the other shoe falling. He assured me it never will. 'My beauty, my love, my Goldenhair – don't you know how it is with us? Just trust me, and we will love and laugh, and the world will be ours.'

I think I almost believe him. He said he will not press for marriage until he has rewon my confidence. He will tell me many things about himself. 'You who understand so well, you will know me.'

Only when I suggested he see a shrink, his face grew tight. 'Are you implying that I'm crazy?' he asked quietly.

'No,' I said, 'of course not. I only meant to help you.'

He shook his head: 'You are the one who can.' And he read me a poem by Stephen Spender in his marvelous, heart-breaking voice:

. . . .
Our angel with our devil meets
In the atrocious dark nor do they part

214

But each forgives and greets
And their mutual terrors heal
Within our married miracle.

Words can undo me. 'We must protect our married miracle,' he said. 'When we go abroad in August, we'll make memories to last us a lifetime.' He said: 'You are my woman, don't you know it? No one else will ever love you as I do.'

When he left, he touched my cheek. His warm hand on my skin can undo me too.

And did.

SATURDAY APRIL 29

This morning, a dozen white roses, and with them, painstakingly transcribed on rice paper in his beautiful hand, this from Dante:

In te misericordia, in te pietate . . .

In thee mercy, pity, magnificence and whatever good exists in any creature are joined together.

Tonight he will come.

Isabel can't go on; having a walking breakdown. Divorce! It's like Death, only worth. Worse. Furious with Dr K. – he shoved her off the diving board; he knew she couldn't swim. He gives her nothing; is as silent and remote as Edgar. She needs warm, compassionate doctor who would help her over this. She doesn't need a doctor; she needs a lover. Dr K. is very married.

FABLE AFTER FREUD

Once upon a time there was a girl who kept falling in love only with married men. This caused their wives much trouble. The girl wanted to be a Wife too and keep house for her husband, but there was a law in the land that a husband could have only one wife. So she went to see the Wise Analyst, who explained that when she was a little girl she wanted to get rid of her mother and marry her father. At first she didn't believe the Wise Analyst, for her mother was already dead, and her father was old and nasty, and she didn't really want to marry him. But after many years of lying on the Wise Analyst's couch, she received an Insight and became cured of running after married men. It takes a very long time to receive an Insight, and by then there were no single men in her age group left, so she kept house for her father, who had become older and nastier.

MORAL: If you want something badly enough, you will get it.

NOTES TO MYSELF

What am I doing? Just realized I've been attributing these fables to Isabel! But she isn't a writer; she couldn't have written them! I got carried away, back to my own divorce, when I used to try to reduce that horror to absurdity by writing fables in my diary.

But Isabel isn't me!

SUNDAY APRIL 30

Together again. Wary after deep pain, but together. A miracle, a resurrection.

'Where do you get your strength from?' he asked. And half asleep, he murmured: 'You give me courage.'

Never before was there such a night. We held hands even in sleep.

He made breakfast which neither of us ate. 'You have your morning face on,' he said.

'It's just that you're seeing me again,' I told him.

We were apart for nine days and nights, nine days' wonder – a mystical number.

I: 'The Nine Muses.'

He: 'The nine Gallicenae, virgin priestesses of the ancient Gallic oracle.'

I: 'The Nine Muses.'

He: 'Nine Rivers of Hell.'

I: 'You're so learned!'

He: 'You bet! And Milton's Gates of Hell – "thrice threefold."'

I: 'Those were the nine days we were apart.'

He: 'Never again!'

Yet I will not talk of marriage. He sees my fear; it saddens him. He told me about a girl he had lived with in Paris after his first wife died. She was a model, made hats, said she loved him, but she would not come to the United States with him, and she would not marry him. Later, he found out she had been in New York for a couple of years without calling him. And he told me about a Swiss girl he met in New York and lived with for three months. She suddenly received a telegram to return to Switzerland. She never wrote to him, but he subsequently learned that she was pregnant and had married someone else. She had a little girl; he thinks it may be his child.

'Don't let me lose you,' he said, 'don't ever let me lose you.'

Tonight he stuck a yellow rose in the teeth of the little bronze dragon.

THE LISTS

One way, Isabel found, to hold on to sanity, was to make lists. They circumscribed chaos. Numbers, objects, legal phrases, medical terms pinned down with neat labels feelings that verged on panic.

She listed *things* they had accumulated throughout the years. The monogrammed towels – their earnest discussions: blue on white or white on blue? Things that had been bought to match, to go with, to be used for. Things received on birthdays and anniversaries; things that stood for occasions, events, a life together.

Each ashtray, vase, kitchen utensil, each sheet and end table would have to be fought for, wrested from him, won from the shambles of their marriage – a trophy of survival.

'Be practical,' her friends said. 'Every little can opener costs money, and you won't have much to live on. You'll need the radio, the frying pan. You're starting a new life.'

She knew she would have to start a new life – with a radio and a frying pan. But she felt so helpless: she had no strength in her hands, she had always had to call Edgar to unscrew the lids of jars. And to reach the top shelf of the linen closet. Besides, she was afraid – a woman living alone, exposed to many dangers . . . One night he had grabbed the broom and went forth in his pajama top, his innocent male legs naked and hairy, to see who was making the noise outside the kitchen door; to protect his mate, his hearth, his home. How would she manage alone, eat alone in a restaurant, a book propped before her?

And what about her wedding ring, her sterling ring from the five-and-dime? It would have to come off, of course, but she had always been superstitious about that. Never in the twenty-none . . . the twenty-nine years of their marriage had she removed it. By this time it would probably have to be sawed off. Would it hurt? Would they give her a local anesthetic?

But that wasn't it, that wasn't the important thing. Dimly she felt, as she was adding to her long lists, that something else was at stake. (She could even smile, when she was with her friends, at her *twenty-none* years of marriage, at her obsession with trivia.) The important thing was that some future judge, in some future court, would award her all these things, the things she needed for her new life. Their worldly goods – with which, by the way, he did not her endow. Strictly for the record, Your Honor, she had worked hard for those worldly goods, had worked for years as a salesgirl in Macy's book department to help support him through medical school and two years of internship. Dressing in the cold darkness of early winter mornings so as not to disturb his sleep, she would go to work, to stand behind her counter, his helpmeet, his wife, his about-to-be-ex.

She dared not omit any small item that might be the key to release her from her intolerable situation. Everything went into the crazy quilt of accounts and complaints and phrases and objects in the chaos that was now her life.

She listed: all the furniture in their apartment; which pieces she needed desperately, which she could relinquish if necessary. She listed: the number of cups and saucers and soup plates; the contents of the linen closet; the records in the cabinet.

She listed: names of divorcees she knew, the amounts of their settlements, their ages, the number and ages of their children. She listed: statistics on divorced women in the city, in the country, in the world; the number of remarriages; the number of suicides.

She listed: the kind things she could remember about Edgar. The time he had given her money for two weeks vacation. The stamps he had given her for the letters she was writing their children in camp; he had come upstairs from his office and handed her a sheet, a whole sheet of a hundred stamps. This went down, carefully noted. She listed his presents on Christmas and birthdays: the perfume, the umbrella she always lost, the annual scarf. His face when he told her their parakeet, Lucky, was dead. The way he adjusted his necktie before facing his newborn son. She listed whatever she could recall of happy times in their long life together. The list was meager, the list was short.

The longest were lists of injuries she suffered daily since she had asked for the divorce. She had a need to set them down on paper for her future justice-dispenser, kind, fatherly, loving, who would read everything and understand what happened and forgive and absolve and avenge. Her long-awaited day in court, when Edgar's lies and crimes against her would be exposed, and her children would see (Dear Judge, mostly the children!) that she had wished only the best for them. Because he couldn't care less, Your Honor. Look how he abandoned them weekend after weekend as he went off to seek his pleasures. Look how he ignored them, denied them everything, even a graduation photograph for $7.98! She herself could not speak up, reply, show cause, justify herself. She could not throw them into a greater conflict of loyalties. But they would learn the truth on that final day of judgment, her day in court.

In the meantime, it was all there, in the two valises which had been fattening in her closet and which were now in her attorneys' office: the evidence that would exonerate and free her. Inside the valises were several large manila envelopes bulging with bills, budgets, grievances, names of women, their photostated letters, money paid him copied from his appointment books, dates and hours he was away, sales slips, income tax returns, snapshots, former standard of living, present standard of living, her debts, her empty bankbook – Balance: $0.00.

Only let it come soon, her day of vindication. She could not go on like this any longer.

She wrote to her lawyers, her Esquires, letters that were cries from the heart. She asked for advice about her children and her future. She apologized for taking up their time. She told them that her husband had changed his will, canceled his insurances, doctored his ledgers, and was strangling her (she saw this literally) with his purse strings. She begged them to do something soon.

In reply, a letter arrived addressed to *Mrs Webber*: 'Please remit for out-of-pocket expenses.' The rest was legal jargon. *Pendente lite:* That was the amount of support her husband was obliged to provide for her until the final settlement. This temporary alimony was important, they explained, because regular alimony was likely to be based on the amount granted.

Pendente lite – it rang obsessively in her head. She began to make lists of their legal phrases: 'Serious marital discord adversely affecting the attitude of the parties.'

'Irremediable disharmony in the common life.'

'On information and belief, the defendant's acts of adultery were committed without the consent, connivance, privity, or procurement of the plaintiff, . . . nor has the plaintiff forgiven or condoned the same by voluntary cohabitation with him or otherwise.'

Or otherwise.

She listed: *belittle and disparage, continuous and repeated, willful and intentional.* Her attorneys were fond of paired words, irrevocably coupled, with no chance of divorce from each other: *Assumes and undertakes. Repeats and realleges.*

She saw their phrases in vivid pictures. 'Dissolution of marriage' was a dissolving grayish mass melting down the kitchen sink. 'Encroaching years' was a terrifying image of approaching cockroaches, crawling, single file, closer and closer.

One morning she had come upon Edgar unexpectedly, rummaging in her desk drawer. How shameful! 'Perhaps I can help you find whatever you need so desperately,' she said. It was only later she discovered he had removed her photograph album. Why? What was he plotting?

'Dear Adams and Gross,' she wrote, she telephoned, she cried, but their only answer was phrases and postponements.

Dearest Jess,

We've talked a lot on the phone these last few days, and I know how hard you're fighting against getting swept once again into your fantasy of Max, or your affair with Max, whatever it was. For all his pleading now, I think you should be wary. I love you too much to see you hurt once more. And I'm afraid for you.

One of my young fans wrote: 'You see through funny eyes, which makes it more sad.' The funny eyes are merely a sense of proportion. A kind of self-protection. I've had to see through funny eyes some of my own inconclusive affairs, to sidestep pain. Perhaps this is the time to tell you about the few mild oats I've sown. The one in my youth who, it developed, was interested only in my feet. My shoes sent him. (I used to think a pederast was a foot fetishist. There's nothing new under the sin.) Or the one who was so amusing, so delightfully funny, that we laughed ourselves smack out of bed. A guffaw is not conducive to romance. Or the man who used to perform his genital ablutions at my bathroom sink with the door to the bedroom open, while conducting an amiable conversation with me. His hygiene made me frigid. Or the man who prided himself on his frankness; he was terribly frank about his faults – and mine. Or the man divorced from a woman whose name happened to be Nina and who, at the very mention of my name, was unmanned. This is a small and sorry collection, I know, but the man I did *not* see through funny eyes I married. And that was a disaster.

Nevertheless, I am now an Authority on Obscenity. Tomorrow I appear on a TV panel on 'Obscenity and Censorship.' Why? Because my book was recently banned from the library of a local high school for obscene language used by my characters! This is a school with cops in the lobby, pot on the stairs, a barricaded principal's office, and graver graffiti than the obligatory four-letter word on the blackboards of our youth. My argument will be a simple story: When I was nine or so I had got hold of a book about prostitution, with vivid descriptions of venereal disease and its resultant rash. I think it was called *The Pit*. My parents allowed me to read any book I wished, reasoning, quite sensibly, that if I understood the book, fine; if not, it couldn't hurt me. What they did not know, however, is that I was fascinated by *The Pit* because it had the most realistic description of measles I had ever read.

I think I'm still armed with innocence. At least, when I read the scraps of paper my schizophrenic correspondent keeps sending me, they make excellent sense to me. 'Children and lunatics' – something you once quoted from Arnold Bennett. It's a cliché, of course, to point out how sane the insane are, but listen to this:

XYZ is the last confidence.

The compound eye has the pulse of the heart.

I'll swap you these for your Varyas! Your description of her party made me feel I'm wasting my time here in San Francisco. Move over – I may be returning to New York now that my movie is finished.

In the meantime, I worry about you. I worry about you and Max, I worry about you and your work. You sounded so discouraged on the phone. But then, who am I to talk? I still keep rereading the reviews of *The Sad Merry* for courage.

Never mind. Whatever you do, it will be all right. You're a strong lady. Or didn't you know that, either?

Much love,
Nina

IT'S ONLY MONEY

Her strength ebbing, her lawyers away, Isabel had turned in desperation to Gertrude. She asked her to see Edgar, to plead her cause. He liked Gertrude; perhaps she would be able to persuade him to see reason: to give his wife enough money for 'rehabilitation' after the divorce. It was her lawyer's word; it conjured up for Isabel a wheel-chair, a hook for a hand.

He might even agree to pay for his children's college, and perhaps graduate school. Who deserved it more than Wendy and Gregory, with their honors, their awards, their sad faces? There is nothing sadder than a sad child, she thought. She remembered a crude drawing Wendy's little school friend had once made of a square coffin with a child lying in it, and the caption, in large block letters: I WISH I CAN DIE.

'Well, what? How did it go?' she asked Gertrude.

Gertrude shrugged. 'Just like you said – he's a stingy bastard.'

'How long did you talk? What did he say?'

'Nothing much. About half an hour. We met at this little coffee shop on the corner of Lex. He put on his going-to-the-poorhouse act. Said he would gladly, if only he had it, but he doesn't. He lives hand to mouth. He explained how he's a lousy businessman, hasn't saved a penny. He also threw in how you're able-bodied and capable of supporting yourself *and* the children. And how generous he has been in the past, and how ungrateful his family is.'

'And you? What did you say?'

'Well, he has this veneer. This surface charm. The lovely manners. He kept saying how glad he is you're not cracking up. He asked if you're *sure* you want the divorce. He talks like such a patient man, such a reasonable man – '

'You didn't fall for it, did you?'

'Of course not. But listen – are you *sure* he has it stashed away? He said he might have to sell his car.'

'My God, he took you in too!'

'No, not for a minute. But you must admit, he does sound like a hardworking man who is doing his best to – '

'Did he say I was crazy?'

'Not in so many words, but – '

'He's been spreading that all over the hospital. He tells this to his women too, I overheard him on the phone. He can't marry any of them because he has this crazy wife who refuses to give him a divorce.'

'Well, we were talking about money.'

'Didn't he promise *anything*?'

'I told him how you were struggling. How you were in debt. So he began proving to me, on a paper napkin, with his pencil, how *he* was struggling and how *he* was in debt.'

'He always knew how to manipulate his finances. If the Internal Revenue – '

'The point is, he was very firm. He claims he's offering you all he can. I think he has convinced himself, that this is the most generous offer any husband ever made to his wife.'

'And the children?'

'He calls them ungrateful. He says they can work, like he did. He says they'll get scholarships to college, they're so bright.'

'My God, my God . . .'

'Listen, don't get discouraged. I'm sure the court will grant you more than he's offering. I'm sure the court – '

'My God. So then what happened? How did you leave it?'

'Well, we got up to go, and he gave me a peck on the cheek and thanked me for having your welfare at heart. Then – as he was leaving a tip for our coffee – coffee is all we had – he dropped a dime under the table and spent about five minutes looking for it. Under the table.'

'My God . . .'

Dear Nina –

Thank you for your calls (what huge phone bills you'll have!), for your encouragement about my writing, for your concern about Max.

As I told you when I spoke to you last, we're together again, but you need not worry. I don't intend to marry him. There are things about him I don't understand; I know only that he makes me happy.

For the time being, I'm all for Varya's proverb: 'Truth is good, but happiness is better.' Much better. It's something I missed in my marriage. When I now reread my diaries of divorce, I marvel at my submissiveness to Charles. I had a good teacher: Leopold von Sacher-Masoch. (In my book, he is Isabel's mother.)

I recall the shock of disbelief of our relatives and most friends: 'But *why*, after all these years?' Even my former housekeeper, Rosie, wept: 'But you and the doctor were so happy! You never even yelled.' Come to think of it, we never did. Maybe that's why.

All I did was appease, appease, and sing for my supper. And for my breakfast and dinner, too. I thought I had nothing else to offer. Max was the first to discover who I was. Before him, I was so unsure of myself, yearning and longing, even as a teenager, for what I couldn't have because it was too good for me. How I envied the girls who wore gunmetal silk stockings with clocks on them (don't be alarmed; they were only embroidered arrows), and high heels clacking down the pavement! (I was allowed only lisle knee socks and flat oxfords.) How I envied their splitcurls! (I wore my hair in long sausages bobbing on my sharp shoulder blades.) How I envied their cupid's bow lips in scarlet lipstick! (I was permitted but a touch of Tangee pomade on weekends.) And how I envied them the tweezed eyebrows, the open, flopping galoshes, the slickers with the boys' initials painted on them, the boys themselves! I used to write letters I never mailed to boys I idolized from a distance. I would never have dared to write to a famous author, the way your youngsters do, or talk back to a teacher, a parent, a husband.

I dreamed of romance and high deeds – and settled for Charles! I mistook his silence for wisdom, his coldness for dignity, his profession for humanity. My dreams misled me.

Now, then – back to business. Your 'inconclusive' lovers remind me that I, too, have a boot fetishist in my past. He was a suave, impeccable gentleman whom I met last winter at an elegant cocktail party, from which he took me to an elegant restaurant, where we had a genteel discussion about politics. After dinner, sipping my brandy on my couch, he became animated for the first time all evening. He pointed to my boots and said: 'Do you have them in white? Any suede ones? What color? High heels? Side zippers? Any with tassels? Show me.' It developed that he wanted to see me model my boots, stark naked. 'Only the boots, nothing else on,' he requested. I managed to get rid of him fast, but I admit I was a bit unnerved.

Do you really plan to come to New York? That's great news! You will, of course, meet Max. And you will meet Varya, head on.

You ask about her relatives. There's Mr Rogov ('hawsband number thrree') – small, bald, impressive. He wears a black-ribboned pince-nez, corrects newspaper typos with a small gold pencil, speaks in one-word sentences, and sculpts in bread. I'll describe his bread studio to you in my next letter. Husband number one was a woolf: 'He only want one thing from woman, then *ffft!* Good-bye!'

Husband number two was a crocodile: 'Give him only to lie in the sun and the stomach full.' Before husband number one ffffted away, he sired her daughter, Nancy-Anastasia. That is, her name was Anastasia, but she changed it to Nancy, with Varya's full disapproval. 'Who Na-a-ncy? What means Na-ancy? Don't like Anastasia, want change name? Good, congrratulations! But why Na-ancy?' Although she had accepted the name, she always translated it in a hyphenated aside. Nancy-Anastasia (now get this straight) is about to divorce her husband, Walter ('Poor Valter') – a nice type, but with whiskers. 'Is Rawshian saying: "The beard is honor, but whiskers even a cat has."' In the meantime, the two are living in Varya's back room, trying to save money for their divorce. When I expressed surprise at this arrangement, Varya assured me: 'Is Hokay. Is Rrawshian saying: "Not everrybody who snorres is sleeping."'

Who else? Did I mention the nervous Second Cousin Lisa? When I asked Varya what Lisa was nervous about, she replied: 'She nerrvous about dying.'

'Oh, I'm sorry – I didn't know she was ill.'

'Akh, no; she healthy.'

'But you said she was going to die?'

'Of course she die. One day – ffft! Everrybody mawst die!'

I wish there were a key to my typewriter for her marvelous r! It had to be worked for: Varya told me that as a child she could not roll it properly, and that her father used to make her repeat exercises about gorgeous grapes growing on Mount Ararat and three hundred thirty-three drummers drumming on three hundred thirty-three drums. I can produce a pretty good r because of my mother, but Nancy-Anastasia speaks in clipped, precise English when her mother addresses her in Russian. 'I sacrrifice my English for Nancy-Anastasia speak Rraw-shian,' Varya says, 'and what happen? I have no English, Nancy-Anastasia have no Rrawshian!'

More about Varya next time. Remind me to tell you about the Emergency Tea and Rogov's prize. In the meantime, dear Nina, please be happy too!

Love,
Jess

MONDAY MAY 15

No entry here last two weeks; they were beautiful. Once more we're inseparable. He's right: this time it's *real*. He comes with flowers and books and marvelous food to cook for us, he comes with little presents and surprises, he laughs again and makes me laugh. 'You make it easy for me to be happy,' he says. He feels so young and rejuvenated that he wants to buy himself new clothes; for some reason this touches me to tears.

Last Sunday morning we walked through the park, swinging hands, singing my 'Weather Song' from *Children and People*:

> Feather weather, leather weather,
> You and I together weather . . .

He knows all the words, and that moves me too.

He makes impromptu dinners, like frankfurters roasted with apples, or we drive to the country to a special seafood restaurant. One night we stayed in bed eating ice cream out of paper containers and watching something silly on TV. 'Of such is the kingdom of heaven,' I said. He shook his head: 'Huxley's people weren't half as happy in their bathtub.'

He's keeping his promise: no mention of marriage. But we're planning our holiday in Europe this August.

Last week, when I had a cold, he gave away our theater tickets and put me to bed with tea and honey and aspirin. He hovered over me like a distraught nurse. I didn't want him to sleep with me, afraid he'd catch my cold, but he insisted on staying here, on the couch. I heard him several times during the night tiptoe into the bedroom to touch my forehead.

He moves me to — I don't know. I wish I were young enough to bear him a child. He thinks he may be father of little girl born in Switzerland to that woman who fled from him. That may be his fantasy, but his need to love a child is very real. He has this image of childhood innocence in a world that is corrupt. He sometimes talks to me with great urgency about my children, as if they were little. 'They're grown people, Max; they're adults: Jeremy is thirty, Jill — twenty-eight. They're private people who live their own lives. They know that I love them, that I'm always here if they need me.' He's not satisfied; is agitated, upset. He wants to do something for them.

'What is it you want to do, Max?'

He changes the subject.

'It's nine-fifteen in the morning, and did I remember to tell you how much I love you?'

Dearest Jess,

Your letter sounded happy again. For this, I suppose, I must forgive Max, even though it was he who caused your unhappiness. But I hope you understand your own vulnerability as well as Max does. Please be cautious. Is there a Russian proverb: 'While walking on air, watch step'?

As for me, of course I'm happy. Why shouldn't I be? Just look at this letter that came this morning:

> I am not in such a high grade or anything so who am I to tell you but I still think your book is great and if you are real, I think I love you.

And lest you fancy that you are the only poet in my correspondence, this rhymed review arrived from a Juvenile Detention Center:

> When I did read *The Sad Merry Go Round*
> This book very interesting I found.
> The authoress Miss Nina Moore
> Writes English which is not poor.

You will be pleased to know that my book is back on the school library shelf, whether as a result of my TV appearance or an enlightened pressure I don't know. I'm told there has been an unprecedented run on it. Perhaps they think it's about measles?

In the meantime, I made the mistake of my life. In a moment of weakness, I allowed myself to be persuaded to accept a weekend invitation at the country home of Lucy Crandon in Walnut Creek. I went up the Creek all right; it was a disaster. Surely, you know of Lucy Crandon, the celebrated author of many travel books, known for her trenchant prose – 'a traveling writer's writer' – the author of the famous *Gaspé Peninsula*? I never read it; it makes me think of a miracle drug for asthma. But there I was, trapped for two whole days. Her home, on lavish grounds, was filthy inside: unwashed glasses and dishes in the sink, no soap, dirty towels in the bathrooms, no hangers in the closets, no drawer space, bedding that looked used. I had brought a hostess gift – some goodies to munch on, just for fun, but that's about all we had to eat all weekend. Two whole days. It rained most of the time. Everything was damp, mushrooms grew on the ceiling, the toilet got clogged, the plumber never showed. We went to a party down the road apiece, came back in the dark – all the electricity was out. My hostess, who had been drinking steadily, was reeling with bottle fatigue as we made our way across the pitch-black lawn. 'Bear right,' she commanded, 'dog shit on left!' While we were out, my costume jewelry was stolen ('We never lock doors here!' Lucy said indignantly) and my cashmere sweater was chewed up. 'I can't imagine how it happened,' Lucy said, while her dog lay on my bed with pieces of wool sticking out of its innocent mouth. All this would have been something to laugh off, but when I got home, I discovered symptoms of athlete's foot in my toes. That night Lucy called to advise me that her doctor told her she had trench mouth, which was contagious. 'Better do something about it,' she said, and hung up. So now I'll probably come down with hoof-and-mouth disease. Serves me right!

I should have stayed home and written a novel. Or a letter to you.

Next week I'm off on another lecture tour, so please hurry with the Varyas! You promised to describe the Emergency Tea. Was it a real emergency, or just a drill, like the kind we had in public school, to prepare us for the Real Thing?

Much love to you – and I guess Max too.

Nina

WEDNESDAY MAY 24, 1978

Quite a while since I wrote here. Time fades when I'm with Max. The clock points to my deadline, but I look away.

I've incorporated some of his Maxisms into my book: i.e., 'Specialist in incurable diseases.' But I've done very little work on it. Most of my energy goes into calming him — he's so irritable these days.

I don't see my friends; he's critical of them, but he tolerates Varya. When we're alone he mimics her brilliantly. The other evening we stopped at her apartment for a drink and some *zakooski* — calf's foot jelly, pickled mushrooms — delicious.

'Here Lapochka and Maxvil!' Varya announced to us.

'That means "hands of cat,"' I said proudly.

'Paws,' Max said. 'You are dear little paws.'

Varya reported that poor Walter had his wallet snatched the day before in the subway by a couple of children.

'*Na byednovo Makara vse shishki valyatsa,*' she said. For my benefit, she translated: 'On poor Makar all — what you call little things fall all time from trees?'

'Leaves? Branches? Caterpillars?'

'No, no! *Shishki!* Little, little!'

'Pinecones,' Max said.

'So. On poor Makar all pinecones are falling'.

'But his name isn't Makar,' I pointed out.

'Still falling.' Varya said.

It was one of our good evenings: Max was less tense. He hints at something special that's being planned for me. Soon, he says, I'll understand how much he loves me, how much he's doing for me.

Last night he was especially tender. This morning he left while I was still asleep; on my pillow I found a card with these lines of Robert Graves:

In time all undertakings are made good,
All cruelties remedied,
Each bond recalled more firmly than before –
Befriend us, Time, Love's gaunt executor!

I wonder if it will.

Dear Nina –

It was good to talk to you, to know that you're back from your lecture tour, and that the hoof-and-mouth disease has sidestepped you.

Max is at his place today, I've done eleven pages on my book, so I can write to you with a clear conscience. To keep working, I bribe myself with little rewards: after eight pages, or four hours (whichever comes first), I allow myself a chocolate bar, or a dish of ice cream, or a letter to you.

As promised: The Emergency Tea. It was called by Varya to announce Mr Rogov's prize. Mr Rogov's prize was for winning the Odd Hobby Contest for his bread sculptures. His bread sculptures are the little figurines he makes in the Bread Studio. The Bread Studio is the small room off the kitchen, where Mr Rogov spends most of his time. Only once was I privileged to see it. He was sitting, stately as an ambassador, at a work table, a jeweler's loupe in his eye, working with a toothpick on a figurine's face. Dozens of little statuettes were lined according to size on the shelf above him, each executed with minutest attention to detail: grotesques with gaunt faces, centaurs, fauns, devils, ogres, and dwarfs. They were all of an unusual bronze color and appeared to be hard as stone.

'How do you get the bread to the consistency of clay?' I asked in a respectful museum-whisper.

'Pumpernickel,' he said.

'What makes them so hard?'

'Baking.'

'And how do you get this lovely bronze color?'

'Iodine.'

Varya treated this with amused tolerance. 'Some haws-band drrunk, some hawsband play all time cards, some hawsband fleert with woman. Rrogov make only with brread. Little peoples.' He hadn't told anyone he had entered the contest. When he won first prize, two hundred dollars, Varya, exploding with excitement, called the Emergency Tea. I came that evening. 'Good morrning!' she greeted me. 'Rrogov – genius! Is meerracle! Walk in strreet – everybody know! Rrogov in rradio, in musei, we all millionairre!' Ever since the item had appeared in the paper, various relatives kept calling up. '*Da, da, da!*' Varya shouted into the phone. '*Preez! Perviy preez!*' Mr Rogov himself, torn between pride and distress that his name was misspelled *Rogow,* sat surrounded by dozens of copies of the newspaper, neatly changing the *w*'s to *v*'s with his little gold pencil.

One of the calls was from a bread company. Nancy-Anastasia took the phone. 'They want you to endorse their bread,' she told Mr Rogov. 'They said they'll make it worth your while.'

'More mawney!' Varya cried, beside herself.

'What color bread?' asked Mr Rogov.

'White, I guess.'

'Impossible,' Mr Rogov said. 'Cotton.'

'So what if cotton? Brread is brread!' Varya decided. Arms akimbo, she triumphantly surveyed the table. 'See, what I tell you? If God want, will be! Here in Amerrica – one-two-thrree – *ffft!* Millionairre!' She picked up her glass of tea and raised it, like a victorious torch, high above her head. 'Tawst!' she commanded, as we lifted our tea glasses. She thought for a moment. 'Health to mawney!' she said.

And did I tell you about Nancy-Anastasia and poor Walter, her about-to-be-divorced husband, who is constantly plagued by tiny pinpricks of fate? 'Wind whistle in pocket,' Varya says. 'Is dear divorrce. Lawyer dear. Mawney dear.' Until they get enough money for the divorce, they're living at Varya's; I often find them at her table. Walter's gloomy face, with its drooping moustache, emerges from a long, thin neck as he peers around, cautious as a turtle. Nancy-Anastasia's expression is one of desperate patience. 'Akh, if I only yawng!' Varya cries. 'I love, laugh, crry, sing — I live! Nancy-Anastasia live? No! I talk, talk, *Kot Vasska slooshayet da yest*! Means: Cat, name Vasska, listens and eats. Means: I talk, talk, no difference. Beautiful girl, but look her face — grreen! Why she don't use rrouge? Why she don't drress sexy?' 'Oh, Mother,' Nancy-Anastasia says wearily, while Walter blinks morosely. Between these two there's a kind of funereal pity, as if the knowledge that they are about to part makes it possible to forgive everything.

I've been observing marriages, seeking comparisons to characters in my book. I talk to people, and I listen. Certain phrases I don't understand, like 'amicable divorce.' One woman told me with pride how she and her husband managed a divorce without any bitterness: amicable division of property, amicable arrangement about children. Amicable hate, I thought, for while she talked, her anger showed like an ill-fitting slip. How come they got divorced, if they were so goddam amicable with each other?

Other current phrases bother me because I see them *literally*. When Marge says: 'Split, and let it all hang out', I see a sloppy girl with flabby breasts in a loose brassiere. A split I see as a real tearing, a ripping. People breaking up I visualize as broken into many pieces, shards, fragments, slivers of glass . . .

What about infidelity? I ask, trying to explain my husband to my novel. Each woman responds differently: some with blinders, some with hysteria, some with curiosity that smacks of homosexual vicariousness, or with screwing around in an attempt to outdo the man. Some just walk away, forever.

One woman gave me a lecture on the joys of being married to a philanderer. She was supremely happy, she said, because her husband's affairs add richness and zest to their marriage, make him a more skilled and confident lover, keep him married to her not through obligation or inertia but through choice. What if he should find someone more to his taste? I asked. – That's exactly what keeps her on her toes, she said, so that she doesn't grow dowdy or uninteresting.

Do you suppose she meant it? How much anguish could have been avoided if Isabel had been able to feel like this!

I remember something Max quoted from Horace Walpole, about life being a comedy to those that think and a tragedy to those that feel. I suppose the same event can be shattering or absurd, depending on who sees it (locksmith hiding in the bathroom, ladder leaning against window). Since children feel rather than think, for them divorce can be a terror. Only time may befriend them, as it did my own children.

One day Jill came from nursery school with a watercolor painting.

'That's beautiful,' I said with pride. 'What did the teacher say?'

'She said let it dry.'

Perhaps that's the secret: to let it dry.

Dear Nina – it's late, and I have wandered from happy Varya to gloomy Walpole, which means it's time to go to bed.

Love,
Jess

CHILDREN OF SAID MARRIAGE

The women who did not step beyond the point of no return, who remained safe in their marriage – how Isabel envied them. Women like Lila. A few months earlier, Lila had started divorce proceedings, but panicked, and put herself into a hospital, while she still had her husband's medical insurance. Isabel had visited her there, lying helpless, everyone sorry for her, including her husband, who came to see her twice, once with flowers. Now she was back with him. All former confidences and intimate details of his villainy stopped short. Lila said she had sacrificed her own happiness for her child, five-year-old Judy. 'If I deprive her of her father, how would she ever relate to other men?'

On this Saturday morning – there was no new evidence in Edgar's desk to photostat – Isabel had come to baby-sit with Judy in response to Lila's call: her husband was away for the weekend on a business trip, and Lila had a dentist's appointment. Would Isabel be a doll? Before she left, Lila had flung a piece of advice to her friend: 'Try to hold on to your marriage, no matter what! For women like us, anything is better than living alone!' (*Why do they always make me one of them?* Isabel thought bleakly.)

Judy was playing in her room. Isabel stopped to look in on the child through the half-open door. Judy was talking into her toy telephone:

'Hello, who is this? I want Mr Aly Money. Hello, Aly? This is the poor wife. Is my husband there? Is he in the basket lawyer? The child needs him to come home right away!'

Isabel had tried to distract her. For a while they drew pictures. Judy crayoned a house; the kind of house children always draw: square face with window-eyes and door for the nose, a top-hat chimney spewing black loops, a round yellow sun above it with orange spokes for rays, and from the door – a resolute path going off the edge of the paper – where?

241

'That's the Poorhouse,' the child explained. 'That's where the children go barefoot.'

NOTES TO MYSELF

No, doesn't come off. Too structured, too pat.

Try dialogue between two children? Judy and the neighbor's little boy, Larry. Both are 'products of divorce' — Judy's mother whispers the phrase ominously into Isabel's ear. The children are playing house, immemorial game of children everywhere. Judy is combing her doll's hair; Larry is crayoning. Isabel overhears their idle prattle — the safe sounds of home. Until she begins to listen to their words.

> JUDY: (*to her doll*) Sit still. I'm doing this for your own good. (*to Larry*) You never lift a finger to help!
>
> LARRY: I'm making a man. I think he's a cop. I used up all the blue. I need a yellow. Have you got a yellow?
>
> JUDY: Daddy took it away. Him and the basket lawyers.
>
> LARRY: My daddy will come home.
>
> JUDY: When?
>
> LARRY: Soon. In the spring.
>
> JUDY: Will he bring you a present?
>
> LARRY: Yes.
>
> JUDY: Will he bring money?
>
> LARRY: Yes.
>
> JUDY: Money talks. I've got this child to take care of. How will I manage?
>
> LARRY: Some daddies have visitations on Christmas.

JUDY: I like birthdays better.

LARRY: Christmas are better than birthdays. My daddy took me to the Planetarium.

JUDY: Me too. You can learn more there than in a restaurant.

LARRY: When?

JUDY: A long time ago, when I was little. Now my poor baby will starve to death.

LARRY: Why?

JUDY: Who will pay the rents? I won't live forever.

LARRY: We got to have money. I don't have a yellow.

JUDY: Life is too hard for me.

LARRY: What will we do now?

JUDY: I don't know.

LARRY: I don't know too.

These are the 'infant children of the parties,' the 'issue of said marriage,' the 'minors,' the 'children of tender years,' Isabel thinks. The children of divorce.

[DIARY]

Strange week – his shifting moods, tenderness, sudden withdrawals. A *déjà vu*: is it happening again? I try not to panic. If I do, we open up something in each other that is perilous.

Even the poetry he brings sometimes frightens me. Like the photograph of a tapestry from the Cluny Museum – 'Woman with a Unicorn.' On the reverse side, he had copied Dylan Thomas' 'Woman on Tapestry':

> I have made an image of her
> . . . With the power of my hands
> And the cruelty of my subtle eyes.

'Why the unicorn?' I asked.

'Because it's only half a cuckold,' was his answer. Weird . . .

Last evening he was displeased by something and went off to sleep at his place. While I tossed in bed, wondering what I had done or said to make him angry, he called up. 'I love you,' he said, and hung up. I fell asleep, safe as a baby.

But I want to be loved because I am me and no one else. No one's fantasy or fairy princess. Peculiar conversation about fairy tales the other night. He pointed out my gifts: beauty, passion, humor, generosity, intelligence, creativity.

'Go on,' I said. 'Tell me more!'

'That's all,' he said.

'Are you sure?'

'Yes. But for a long time they were all useless.'

'Until Prince Charming came?'

'I doubt it,' he said. 'Did you know that in an earlier version the prince rapes and impregnates the sleeping girl?'

'Would she have been better off asleep?' I asked.

He didn't answer.

Last weekend he said he was too busy to see me, avoided my calls (his phone off the hook). I was desolate. Sunday night he appeared, looking great; said he was in the country, visiting friends. (What friends?)

'You seem upset,' he said. 'Why are you upset?'

What a small word to use for my distress! I don't know where I am or who I am with him.

In bed, hot words and lust — but loving too, deep loving. 'Fucking is God's work,' he says. 'How can you doubt me? Look what we do together! Was ever woman so laid out?'

Then he withdraws, says he's uncomfortable because I don't express my preferences, because I make too great an effort to please him!

Saw Dr Schrank. He said: 'His behavior is irrational and contradictory.' As if I didn't know it! He thinks because I lost my father when I was little, I'm drawn to white-haired men. 'Not white — silver,' I correct him. 'Besides, my father's hair was dark when he died.' He thinks Max needs help. When I suggested that to Max, he said with a shrug: 'There's nothing wrong with me. The problem is yours.'

FRIDAY JUNE 2

Awful — last night was awful. I had asked him to stay with me — he was reluctant. When I pleaded, we went to bed. But he didn't embrace me; he lay there like a stranger, his left arm over his eyes. When I moved toward him, he said quickly: 'Don't touch me!' . . . Then, more gently, he said he had a momentary spasm in his chest. He dismissed my concern, turned his back to me. It opened up all those loveless nights when I saw only my husband's back.

'Max — turn to me — I feel sick to my stomach,' I said.

'Go to the bathroom and either move or vomit.' He actually said that.

I got out of bed and sat on the living room couch. Was this the end of us? Was this what I had been dreading?

I expected him to follow me to the living room, but he didn't. After a while, I heard the even sound of his breathing.

I must have fallen asleep too, on that couch, for I had a strange dream. I'm in charge of two small children I had volunteered to take home, but I've taken the wrong turning. I realize it as soon as I see the narrow steps leading down to a precipitous path, but the children have run ahead and I must follow them. I'm calling them, though I don't know their names yet. I can hear their shouts, far away. I want them to stop and wait for me, but I can no longer see them, nor any houses, nor even a path, only a thick fog, and I realize it's dangerous, and that I am lost . . . I awaken to see someone outside is trying to break into the front door. The door is open a couple of inches, the man outside is rattling the door-chain. I'm terrified. The chain is almost off when I glimpse his hand. He is thrusting it into the room, holding a broken champagne bottle, its jagged edge towards me. I try to scream, but can't make a sound . . . and I awaken again.

How phallic can a dream get?

This morning Max appeared cheerful. He said it was my fault for insisting he stay over. 'There's no use in your trying to manipulate me,' and he left, as if nothing happened.

Later: Delivery boy just arrived with flowers — a splendid burst of spring flowers (then we're off roses? I thought dully) and a note written in his hurried scrawl, so unlike his meticulous handwriting. I'm copying it here, just correcting the strange misspellings:

Darling, darling, my own, all will be well, be calm. All will be glorious, as it always is with us. Blue

246

skies, green winds, golden hair . . . We will have five
weeks to love each other. Know this as I know it.

Your Max

What happens to us now?

NOTES TO MYSELF

Isabel's marriage – all those years on wrong train.

When Edgar goes off for night or weekend, he tells her: 'I can sleep better there,' and wonders why that should 'upset' her.

Attempt at communication ends in spurt of hate.

Role of living-room couch in marital disputes.

'I'll come to your funeral if you'll come to mine.' Why did I write that? What does it mean?

Overheard from open window: Woman: 'Go to hell!'
Man: 'I'm there already.'

Fall from grace.

Duress.

Give Midge (Marge) bigger role.

Something bound to float up from the unconscious: a nugget, a fish –

Can't think – sitting here over an hour, can't concentrate. I give up.

FRIDAY JUNE 2

Still punchy from last night and this morning. Can't work.

Varya sees it; she comforts me with *pirozhki* and proverbs: 'To mouse, cat is lion.' I'm a mouse all right, but I don't think Max is a cat. A warlock, more likely; a changeling.

I'm remembering how kind he was when I had a backache. 'Definition of woman,' he said; 'a creature with two legs and backache.' Yet he came with roses and a bed board. He bought a special backrest for the seat of his car. He cooked for me and read to me —

Maybe I did overreact last night. After all, what happened?

Dear Jess,

A brief note on my return from my lecture tour, in reply to your rich letter of May 27, and your comments on marriage.

I'm a realist; I take for granted high infidelity these days. I see all those gray Lotharios, very married, making out all over the place. But I wouldn't want to be married to one.

It's hard to believe the woman who claims she's so happy because her husband is a philanderer. We aren't as liberated as all that. A young girl writes me:

> I don't want to stunt myself, but about Womans Lib I'm ½ way.

I myself am nine-tenths. What's your ratio?

Letter follows, as soon as I catch up.

Does Varya have any more relatives? Don't keep them from

Your loving
Nina

ALPHABETICAL GROUNDS

If only she hadn't called off the detectives three and a half years ago, she would be free now, her suffering over, her children's future assured.

When she first began to sleep on the mattress on the living room floor, the children had to step over her on their way to the kitchen in the morning. That's when Gregory's eyes began to hurt, so that she had to read his schoolwork to him. One terrible day they had called from his school: he had gone blind, they were sending him home. Isabel rushed him to the eye doctor, who took her aside and told her there was nothing wrong with the boy's eyes or glasses, but that he couldn't, literally couldn't, bear to see what was going on at home. 'Do something about your divorce, and fast,' he warned her. 'When these symptoms clear up, others may appear. What are you doing to this boy?'

Isabel had reported this to Edgar, the son's father, the doctor. Edgar hissed at her: 'You won't be satisfied until you've made a psychotic out of him!' and went off on his weekend. Why was she always surprised anew? Why did she always hope that this time he would be different?

Even at Gregory's graduation that spring, when he won a scholarship, his father ruined the boy's triumph by telling him he had no money to supplement it. Isabel had to stand silently by while Gregory's lips quivered: 'But it was promised me . . .' His father didn't wait; he bolted out, while Isabel tried to reassure her son: '*I* promise you college. You know Daddy is a little peculiar about money. Don't worry, you'll go.'

A little peculiar. At the mention of money, Edgar's knuckles turned white and his face muscles began to twitch. She was sure he must be insane when he said to her: 'You can no longer entertain your friends with champagne, and you must stop having lunches at the Chambord.' What friends? What champagne? She had never set foot at the Chambord.

Now Edgar took off every weekend, leaving no money for

food. 'Did your lawyer advise you to starve us?' she asked. He gave Katie three dollars and said: 'Let me have the change.' It would be ludicrous, Isabel thought, were it not so terrible. If it were something read in a book, no one would believe it.

She could not understand why Katie was staying on, pale and sad, bringing food from her home, lending Isabel a few dollars: 'You need it more than I.' Was it devotion or masochism, like her own? The other day Katie handed her a letter from Edgar which he told her to deliver to Isabel in the next room. It accused Isabel of 'causing cockroaches to appear in the apartment.' Katie began to cry. 'If he saw a cockroach in the kitchen, why didn't he tell me?' But Isabel didn't even get angry. *Just let me off the hook fast!* – she begged Adams and Gross for deliverance.

'Get off the pot,' Adams said in simple English, 'and we'll catch him in' – he added with sudden delicacy – 'in the act. You ready for the detectives?'

'Yes,' Isabel said. 'Yes, please.'

For the first time in her life she would fight. She would not lay down her weapons now.

To steel herself for it, she sat down to make a list, alphabetizing various grounds for divorce in other states, with asterisks for those that applied to her:

    abandonment (see desertion)
    *adultery
    alcoholism
    attempted murder
    *cruel and inhuman treatment
    desertion (see abandonment)
    drug addiction
    felony
    fraud
    imprisonment
    incest
    *incompatibility
    *indignities
    insanity

*mental cruelty
*nonsupport

Adultery. But there was no other way, absolutely no other way. 'God help me,' she heard herself say her mother's words. But she added her own: 'For my cause is just.'

NOTES TO MYSELF

Piling it on? Edgar losing credibility, Isabel — sympathy? Gregory's blindness — too much?

Instead, illustrate Gregory's sensitivity with one brief touch, more muted, more tender than this? Perhaps Isabel remembers how once, when Gregory was three and she was reading *Mother Goose* rhymes to him, he suddenly burst out crying.

'What is it, darling?'

'I don't want Jack to break his crown!' he sobbed.

Recapture my feeling when Jeremy, as a child, cried: 'It's only a story, it didn't really happen!'

Difference between writing and merely narrating. In Fiction Workshop, I keep looking for the telling detail, the word, the gesture that illuminates character.

Find it for myself now.

SATURDAY JUNE IO

Over a week since I last wrote here, since that terrible
night I spent on the couch. Max says I'm overreacting to
it, that any day now it will be revealed to me why he's
been under such pressure. That he loves me as no man
ever has or could. That all will be well with us if we only
remain calm.

Calm. That's a word he keeps repeating.

I worried about his heart, the spasm of pain. He's fine,
he tells me, superbly healthy.

Was that the second shoe I was dreading? 'Now that
both shoes have dropped,' I say to him tentatively, 'we
have nothing left to fear.'

'What about socks?' he says. We laugh again, and we
make love. Each time is like the first time; each time is
new and beautiful, but I'm wary. I feel like a convalescent
after a dangerous, recurrent illness.

He brings me flowers and poems and presents. He even
brought one for Cat: a catnip mouse beautifully gift-
wrapped, with a card written in Aramaic. 'No use
translating it to her,' he said; 'it loses a lot in translation.'

At times he's distant, grim, preoccupied with something I'm not allowed to know. Spends more time in his
office, says strange things. I'm so hooked now, I become a
beggar, pleading for love.

Marge says: 'You're nuts. If a guy hurts me, I split.
Who needs it?' It sounds so simple. Like Jeremy at two,
when Jill was born. He took one look at his sister and
said: 'I don't *need* her.'

I can't say that about Max.

SUBJECT DEPARTED PREMISES

This time there would be no last-minute weakness, no eleventh-hour abdication. Both children were away in college; there was nothing to stop her. She borrowed the money from Jim and Hilda – $150 a day – to 'initiate surveillance.'

This time he did not go out of town. The detective's preliminary report, accurate to the hour, to the second, with detailed description of everything from the subject's car to the location of a telephone booth, informed her that: 'Pursuant to instructions from Mrs Webb, a surveillance was initiated on the above-captioned subject on November 17 and 18, 1965,' and went on to describe how subject departed residence . . . entered car . . . made phone call from booth . . . parked car . . . walked to . . . entered apartment building at . . . took elevator. Subject departed building in company of a blonde female approximately 5'5", 35 yrs. of age. Subject and female window-shopped . . . entered restaurant located at . . . departed restaurant . . . entered building, took elevator to second floor, and entered apartment 2H. This apartment is listed to Rhoda Barnes. An observation from across the street revealed subject and female in apartment, which was visible from the street. At 1:04 a.m. blinds were drawn tight. At 1:33 a.m. all lights in apartment were out. Nobody entered or left the building until 3:12 p.m., when subject left the building, entered his car, and departed the area. Respectfully submitted . . .'

Respectfully! But this was just an exploratory, as they say in the operating room. Above-captioned subject would be surveilled the following weekend. For her $150 she learned a new name: Rhoda Barnes. A name that wasn't even on her neatly alphabetized list!

The next surveillance was initiated at the residence of Rhoda Barnes. Isabel had to accompany the two detectives 'for purposes of identification.'

'You mean, I have to walk into the room, *see* them?'

'That's the law.'

They had a camera with them; they would take pictures *in flagrante delicto*. Isabel tried to stop her knees from trembling; it was unreal, it couldn't be happening –

The main detective, she guessed it was, looked at her.

'Listen, we'll call you just before we nab him, then you can come down to join us. Stay right by the telephone, we'll call you.'

A reprieve. For a while, at least. She paced the bedroom floor, her eyes on the telephone. She kept looking at the time. Six o'clock. Seven. Dinner time. Were they surveilling the restaurant? Had they, perhaps, lost track of him? Eight. Ten. At eleven-forty they called her and asked her to meet them: they would be in their car at such and such address.

She took the subway, found the car, sat huddled in it, trying to make herself invisible. The detectives filled her in: the subject and female previously described departed the female's apartment building, entered the subject's car, and drove away. They stopped at a florist's, the female departed the car, purchased a bouquet of flowers, and entered the subject's car. They drove to another address, entered that building, subsequently departed that building without the flowers, entered the subject's car, and drove back to the female's building. Subject parked the car, they departed the car and walked to a newspaper stand, where subject purchased the Sunday *Times*. He was also carrying a man's shaving kit. They entered the female's apartment at 11:32 p.m. That's when they called her.

She wondered, vaguely surprised that it could occur to her at a time like this, with whom they had dinner, for whom they had brought flowers. Was it one of their mutual friends? The address was not familiar to her.

The window the detective pointed out to her was the bedroom; it was on the second floor, facing the street. It was dark. The point was – how to get in. 'Make entry' was the way they put it. Surprise them in the act. They might try breaking the lock on the front door, but by that time the subject and female would no longer be in the act. They would have time to dress and pretend to read books. Even then, all that the detectives were obliged to prove was 'disposition and opportunity.' He was disposed, and the opportunity was there. Perhaps they could find some way of entering through the open window, right into the bedroom? The detectives conferred about that for quite a while. What they needed was a ladder, something to stand on, to scale the wall. One of them stepped out of the car to reconnoiter.

There is no other way to do it, Isabel said to herself; *this is the only way.* She tried not to imagine them in bed behind that window. She suddenly thought of Lucky, the parakeet, and how Edgar had said, 'He is dead.' If he only knew that she was at this moment just a few feet away . . .

The second detective returned, jubilant. 'We've got it!' he said. He had found a ladder leaning against the wall in an alley a block away, apparently left there by some house painters. What a stroke of luck!

By this time it was four in the morning. She had been sitting in the car for over four hours, and she hadn't cracked up. This was the culmination of all her suffering, ever since she had called off the first detective. This was her last chance.

The detectives had set up the ladder against the wall, right under the window. One was climbing up after the other. 'For a witness,' she thought dimly, grateful they did not make her climb up with them. 'It's okay,' the nice one had said to her. 'You can stay right here in the car.'

As from a long distance, she heard sounds: a shuffle, a faint 'Help' in Edgar's voice she hardly recognized, and in another minute the two detectives emerged from the front door of the building. They quickly got into the car and drove off. 'Where to?' said the nice one.

Where to? It was a question that hadn't occurred to her. She certainly couldn't go back home to face him. She would ask her lawyers in the morning where to move. It *was* morning; it was almost dawn. She asked them to drive her to Martha's; she would stay at Martha's until it grew light.

Martha took her in, gave her hot chocolate, made her lie down for a couple of hours until it was time to call her lawyers.

She called Adams as soon as he got into his office. He told her to go back to her apartment.

'But how can I, after what happened?'

'You can; we'll prove you had no money to live elsewhere.'

'But I can't – '

'We'll get you on the court calendar as soon as possible. In the meantime, get a lock for your bedroom door and lock him out. To show there's been no condonation.'

'Lock him out?'

'From the bedroom. You can't lock him out of the apartment because he claims it's part of his office.'

'But how can I – '

'Get a good strong lock.'

She was terrified to go back, but Martha went with her and stayed with her, waiting for Edgar to come up from his office. She heard his footsteps. Martha put her arm around Isabel and held her close.

Edgar stood in the doorway and looked at her with icy hatred; his lips were white. 'That was a contemptible thing to do,' he said, and walked out with his weekend bag.

At least, he didn't kill me, Isabel thought.

While he was away, Martha helped her take out his clothes and toilet articles from the bedroom and pile them up on the marble staircase leading down to the office. They worked fast. Isabel called a locksmith, and when Martha left, she locked herself inside her bedroom and waited.

The detectives' report came three days later:

4:05 a.m. Entry was made into apartment 2H via the second-floor window. The subject and female were sleeping in a convertible bed located on the left wall of the room. The subject awakened and jumped out of bed. He was nude. A second later the blonde female companion previously identified jumped up. She was also nude. The subject's clothes were draped over a chair on the right side of the bed, his shoes were alongside of the bed, the newspaper he had purchased was on the chair and had not been disturbed. Investigators left through the front door which was double-locked and secured with a chain. Apartment 2H is a one-room apartment, and no other persons were present in the room. Respectfully submitted –

His shoes, it was his 'shoes alongside of the bed' that unnerved her.

As for the photograph of them in bed, it never came out, Adams told her; but she was not to disclose this to anyone. Let him worry, he said.

Dear Nina –
Guess what! My publishers have assigned an editor to
me. Since my book is due in less than six months, they
thought I might be ready for 'editorial assistance.' I talked
to someone named Arlene Sherman on the phone, who
offered her help; I said I would drop her a note. The
problem is twofold: first, I don't want anyone to work
with me on it at this point, and second, I'm not sure how
to address her.

> I wonder who *this* is –
> A Miss or a Mrs.
> Whoever it is,
> She must be a Ms!

Besides, I've always done my best work alone. When I
was eleven, for example, I was writing my five-act drama
without any editorial assistance. It was called *She Died
for Love.* It's true that I never finished it, but it was for
lack of space rather than imagination. You see, I had one
of those lined paper notebooks, and I got so involved in
the description of my *dramatis personae* (there were
twenty-eight of them) that by the time I was ready to
write Act One, Scene One, the notebook was filled up and
it didn't occur to me to get another one. I described in
minute detail all of my characters: their names, ages,
color of hair, of eyes, of shoes, of socks, their dress,
jewelry, previous misdeeds, future plans, and so on; and
since I wrote with a pencil that turned purple when wet
with the tip of the tongue, I had quite a number of purple
passages. I wish I could find that notebook now; my
inspiration, in those days, flowed unblocked.

But I *have* been working on my book. Max has been
rather busy and distracted; he spends more time at his
place, so I can work undisturbed. I've been writing about
children of divorce, legal jargon, obsession with *things.*

I've been dipping into my old diaries (it's true, a scar *has* no heart!) to see what else was happening in 1966 besides Isabel's divorce. That was the year when the young were in power; the year of the hippies and Beatles; the year when Masters and Johnson perfected Freud's discovery: sex.

Varya drops in occasionally and encourages me. 'But why take so long?' she asks. 'Akh, if I only know English, I write book, one-two-three – *ffft*! Plyenty customers!'

She stepped in the other day on her way to the auction, her purple velvet beret at a rakish angle over one ear. 'My hat I keep because today is aukzion!' She pirouetted: 'You see how I dress?' I saw. She wore a tight satin dress; her small feet in tan socks over her nylons were squeezed into high-heeled patent leather pumps; she carried a huge pocketbook in the shape of a straw basket. 'Well, how?' she asked. 'Look harder!' I looked harder: she wore a black velvet ribbon tight around her neck, as well as a gold locket on a chain, and over this – a pearl necklace.

'Your pearls?' I asked.

'Akh, no! Look on dress only! Is beautiful – in morning green, in evening – *ffft*! – blue!' (Varya never describes a color simply, but: 'From far – gray; you come close – black and white checks!')

She takes pride in her auction finds: a rhinestone tiara, a three-legged stool, a parasol 'for the rainy season.' But this time she had a complaint. 'Last week I buy naked lady lamp, very sexy, but when bring home – no good. No light! *Sela v galoshu.*'

'Sell what?'

'*Sela v galoshu.* Means: sat down in a galosha.'

'A galosha?'

'A galosha. Is like rubber shoe, put on when rain, when snow . . .'

'I know, but . . .'

'Means – look, I show you.' She grabbed an ashtray from the table and held it up. 'I think this – diamond. Hurrah, congratulations, I buy. Take home – look again – is only ashtray! *Sela v galoshu.*'

'I see,' I said uncertainly. 'A mistake? A disappointment?'

'Eh,' Varya cocked her head dubiously. 'In English have no good word.' She nudged me with her basket: 'With Maxvil – how?'

'What do you mean, how?'

'You go marry? No?'

'No,' I said. 'I don't think so.'

She nodded. 'Is Rrawshian saying: "Not for hat only is head on shoulders."'

'You disapprove of him, then?'

She shrugged: 'I never go marry with Maxvil.'

'Never?'

'Never!' She bustled out.

That leaves the field wide open to me. Don't worry, as I told you before, I don't intend to marry him. But we *will* have our holiday in Europe this August, and I'm counting the days.

I miss your letters. You did tell me on the phone about the staggering offer you received: three quarters of a million dollars!!! How much is it in money? I mean, in one-dollar bills? How many valises would they fill? (I have valises on my mind these days because the climax of my book will depend on Isabel's two valises of evidence against Edgar!)

But dear, dear Nina – if that TV series they want you to do is something you don't believe in, if it's something that

262

might betray all you've been doing for the angry young-sters in our country, then where's the conflict? Why are you so troubled by this decision you have to make?

You once said that astronomical sums exist only on paper, and you pointed out the dangers of taking success too seriously. Remember the letter from that prisoner. Remember the words of the schizophrenic young man, and watch out for the rubber eye! And remember the child who wrote: 'I'd rather read you than TV.'

But whatever decision you make, it must be the right one for *you*. And whatever decision you make, know that I love you.

Your
Jess

P.S. A selfish question: If you do the TV series, does it mean you will not be moving to New York?

DOMESTIC CASE

The evening Edgar returned, he came upstairs, tried to open the bedroom door behind which Isabel was hardly breathing, and finding it locked, furious, threatened to break it down. In a few minutes, she heard him on the other side, unscrewing the doorknob. She panicked. The doorknob wobbled, loosened. In desperation, she called the police.

Two cops arrived. Isabel opened the door of the bedroom and told them she was afraid for her life. Edgar began to complain to them: how hard he was working, how he had no place to sleep. Isabel, surprised at her calmness, pointed out to the policemen that there were several couches in the apartment and downstairs, besides the two beds in the children's unoccupied rooms. She explained she had locked him out on advice of her attorneys. The cops shrugged indifferently, offered to escort her to a hotel, but she stood her ground. The cops said that since he had committed no crime, there was nothing they could do. They mumbled something about a 'domestic case,' and left.

She locked herself in again, went to bed, and stayed awake most of the night listening in terror for his footsteps. In the morning she heard him come up and begin to unscrew the doorknob again. She crouched against the wall. The knob on the bedroom side fell down, with the metal rod, the long 'pin' attached to it. She found she could put it in and lock the door with it. She could slam the door when she left the bedroom; he had no way of opening it. For once, she thought wryly, she didn't get the short end of the stick, but the long one. As long as she was in possession of the doorknob with its pin, he had no access to the bedroom.

All week she carried the doorknob with her wherever she went, at first in her pocketbook, then, afraid he might find it, on a rope around her neck. She knew he was in a rage about it and was scheming something.

On Sunday, some instinct warned her not to come out of her locked bedroom unless there was someone in the house; she heard him moving about outside her door and she trembled with fear. It was Katie's day off. She waited all day, hoping he would leave so that she could emerge and get some food, but she heard his breathing just outside the door. She picked up the telephone – her link to the outside world – and called up Katie. She asked her to come, since Katie had a key to the apartment, and to stay a few minutes while Isabel left the bedroom to get something to eat. At five-thirty Katie arrived and Isabel let herself cautiously out of the bedroom. He was gone, but Isabel was shocked to discover that he had put some metal soldering into the keyhole from the outside, so that she could no longer lock her door when she went out. Katie cried when she saw what he had done; they were both frightened.

Isabel tried to scoop the metal out, but it was solid; he must have done it during the night. Katie brought her coffee and scrambled eggs and Isabel locked herself in again, imprisoned in her bedroom. She asked Katie before leaving to push the button on the outside door so that anyone who came to her rescue could walk in. If things got rough, she could call someone.

In the evening, hungry again, she called Martha, who came with a hamburger for her in a brown paper bag. She told her that Edgar, who was back in the apartment, had waved her toward the bedroom door, saying graciously: 'Go right in,' but waiting outside, ready to pounce. Isabel took the hamburger quickly and locked herself in again. 'He must be insane,' she told Martha later on the phone.

The following morning she phoned the locksmith to come and put a new lock on the door. Now that Katie was in the apartment she was less frightened.

The locksmith came at noon. Apparently Edgar had intercepted her call on the extension and had instructed the doorman not to let him in. The locksmith – a kind, sympathetic man – came through the back door with his tool box, but before he could begin, Isabel heard Edgar's footsteps on the stairs. She told the man to hide in her bathroom. Edgar came prowling around, though there were patients in his office at that hour.

'Did the locksmith come?' he asked.

'What locksmith?' she said. She had opened the bedroom door, and asked Katie to pretend to clean the bedroom so that Edgar would see there was no one else there and go down again. But Edgar remained upstairs.

Suddenly, to her horror, he brought a hammer and began to hammer nails into the inside frame of the door, so that now she would not be able to lock it from the inside either. He kept banging the nails in, then he sat around in the foyer for some fifteen minutes, while Isabel kept whispering to the locksmith in the bathroom that soon her husband would have to go down, since he had patients waiting.

The locksmith was so angry at what her husband was doing that when at last Edgar went downstairs, he told her he would be glad to testify in court for her. He promised he would return as soon as Isabel called him to say the coast was clear. He said he would give her a lock for which no one would be able to get duplicate keys. He left his toolbox, which she hid in her closet. She would have to wait now until Edgar was out of the house, since the noise of the drilling would alert him.

An hour later the locksmith called. She said she would call him back; she knew Edgar was listening in on the extension in his office. She ran down to the corner drugstore, which had a public booth, and called the locksmith. He said he needed his toolbox. She went back, put it into a valise, and carried it – it was very heavy – to a place two blocks away, where he was waiting.

A couple of hours later the locksmith called her again, very upset. She dashed out to the public booth to call him back. He told her her husband had phoned and offered him double the money Isabel gave him if he would not put the lock in, or else, if he would give him a duplicate key. The locksmith said he told Edgar he would think it over; in the meantime he assured Isabel he was on her side, and would try to get proof on a recording device he had on his phone of her husband's attempt at bribery.

When Edgar left for the evening, Isabel called the locksmith and had him come to remove the nails and install the lock, the kind her husband couldn't possibly tamper with, though she was worried about the expense. She asked Katie to spend the night, to sleep in Wendy's room. She was afraid of what Edgar might do to her; she explained to Katie that he was irrational.

The lock disfigured the door, but Edgar had already started it by unscrewing the doorknobs, soldering the keyhole, and hammering in nails. Now she noticed something new, some additional harm he was planning. For some reason, he had unscrewed the doorknob from Wendy's closet. What did he have in mind? She also discovered he had put some kind of moist white plaster into the indentation on the side of the bedroom door, either to make a plaster cast of the lock, or for some other frightening purpose. The stuff had hardened. But now Isabel had no need of the doorknob around her neck to get in and out of the bedroom; she was safe behind her new lock!

Not as safe as she thought: During the night she heard him prowling outside her door again. Next morning she called the locksmith, who said he could attach a padlock arrangement with a combination over the keyhole that would prevent her husband from soldering it. In the meantime – since Edgar could do the soldering only when she was *inside* the room, otherwise the whole door would have to be taken off its hinges – she pretended she was not in the room. Lights out, she spent night and day in the locked bedroom, hardly breathing, calling no one – let him wonder!

On Sunday he saw she was home. Afraid to lock herself in the bedroom, she slept, fully dressed, in Wendy's room. The following night she slept in Wendy's room again, since he was home, waiting for her to get into the bedroom so he could solder the keyhole. She would outwit him at every move.

If only he had left the door alone, this whole business wouldn't have been necessary, she thought bitterly. If only he had been willing, three and a half years ago, to provide for her and the children, the hiring of the detectives, the raid, the whole nightmare horror would not have been necessary either. He had forced her into every action she'd had to take.

TUESDAY JUNE 20

Last ten days together – mostly good.

One warm day last week we drove to Eaton's Neck, to a private beach of someone Max knew who was away, who had invited him to use the facilities. Completely deserted spot, remote, beautiful. We took our clothes off and cavorted like naked children, frolicking, splashing each other. We rode the waves, we raced from one end of beach to the other; we made love on the hard sand to the sound of pounding surf. He had brought French bread and cheese and fruit and a bottle of wine, and we said silly, funny things to each other, and he mimicked an old professor of art he had known, and it was a day of such innocence and radiance that it was impossible to imagine anything beclouding our happiness.

He had two cameras with him, and he took lots of photos of me naked, running in and out of the water. He has won prizes for his photographs, so I thought these would be special. But a couple of days later, when I asked him about them, he said none of the pictures had come out. His cameras were defective. 'Both of them?' I asked in dismay. 'Both of them,' he said, unconcerned. 'But we have all the pictures in our memories.'

He was tired that day. We stopped at a hardware store for some light bulbs – he became very upset that the price had gone up, very agitated – shouted at the clerk. Later, he said he had to sleep alone, at his place.

That night I dreamed of a banquet. I saw a long wooden table of gnarled wood – with nothing on it – no dishes, no silver, no cloth – just the grains of wood and empty benches on either side. I had come to the banquet too late or too early, or on wrong day, or to wrong place . . .

Yesterday, when I asked what plans he had for our

long July Fourth weekend, he pretended to be annoyed. 'You don't seem to have much concern about my money problems.'

'Do you need money, Max?'

He moved his forefinger sideways in front of his face: Taboo!

I'm sure he said that to put me off the trail; I know him! He's planning a special weekend for us, perhaps at a beach. I know he recently bought himself some summer clothes. He doesn't like his surprises to be spoiled.

On my birthday next week he's taking me to the ballet. Is it possible that in one week, on June 27, I'll be – fifty-seven? Almost sixty? It seems absurd; I can't believe it! My face in the mirror is that of a young, radiant woman. Varya tells me I never looked better. '*Krov s molokom*,' she says, kissing her fingers. 'Means: blood and milk. Means: very beautiful.'

I've been writing for a long time, time I should have spent on my book. But here I can speak freely, without having to impose order on chaos, invent cause and effect, rewrite my life.

I suppose, in a way, I can speak freely to Nina, too, but our letters have struck a tone that's hard to change. And a tactful reserve, a kind of civil candor. *Social* truth.

So many ways of approaching truth – in private, in public, in fiction. And what is *the* truth?

Varya says it's like the right note struck on the piano: the ears know it, and do not wilt.

Dearest Jess,

Thank you for your letter of the 13th and for your wise words. My conflict is a difficult one. TV or not TV, that is certainly the question; but the problem is far more complicated than it appears to you. There are enormous pressures upon me to say yes, not only for the money. This may be an unequaled opportunity for me to reach vast audiences, many more people than any book or lectures can. My name, after all, bears some weight, and my influence can be considerable, since they want me not only to be in charge of writing the series, but to appear in it as well. Unfortunately, as I told you on the phone, I have no autonomy. 'They' have the last word, though they assure me of their respect for authors. Come to think of it, I had very little to say about my film, but they did it creditably enough, as you'll see when it gets to New York. Perhaps this, too, will be done well, in spite of sponsors, big business interests, and the proposed title: *Kids & Co.,* which sounds as if it might veer between slapstick and trivia. I don't want to phony up my act and betray the kids, yet I hate to let a chance like this slip away. I'll probably accept.

Speaking of titles, I came across the sad merry-go-round — not in italics or caps, not even in quotation marks, in a political article. This is heady stuff, as is the standing ovation I received last week in Santa Fe.

It's when I come home from all that public love that I feel most the lack of a private one. I let myself in with my key and I greet my chairs, my sofa, my stunning view of the bridge, and my plants. I remember how at a dinner party once, when all the women were talking about their children and grandchildren, I said — not to be outdone — 'I have a plant home, and you should see the amount of water it takes!'

What I'm saying is that though I am loved by many

people I don't even know, I would rather be *in* love like you. I'm not referring specifically to Max, who may or may not be all you think, but I envy your being in love. I think it's much more important to love than to be loved.

With which thought I will leave you now —

Much love,
Nina

P.S. It seems to me that the measure of success is: how long the newspaper obituary will be.

P.P.S. Sent you a birthday present I think you will like!

NOTES TO MYSELF

For contrast, invent dialogue between Isabel and Midge, who can't understand what all the fuss is about. 'So what? So get up and go. Who's stopping you? Find a room, get a job, what's the big deal?'

Or bring in Teresca (by another name): her narcissism can't admit anyone else's suffering. She says: 'Did you know that gelatin makes the nails grow longer?'

Isabel has lost her sense of humor (proportion) totally. Her lists and her mind cluttered with jumble of large and trivial issues. Her affection can find no outlet — not in the children, not even in the cat.

In short scenes, imply this. Remember ruthless art of leaving things out.

Yet, her resilience. Like toy I had as child in Kiev: *Vanka Vstanka*: Vanka-Get-Up! A little wooden boy on a round weighted base; no matter how many times he was pushed down, he always sprang up, his foolish painted smile impassive. No matter how many times Isabel says she can't go on, she goes on.

Lawyers again. How they muddy up what was, in the beginning, simple. 'We demand, they refuse, we submit, they allege.'

Irrelevance intrudes, as it does in life. She still frets about the red chair he had removed from the living room. A relative complains to her that Edgar will no longer treat her free of charge. She misses the evening paper he used to bring upstairs, folded a certain way. She steals in triumph two quarters from his coat pocket.

Dear Nina –

It has arrived! This morning, the day before my birthday, the beautiful electric typewriter you sent has arrived, and I love it! I'm confident it will know exactly where to put one word after another. And it's such a relief not to have to stop every few minutes to unravel the ribbon or bang on the machine to get a key unstuck! My old typewriter is retired to the floor of the linen closet, and I'm writing to you on my new one. Aren't the sentences pretty?

> I am now the happy owner
> Of this gorgeous Smith-Corona!
>   Upper case and lower case,
>   Every letter in its place,
> Waiting patiently for me
> To combine them, A to Z . . .

My only problem is an old one: guilt at your extravagance!

I appreciate how difficult your decision about the TV series must be, but I'm sure you'll make the right one, as long as you don't lose your sense of humor. It's one thing to say with a laugh: 'My name may not be unfamiliar to you' (I quote you), and another to mean it. You are both my sometime pupil and my model. By the same token, you once said I keep you on an 'even kiel.' Don't you disappoint me too!

I can't wait until August; Max has been so tired lately, he needs a vacation more than I do. In the meantime, I've been working on the craziness of divorce. First, I put my Isabel on a mattress on the living room floor; then I locked her, a prisoner, in her own bedroom. I remember, in the insanity of my own divorce, when Charles was sleeping in the living room, how he once tied one end of a

273

long piece of thread to a little bell on the table next to his couch, and the other one to the handle of our brownstone front door, which opened *out* instead of in. When I came home in the evening and opened the door, the thread would pull the bell off the table and wake him, so that he would know the exact hour I came in!

The more I can laugh at things like that, the less the pain.

This is *my* thought for the day.

Is it possible that tomorrow I'll be fifty-seven? How did I get to be that old, when the day before yesterday I was nineteen? Varya says: 'Look in meerror – yawng, count on fingers – not!' I will not count on fingers. Max is taking me to the ballet tomorrow night. We haven't gone out much lately.

I was interested in your P.S. – that success is measured by the length of published obituaries. Did I tell you Teresca has written her own, a heartfelt tribute, which she keeps clipped to her best studio photograph on top of her desk 'just in case'? If I were to write my own epitaph, I would ask you to

> Tell all my friends who write or phone
> That I have gone. Address unknown.

I am, as always, modest – in death as I was in life:

> So give me neither tears nor praise,
>   But just a brief, ironic sigh.
> For one who always shunned clichés –
>   How unoriginal to die!

> I want no sentiment sublime,
>   No promise of eternal bliss
> In lofty prose or flowery rhyme.
>   What I would really like is this:

> A simple stone, and just one line:
> The year:2069.

Now why, on the eve of my birthday, should I think about death?

Varya once told me about a friend of hers, a woman in her seventies, who had died. The widower, a man of eighty, remarried within six months. 'You see, Lapochka,' Varya said, 'it doesn't pay to die!'

It sure doesn't.

Thank you again for the typewriter, for your friendship, for your love.

Your
Jess

VIVAMUS, MEA LESBIA

Isabel did her best to avoid Molly, but on this particular afternoon they had their confrontation. Isabel had gone to her mother's to persuade her to go to the hospital for tests, and found Molly there.

'Doesn't she look beautiful?' her mother said to Isabel.

If you only knew, Isabel thought bitterly.

Her mother agreed to go to the hospital 'one of these days,' she said, although the tumor, which had grown unmistakenly in her abdomen, was certainly benign.

'Did Jesus make the diagnosis?' Isabel asked, and was immediately sorry. She was never at her best with Molly.

'I will do it only for you,' her mother said. 'My children are all I have.'

Somehow Molly had managed to leave at the same time Isabel did. They found themselves in the elevator together.

'I've been wanting to tell you – ' Molly began.

'I don't want to hear about it.'

'It's not . . . I mean, I've always admired you so much! The way you look, your voice, everything about you. I wanted to be like you, and it . . . With him, it made me feel closer to you.'

They were on the ground floor now; the elevator door slid open. Isabel nodded to her sister-in-law and walked away briskly. She suddenly remembered a line from Catullus: *'Viva- mus, mea Lesbia, atquamemus.'* Strange, she remembered nothing else from her college Latin, and she had not thought of this line for some thirty years. She felt a surge of pity – she wasn't sure for whom.

How can a mother name her baby boy Quentin Vincent? she thought, *and why doesn't she go to the goddam hospital?*

But that wasn't it; she meant something else, she didn't know what.

Title too obvious? Besides, Catullus' Lesbia was not homosexual.

Glad I decided not to satirize Q.V.

But are some of my other characters slipping out of their roles?

Dearest Jess,

Just returned from a talk in Wisconsin, to find your thank-you-for-the-typewriter letter. What's this about guilt? Don't be a postnatal drip, and accept your birthday gift gracefully. May the keys ring merrily and swiftly, and may your book grow and grow.

Max had called to invite me to your surprise party, but I couldn't cancel my speaking engagement, made almost a year ago. What a pity! I wanted so much to be there with you. Send me a detailed description, including the loot you got.

They gave me more time to make up my mind about the TV deal. I hope you don't think I'm getting corrupted by success? You wrote that you didn't want me to disappoint you too. Why *too*?

In any event, I'll try not to disappoint you. Nor my young fans. Look what I found among my mail:

> I am unable to fine you in my liberry. Please excuse my typping because I didn't get typping in school I got jurnalism & cretive writing instead.

Do you suppose they've banned me for obscenity again?

You once told me you're keeping a scrapbook of Nina Moore. Well, I'm keeping the verses of Jessica Proot in a special notebook. One day, I figure, they'll fetch me a fortune!

Or perhaps we should publish our correspondence, under the title of *Life and Letters*? I believe all titles should be appropriate to the author's name. Like:

The Chairs, by all the Sitwells
Portrait of a Lady, by Trollope
The Chess Game, by Hugo, Victor.

Never mind. Happy birthday once more, and tell me all about the party!

Much love,
Nina

FRIDAY JUNE 30

Evening.

Now I know, I know he really loves me! How could I have doubted this magnificent man even for a moment? What he did for me was spectacular! Who else is capable of such caring, such munificence?

I must write it down carefully, exactly how it happened.

This was on my birthday – last Tuesday. And I suspected nothing! All day he was irritable and distracted on the phone – had sent no flowers that morning – had no time to see me during the day, canceled our dinner before the ballet, but he came after dinner, with a single yellow rose to pin to my shoulder. We wore evening clothes: he black tie, I white chiffon, and off we went in his car (the color of my eyes). We sat in the fourth row center – always the best for Max and me; we deserve it, he says.

After the first twenty minutes of the performance, he suddenly clutched his heart and whispered to me that he was in pain; we had to leave at once. I got panicky, but he kept assuring me he was all right; all he needed was to take some pills in his medicine cabinet at home. He wouldn't hear of my taking him to a hospital; he wouldn't hear of my calling a doctor; he wanted only to get home for his medicine. He said he knew what it was; nothing dangerous, but recurrent.

So that was why, I thought, he has been so tired at times! That's what was troubling him the night he wouldn't let me touch him in bed! And that was why he had wanted us to break off, to protect me from himself!

Full of love, compassion, anxiety, I supported him as we staggered up the aisle. He told the concerned usher it was all right, and handed our ticket stubs to two over-joyed standees. He wouldn't let me call a taxi, but insisted on driving his car himself, driving with one hand, holding the other over his heart – an endless trip, back to his apartment.

He took out his key, opened his door – and suddenly the dark blazed with lights, and a hundred voices, it seemed, shouted: 'Happy Birthday!' Faces of all my friends swam into focus; people kissing me, people laughing, the popping of champagne corks, flowers everywhere; a table spread with food; a heap of presents in colorful wrappings in the corner – it was overwhelming. Suddenly I thought I saw – yes, it was Jeremy, standing shyly behind some people! My knees buckled as I fell into his arms; he had to hold me up. A moment later, I couldn't believe my eyes – there was Jill, looking lovely and beaming with all her dimples . . . It was too much! I was hugging and kissing my children and laughing and crying at the same time. Too much! Max had imported them for me: Jeremy from Chicago, Jill from Los Angeles. He had called them, sent their plane tickets, it was like a dream! That was his most fabulous surprise . . .

Has anyone ever known a man like that?

The whole evening sped by on waves of high feeling. Toasts were made to me, I was feted, I was loved. And it was all created by Max! He told me later he got a list of my friends from Carrie and had spent weeks preparing for this, taking infinite pains to make sure it would be a surprise. They had all been waiting for us in his apartment for one and a half hours. The children had flown in that morning; he had them go directly to his place. When I explained what Max had done, pretending a heart attack and driving back from the theater, everyone seemed amused, except humorless Gilda, who said: 'Why did he have to put you through that? Why didn't he just say he forgot something at his apartment?'

Suddenly the lights were dimmed and a huge cake, the biggest I've ever seen, was brought in. It was in the shape of a gigantic book: the exact replica of the cover of *Children and People*, in the same colors and script, with the same figures of children and animals, with my name below, done in icing. Max told me later how much planning it took to get it done exactly right: how he had brought my book to the baker and made several trips there to supervise the inscription. He said he had been preparing for this party for weeks; that's why he has been so tense lately. 'Now do you believe that I love you?' he kept repeating.

My friends were toasting both of us. 'What a fantastic man!' Carrie said, hugging me.

He is, indeed. And I will never doubt him again. I will not be afraid to marry him. He *is* my man! To bring my children to me, that took such rare loving!

After the guests were gone we sat talking. Max was as excited as a child that the party had gone without a hitch, that everyone had a good time, that he had pleased me, that I had Jeremy and Jill with me. They were spending the night in his guest rooms, and he hovered over them like a doting nanny, putting them at their ease, drawing them out. He whispered to me that I would have to spend the night at my place, alone, because it wasn't proper that the children (at twenty-eight and thirty!!!) see me sleep in his home. He meant it – he used the word 'proper'; he's intensely serious about things like that. I would see Jill and Jeremy early in the morning, when they both had to leave; he offered to drive us all to the airport. In the meantime, there they were, my children, chatting and smiling, as if the difficult months and years of the divorce had never been. I felt our ugly history erased. Perhaps the fact that I was loved, that I was happy, relieved them of their own guilt. All this because of Max, my ultimate surprise giver, my miracle maker.

He was very tired. He took me home and went back to sleep, to arise at crack of dawn next day – that was Wednesday.

He picked me up early and made breakfast for me and the children, taking great pains with fresh orange juice and mushroom and parsley omelet and specially ground coffee. We were a family – a feeling I haven't experienced in years. Then we all drove to the airport, and – at the very last minute, so that they couldn't refuse, Max slipped his presents into their hands: for Jeremy – a special pen; for Jill – the coral necklace he had once shown me. He thrust it upon her, over her protests. She didn't unwrap it, and it wasn't until we were on our way home that Max told me what he had given her! He answered my unasked question: 'Because she is her mother's daughter.'

Jeremy's plane left first; he hugged me warmly, and said: 'Take care!' Max and Jill and I sat in the airport cocktail lounge and talked until her plane took off. She, too, seemed pleased, more affectionate, and it was all Max's doing.

He drove back with one arm around me and said he had never felt so close to anyone. 'I did good,' he said, smiling his beautiful smile, 'I did good to bring you your children.' We were so close, he was even able to mention his financial problems to me. He had been worried about some business deal that had come up unexpectedly, for which he needed immediate cash until after the July Fourth weekend: $9,000 or $10,000 he couldn't put his hands on at such short notice. I offered to lend him my savings – I still have over $9,000 in the bank – but he wouldn't hear of it; he was shocked by the suggestion.

'It's only for a few days,' I said, 'and I don't need it right now. I can easily get it out of the bank tomorrow.'

He was adamant. 'It's improper for me to borrow from you. It might spoil something between us.'

'That's only your silly pride,' I said. 'Don't we share far more important things than money? Haven't you given me everything, including yourself? Nine thousand dollars is a trifle; it would make me happy, for a change, to be able to do something for you!'

'I'll have to think about it,' he said. 'I can't bring myself to borrow money from the woman I love.'

'From whom better?' I asked.

He said he would let me know the next day, but he didn't want to talk about it anymore. Talking about money seems to upset him.

Yesterday, when he came over, I silently handed him a manila envelope with $9,000 in cash, which I took out of the bank in the morning just in case. He bowed and kissed my hand and said simply: 'Thank you, Goldenhair,' and we talked about the party some more.

'Did I please you, did I really surprise you?' he kept asking. 'Do you think Jill and Jeremy liked me?'

As for the money, he'll return it after the weekend, when banks reopen, yet he insisted on writing an I O U for it.

'That's ridiculous,' I said, 'why do we need it, we of all people?'

But he said it was necessary; it was businesslike; it was the only way he could accept the loan.

'All right,' I said, laughing, 'put down "IOU" right here' – and I handed him a scrap of paper.

But he wanted to write it on his own stationery, to make it 'legal.' He'll bring it tonight, after transacting his business. Poor darling – I think he was embarrassed about it. We were both relieved not to talk of it anymore.

We had a lovely day – except for one moment, when he discovered the new typewriter Nina had given me for my birthday. He had wanted to give me one. He actually kicked my typewriter table as we were leaving. But the evening was one of our special Max-and-Jessica evenings: we went to the movies, had a pizza on the corner, laughed like kids, holding hands on the street. Then he was suddenly very tired; he confessed he hadn't slept for several nights. 'You don't know how much the party took out of me,' he said – and we parted until tonight.

I expect him any minute now (he said he might be a bit late), and then we're going to have the most glorious July Fourth weekend, starting tonight! We'll have four whole days together! Though he said nothing about his plans, I have a feeling he went home to pack. We'll probably go to some remote beach, and we'll be together until Wednesday. I know he has recently bought new luggage, and I – I'm practically packed, all set to go at a moment's notice.

At last I am ready for him. For anything, for everything with him. I am no longer afraid.

Dear Nina –
I haven't heard from you since your letter of June 20, but I must share with you the fabulous surprise Max gave me on my birthday! It was the surprise of all surprises! He thought of the most brilliantly clever ruse to make sure –

I thought I heard him at the door, but no. I expect him any minute. We're to spend the long July Fourth weekend, I suspect, in some lovely romantic spot. I'm on to him and his surprises! But that party on the 27th was stupendous! He went to such pains to surprise me – took me to the ballet, pretended to have a heart attack, drove back to his apartment – he had been planning it for weeks! You can imagine how overwhelmed I was to see not only most of my friends there – but Jill and Jeremy! Yes, he had sent plane tickets to both, had put them up in his apartment the morning they arrived and kept me from knowing it until that evening. They spent the night at his place, and the following morning he drove us to the airport. He gave each a lovely present, and he made me feel, for the first time in years, really close to them. Have you ever known such a man? He said he called you to invite you, but you were away on a speaking tour. Had you been there, I would have been surrounded by all the people closest to me.

And the birthday cake! He went to the trouble . . .

I keep listening for his key in the door; he's late.

He had the cake made in the shape of my book, with the title and cover reproduced in icing. Champagne, marvelous food, laughter, presents, and my children, my children with me. Dear Nina, I never loved him more.

After the guests were gone, we opened presents, and he

was so delightfully funny, he made Jill and Jeremy laugh
as I haven't heard them laugh in a long time. 'Here,' he
said, holding up a package, 'is a gift that knows in
advance it will be returned or exchanged!' Another, from
Teresca, looked vaguely familiar. He suggested I compose
an acknowledgment in verse, which I made up on the
spur of the moment, but which will remain forever
unmailed:

> Your gift is lovely; I shall prize it.
> You know my taste, Teresca, dear!
> I cannot fail to recognize it —
> It's one I gave to you last year!

I know it's uncharitable, but we laughed so well together,
it was like having a family again. It *was* my family,
because I will, I will marry him. I am no longer afraid. We
were so close, he was able to confide some of his financial
problems to me — and he even allowed me to lend him
some money. We'll probably be off first thing in the
morning for our weekend together — I'm all packed and

It's getting late. I wonder what's detaining him.

What was I — oh, Teresca. I must sound incoherent; it's
just that I'm happy! I was telling you about Teresca. Do
you remember the way she talks, in unfinished sentences?
'Call me, I won't be home, but until.' Someone at the
party said how well I was looking, whereupon Teresca
took me aside and advised me not to waste a minute, to
begin at once to preserve my beauty: 'You're sitting alone
on the toilet, no one sees you, go like this.' She started to
pummel her face: back of her hand under her chin, palms
slapping her cheeks, fingers patting her neck. 'You're all
alone in an elevator, you must always.'

Did I mention I saw your movie advertised? It's opening
in two weeks. When your name appears on the credit line,
I'll applaud like anything!

And in just one month, Max and I are going on our European holiday — a *real* honeymoon!

Now I'm going to call him, to see what's delaying him. I'll write to you after our weekend, wherever he plans to take me. And do, please write me about yourself: your decision about the TV series, your fan mail, your new award. I read that you were honored at UCLA with a degree. Are you a double doctor now? Double or single, I congratulate you. I am happy for you, my Nina — and you know what? I am happy for me!

Your
Jess

COUNTERATTACK

One morning Adams called Isabel to inform her that her husband was now countersuing.

'What does it mean?' she asked, numb with apprehension.

'It means he's filed a counterclaim. His charges against you, to muddy up the water,' he said. 'To drag it through court. You'd better get down here soon as you can.'

When Isabel arrived at his office, Adams gave her to read twenty-one pages of Edgar's accusations, pages of such outrageous lies, such sickening filth, no one but a maniac, she thought, could have concocted them. He painted her as an unfit, depraved, unbalanced creature who couldn't be trusted with money because of her extravagant shopping sprees. He said she was guilty of lewd and lascivious conduct with a number of unspecified men in a number of unspecified locations. He claimed that she had entrapped him with a woman, and in the past had condoned his affairs and had procured women for him.

So that was the reason for his 'confessional' that long-ago weekend in the country! To prove her an accessory, to make her his accomplice! How diabolical! Or had it been unconscious cunning? Was he sincere at the time, and was he now debasing a once genuine feeling to besmirch her and save his own skin?

In his counterclaim he presented himself as a paragon of nobility, devoted father, good provider, a most abused man. His charges were so full of contradictions, if she could only laugh, she thought, they would all disappear. He denied his own adultery, yet called her 'an adulteress many times over, at least equal to mine.' He claimed she lived behind locked doors 'to establish the fiction that we're living apart'; at the same time he complained that they had lived separately for years. He wrote: 'She reaps the following benefits: rent, maid, all utilities, laundry, cleaning, and every other incidental paid for by me.

Food is provided for her. She has more clothes than she can possibly use because of her extravagant shopping, and she frequents a psychiatrist for self-indulgence, the way other women go to the movies.'

Only a madman could do this, Isabel thought. But that wasn't all. He mentioned a photograph of her in a lewd pose in the nude with a nude man, which he was ready to produce in court. So it was for this he had stolen her photograph album! For the snapshot the four of them had taken one summer, as a lark, naked on the beach, their arms around each other. Two couples romping by the sea. He had cut himself and the other woman out – and that was his evidence! By this time she was feeling so ill that Adams told her to go home.

'What will I do?' she asked.

'Borrow more money until the temporary alimony comes through.'

'But these lies, these charges – I must answer them!'

'You don't have to do it now,' Adams said. 'All the judge wants to know is – do you need temporary alimony or not. The rest will come out in court. This is just for the money.'

She went home seething with outrage. There was no one to talk to. Martha was away. Her mother would only flagellate herself at this new punishment from God. Besides, she was very ill, though she was still postponing going to the hospital for tests. Isabel didn't know where to turn. She thought of dying, but she could not; she had to fight for her children's future. *They're all I have*, she thought. *I mean, I'm all they have*. She was shocked to find she had used her mother's expression, which had always made her squirm with guilt.

All she could do was wait for the temporary alimony. Her proof that she needed it: the accumulated bills of the past eight months, which Edgar had never paid, and which kept piling up on top of the mantel, displayed like so many pale and angry Christmas cards, one overlapping the other. Isabel had them photostated to show they were the same bills, month after month – for household necessities, for the children's clothes. She had made no new purchases – except one: Edgar didn't know she still had a charge account at Macy's. She bought three pairs of stockings for $3.88 and a pair of shoes for $14.95.

Let him kill me for it, she thought. *It might be better than this.*

A few days later Adams phoned to inform her that her husband had hired Ridley. Ruthless Ridley, he called him. Edgar had paid him $7,500 as a retainer, Adams told her gleefully. Engle had bowed out, he said. She saw the man bowing out of Edgar's office obsequiously, as before royalty. 'Ridley plays rough,' Adams said. 'Now we'll see some action.'

She waited, behind her locked bedroom door, like a trapped animal; the more she struggled, it seemed, the tighter the trap.

Two days later Gross called her.

'The judge made a mistake,' he said. 'Temporary alimony was denied because you're still living in the same apartment with your husband.'

'A mistake?' she repeated dully.

'Yes – it's true of a separation, not a divorce action. He made a mistake. We'll have to appeal.'

Isabel kept nodding into the telephone: 'I see.' She saw nothing. Gross explained they would file for temporary alimony in the Appellate Court, which would meet sometime in the spring. Even if the judge should reverse the decision, Gross didn't know how much Isabel would get.

'When will it be over?' she asked.

'Only after the Appellate Court, when we'll be scheduled for a regular trial.'

'When is that?'

'Hard to say. Courts are jammed in the spring and closed in the summer.'

'What am I to do in the meantime?' she whispered into the phone.

'Go to all the stores for photostats of his letters saying he cut off your credit. Get all that to me for the appeal.'

'How am I to live?'

'That's your problem,' Gross said.

NOTES TO MYSELF

On paper, is Edgar believable? Is this someone Isabel could once have loved and married? Make clear he's fighting for his life: her entrapment. She's fighting for hers: her freedom.

When she upsets careful balance he has achieved in marriage, he goes over the cliff. At the same time, he is now out for blood . . .

Adams and Gross? In my own life – far more crude and callous. Had to tone them down to make them believable.

Strangely enough, the 'true' scenes seem invented; invented scenes, true. That must be what I mean when I talk to my students about fictional truth.

[DIARY]

In panic all this holiday weekend. Something happened to Max. He never came last Friday night. Hasn't answered phone, though I called every half hour, all night long. Have been calling all weekend – he's not in. Called his garage: his car is there, it was never taken out. Went twice to his home; regular doorman on vacation, substitute doorman just shrugged: 'Mr Mahler comes and goes, sometimes for a long time. No telling with him.' I can only suppose he had to go someplace in such a hurry he couldn't get in touch with me. But why didn't he take his car? Something dreadful happened to him, I know. I see him mugged, lying unconscious or dead someplace after a heart attack. I'm going out of my mind. Called hospitals. Called police, too, but they just took my name and his and suggested I wait till after the weekend. They said: 'Many men go off on a drinking binge on a holiday.' My Max, on a drinking binge!!!

Every moment I think I hear his footsteps in the hall outside. I keep listening for phone to ring. Can't write anymore. Can't do anything . . .

THE CREDIT DEPARTMENT

The blow was severe; since Isabel was denied temporary alimony, she was worse off than ever. Obeying her lawyer's order, she went to each of the stores in which she had for so many years enjoyed the prestige of credit, the fashionable Fifth Avenue stores where courteous salespeople showed *Moddom* where she could find what she was looking for. She now entered these same stores, these same elevators a different person. A supplicant, a pariah. She found herself on a floor where she had never set foot before, in the upper mechanism of the store, in an undecorated, forbidding place: The Credit Department. Here no-nonsense business was transacted. With contempt she either saw or imagined, the people behind their desks made short shrift of her. Her rank in the community of merchandising had been canceled, here and elsewhere. One store told the others; she was now *persona non grata*, not to be allowed in, not through the front door, anyhow. She suspected that some invisible camera had already photographed her; perhaps they had also caught her fingerprints on the desk. The message was sent out: 'Her husband is no longer responsible for her debts.' No longer responsible for her bed and board, her life, her death.

In store after store she was met with indifference, even rudeness. She was asked to go from one desk to another; she was made to wait for a long time for one or another of the minor executives, a woman so sullied, she had to be kept away from the downstairs selling floors, kept here indefinitely, while those miserable letters were exhumed and copied.

Only in one store, more modestly situated off Fifth Avenue, was she treated with sympathy and understanding. Behind the wicket in the Credit Office, a middle-aged black woman looked at her, really looked, and smiled, and said: 'I know how you feel, dear. I was divorced, too, when I was young, and left to care for three children. You'll be all right; it will be all right for you.'

She had called her *dear*. It was not familiarity or condescension – it was a warm, affectionate greeting, woman to woman, ex-sufferer to sufferer. Isabel left the store feeling that somehow, she, too, would come out all right. Others had told her that, but she believed this stranger, this smiling black woman who was nice to her when she didn't have to be. Nobody had to be nice to her anymore.

Dearest Jess,

Your letter of June 30 *was* a bit incoherent, but who ever thought happiness sprang from logic?

That surprise was certainly a surprise. What a bizarre introduction to such a happy evening: a heart attack!

I wish I could have been there. I'm glad you were with your children. Too bad you couldn't spend more time with them, as long as they were in New York all day.

You wrote that now you will marry Max. Was that euphoria, or did you really mean it?

Where did he take you for the July Fourth weekend? I spent it at the – I believe the adjective is palatial – home of the vice-president of the network in Brentwood, together with a couple of business bigwigs and their wives. Presumably, it was a social invitation, but I thought it politic not to refuse. Discretion is the better part of dollar. (Anyone in the EGG would know that quotation!) We spent the time 'throwing it around,' that is, my possible participation in *Kids & Co.* There was soap in the bathrooms, plenty of electricity, and no shit on the lawn, yet I was uncomfortable. The pressures are great. They have now upped their offer to a cool million (why cool? in contrast to hot money?), they promise not to vulgarize the scripts or tamper with my words, but they won't put it in writing. They have the last word. That's what worries me: it's often different from their first! I will have a major role in the writing, I will introduce each segment myself, and I will be seen by millions upon millions of people. 'Do you realize how much *good* you can do?' they keep telling me, appealing to my nobler side. For an hour each week we'll be 'rounding out' the problems of the teenagers in our society. Rounding out? I think none of them has ever seen a real, live teenager. It sounds a bit like that five-minute TV spot I once turned down, but longer and more expensive. On the other hand, they may be right; I can make a real 'input'. I think they mean impact.

It's the opportunity of a lifetime and I'd be crazy to refuse. But I must be more conflicted about it than I thought: I even had a dream. I'm all alone in an automatic elevator, not even preserving my beauty by slapping my cheeks, when the door slides open – on a blank wall. A solid wall, painted an institutional dull gray. Obviously, I'm stuck between floors. What to do? I did the only intelligent thing: I woke up. Ask your shrink what it means. I think an elevator is supposed to stand for something significant, like sex.

Yes, I got myself another degree. I am now Doctor Doctor Moore. Just remember that!

And remember that I'm rooting for you.

Much love,
Nina

P.S. Can you decipher this latest from my schizoid?

$$29 = 29 = 11 = 2$$
$$33 = \text{Face}$$

THE PORTENT

It was her spring of the pay telephones. Since her phone was tapped, she would sneak out of her bedroom, and call from the telephone booth at the corner drugstore, or, if that was busy, from the stationery store; call friends, lawyers, while spring came on silent feet. She perceived dimly the blossoming trees, the discarded overcoats, the gentle days and long, mild evenings, but she had no part in them. She waited only for the Appellate Court decision, half aware of the season – all the seasons she had missed. In a few weeks she would be fifty. Where had her life gone?

NOTES TO MYSELF

No – overwritten. Comb out clichés (blossoming trees, etc.) and write it simply, with no strained metaphors. Just say what happened in the spring of 1966, and how it ended, how it is ending, continues to end.

THE PORTENT

She waited for the Appellate Court decision amid accumulating bills, but she dared not panic. Where else could she borrow money? Her lawyers did not allow her to look for a job. 'Then he'll get out of paying you anything,' they warned her. They had never met a customer like him, they said. Adams called him a bastard. She was glad he said it for her. 'Does he have a relative, a friend, a priest, someone who can talk to him?' he asked.

He had no relative, no friend except his women lovers, no priest. His parents, now dead, had abandoned him as a child to an elderly aunt while they were off on their anthropological digs. There was no one to talk to him.

All she had was her ammunition: the two valises now at the offices of Adams and Gross, with evidence that would detonate in the courtroom; that would explode, expose him, exonerate her, and free her at last from the purgatory in which she had been living for four years now.

The worst blow came the evening she had dinner at Ellie and Bart's. Bart told her he knew Judge Greene, who had denied her temporary alimony. They had been classmates in law school; he and his family spent their Sundays at the same club. 'Why didn't you tell me you were applying for it?' he asked. He said it was her lawyers who had made the mistake. Then and there he looked up in his lawbooks a case to prove it: Berman vs. Berman. It clearly stated that a wife may stay in the same apartment with her husband in other boroughs, but not in Manhattan. Isabel should have moved out right after the raid. She had been ill advised.

But this was untenable! How could she survive this knowledge? All those nights behind the locked door, the soldered keyhole, the cops, the doorknob, the children's hostility, all that was unnecessary! Her suffering was unnecessary! Had she engaged Bart instead, she would not have had to pay $1,500 to Adams and Gross, and she would now be living away from Edgar, without the horror of the countersuit – no, it was too terrible to encompass. Those two charlatans who had done this to her had to be exposed. That they should be allowed to wreck people's lives – it was monstrous! She was beside herself. But there was nothing she could do now except wait. She had waited this long, she would wait longer; she would not break down.

At least both children were away in college. Wendy, after having been refused by all the colleges of her choice because her father had written on her applications that she needed a full scholarship, was accepted at Winnetka, only after her father relented and agreed to pay for her first year.

But he was not sending Wendy enough money. Isabel found

a heartbreaking letter from her on his desk on Saturday, explaining to her father how frugally she was living, how little she was spending on food and incidentals, how she had to borrow from a friend for books. Apparently Edgar never replied, because a few days later Wendy called her mother to ask her what to do. 'Call daddy collect,' Isabel said. 'You're still on speaking terms with him. Maybe he just forgot.'

Wendy replied in a letter:

> My speaking terms with Daddy are not so good. I got tired of trying to be nice, so now he threatens to cut me off. He is still sending some money, but very hostilely now.

Hostilely, Isabel thought, *hostilely*. Is there such a word? She put Wendy's letter into her pocketbook and wrote her not to worry; any court would make a father, a professional man, educate his children.

Suddenly Isabel received a call from Adams and Gross. Their secretary asked her to come down to the office. It was urgent; it was about money. Elated that at last the Appellate Court had come through, she rushed downtown.

Only Gross was in. He presented her with a paper to sign.

'What is it?' she asked.

'Disbursement for appeal.'

'What does it mean?'

He explained that they were asking the court for $250 for printing costs on the appeal, and $65 for paper.

At last, she thought dully as she signed her name, Adams and Gross were doing something.

A week later Isabel was eating her dinner – cold chicken Katie had brought from her home – when Edgar walked into the dining room looking triumphant.

'I see your lawyers lost the case in the Appellate Court,' he said.

'They did?' she asked, dumbfounded.

'This is a portent of what's to come,' he said. 'This is what will happen in court. Why don't you drop the divorce?'

Isabel called Adams – no answer. She called Gross – not in.

She waited all day – they didn't call. She knew only that she must not go to pieces.

When Adams did call a few days later, it was to tell her that her husband was now asking for a jury trial. It was but another delaying tactic, he said, nothing to worry about.

NOTES TO MYSELF

Katie's cold chicken – overdoing it? Fallacy of 'That's how it was.'

Good I gave Edgar bit of background. Do more? His childhood deprivations?

In what tone of voice does he ask her to drop divorce?

Of course, Charles made a fuss about Jill's college, but he did pay for it. And when Jill quit art school, she said it was only because she had lost interest. Switching from fine arts to textile designing – wise decision.

SATURDAY JULY 8

Today a note came written on the plane – a thin blue sheet with *Air France* on it and printed under it: *'en plein ciel, le.'* In full sky. In flight. He was in flight. Only two and a half lines: 'Urgent call. Situation demandes immediate presence. Will be gone for a while. Love, Maxwell.' That's all. It reads like a telegram. Handwriting – sloppy and careless, perhaps because of air turbulence. The word 'demands' misspelled. He signed not 'Max' but 'Maxwell.' He did sign 'Love.' He did write 'Love.'

Now that I know he's alive, I'll be getting a real letter in a day or two, or a call, explaining everything. 'How could you doubt that I love you, Goldenhair?' he'll say. He'll come for me, or – more likely – send for me to join him in August, as we had planned, and we will walk the crooked, cobblestoned streets of old cities, we will sail in the moonlight, we will make love and laugh, and all will be as before. I must think that. But I understand nothing. What 'desperate situation'? What does 'for a while' mean?

My friends still call to congratulate me on that stunning surprise party. I say he was called away on urgent business. Yes, I say, a wonderful man, a rare human being. Carrie and Gilda are in my confidence. Carrie gives me unquestioning, unconditional support; she assures me he loves me and that soon all will become clear. Gilda spouts psychiatric jargon: 'psychological liar, paranoid schizophrenic, psychopathic personality.' She says she never trusted him. She says he never loved me: he's incapable of real feeling. Good mimic – he mimics love, she says. Lives in his own fantasy, can't face reality. 'He saw you were easy, so he took your money and ran,' she says.

I cannot, will not believe this. I know as only I can

know he loved me. Loves me. He'll return the money; he'll send an IOU. We'll spend our holiday together.

But where is he, and why?

Varya sees how distraught I am. She says: 'Misfortune came – open the gate.' She tells me to accept pain as I accepted joy; without either, one can't be alive, she says, and she brings me borscht.

Made appointment to see Dr Shrink. Schrank. I must understand this.

No mail tomorrow – so I'll probably get a letter on Monday. Or a call. In the meantime –

MONDAY JULY 10

Just saw Schrank. Doesn't think Max is a con man, just disturbed. I offered him Gilda's diagnosis; he shrugged: 'What difference do the words make? His behavior is puzzling. But so is yours: How come you always put yourself in the position of a victim?'

No help there, either –

This morning's mail not here yet.

NOTES TO MYSELF

Do hospital scene. Isabel's mother has agreed to go for tests only; they show she's 'riddled with it' (Edgar's words). But she will not face it, refuses surgery, waits only for miracle of God's forgiveness. She keeps in her bed, over nurses' strong objections, her worn, unsterile New Testament in its rubber band, and the bandaged mummy of what was once a small wooden cross Vincent had made for her in fourth-grade woodshop. Through the years it had cracked and splintered from constant touching and kissing; her mother kept wrapping it in layers of surgical tape, so that now only bare outline of cross showed. The pigeon feathers were confiscated as disease carriers.

She blesses Isabel with the bandaged cross, opens her Bible, reads the line: 'He that endureth to the end shall be saved.'

Show that her mother, though a suffering woman, was grateful for any little joy that came her way. She is now overgrateful for Isabel's visit. She tells her Edgar had come to see her in the hospital, 'though it's not my specialty,' he had said.

Her mother never leaves hospital. Write deathbed scene: she is still convinced God will save her. 'O thou of little faith, wherefore didst thou doubt?' she says to herself as she lies, arms stretched out with tubes puncturing them on either side, between two other patients in the semiprivate room. When Isabel comes, she weakly lifts one arm with the intravenous tube attached to it, and makes a sign of the cross over her daughter. 'God told me . . . You . . . Miracle,' she whispers. 'Seek and ye shall find' . . . Her face is illuminated, transformed; at that moment, Isabel believes her.

Only once, just before she dies, she looks at her

daughter with terror. '*Eli, Eli, lama sabachtani?* . . . My God, my God, why hast thou forsaken me?' she cries.

No, I can't do it. Come back to this scene another time.

WELCOME HOME!

The grim game of musical beds was now the focus of her days: who would outwit whom, who would sleep where? The new lock made it possible for Isabel to sleep in the bedroom, as long as Edgar did not know she was there. He took to sleeping upstairs, in Wendy's room, instead of in his office, probably, she thought, to be able to stalk her more closely.

With the children home for the Christmas holidays Isabel would be able to tell them that at last they were going through with the divorce. She would say nothing more; she would protect them from the ugliness their father was creating. But Edgar had no such scruples: as soon as Gregory arrived, pale and distant, hardly greeting her, just allowing his cheek to be pecked, Edgar whisked him downstairs to his office and kept him there for over an hour. When Gregory came upstairs, he darted into his room, closed the door, and when Isabel knocked, told her gruffly he was busy and did not want to be disturbed. Later that day, when she entered his room, he put down the book he was reading and glared at her, waiting for her to leave.

Whatever Edgar had told him about her, Isabel knew that she could never tell Gregory her side, never accuse his father of anything, never throw her son into worse conflict. Edgar knew this too, and was counting on it.

At the same time she realized it was her own rage she feared; her tightly-leashed, murderous rage at Edgar had kept her silent.

Have I lost my son then? She closed the door of his room behind her.

Wendy arrived that evening, after a twenty-two-hour bus trip through snow and ice. Before she even unpacked her bag, she saw her father's things in her room, and began to move them out. When Edgar came upstairs, he made a scene: he refused to give up her room. He told Wendy she would have to sleep with her mother in the bedroom. (This, of course, Isabel knew, would make it possible for him to get in and tamper with the lock!)

He began to use all the old weapons so familiar to Isabel, with that whine in his voice she knew so well: 'I'm working too hard, I need my rest. Do you know how many of my friends are dying of heart attacks?'

'Your friends' heart attacks have nothing to do with my room,' Wendy replied, standing tall and straight, facing up to him.

'I'm working so hard, supporting six people,' he was saying. (How did it get to six? Isabel thought. Katie? Her mother, and her fifteen dollars a month?) 'I can't sleep on the couch.'

'Mommy did,' Wendy said.

'Your mother probably put you up to this.'

'I got here just a few minutes before you did,' Wendy said.

'You don't know how exhausted I am.'

'In that case,' Wendy said, 'you can sleep *anywhere*.' (She must know where that 'anywhere' was; bless the girl, she was taking her mother's side, she was not giving in!)

'I haven't had a vacation in years.'

'Your skiing weekends are your vacation.'

'I haven't been skiing all winter; it's your mother's fault.'

'It's your fault, too. And I don't care whose fault it is, I want my room. I'm tired.'

'I'm more tired than you,' he said. 'I'm thirty-five years older than you!'

(It would be ludicrous, Isabel thought, if it weren't so monstrous.)

'Don't you love me?' he asked.

'Don't try to appeal to my pity; I want my room.'

'It isn't really your room. I pay the rent.'

'In that case I'll move out.' She meant it. She would sleep at her college roommate's, whose parents lived in New York.

While her father was saying that he was not to be pushed around and that she was hard and unfeeling like her mother, Wendy walked firmly into the kitchen, opened the refrigerator, took out a plate of jello, began to eat it, and began to cry.

Having made everyone miserable, Edgar told Wendy she

could sleep in her room 'for the time being,' and went down-stairs.

Isabel went to bed behind her locked door, but she could not sleep. She thought of her daughter with pain, compassion, pride, and the hope that they might be friends one day. She believed Wendy respected her now that she had at last taken this step toward divorce. But Gregory was lost to her. She was helpless; how could she tell a son the truth about his father?

NOTES TO MYSELF

Pleased with Wendy. Pride by proxy. Refreshing, after all the victimization.

Almost sorry for Edgar here, but had to set him up for sake of scene. Would reader accept this?

Tried to camouflage Charles. He must not be recogniz-able, for his own sake and the children's.

Dear Nina —

Haven't written to you in a couple of weeks. Just before the weekend of the Fourth, Max got an urgent call and had to go abroad in a great hurry. He wrote me about it. I'll probably join him in August, as planned; in the meantime, I'm working, or trying to, and missing him.

Saw your film yesterday, saw it twice. There was a line a block and a half long, lots of young people, scattered applause and whistles of approval at the end. I liked it, I really did, even though it can't come close to your book. I thought the kids in it were heartbreaking.

I was too involved with Max to respond to your letter in which you speak of coming home to greet your view of the Golden Gate Bridge. I can understand that kind of loneliness. And I agree with you that to love is more important than to be loved, even though love risks pain. Bad pain.

In my book, I'm distilling some of the pain of rejection, pain of regret. Do you remember Robert Frost's 'The Road Not Taken'? The road taken always means the road *not* taken, never taken.

Your decision about the TV series is a tough one; I hope you resolve your conflict soon. There's nothing worse than the paralysis of indecision — I know it well, having lived through it in my divorce, having written about it in my book. Nancy-Anastasia and Walter have solved their problem by making a decision: they're about to move into their own place. According to Varya, their marriage had been very dull; they were bored with each other('ears wilted'), until the moment they decided on a divorce. Suddenly they had something to talk about, to plan for — a common goal. 'Is more interesting,' Varya told me, 'talk all time divorce, what lawyer, where mawney.' She's delighted they're moving: 'Better for baby,' she said. 'Is she pregnant?' I asked. 'Akh, no! But if God want, yes baby! Name Kolya, for killed Uncle Nikolai!'

You know, now that I'm fifty-seven, I suddenly *feel* my age. There seem to be so many *young* people around! In our culture, there's something unseemly, almost obscene in a woman in her middle or late fifties having a passionate, romantic, erotic affair, though it's impressive in a man.

The older I get, the more I seem to recollect my child-hood: disappointments, mostly. I remember lying in my crib – I must have been very little – and looking up at my father, who was standing in the room, when I realized with a shock that his head did not reach the ceiling! There was a big space between his head and the ceiling, and I felt bad about that. I don't remember much about him; he died young, a dim, romantic figure.

Your dream about the stuck elevator is fraught. Had I dreamed it, I would have gone into a panic of claus-trophobia. I've had it ever since I was a child. I used to ask my mother again and again to be sure not to bury me for several days, to make certain I was really dead.
Dear Nina, I feel a bit low. Will write again when I hear more from Max. In the meantime,

Love,
Jess

P.S. Maybe an elevator means an elvator? And everyone knows that 33 = Face!

NOTES TO MYSELF

Try mother's death scene again? Perhaps more objectively, in brief vignette: nurse removes wristwatch from her mother's wrist and says: 'She won't need this anymore.'

Show Isabel is now truly alone: now nobody *has* to love her.

She tries to reach her children —

MADONNA AND THE CHILD

Alone and frightened, locked inside her bedroom, Isabel was overwhelmed by a need to be close to someone, to be near a living, breathing being. She cautiously unlocked her door; Edgar was away. Behind their closed doors Gregory and Wendy were asleep, her children whom she loved, home for the holidays. When they were little, if one of them awoke from a nightmare of tigers, she would pick the baby up and hum a wordless tune of adult reassurance, loving comfort. Mommy was there, all was well, no terrors lurked under the crib.

Now she needed that reassurance, that comfort. She couldn't go into Gregory's room. He looked at her with open hatred these days; he was lost to her, lost. But Wendy, who had defended her when she came home, was still hers. She stood outside the girl's door, listening to her breathing, recalling the soft, warm baby cheek pressed to hers as she held her with fierce protectiveness, safe from all harm. Now she, the mother, was frightened of the bogeyman, of the dark, of something bad that was going to happen. Perhaps that was the reassurance her own mother had needed, when she used to come to bless her in her bed each night, Madonna and her child.

She would tiptoe into Wendy's room, touch her lightly, kiss her, surely Wendy wouldn't mind that. She would not even wake her. Just to be close to her, in her room, was enough.

She entered the sweet-smelling room, looked at the sleeping face she had loved for eighteen years, touched Wendy's cheek. Wendy stirred, opened her eyes, shrugged her mother's hand off, and said sullenly: 'What do you want?'

'Just to be near you,' Isabel said. 'I just have a need – '

Wendy turned her back to her. 'I can't sleep with you here,' she said.

Isabel left, closed the door softly behind her, walked into the living room. There on the couch, curled up into a cozy, furry arc, was Clara, the cat. She was relaxed, warm, breathing softly

– a living thing. Isabel sat next to her, patted her head gently, rubbed her neck under her chin, caressed the cat with little whispers of love, breathing softly into the warm fur. Clara stood up, stretched to twice her length, jumped off the couch in one graceful soundless leap, walked slowly away, leaped on the chair across the room, curled up, and fell asleep.

Isabel returned to her bedroom, locked herself in once more, and lay down with her pain.

NOTES TO MYSELF

Have I written this scene with too much relish?

Can't dismiss Isabel's children from book; they insist on being.

If I were to ask them what they're feeling – what would they say?

Wendy – that she was trying to protect herself.

And Gregory? 'Don't you know it wasn't hatred?'

Dearest Jess,

I was sorry to hear Max had an emergency call: where, why? When is he returning? Or are you joining him someplace? Your letter of July 15 is vague – and sad. I can imagine how much you miss him. Is he sending you daily poems? Has he left a standing order with his florist for your roses?

I've been frantically busy; will call you in a day or two. In the meantime, you'll be glad to know I've made a decision. Call me madman, but I turned down the TV series! The danger of a shoddy program seems to me greater than the possibility of an honest one. I'll probably spend the rest of my life in genteel poverty, nodding by the fire, watching the embers, and letting sleeping logs die . . .

But not yet. There's a strong chance that *The Sad Merry* will be a Broadway play, and that I'll be moving to New York this fall, for several months. How wonderful it will be to see you!

What else can I say to cheer you up? How about a few lines of the latest comments from my young fans?

> It's important to kick the habit because you may be president some day.

> Dear Nina, your book is no shit!

I'm sure if anyone can make Nancy-A have a baby, it's Varya! I sympathize with Nancy-A's boredom with her husband, when they had nothing to talk about. A dull marriage can be worse than a miserable one: it never pains but it bores.

I wish you swift completion of your book, and all kinds of good and special things. Above all, I wish you no disappointments.

Love,
Nina

314

TO WHOM IT MAY CONCERN

Dear Sir, yours of the whatever received and duly noted. Dear, dear Sir, please do not send me any more bills and do not threaten me with any more threats; I've just about had enough. Also, To Whom It May Concern: I cannot go on, I simply cannot go on like this. Your letters keep coming, and I am not strong-minded enough to throw them into the wastebasket, therefore, dear Sirs or Madams, I am obliged to read the terrible things you say about me and my husband, my ex-husband, I think, though I am not yet completely exed out, since the divorce is not final, just the separation, so called. I say so called, because we are still living under the same roof, the same ceiling, even, though we are, in legal parlance, 'separate and apart.' That means we do not cohabit with each other. That also means that he, my almost ex, is refusing to pay these bills, though he is responsible for my debts as long as we are still married – legally, that is. Besides – I have this on advice of counsel – these purchases were made many months ago, when he was certainly responsible for my debts. Not that they are strictly speaking debts. You will see, if you examine the bills – herein photostated – that the purchases were made not because of vengefulness, which is what you imply in your letters, but in order to buy 'necessaries,' as they say in the trade – the legal trade, that is; necessaries, mind you, not for me, the 'extravagant wife' he claims he is saddled with, but for my children, our children, children of said marriage, children who had sprung up from my loins, sired by him in the days or nights when he could still sire. One is for a winter jacket for our mutual son, Gregory, whose old coat was ripped clear across the back (provided on request, as Exhibit B), and another is for our mutual daughter, Wendy, for shoes, skirt, and woolen muffler. The winters in these parts, dear Sirs and Madams, are cold and rough. Very cold, very rough.

Sincerely yours,
Isabel Webb

[DIARY]

All this time — living in terror. Something terrible happened to him, I know. His heart? Dangerous mission in some distant country? Smuggled money? Arrest? Car accident on a treacherous foreign road?

I wait each day for the letter, the phone call, the cable. My only news so far — the note from the plane, 'in full sky,' in flight. In flight from me. And not another word.

Gilda thinks he's a con man, but that's absurd: the sum was too trivial for all the effort and time he spent! He could have gotten ten times that amount easily, from any number of rich women.

Varya embraces me. 'I don't know where to turn,' I say to her. 'To God — too high; to Tsar — too far,' she tells me. 'Live with self better.' She urges me to work on the book.

I suppose I must, especially now, if there *is* a danger (I don't dare believe it) that my money is gone.

Talked to his doorman again — the regular one. He expects Mr Mahler in the fall. Says he often goes away on business quite suddenly. Says he was instructed to water the plants in his apartment. So he took care about the plants, but he couldn't call me, spare me!

Gilda is going to lend me a book on the psychopathic personality, a clinical study. I'll find Max in it, she tells me. These people, she says, are charming, persuasive, attractive, cultivated, and intelligent. But they're incapable of feeling love or guilt.

No. This can't be my Max. He was a tortured soul. Did I say 'was'? Already I mourn him as if he were dead. I think I almost wish he were; that he had died of a real heart attack the night of my birthday in that theater — and left me a memory unsullied.

I can't believe Gilda's explanations. And I will not believe he was after my small sum of money. He'll explain everything to me, as he did that other time.

I know he loved me, will love me again. All we need is to see each other. To touch. A man can't make such love to a woman without loving her.

Later: The phone rang – but it wasn't long-distance. It was a wrong number. A child who sounded Puerto Rican was asking for his mother.

I can't be angry. If it's true this is the end of us – whatever the reason – there's no room for anger in the total grief for my loss.

But I won't accept it. It's not August yet. I know the magnificent surprises he's capable of. I'm sure he has something very special planned for us. Any day, any hour now he'll come, call, send for me. Otherwise – I understand nothing.

People are still phoning about that great party he gave for me. I tell them our plans have changed, that I may not join him abroad until later. He's fine, I say; I'm fine; yes, I know how lucky I am.

Carrie comforts me: 'If it was only money he was after, then you're well rid of him. But if he loved you, and I'm sure he did, then he's a very sick man, and you're well rid of him.'

His robe in my closet, his slippers, his shaving things in my medicine chest, 'uncontaminated' by anyone else, his books – cry for him. His unseen presence is everywhere. Today I pressed my face to his robe; I heard myself say: 'I can't live without him!'

(My life seems to echo my fiction!)

I try to work on my book. I try to write Nina funny rhymes about him; they don't come.

> He put his head upon my breast
> And read me verse and book . . .

The only rhymes that occur are 'befouled our nest' and 'crook' – I can't.

I must be patient; he always told me that.

Dear Nina –
It was good to hear your voice, to know you're back from
your vacation, looking gorgeous. Who told me? You did.
I forgot to ask if you came back with a romance under
your belt?

I appreciate your warning on the phone, but it was
unnecessary, because it's based on the assumption that
Max isn't coming back – which isn't so. Nor am I
'romanticizing' him, as you suggest.

Today is the eleventh hour. Tomorrow is August first;
knowing him as I do, I'm almost sure he'll swoop down
upon me in a day or two and whisk me off, just as he had
promised. In the meantime, I lead a chaste and celibate
life. I retire early, and get up to work when I can't sleep –
which is often.

> Roses are red, lilies are white;
> Early to bed, up in the night.

I miss him terribly, of course. Cat comforts me: just now
she wordlessly offered me a piece of cellophane. You
comfort me. Thank you for your concern and for your
offer of money. I keep telling you I have enough until he
returns and repays his loan. No need to worry; as you see,
I'm chipper. And don't you *dare* make an unworthy pun
out of that!

Your call came, as a matter of fact, while I was writing
about the role of the telephone as the instrument of the
lonely. It keeps coming up in various segments of my
book: as a lifeline, a coiled umbilicus. As an electronic
taped message that ends in a beep. As a faint echo of what
is happening elsewhere.

The other day my phone rang. A child's voice, in a thick
Puerto Rican accent, asked timidly: 'Who's this?' –

'Whom do you want?' I said. Silence. Impatiently, I repeated: 'Whom do you *want*?' Pause. Then, so softly I could hardly hear, the child said: 'Mama.' – 'She's not here,' I said. The click of the telephone on the other end was so final.

Another time, in a dream, a friend telephoned me, someone I had once known but had not seen for a long time. 'I hear you died,' she said. I made no reply. 'I'm sorry,' she said; 'when is the funeral?' – 'I don't know,' I said, 'they never tell you these things.'

How did we get from the subject of Max to death? 'You cannot ride far in a coffin,' Varya used to say. Max liked to make up absurd proverbs, just to confuse her: 'You cannot cook borscht with your elbow.'

She no longer gives me proverbs, but glimpses of courage: How she escaped from Russia when escape was impossible, alone, with a two-year-old daughter. How she made her way here, struggled, married a Russian ('American man have no sawl; only beezness and bezballs'). And how she is even sexier now than as a young girl. As proof she produces a photo of young Varya in a sleigh, waving a fur muff at a papier-mâché mountain.

Max had fun with Varya; he understood her logic. She once gave him directions: 'You know big drugstore across street on corner?' Max nodded. 'Is not there,' she said. It's the same logic, he told me, that he found in his *dezhoornaya* in Moscow (that's a kind of concierge or matron on each floor of the hotel, who handles keys and messages and mail). One day his *dezhoornaya* said to Max: 'I have in my pocket a cable for you from America for three days now.' – 'Three days? Why didn't you give it to me sooner?' – 'You were having such a good time,' she told him, 'I didn't want to spoil it if it was bad news.' – 'Then why are you giving it to me now?' he asked. – 'Maybe it's important!' she said.

319

Dear Nina – I'm just making conversation. I'm treading water. If I don't hear from him soon, I'll know what I think I have known all along. Why is it the inevitable so often masquerades as the unexpected?

Love,
Jess

STRICTLY CONFIDENTIAL

It was incredible, it was a true miracle; the miracle her mother had promised, and promoted, now that she was closer to the source! A door to freedom swung open to Isabel by Dorian herself! At a time when Isabel was at her lowest, most hopeless, after her mother's death, after Edgar's countercharges, after her temporary alimony was denied, this totally unexpected gift had fallen into her hands.

She knew Edgar had discarded Dorian, from the letters in his desk and from Dorian's frantic calls. She had heard her plead with Edgar for a kind word, just as Isabel used to, before they were married. Twice she had called Isabel directly, but Isabel had hung up on her. For some reason, this time she didn't.

'I want to help you,' Dorian said. 'I want to be your friend and help you get rid of that pervert who's destroying your children.' She was suing him, she said, for malpractice, the Mann Act, perversions and drugs, and she wanted to be Isabel's ally in helping her get a divorce. She had names of hotels and motels, restaurants, witnesses; she had proof of his finances, and she would be glad to share this information with Isabel. She made an appointment to see her on the following day; she lived only a few blocks away. 'You sound so much nicer than I thought,' she said. 'You must get rid of him before he squanders all his money and your children have a breakdown!'

Hardly able to believe her luck, Isabel called her lawyers at once. Adams advised her to take careful note of everything: the furnishings in the apartment, what the girl said, to remember everything but to say very little. 'Just get the girl to talk,' he said.

The following day, at the appointed time, Isabel

NOTES TO MYSELF

No, opening too slow, Important scene. Start again, this time inside Dorian's apartment. For emotional identification, try first person.

So this was Dorian – tall, flashy, attractive redhead with too much makeup, but warm, very cordial, and not stupid. I petted her gray poodle, nice and civilized, two women wronged by the same man, and observed the furnishings, as my lawyer had advised. I was shocked to see my little green alarm clock, which I thought I had lost, on her mantel. My transistor radio was there too, and the glass lion from our coffee table. She bolted the door; she said she had to, since my husband had, surreptitiously, under pretext of walking her dog, made a duplicate key.

She seemed surprised when she saw me. She told me she didn't expect me to be so attractive and sane, after all he had said about me. She wondered how I could have stood it for so long, when she got out of it in a year and a half with her life. He's a man incapable of feeling, she said; a man who feeds on the unhappiness of women. His own lawyer, Engle, to whom she had referred him, refused to have anything to do with him: he thought him contemptible.

I listened carefully, nodding, saying nothing, remembering everything. I dared not muff it this time. I must not let this God-given opportunity escape. She was telling me things no one else could possibly know: about my abortion and our wedding, and about my mother – 'Your crazy mother and her pigeon feathers,' she said. He had called my mother crazy . . .

She knew about our friends, she knew about our children. Gregory had been to her apartment, she said. His father had brought him, and Gregory had cried. Why was he in her apartment? He *cried*? She said his father took him into his confidence, told him terrible things about me; his father . . .

It's hard to go on, but I must. I must hear her out, hear all of it.

She stood on a chair to reach the top shelf of a closet and took down a big box with all the evidence she had collected against him in order to sue him. She had lists of places where they were registered as man and wife; lists of restaurants where he took her; lists of gifts he had bought her. She showed me a brown suede jacket he gave her, which cost $280, she said (and Gregory's graduation photo only $7.98!). She told me he made close to $70,000 a year; that's what he confided to her, asking her not to mention it to anyone. She said she had lived in my bedroom during the two weeks I was away and the children were working in camp. She slept on my side of the bed (he told her), while he put my photo with Gregory as a baby face down on the bureau. She told me that the morning before I returned, our housekeeper Katie found her in bed and had cried. She told me how he had opened my drawers and made her wear my underwear, and how he made her 'insensible' with drugs and liquor. He had made her an addict, she said, so that she depended on him for her supply of drugs. 'Did you know he has a whole store of drugs in his office, that he injects morphine into the addicts that come to him, that he has affairs with patients, that he had an affair with his nurse, Florence Wyle? He fired her,' she said, 'because she knew too much.'

Florence – who was always so sweet to me, I had even bought her a present –

I knew I must not speak my own feelings; I had to listen. But Gregory . . . How dared he take him to her apartment, make him a party to this, make him cry? I realized, as if for the first time, through the words of this young woman, how Edgar had wronged me. If Dorian felt this rage against him, what about me? What's Hecuba to her?

She kept saying how different I was from the way she had imagined. He told her that I refused to give him a divorce, that I was seeing a psychiatrist seven days a week, and that I slept with Indians and lesbians.

Indians? Lesbians? Was she insane? Was he? But if she was making this up, how did she know about my mother, my abortion, our reading group?

'About Gregory – ' I said.

She told me she had asked Gregory if he wanted her to be his mother, and that's when he cried. She used to telephone him at college, but he would say: 'I don't see the point of your calling me,' and hang up.

'That poor boy is so torn, he'll have a breakdown if you don't get rid of your husband fast,' she said. 'And your daughter – what will become of her with a father like that?'

There was more. He went to Nassau, she said; when she

phoned him there, she learned he was registered with some-one else as his wife, and he was furious with her for calling.

He gave her my books to read. He bought her a $310 skiing outfit and took her to a skiing resort where she froze and was miserable, she said – she doesn't ski – and he told her that she ruined his weekend.

'Wouldn't it be ironic if we were friends?' Dorian said. 'You're nice, I want to help you. Your children must not suffer. I'll go to any lawyer of your choice. I'll testify for you.'

My children. No wonder they're so hostile to me, answer in monosyllables, avert their eyes, shut themselves away from me in their rooms. One day I must write a letter, 'Dear Children,' to be opened after my death. 'Dear Children,' I would say, 'we might have been friends.'

Perhaps Dorian was lying, perhaps it wasn't so? But she was privy to my life and its secrets. She told me how they used to make love downstairs on the couch in his office, to the sound of my footsteps upstairs. She said it seemed to turn him on. And how he had attached a special extension to my phone so that he could listen in on my conversations with my friends. He promised to marry her as soon as I gave him a divorce, she said. But he cooled toward her and changed completely. She had gone to her own doctor, who told her Edgar should have his license taken away for the harm he had done her with drugs.

She would not let me take with me any of the material in her box, the 'strictly confidential' material, she called it, because she was afraid he might find it at home. But she said I might come the next day and copy it, and she would sign it. I arranged to come with my portable typewriter, and as I was leaving, she threw her arms around me impulsively and kissed me.

This was the miracle! The woman scorned, who handed me everything I needed. Here it was, in the palm of my hand! My hand that was shaking with rage at what he did to Gregory . . .

The following day Dorian called me on Wendy's not yet disconnected phone, to tell me she couldn't see me; something had come up. She would call again and let me know when I could come.

Was it all a mirage, then? Was this another failed miracle? Did she change her mind? Was she advised not to see me? Was it all for nothing, then, my smiles, my sympathetic nods?

She called again, made an appointment for the following day, but provisionally; she had to go someplace for an audition, for a nightclub job. Just when I began to despair, she called to say she was ready for me to come.

I almost ran there, my portable typewriter in one hand, and pad of paper in the other. I set up my typewriter on her coffee table; there was no other place for it. I had to kneel on the floor in order to reach the keys; I couldn't reach them from the couch. Kneeling, I copied down all the documents she showed me, word for word, the names, the dates, the accusations. This took a long time. My knees were numb, my arms weary, but I got it all down, and Dorian signed her name on the bottom of each page. She asked me to add this sentence, which she dictated:

> I, Isabel Webb, know about these things because they were told to me by Dorian Larrabie and we are collaborating for the exposure of Dr Webb and for the purpose of my seeking a divorce from this man. Miss Larrabie and I have spoken and we both agree to be truthful and cooperate with each other.

Another crazy one? But even if she is, this is hard evidence. Together with all the material I had amassed in the two valises, there is enough here to – what? To give me only what I deserve; freedom from him, and enough money for me and my children.

No, she couldn't be crazy. Some of the paragraphs I had copied sounded not only sane but legal. She had probably already consulted an attorney:

CHARGES: *MALPRACTICE, FRAUD,*
PREMEDITATED CRIMINAL
ASSAULTS, MANN ACT

With painful and careful consideration concerning the severity of the following accusations and with the knowledge of the inevitable repercussions they will have upon his career and reputation, I find no other alternative than exposing this man who, as my doctor, malevolently perpetuated insidious, calculating deeds which ruined my physical health and my psychic stability.

He was over fifty, I was twenty-two. He used his status as a physician, combined with carefully developed charm, to undermine my resistance and subject me to a kind of paralytic depravity . . .

Surely, it would stand up in court?

I called Adams, told him what I had, and he advised me to put it into a large envelope and mail it to his office, registered. This will be the prize of all that's waiting in the two valises now in their office!

NOTES TO MYSELF

Is Edgar becoming too much of a monster?

Does this double distortion serve a purpose in Isabel's story?

Perhaps the important thing to him was the response of women he made love to, because he himself was incapable of feeling. Would this make it easier to understand him?

WEDNESDAY AUGUST 2

I know he's well. This card came from Rome, a picture postcard: reproduction of Michelangelo's *Pietà*, from the Basilica of St Peter. On the back – just two words: '*Sans paroles.*' Not even a signature. I study it: the handwriting – his small, calligraphic script. The postmark. The legend, printed in fine type in four languages: Italian, French, English, and German. On the other side – photograph of the statue: the Virgin Mary holding the limp body of Jesus, dead in her lap amid folds of marble. Mary looks so young, and Jesus – why he resembles Max: the lean, ascetic face, the long, loose body. His right hand hangs limply down; his left rests in Mary's lap. I look at his feet. Wasn't one of them broken a few years ago by vandals, and mended? Yes, in 1972, I think. It was restored so well I can't find which foot it was; can't see the crack. Or was the photo taken before the break? Is that why Max has chosen this, of all the Pietàs, the one with 'clay feet'? Symbols too obvious; I don't even need his '*sans paroles.*' I know what he's saying to me. ('*In te pietate . . .*')

I think of Mother and her Jesus; I think of miracles.

At least, Max had made contact. At least, he let me know he's in Rome. At the moment of writing the card, at least, he was thinking of me.

So there will be no holiday for us in August. Or ever? How is it possible, then, that I'm still expecting a letter, a call, a cable? I'm still ready to join him. I'm still vacillating between hope and despair. And I still love him.

It's only August second. Tomorrow everything can change.

Dearest Jess,

In your last letter you ask if I've returned from my vacation with a romance under my belt. Have they moved it lately? But no, no romance under my belt or any other garment. I'm dedicated to my art.

You're a gallant lady. But you don't have to be, with me. On the phone we talk about my movie, we talk about your book, we talk about my coming to New York for my play, we talk about Varya and your brother, we say funny things to each other all evening — quips that pass in the night — but we say very little about Max, and I know you don't feel all that funny. You're protecting him. You don't have to. He may not even deserve it.

When I first met you in New York, right after your divorce, I saw how wounded and frightened you were, yet how courageous too. You had picked yourself up and brushed yourself off and started your Fiction Workshop and began to survive. I've admired you ever since. Just thought I'd tell you.

I know you're still hoping to spend part of the summer with him, but I wish you could get away now, away from the muggy heat of New York, someplace where it's cool and serene. And I wish you would accept the enclosed check. Stop saying no; you can pay me back with the money that will pour upon you when your book is published.

It does look as if I'll be in New York some time in the fall. I'm subletting my apartment with the Golden Gate Bridge in the window and moving to a suite at the Pierre, but of course I'll haunt your doorstep, and Varya's. You may as well be prepared.

Until then, whatever words I may say to you on the phone or in my letters, they are prompted only by love. I may be safer with puns: perhaps the pun is mightier than the word.

Dear Jess – I don't want you to be hurt.

Love,
Nina

Dear Nina –
I'm returning your check, with gratitude. I don't need it at this time; Max is coming back soon to repay his debt. I really think it was unnecessary for you to compare his trip to my divorce, or to speculate on what he may or may not deserve.

Of course, I'm delighted you're moving to New York. You'll meet Varya, *and* you'll meet Max. By the way, he sent me a beautiful card from Rome: Michelangelo's *Pietà*. I'm sure he has written me letters that have gone astray. Mails have been notoriously unreliable lately, especially from abroad, especially from countries where there is political unrest.

He will return – if not in August, then first week in September. In the meantime, I must work. I must *make* my book happen. Yes, it would be lovely to take a vacation instead of being stuck here in this sweltering city. Yet I must –

> For nature can provide a tree,
> A sandy beach, a summer sea,
>   A mountain or a cooling brook –
> But only man can make a book!

I suppose today it should be 'a person' instead of 'man,' but it won't scan. Strange things are happening to our language: the word 'mother' has become an obscenity; the word 'man' – a symbol of male chauvinism. How about: 'But only I can make a book?' No – too self-aggrandizing. Besides, it sounds like a bet on horses. How's this: 'But only I can write my book'? For that's true; I'm the only one who can write my own truth.

Each night I cross off the calendar date; each day brings Max closer to coming home. For I'm sure he'll come home. I think so.

> My calendar is crissed and crossed;
> Each day is *won* when it is *lost*!

Yet admittedly, what lies ahead is unknown. Else why should tomorrow rhyme with sorrow?

Yours,
Jess

P.S. Or sex with ex?

TUESDAY AUGUST 15

Nothing new. Again an entry, preceded by blank pages.

Last two weeks – silence. This was the month we were to be abroad together, making memories. What happens to a memory unborn?

I'm afraid he's in grave danger. Anything could have happened to prevent him from writing or calling me. Yet I have the strangest feeling that soon – very soon – I'll hear his voice on the phone, and everything will be explained. There are still three weeks left of our proposed holiday. There is still hope.

Like Isabel, who has foreshadowed me, I run from friend to friend for words of comfort or advice. Carrie says she's sure he loved me. Gilda thinks he's a CIA agent, or a con man, or a psychopath, or all three.

Marge says: 'You got off cheap. How come you keep getting involved with loonies? Why can't you get yourself a nice unloony, a guy who's together? Or is that maybe too dull for you?'

Nina offers me money. Such lack of faith! She of all people should understand.

Varya keeps dropping in to make sure I have something to eat. Says nothing about Max. Not even a proverb.

The shrink tells me not to blame myself: 'You couldn't have helped a man so disturbed. At least,' he says, 'your capacity for love is unimpaired.'

That's some news! When your arm is amputated, it's no comfort to be told that your capacity for pain is unimpaired. 'Impair it, impair it,' I cry, 'and let me stop suffering!'

The children write more often than they used to; they ask about Max and send him regards. I think they could have loved him.

What do I, Jessica, think? I think — I don't know what I think.

Yet I do not disbelieve in miracles; I am not my mother's daughter for nothing.

INADMISSIBLE EVIDENCE

All week she waited to hear from Adams and Gross about her unexpected miracle: Dorian. Finally she called her lawyers to ask if they got the material.

'Yes, we got it,' Adams said.

'What are you doing with it?'

'Nothing.'

'I mean – how are you using her information? All those places and dates?'

'Forget it. It's inadmissible evidence.'

'Why? How? Why?'

'We checked her out. She's a nut. She tried twice before to sue two other doctors who took care of her. One case was thrown out of court, the other never came to trial.'

'A nut?'

'She spent six months in a psychiatric ward. A real whacked-up dame. Forget her.'

But how could that be? So many things Dorian had told her were true; no one but Edgar could have reported them to her. She had been so open, so eager to help. She had names, places, dates, witnesses. All that evidence Isabel had copied on her knees – inadmissible?

Perhaps Adams and Gross had gone to Edgar with it, and he had bribed them not to use it? It was like him; he had tried to bribe the locksmith, he may have bribed the judge who denied her temporary alimony. He would spend thousands to avoid giving her a penny. It was terrifying. Was Adams really on her side, was he telling the truth, was she paranoid, going crazy herself? Was Gregory never in Dorian's apartment, crying? Was she, Isabel, never in Dorian's apartment, kneeling in front of her typewriter? Was she cracking up now, at the eleventh hour, just as Edgar hoped she would?

She called Dorian; there was no answer. She called again and again, but Dorian had disappeared, as though she had never been. Isabel went to her house. She walked nervously up and down the street, finally entered the lobby and asked the elevator man for Miss Larrabie.

'Moved out,' he said.

'Where?'

'Can't say.'

Dorian can be forced to return, Isabel thought wildly. She must be subpoenaed, wherever she was, and the doorman, too! Besides, she didn't need her; she had enough evidence in her two valises to make up for ten Dorians. She would not break down. She would see this through, and she would triumph.

One good thing – what was it – yes, maybe Dorian had made it up, about Gregory crying in her apartment?

Dear Nina –

I realize your calls are prompted by your concern about Max, but you needn't worry. And of course, your calls are as welcome as your letters, but not *in lieu* of. There's no way one can reread a telephone call, except, of course, by tape recorder. I once went to great expense and trouble to have Charles's phone tapped for evidence my lawyer needed, only to be privy to patients' complaints about insomnia. In my book, naturally, I make Isabel's eavesdropping on Edgar more dramatic.

I don't know why I'm saying all this. Yes, I do. I'm so angry, I'm trying to hide it. At whom? Not at you, really; at something I'm not sure I recognize. I must face what seems so obvious to others. Marge tells me: 'Stop being a patsy – you've been took!'

And Varya, although she thinks that he'll come back 'when lobsters will whistle,' tries to distract me with elaborate nostalgia about the old days in Leningrad, the big snows ('You call your American snow *snow*?'), the air like wine, the promenades on Nevski Prospekt – and she gives me a rhyme: 'Billo da splillo'–Was, but swam away. She wants me to forget Max.

I started several times to write funny verses about him, to exorcise the pain with humor, but the humor turns out to be too bitter for laughter.

> He laid his head upon my breast
>   And quoted verse and book;
> Then he befouled our little nest
>   And fled like any crook.
>   I think that I've been took!

No word from him since his card from Rome three weeks ago. Perhaps some accident has befallen him; perhaps he is behind some impenetrable iron curtain; perhaps I'm still rationalizing and hoping. In just two weeks he will, he must be back, and then I'll know.

I don't remember – did I tell you on the phone how glad I am you made the decision to turn down that TV offer? You're responsible to the young people for whom you have spoken, and you can't allow anything to debase what you mean to them.

Love,
Jess

P.S. Please pray that lobsters should whistle.

THURSDAY AUGUST 31

He hasn't returned. Should be back in a week – that's when we would have come home from our vacation. At the thought of seeing him, hearing his voice again, I –

Even if we're through (I'm beginning to admit such an impossible possibility), at least I'll know he's all right.

In a way, the money is a test. If he returns it, that means he loved me. If not, I need shed no tears, except for his sickness. Con man or lover? Some test!

The money isn't important, if I could be sure that he really loved me, that he was not pretending. But if it was all an act – a mimicry of love – ?

What dragons? What missions?

No.

Remember what that old surgeon told Charles when he was starting out in practice: 'Better to live without a diagnosis than to die with a diagnosis.'

When he returns, I'll understand everything, and perhaps I'll be ashamed I ever doubted him. Perhaps having borrowed the money, he couldn't face me. Maybe he felt emasculated, he the giver rather than taker – like the time he was upset because I had sent him a book. Maybe he's unable to repay it yet, and it makes him uncomfortable.

How can I believe what I am saying? Maybe he spent my money on his vacation with someone else? Maybe he wants nothing to do with me now? *The Pietà* was eloquent enough. Am I the Virgin Jessica? The Saintly Madonna of my book? Is he forever dead in my arms?

What nonsense all this is! I need only to be in his arms, and I'll be safe again.

I can fight for him again. I did once before. I must not panic. I must be calm; calm is a word he liked.

I want to send him loving notes, reminders of all we

were to each other. Instead, I send him clever rhymes to greet him on his arrival. I send him funny Welcome Home cards.

I've lost my pride but not my hope.

FRIDAY SEPTEMBER 1, 1978

LETTER TO BE UNMAILED:
My very dear, My Max —

I write you letters that will remain unsent. I talk to you on these pages, but they do not answer. I cling to scraps of memories of you — my drowning straws.

Everything reminds me of us. My darling, I cannot bear it. I am doing badly. You once said I had courage — where is it now?

It was a mistake to lend you the money. You will be angry it wasn't more, you will despise yourself for taking it, you will avoid me to avoid guilt. Yet you gave me more than you reckoned. And if the dream is over, I did have the dream.

Any day now, you will return and we will have our obligatory scene: our confrontation.

What I really think is

['BOOK']

Dear Children –
I have shielded you all your lives, in the hope that

Dear Wendy and Gregory –
I can't

NOTES TO MYSELF

No – Isabel wouldn't want to fill them with guilt in
such a letter –
But, of course, it's to be *unmailed* –

[DIARY]

Not back yet. Something must have happened to him. I call daily – no answer. I inquire at his house – no sign of him.

He should be back tonight, or tomorrow at the latest. And then –

Dear Nina –
Just a few lines, since I promised on the phone to let you know. He's not back yet – no one knows where he is. I'm really worried something terrible has happened to him.

My book lies heavy inside me, like a monstrous fetus, long overdue, undelivered at term, with difficult labor ahead. I wonder if it will be born alive, or stillborn . . . Too late for an abortion: the contracts signed, the advance gone. I keep hoping for some eleventh-hour miracle, when it will get done all by itself, nice and neat. In spite of everything, I'm trying to work on the tightening noose, the mounting craziness, the ultimate court scene and the two valises . . .

Cat suddenly went wild – she does that sometimes, for a moment or two, for no apparent reason. Back arched, fur up, tail flailing, she has just leaped, demented, from window ledge to the top of the bookcase, staring with fixed emerald eyes at some mad and private vision.

It will be good to have you here – I think you said second week in November? I can wait; I'm used to patience. On my tombstone let it be writ: *Patience and Gratitude.* I've been grateful all my life – for crumbs, for stamps, for a kind word. All through my labor, instead of screaming like a normal primipara, I kept thanking the anesthetist.

I'm full of images of parturition today. What would your schizoid say to that?

Your
Jess

[DIARY]

He's back. Now I know it's hopeless. I've lived with fear of this for so long, yet I wasn't prepared.

When I called him today, as I have for days, he answered! I went so weak, I hung up. A moment later, when I was able to dial again, I forgot the last two digits of his telephone number. The number I knew by heart. I had to look it up in my address book.

'Hello, Max,' I said.

His voice was courteous, impersonal. 'Hello, how are you?'

As if I were some casual business acquaintance. His Goldenhair. His life-giver, his old mire-lifter.

I found myself speaking in the same tone. 'How was your trip?'

'It was difficult,' he said, 'but necessary.'

I thought we should see each other; there was unfinished business between us.

Was there? he asked. He was very busy; leaving shortly again.

I was surprised to hear myself say: 'Your things are here: books, clothes – you might want to pick them up.'

He thought he might, when he had time. He would call me.

How carefully I hung up, my hand quite steady.

It's over, then. I understand nothing.

It isn't fair! He owes me – what? Not the money, that's unimportant, that has only beclouded something between us. He owes me – a memory. He's *responsible* for us.

The odd thing is – I didn't recognize his voice, at first. Did he sound different, or had I forgotten?

Right after I hung up, I began through a blur of tears to write him a letter. I wrote we owed each other the dignity of a decent parting. (My errant fingers almost wrote: 'a decent burial.') I wrote: 'I think we both overloved. A stiff price was exacted – and paid.'

No, I couldn't mail it – too guilt-provoking. He might think 'stiff price' referred to money. I wrote, instead, the words of Robert Graves:

> Since now I dare not ask
> Any gift from you, or gentle task,
> Or lover's promise – nor yet refuse
> Whatever I can give and you dare choose –
> Have pity on us both: choose well
> On this sharp ridge dividing death from hell.

I wait for his call. Only I must stop crying.

['BOOK']

NOTES TO MYSELF

Isabel's thoughts:

How did she get where she was?

She had hired detectives, called off detectives, hired them again, jumped off the diving board, and for four years remained immobile in the frozen leap, while Edgar changed into an enemy before her eyes.

How unimportant money was to her when she married a poor medical student, how eagerly she had given him all her earnings. Now money was what it was all about.

Once Edgar had cried: 'I want to be happy with you!' But he didn't know how. Once she had wanted more than anything to be married to him. Now, her struggle to get unmarried was a struggle unto death. One of them would have to die on the Day of Judgment, in court. Would it be she?

THURSDAY SEPTEMBER 14

He hasn't called. I waited three days, and he hasn't called. I'll call him. In a little while. I don't understand what we're doing. How is it when we talked, we took it for granted that it's over? Why?

Later: I just called. Line busy. But this is brutal – to have given me so much, and to take it all away. How *dare* he not want me!

How did I ever find him, in his foolproof disguise, the same pain-giver?

All the signs were there; I can see them now. Even his poets were spelling it out for me! 'No god can ask thee to his table/No goddess to her bed.' He knew what would happen. It must have happened to him before. His young French wife who died long ago. His second wife who fled from him. The two young women he told me about who ran away from him.

When he was shouting it from the rooftops, I didn't listen. This goddess took him to her bed – and then some.

Poor Max – he worked so hard for love he couldn't keep. No man worked harder.

I should have fled from him at the first sign. I should have fled without a backward glance. Lot's wife got what was coming to her.

I'll try to call again.

Just spoke with him. Kept my voice cool: 'Do come by and pick up your things, and let's say good-bye.' No mention of love. No mention of money. He said: 'Don't pressure me,' but he did agree to come next Monday evening. I'll see him Monday. I must live through the next four days.

Someplace inside his skin there is still the Max who

loved me. Perhaps when we meet he'll realize — realize what?

'Was ever woman in this fashion wooed?' he once asked me. Was ever woman in this fashion lost?

['BOOK']

IT BEGINS

Something was happening. Isabel found her bedroom lock tampered with again. Edgar must be getting frantic. Why?

She called the locksmith from an outside phone. He said it looked like a professional job. He suggested the safest lock, made of bars across the door that her husband would not be able to remove. But then the mirror on the inside of the door would have to be broken. She couldn't do that; Edgar would be furious! The locksmith shook his head: 'I feel for you, lady,' he said. 'You change your mind, just call me.'

She put a heavy chair against the door and sat in it all night.

In the morning Adams called. 'Move to a hotel at once,' he said. 'Be in Room 406, Supreme Court, tomorrow morning at 9:30.'

'Is it beginning?' she asked, her knees shaking.

'You may never see your apartment again,' he said.

She was doing everything fast now, with jerky motions: she dialed a hotel, the first that came into her mind, the Savoy Hilton, made a reservation, like anyone else, she thought wildly, began feverishly to pack a few clothes.

Edgar knocked on the bedroom door. 'Open the door,' he said. 'There's a leak in the bathroom seeping down into my office. The super and the handyman are coming up to fix it.'

She looked into the bathroom – no leak there. *He must be desperate to break in,* she thought; *he must have learned about the court too.*

While Edgar was banging on the door, Adams called again, to say the process server was on his way to serve her husband with a summons. At the same time, Edgar was shouting through the door that the super was on his way to break it open. Isabel raced to finish packing: nightgown? sweater? umbrella? She kept dropping things, the pulse beating at her temples – hurry, she must hurry –

The process server arrived. She unlocked the door and saw

him hand Edgar a summons. She stood, irresolute, valise in hand. The process server offered to drive her to her hotel. Gratefully, she nodded, told Katie she would keep her informed of her whereabouts, and drove off with him, her rescuer.

Only when she was registering in the hotel, things slowed down. The potted plants, the beige carpet, the soft, polite voices, the courteous busboys – she was in another world now. She felt, for the first time, like a normal person, like all these normal people in the normal hotel lobby, leading normal lives.

She signed her name on the register.

At last it had begun.

Dearest Jess,

Now that Max is back and you no longer need to worry about his safety, perhaps you might give some thought to your relationship. I don't know much about him, but I do know about you – trusting, romantic, vulnerable Jess. Your great disappointments grow out of great expectations (have we thought of *that* as a title for your book?). I'm trying to protect you from the pain that lies between expectations and reality. This is what I wanted to say on the phone, but I needed to choose my words as carefully as possible, and I can do this only in a letter.

If you're angry – at me, at Max – go ahead and express it, even if only in your verses. And if you need money, I keep telling you to borrow it from me. Your credit is good: that courtroom scene alone, which you hint at, should be worth the price of the book, and the two valises you mention are certainly better than one.

I'm glad I'll be with you soon. I, too, need a friend. There are many problems with my play, though it's in good, professional hands. I'll be able to collaborate on it in New York. I plan to come in mid-November and stay six months to a year. My apartment here has been sublet to an eager lady who, I'm sure, can't wait to put artificial flowers into my fireplace.

Eventually, the play will be a musical. I meant it when I said you will write the lyrics. By Moore and Proot. Note the order of billing. Or do you think we have too many oo's here?

Guess whom I ran into the other day? No, try again. You're way off! It was Sanford. Do you remember Sanford Something from our Fiction Workshop – a round, earnest young man who was determined to 'crack the writing game'? Well, apparently he has: he writes releases as a PR man for some company out here. In only six years he got enormously fat and grew a luxuriant beard, which covers a multitude of chins. Sends you his best. Says with you he 'really learned something.' He meant it, and it should make you feel good.

You ask about my schizoid fan. A month ago he sent me his last communication:

A man is a measure of his own cross.

Since then – silence. I've been trying to trace him: he left the institution, but no one could tell me, when I phoned, if he fled, or was discharged, or left this world altogether. I could get no further information, even when I introduced myself as Doctor Doctor Moore. Something to do with their records.

Dearest friend, I wish – I wish so much for you!

Love,
Nina

WEBB VS. WEBB

This was it, at last, the day of divorce.

Everything was happening fast, yet in slow motion. At 9:30 Isabel appeared in Room *406* of Supreme Court. Gross was already there, and the two detectives who were at the raid. 'This is your husband's day of reckoning,' Gross said. Isabel sat and waited, not knowing what was happening, what to expect.

Gross pointed out Edgar's two lawyers, who sat on the other side of the room. But Edgar wasn't there. Why wasn't he there?

The judge appeared: Justice Karp. Some cases were called; some postponed. Suddenly she heard: 'Webb versus Webb.' *That's me,* she thought, *I am Webb versus Webb.*

Gross said: 'Plaintiff ready,' and walked up to the judge's bench. Edgar's lawyer came up too, and said something; she heard the word: postponement. The judge looked annoyed. Then the judge and the lawyers went into another room, and again Isabel waited. She had no idea what was going to happen.

Gross came out and told her to call up a friend who would have to identify a snapshot of Edgar he had in his attaché case: it happened to be one of her husband with a girl in a bikini.

'Why?' she began to ask.

'Do it now!' he ordered.

She walked to the pay telephone in the corridor to call Jim, whose office was nearby, and she waited until he came and identified Edgar on the snapshot. Suddenly there was a flash, then another. Photographers. To her horror, photographers were taking pictures of her. She saw Edgar's lawyer point her out to them. She tried to hide her face, but Gross told her to cooperate with them.

'Who are they?' she asked.

'They hang around courts. You better cooperate with them. They'll take pictures anyhow, and if you don't go along with them, they'll slant the story against you.'

'What story? Why?' But she had already stepped into the nightmare. She went through all the motions, standing, sitting, smiling, poised, unruffled for the benefit of Edgar's lawyers, who were, she knew, sizing her up. He must have told them that she would crack under pressure. Well, she wasn't cracking. She was cooperating.

She asked the detective if the pictures were going to be used. He said probably not until the trial itself. He added that the court clerk, and sometimes the judge, gives out affidavits to the papers. The judge was closeted with the reporters. Would he give them the affidavits with those filthy accusations Edgar had made up about her? Impossible!

For a long time she heard her lawyer and Edgar's arguing in the judge's chambers. She sat with Jim and waited to wake up from the nightmare. The judge came out with the lawyers; she caught his words: 'If he's so proficient as a lover, why does she want to leave him?'

Gross told her the judge had awarded her $400 until the new date of the trial in a week. Edgar's lawyer kept running to the telephone to call him; he reported that his client would need a day to raise it.

Suddenly they were all leaving the courtroom, Isabel grateful for Jim's arm to lean on. Edgar's lawyer approached Gross and asked if he could speak to him; he looked uneasy. Four hundred dollars! All that money for just one week! Maybe now she would get enough for herself and the children. Maybe at last it was turning her way.

FRIDAY SEPTEMBER 15

I still know nothing. Two brief telephone conversations with a stranger with Max's voice. He could have been anywhere: in Chile, in Amazonia, in Argentina, wherever there was trouble, wherever he was needed. Or he could have been basking on a faraway beach with someone lovely and young, someone he may have brought back with him, someone he may one day cross the street to avoid.

And I, his Jessica, his love, how did I slip out of his fantasy, and how can he forgive me for it?

And how can I stop loving him? Falling out of love is much harder than falling in love.

Love is not a potato, that's for sure.

September 22, 1978

Dear Nina —
You admit you don't know Max, yet you give me a
long-distance diagnosis of our relationship. I don't need
any more gratuitous advice. Everybody has been getting
into the act, dishing it out – Gilda, Marge. Varya says
only: 'Must work, Lapochka.'

I just realized that Lapochka, a Russian term of endear-
ment which means literally 'little paw of cat,' is *catspaw* –
a dupe, a person *used* by others. And so I have been. I
think I've been ill used.

I'm tired of everyone being so wise about my life. So –
just continue to write your funny letters, be sympathetic,
be encouraging, but stay out of my relationship with
Max; I have enough pain to deal with on my own.

I admit things are going badly; who better than I can
know how badly! Even my silly verses can't compose
themselves without bitterness:

> There is a fly in every ointment,
>   On every foot there is a corn;
> For every joy – a disappointment,
>   On every rose – a hidden thorn.
>
> On every purchase there's a tax,
> And in my great romance with Max
>   I got the ax.

I'm angry, and I have a right to be. He has been avoiding
me, postponing our meeting, playing a game I don't
understand. We did set a date for this Monday, when he
is to come here, and I suppose bring my money and say
good-bye. Unless – unless I can get him to explain what
happened.

I'm working on the last scenes in my book: total de-

355

terioration. Rereading my diaries of divorce, I see no trace of brightness or humor; I had canceled myself out in my marriage. As a matter of fact, it isn't easy to be bright or clever now. The past impinges on the present, the present opens up the past.

I remember Sanford Something; he had trouble with sentence structure. He sends me yearly Xmas cards with: 'Have a merry!'

As for our musical, I'm not at all sure I like the billing. How does this strike you: Proot and Moore?

Love,
Jess

DAY IN COURT

From the moment she stepped into the courtroom (Edgar not there, the flashbulbs of photographers, the judge secreted with the lawyers) to that evening in the hotel coffee shop, when she saw in the tabloid her grinning face, and under it the lurid caption . . .

No. Start again.

Idly leafing through the newspaper in the hotel coffee shop, the hamburger cooking on the grill – her first solid food in days – her heart froze to see the photograph, her grinning face over the filthy accusations, printed for all to read, thousands of people in subways, on streets, in their homes, and her children . . .

No.

She walked out of the coffee shop, the floor tilting under her, the hamburger still sizzling on the grill, and she knew it couldn't be happening. But it was. Wednesday morning she was still in her apartment. Thursday morning – in court, Thursday evening – splashed all over the newspapers . . .

She called Dr Kellerman, to see her, to save her from dying. He said he was busy: he had fourteen people coming to dinner that evening. But he advised her not to be alone, to call her friends to stay with her that night.

Her brother came to the hotel, her friends. 'No one reads this paper,' they said, and 'People forget.'

She was shaking. She couldn't stop shaking. She called her children, so that they wouldn't learn it from the papers or from others. Wendy said only: 'Where did you get the money for a hotel?' Gregory was silent, until Vincent picked up the phone and said: 'This is the time for understanding, Gregory. Talk to your mother – she needs you to talk to her.' After a long silence, Gregory said: 'Don't worry,' and Gertrude was crying, and Martha slept over in her hotel room to make sure she wouldn't jump out of the window, and then –

Then the court.

She was staying at Rose's now, in the little maid's room off the kitchen, so that she wouldn't be alone. Rose, who had promised to go to court with Isabel, backed down the last minute. Isabel went alone, by subway, lulled by librium and steeling herself to face it. When she got there she waited in the gloomy court-room, until she discovered she was in the wrong room. Her lawyers never told her the room was changed. She ran in panic up and down the corridor, as in her old nightmares; someplace they were waiting for her, but where? She called Adams' office; his secretary didn't know the room number. Finally she located a clerk who helped her find something called Calendar of Events. There she found the room, the event. Adams, looking grim, said only: 'This judge is a husband's judge.' A jury was there – for another case which was still on.

'What does it mean?' she asked him.

He looked at her as if she were an idiot. 'It means,' he said, 'that ours is postponed till tomorrow. Be here at ten.'

Next morning – again the subway, again the court. Again it was postponed. The jury case was still on. When she returned, Rose cried: 'Oh, no, not again! But you've got to be strong, hold out for a lot of money. The judge is sure to award you a good settlement after twenty-nine years of marriage and two children. Because you supported him – be sure to tell him – and he ruined you by those false accusations in the paper. Remember all this.' Isabel tried to memorize what Rose was saying, took more librium, held on.

Adams called: 'Your husband has dismissed the jury.'

Isabel sobbed in relief. 'That means –

'But not the charges,' Adams said. 'This is routine. He's just been trying to scare you. Be in court tomorrow morning.'

She was up most of the night, rehearsing what she would say.

358

Toward morning she fell asleep for a few minutes, and awoke to a fragment of a dream. Edgar was dead, but he didn't know it; it was because of her mother's incantations. He was sitting at the breakfast table reading a newspaper instead of going to the funeral parlor, and when she awoke, she saw there were still three hours until court time.

Dearest Jess,

I'm answering your letter the day I received it. You asked me not to involve myself in your affair with Max, but of course I must. We're not going to hide behind funny words. I love you, and I want you to protect yourself from pain.

You don't want to hear this. I realize I'm taking a risk – but there's a greater risk in failing to say something that may save you from greater pain.

When you first met Max, before you began to fantasize him, you wrote me there was something about him you didn't trust. You called him a weird duck, a poseur. Dear Jess – pull out of it! Look at him realistically, at what he is, not what you want him to be.

One day you'll be happy again, not necessarily because of a man. It's only in fairy tales that happiness is something one receives, is presented with, gift-wrapped, price removed. One day you'll be able to see your affair with Max with humor. You may even laugh about it. Where there is humor, there is no room for despair. For sadness, yes, but not despair.

I'm eager to learn what happened to Isabel, so please finish your book.

My friend, my teacher, my future collaborator, I will be with you soon. In the meantime, if you really want me to pray that lobsters should whistle, I will, though I'm not sure I want to be around when they do.

All my love,
Nina

P.S. Moore and Proot, or the deal is off! I wasn't born yesterday. I happen to have – an Italian journalist told me – a man's head on my shoulders. It's my last offer – take it or leave it.

THE TRIAL

Trying to hold on to her ebbing strength this third morning in a row, Isabel went back to court. Edgar's offer was still only four and a half thousand a year. In the subway she kept trying to divide it: long division, short division, how much is that per week, per day? How much does it cost to stay alive? Suddenly startled into panic, she thought: What if Gregory needs a dentist? Wendy – a winter coat?

In the courtroom, Adams said: 'I'll wager he'll go to trial.' Swiftly, so fast she didn't realize it was happening, her detective is sworn in: the trial begins. Edgar – on the stand for a moment – admits adultery. Mention only of 'a woman, nude.' His lawyer asks Adams for the financial statements. All those photostats of ledgers, check stubs, appointment books, bills, lists, and figures it took Isabel four years to accumulate in the two valises – where are the two valises? Why didn't her lawyer bring them?

Adams tells the judge they are not prepared because they had expected a countersuit. Edgar's lawyer says – no, the countersuit only after the whole financial picture is presented. Adams says his partner, Gross, has the financial information but he is at present trying another case and won't be ready until tomorrow. The judge is angry at the delay. Postponed till tomorrow, 10 a.m.

Adams takes Isabel aside and tells her to go to see Gross in his office that evening at seven-thirty, to go over the figures.

She returns to Rose's, tells her: 'The trial has begun. I'm holding on.'

MONDAY SEPTEMBER 25

Couldn't bring myself to open this diary since – when? Ten days ago. He didn't come last Monday. Called it off. Pressure of business, he said. He'll come tonight. His voice was calm and businesslike. He was a stranger, an impostor impersonating Max.

I won't fall apart. I'm holding on. I've waited so long now; almost three months since I saw him. This past week – the hardest. But tonight we'll be together, we'll talk, perhaps we'll even

Later: That was the phone. He can't come tonight. He has been called away. But he will definitely come on October 9. That's in two weeks. Two weeks from today. He was apologetic but firm. 'You don't understand,' he said, 'I must not be pressured.'

All I kept saying was: 'Yes, of course.'

'The ninth,' he repeated. 'Not the real Columbus Day, but the day it's observed.'

What was he trying to tell me? This time he sounded more like the Max I know: 'Forgive me,' he said, 'you have no idea what I've been through. No idea.'

Yes, of course. I hung up first.

Suddenly I'm angry. And the money? What about the money? Nine thousand dollars – have I lost that too? Strange – this is the first time I want my money back. He'll bring it. He won't be able *not* to return it. Whatever his problems, he is – what? I don't know what he is.

I'm trying to see where I, perhaps, have erred. Did I cancel myself out, as Isabel did in my book? Was I like her, too submissive, too scared? Didn't I value myself enough? He said I was walking on eggs, afraid of losing him. Is that why?

The characters in my book help me see myself and Max

more clearly, and loving Max illuminates for me my Isabel and Edgar. Perhaps the terror in any relationship comes with the first realization that there *was* no relationship all along; and the anguish comes with refusal to accept this.

If I didn't have my book to work on, I couldn't survive the waiting.

THE TWO VALISES

That evening Isabel goes to Gross's office. He is not there; he is in the restaurant downstairs, having his dinner. She goes down, finds him, he waves her to a chair next to him. Swallowing her nausea, she sits down and waits for him to finish eating. He is in no hurry; when he is through they go upstairs, and she mentions the two valises.

'What two valises?' he asks.

'You know, the evidence. The two valises I brought you nine – no, ten months ago. All that material.'

She realizes with horror he had never touched them. He finds them now, one on top of the other, covered with dust, behind the filing cabinets, just where they were left. But how is it possible?

He opens them for the first time, quickly sorts out the papers, casting aside all her lists and letters of anguish, everything but the figures. He starts adding them on his machine, sees the total, and gets excited. He calls up his assistant, a young man who arrives shortly, and they spend the next four hours, until midnight, adding up figures with mounting excitement. 'Son of a bitch makes over sixty thousand a year – !' Gross says. 'We were right!'

He sees Isabel's letter, sent by her to herself, registered and unopened. She explains that's the letter protesting the income tax figures: she had written that she signed the joint returns under duress. She knew the figures were incorrect, but she was blackmailed into signing: 'Or no camp for Wendy!' Edgar had said. Gross is delighted. He adds up some more figures. 'Look at the money he's been raking in!'

After midnight he hands Isabel a handsome document in a blue cover she had never seen before, with all of her expenses and rebuttals of his figures and denials of his ugly accusations on neatly numbered pages, like a thin paperback novel.

It has a title. *Trial Brief.* Adams tells her to go home and memorize the figures in it. 'How much for food? Parties? Cleaners?' he keeps firing at her. 'Be sure to say in court your husband told you he was making over sixty thousand a year.'

'But I'll be under oath,' she said. 'Isn't that perjury? He never admitted that to me.'

'Don't be a child!' Gross snapped. 'What's the matter with you?'

She went back to Rose's, reeling with fatigue and terror. 'Do your homework for tomorrow morning!' Gross had shouted at her as she left. She was faint, dizzy with rage. In all those months, her lawyers had never bothered to look into those two valises! How could they even begin to negotiate? It was unthinkable –

She was up all night, until the windows grew light, fighting her nausea, memorizing the figures, trying to anticipate his lawyer's questions: How much for food? How much for gas, electricity, entertainment, clothes, telephone, home expenses, office expenses, insurances? Gross? Net? Deductibles? Figures she didn't understand; she was never good with figures, and besides, he had so manipulated his finances that she couldn't make them out. Numbers swam before her eyes; she felt sicker and sicker.

And what about all his lies? She would have to reply to them: that she had procured his women for him (connived? colluded?). That she was guilty of many adulteries at divers times and divers places with men he was ready to name. That she had posed in the nude on the lewd photograph available to the court. That she had gone on extravagant shopping sprees, lived in luxury in a Park Avenue duplex, went to an expensive psychiatrist, and presented the fiction that they were living apart. She would have to memorize numbers, charges, counter-charges, answers, and it was almost morning, and she needed all her strength for the ordeal in court.

'It's only figures now,' Rose said before she left. 'Be strong, it's almost over. You'll get fifteen thousand for life, and your children will get their education, you'll see.' Isabel nodded, took a librium, went to the subway, head high. It's almost over.

She enters the courtroom, dimly sees Adams, says to him

groggily: 'Is it too late to negotiate?' He looks at her. After a moment, he says: 'No. Will you settle for four and a half thousand?' Isabel hears herself say: 'Yes.'

Gross rushes in and says to Adams: 'We've got him! Only thing is – it's too late to subpoena the nurse. This is in her handwriting.'

Isabel smiles at him weakly and says: 'We've decided to negotiate.'

NOTES TO MYSELF

Too painful to write this. Will come back to it later.

'You – you want to negotiate, now?' Gross asked.

'Yes,' Isabel said.

Then the ballet began, the crazy dance of lawyers. Back and forth they kept running, to Edgar's end of the courtroom, where his lawyers sat, back to Isabel, and again to his lawyers, while the judge (Karp? Goldleaf? her mind was fuzzy) sat silent and impassive, reading *The Wall Street Journal*, patiently waiting for them to make their final pleas and concessions. Only once did he speak; Isabel heard him say: 'After all, they must be married over twenty years.' (She learned later that the judge was on her side; Bart had talked to him about her.) But she kept saying *yes, all right, yes,* for two and a half hours, nodding and smiling and saying *yes,* only to be free of him, only to be out of there.

Was Adams conspiring with his lawyers? Bribed by Edgar? He told her nothing, explained nothing, protected her from nothing, only kept reporting to her, as he shuttled back and forth on the courtroom floor:

'Nothing for the son, he's on scholarship, two thou a year for the daughter until she's twenty-one.'

Isabel said: 'Will he pay for her final year in college after she's twenty-one?'

He ran back, conferred, returned: 'No.'

'Will he pay anything for his son's graduate school?'
'No. He says he'll get fellowships.'
'Will he pay my debts?'
'No, let them sue him.'
'Will he pay my loan to the bank?'
'No.'
'Insurance?'
'No.'

She nodded. Adams said: 'That's four and a half thou *before* taxes, in weekly payments.'

'How can I live on that?' she asked.

'That's the way they want it.'

She recalled vaguely the many long discussions she had with friends and other lawyers about the necessity of a lump sum with a man like Edgar, so that she need not keep begging for payments. But she said only: 'How much would that be, then?'

Adams explained: so much per week, 'and *he* insists on paying the two thou directly to the daughter.'

Isabel stood there, in the corner of the courtroom, nodding, but suddenly it occurred to her to say: '*I* must get the checks for the draught . . . for Wendy. I can't trust him to send them to her.'

'They say no,' Adams reported.

Isabel remembered Wendy's letter which she had thrust into her pocketbook, the letter in which Wendy wrote: 'Daddy threatens to cut me off.' She took it out and gave it to Adams, who ran to Edgar's corner, ran back: 'They say yes.'

It got faster and faster and stranger and stranger. He had become the plural enemy, *they*, who lay in wait to defraud, demean, and destroy her.

'What furniture do you want? Write it down here.' Adams said, and all the long lists she had so carefully compiled during the last four years flew out of her head. 'The contents of the apartment' was the phrase; she tried to visualize the contents. What did her bedroom look like? What was in the living room, the dining room? She had to hurry; she had to write it down fast. Feverishly she jotted down what pieces of furniture she could remember, while Adams kept dancing to Edgar's corner and Edgar kept crossing out the items she wrote down: 'Bed.'

'They need it,' Adams said, 'because it's part of the head-board and can't be disconnected.'

'Table?' she wrote.

'They need it for eating.'

'Chairs?' She thought crazily of the Three Bears: 'They need it for sitting,' and she saw 'them,' Edgar and his lawyers, sitting on her chairs, eating off her table, sleeping on her bed . . . *That's what it's like to go insane*, she thought. And won't she need the pressure cooker? She thought they had one someplace, and thought she had never used it, surely she would need it to make quick meals? And what about the piano? Why the piano? She knew only that she had to insist on the piano. *And* the piano stool. She made that quite clear, waiting for the miracle that would set her free.

And the miracle happened. She got the piano, piano stool, her desk, two chairs, one or two other things, and the judge (Goldleaf? Karp?) put aside his *Wall Street Journal* and read it aloud, and it was written down by the court clerk, and it was so done.

Her relief was indescribable. She was free, at last she was free! She looked for her lawyers, but they had gone to talk to the reporters. She walked to the subway, rode back to Rose's, entered, and said: 'I'm free!'

'How did you make out?' Rose asked.

'Four and a half thousand for me, minus the four hundred they gave me before, and two for Wendy until she's twenty-one, and some furniture. And I lost my apartment. That's it.'

Rose began to cry. 'No, no, how could you?' But Isabel, euphoric and numb at the same time, walked out and began to walk on the street, street after street. It was over; she was free!

FRIDAY OCTOBER 13

It is over. Finished.

He did come last Monday, and he spent exactly fifteen minutes here. Perfectly controlled, pleasant, courteous. He shook my hand; when I was about to embrace him, he drew back: 'Don't make it harder.' Refused a drink. We sat for a while, for an eternity, making conversation about Columbus Day. Cristoforo Colombo, he called him, who didn't know he had discovered America. 'Do you know the impressive, all-inclusive title he was given?' he asked. 'Admiral of the Ocean Sea, Viceroy, and governor of whatever he might discover.'

Senseless talk with a stranger. No looking into each other's eyes, no mention of who we were and what we've been to each other. It was absurd for me even to try to reach him. He was gone, as he sat there, hands clasped on his lap, paying a duty call.

I had the package ready: his robe, his slippers, his pajama tops, his shaving things, his cologne – a neat bundle, in a shopping bag from Gristedes. He winced as I handed it to him, but took it and got up to go. I offered to return his gifts, his hassock, Chinese vase, Aladdin's lamp.

'No,' he said, 'don't do this.'

'But they're yours,' I said.

'They were ours,' he said. He was at the door now.

I took a deep breath, gathered my courage:

'The money,' I said. 'The nine thousand I lent you. I really need it now.'

He looked so stricken, I added inanely: 'You never gave me an IOU, you know.'

'What are you doing?' he said. 'Why are you doing this?' He looked like my old, tormented Max.

'Are you ... Will you return it?' I asked.

His voice broke: 'How can you say this? Who do you think I am?'

He was opening the door; he was leaving.

'Max!' I cried. The cry was wrenched from me; my arms, my arms opened to him – but he was at the elevator now. He put his forefinger up and moved it back and forth in front of his face in a pained prohibition.

The elevator door opened.

'Be well,' I said.

And he: 'You too.'

He was gone. And I still understand nothing.

Like a robot, I walked back into the bedroom and opened the closet, to make sure his robe was gone, the robe I handed him in the bag from Gristedes. I glanced into the mirror and was shocked to see how old I looked. I kept walking back and forth. Why hadn't I dared to ask all the questions that needed to be asked? To speak my feelings? To demand my money? Why did I sit like an idiot, an old and ugly idiot, chatting about Columbus? Why did I insult him by saying that about an IOU? Why didn't I plead for us, as I had done once before? Why didn't I scream, make a scene, beat the walls with my fists?

Then I sat by the telephone, the one on which he had the cord extended so that I might answer it more quickly when he called. I was sure he would call me as soon as he got home, tell me what a dreadful mistake this was. I waited for a long time, but the phone didn't ring.

That was four days ago, the ninth of October. The mystic number nine. And nine thousand dollars. And today is Friday the thirteenth. What does it mean?

It means I'm going crazy. My shrink doesn't think so. Neither does Carrie; she tells me I'll be sure to meet someone worthy of me. Gilda says he has no intention of repaying the money; she says I had to pay that sum to be free of him. But that means he never loved me. How can I live, believing that?

I must accept the fact that it's over, if it ever was. All

370

the king's horses and all the poets who ever were cannot make it whole again. Perhaps by loving him so deeply I frightened him away. Perhaps the money threw him out of balance. Perhaps the victim always recognizes the killer behind the kindest smile.

Dear Nina —
Apparently I didn't make myself clear in my letters and in
our phone conversations. Why do you insist on lecturing
me? It's pointless to warn me against Max. *Finita com-
edia.* Or rather, *tragedia.* Depending on whether you
think or feel.

He came a stranger and he left a stranger. I seem to be
always running after him to the elevator, and each time
he plunges down, down, away from me. This time for
good. I need no advice, except possibly Varya's: to finish
my book and become a millionaire.

She's looking forward to meeting you, and is already
planning a Russian feast in your honor.

Yours,
Jess

PLAINTIFF PREVAILED

Isabel's euphoric relief did not last. A couple of hours after her walk through the streets of the city, the reality hit her. *No, No! What have I done, after all the years of preparation, after all the pain and humiliation – No!* She kept unreeling the reel, starting from the moment, that last moment when she entered the court and said: 'Negotiate!' She refilmed it: This time she stood strong and confident while Adams and Gross presented their evidence. Edgar's lawyer was helpless as she parried his thrusts. She told the judge all that Edgar had done to her, and the judge examined all the papers in the two valises, every single one of them, and awarded her fifteen thousand a year and three years of college for Wendy, and graduate school for Gregory, and the apartment and all its contents, and the money in a lump sum, and Edgar was exposed, and she triumphed, and then –

The enormity of what she had done overwhelmed her. To abdicate the last minute after all she had gone through? To end up, at the eleventh hour, with this? Why had she waited for four years to do it right? Why did she have to sleep on the floor, give all that money to lawyers and detectives, ruin her reputation, lose her children? This sum he would have given her anytime, over the dinner table. And her home? Where would she sleep?

Gasping for breath, staggering with rage at him, at them, at herself, she wanted only to jump out of the window: the ultimate victim. Irreversible. One leg first, then another – and no way of getting back. Like Dr Burr. But 'You can't do it in *my* house,' said Rose.

So she didn't.

Dearest Jess,

It wasn't until I talked to you on the phone last night that I realized how bad the situation is: that he hasn't returned your money. Where do people like that come from? Listen, have you consulted an attorney? Would you like to be referred to an honest one? I know how you feel – felt – about Max, and I realize it's hard to prove a cash transaction (you did say you had given him cash?), but you've got to be practical, and he mustn't get away with this.

I know, I know; I just had to get it off my chest. We'll settle for whatever gives you least pain. You can speak your pain, as you spoke your anger. You're entitled to your anger, but perhaps you're directing it at the wrong target?

Dear Jess – you don't have to be clever, you don't have to be funny, you don't even have to sing for your supper. You'll be fed without a song, bright as your songs are. You are loved.

As long as we kept our correspondence light, with puns and rhymes and anecdotes, there was no danger of touching where it hurts. But there are times when it's necessary to reach out – and I'm here for you, and soon I will be with you.

We'll pick up where we left off six years ago. I may even take a refresher course in your Fiction Workshop. Maybe you'll get me started on book #2, as you did on book #1? My involvement with the play will not take too much time. When I said 'collaboration' I used the word loosely. I have the right of script approval, which is important, and I have a voice in casting. I wonder what happened to the girl with Titan hair who once wrote to me? Here is her big chance. Perhaps we can write in a part for Varya? She's a natural.

Write to me soon, dearest Jessica; I need your letters.

Much love,
Nina

YOU DON'T KNOW HOW HAPPY YOU ARE!

The day after her divorce another story appeared in the tabloid, about detectives, the ladder, the raid, with the names of her lawyers spelled out clear and bold. So that's what they were telling the reporters in court! Betrayers! Murderers!

She was told Edgar was complaining to everyone that she had given out that information; people asked her how she could do this to him, to her children. Her children. If only Wendy would call, if only Gregory would write. But she had lost them, perhaps forever.

Homeless, rootless, searching for an apartment to sleep in as far away from Park Avenue as she could find, Isabel zigzagged up and down the streets of the West Side, looking for a Vacancy sign. Most of the places had none; those that did she could not afford. But she kept going from building to building, ringing the super's bell, asking the doorman: 'Any vacancies here?' One doorman in front of a large building gave her a strange look. 'Lady,' he said, 'if there was a vacancy here you wouldn't want it. This here is a hospital.'

That would be good, Isabel thought: to lie down in a clean bed, to be taken care of, have nurses look in on her, have everything done for her – that would be so good! But she couldn't afford it.

Other women get divorced, she thought, yet most remain in their own home, on their own street. Their pain is cushioned by their children, by small comforts. But nothing was made easy for Isabel. She had lost her telephone, her closets, her red chair, her cup, her coffee pot. She had lost her cleaner, her grocer, even her housekeeper Katie, whom he had bribed to stay on with him in the duplex. Everything was gone, irretrievably.

At least her mother did not live to see what happened to her daughter – for all her faith in feathers from the sky, for all her promises of miracles.

The days were manageable; the nights were bad, with *NO! NO!* screaming inside her as she kept replaying the scene. She enters the court, does *not* say 'Negotiate.' A sympathetic judge (friend of Bart's, why, he had even said: 'They must be married over twenty years') reads Edgar's ledgers, neatly photostated and wheeled in on a cart, like a hotel Room Service tray. Recital of witnesses: Katie, Dorian, even the nurse, who was subpoenaed because of her handwriting. Exposure, public and loud, of all his lies, infidelities, financial frauds. She is exonerated in the eyes of the readers of the newspaper. She is forgiven by her children, who come to her support, realizing how noble it was of her to keep silent all those years.

The nights were bad.

Martha says: 'You don't know how happy you are!' She found Isabel an apartment: one room, small bath, wall kitchenette – ninety dollars a month; a luxury, after her marble prison. Here Isabel gets obscene letters from cranks and perverts who have read the lurid newspaper stories, in which her old address was given. Edgar forwards these to her, together with all the old unpaid bills.

Now her lawyers are worried about their three thousand dollars Edgar was to pay them according to the court judgment. Adams says if he doesn't get it soon, he will make it 'contingent on alimony.' 'How can you do that?' Isabel asks. 'You know my financial situation.'

The cost of war turned out to be thirteen thousand dollars: to court, to lawyers, for 'printing costs' of those fine booklets. That would have paid for four years of college for Wendy.

Each day holds its own ration of pain. Unpacking the boxes in her new apartment, Isabel finds Edgar's old love letters, his words when they were young. And snapshots of the children when they were little. A jewel box neatly labeled: *Gregory's First Tooth.* A small pink candle from a birthday cake. Wendy's drawing of a valentine, in waxy red crayon. A wallet of some heavy material, unevenly stitched, and in it a card: 'To Momie with love.' A graduation program. A history of hopes, mementos of the time when the past still had a future.

The pain doesn't end: Isabel has learned that when Gregory

377

was home from school he was living in her old apartment with his father. When Wendy comes to New York, she refuses to stay with her mother, even though Isabel has 'custody,' whatever that means, and has bought a cot for her. Wendy stays with her girl friend, says on the phone she is 'coping,' but sounds remote and sad.

What have I exchanged – for what? I, Isabel Webb, am free. I can call myself Isabel Barshak, as I did when I was a girl. A fifty-year-old girl, starting life all over again. I don't know how happy I am.

Dear Wendy and Gregory –
  I write this because I don't want to

NOTES TO MYSELF

No. Using children again –

Struggle: inner and outer.
Fish on dry beach, horse fallen in snow.

63 nembutals. Vengeance in a bottle.
There is no substitute for death.

Character is destiny.

Change possible?

DIVISION OF THE SPOILS

With Martha for support and the movers waiting downstairs, Isabel returned to her home, *his* home, where she used to live, to get the things allotted to her by court, the things he hadn't crossed off her list. Past the doorman (snickering?), the elevator man, with eyes averted. Edgar greeted her: 'That was a good picture of you in the paper.'

The bedroom door, mangled from months of raging battle: broken locks, raw nails, soldered keyhole, was off its hinges. She saw large faded rectangles on the living room walls, where their paintings had hung. The bookshelf looked like a huge mouth with missing teeth.

Katie suddenly grabbed the vacuum cleaner and began vigorously vacuuming the bedroom carpet. 'Will you come back, Mrs Webb?' she had asked that morning when Isabel had called to arrange the hour; 'will you be here when the children are home for their vacation? Why don't you make up with the doctor and come home?'

The doctor must have worked fast: he had removed and hidden someplace all the good glassware, silver, kitchenware, linens, even ashtrays. *Must be in his office, on the examining table,* Isabel thought crazily. He brought the kitchen stool into the foyer and sat, tight-lipped, list in hand, checking off each item. Chair. Another chair. Piano stool. Bones of contention. His and hers. *Possessions of the diseased,* she thought. *Deceased,* rather. The nurse's words, the moment her mother died, when the nurse had removed the wristwatch from the limp, dead wrist: 'She won't need it anymore.'

There was one thing Isabel needed desperately: the glass fruit bowl. She had to have it for the parties she would be giving, the men she would entertain at dinner. The bowl was gone.

'Not on the list,' Edgar said, making sure she didn't get away with an extra pillowcase, an undeserved spoon.

Wendy's painting, the one that won the prize? Her Aunt Mary's hand-knitted bed throw for the cold winter nights? 'Not on the list!' he kept saying, as he sat, leaning forward on the kitchen stool, straining to see the titles of the books Isabel was taking, those that were left on the shelves. She held up each one, like an auctioneer. Her own reference books? Books inscribed to her by her friends? Whatever he claimed was given to 'both of us' she let him keep. They were no longer 'both of us.'

The linen closet was all but empty. 'Where are the blankets for Wendy and me?' she asked. That was on the list, she was sure blankets were on the list, for Wendy was to sleep on the cot in her room when she was home from school. 'There are two blankets there,' he said, crossing the item off his list. Only two? Never mind, Isabel thought, let him have whatever he wants, only get out, get out fast into the air outside. Martha stood by, silent and embarrassed.

But he carried on about the piano. He said the movers would not be able to get it out of the door. If it was to be moved through the window, then she would have to post a bond. He couldn't afford any more damage to the apartment; the bedroom door would cost him a fortune.

Hurry, she had to hurry. She was feverishly throwing her clothes and papers into a valise. Surely, he did not need her skirt, her blouses? What else was there to salvage from a lifetime of accumulated possessions? (It was such a sad, cheap, dirty-faced nickel-plated wristwatch.)

There was no problem moving the piano. The following week she sold it, to pay for the movers and her first month's rent on her one-room kitchenette apartment. Hers. With no other footsteps in it but her own.

NOTES TO MYSELF

Edgar? He's caught in it. Major battleground. Can't retreat.

Isabel? Her timing always wrong. The ultimate irony:

Had she waited four more months, until September of 1966, a new law would have made it unnecessary for her to sue for adultery in New York.

But why am I building these scenes? Wasn't courtroom end of book?

My words in Fiction Workshop: Swim, with inexorable breaststroke, toward that raft.

I've been pointing the story toward court scene, structuring climax upon climax until the ultimate anticlimax: her abdication. Parallel? Life with its climaxes, and the ultimate irrelevance: death.

But Isabel is alive. There must be more to her story than this. There's another raft, beyond the first, far more important for survival. Isabel is a survivor. She did *not* swallow her nembutal pills when she felt she could no longer go on; she only counted them again and again for comfort, as a nun counts her beads. She did *not* put her second leg out of the window when she lived at Rose's. Whether I wrote those scenes or not, I know she wants to live.

Now that she's stripped of everything, how will she manage? The divorce is not the end – it's the beginning. Of what?

THURSDAY OCTOBER 19

No word. No check. No IOU. No Max. I keep going over and over it in my mind: When did it happen? Why? How could I have saved us at the end? What should I have done?

It was all so fast, so stupid. The very last words we said to each other, after all the glorious poetry we fed on: an inane 'Be well,' a banal 'You too.' Is this it then, is this how it ends?

For six days now I've been *willing* the phone to ring. Several times I picked up the receiver and put it down as if it burned my hand.

Twice now I thought I saw him on the street; when I came closer, I saw it was someone else, a stranger.

I dream of him. I know it's of him, though on awakening I remember nothing but loss.

Gilda lent me a book, a clinical study of psychopathic personality. I haven't looked at it yet. Better to live without a diagnosis.

'You can do somersaults,' Gilda says, 'you can stand on your head – you will not move him. He can't see. He has no retina!'

I know him better than that. I know how deeply he can feel, and I can guess what tight control he must have exercised last Friday night when he was here. He must be suffering now, as I am.

All day I've been adding up columns of figures: the approximate cost of all he has spent on me. Birthday party: plane fare for my children, caterers, food, champagne, that fabulous cake. Theaters, ballets, movies, restaurants. Liquor, wine, soft drinks.

Flowers – all the roses, the roses of different colors, the plants, the spring flowers. Records, books. Caviar. Asparagus, truffles, hothouse fruit, groceries. Blanc de Chine vase. Aladdin's lamp. Replicas of animals in my book. Royal Copenhagen kitten. Hassock, Japanese prints. Dragon cigarette lighter. Jill's coral necklace, Jeremy's pen. Silver flower vase, bed board. Backrest for the car.

I keep adding the figures, trying to make them come out to nine thousand dollars. But they don't.

I add more: catnip mouse, telegrams, postage. A Chinese brush holder to hold my pens and pencils. Gasoline, phones, tips.

But I can't make it total nine thousand.

And what price for joy in the morning, love at night? How much per hour of happiness? Perhaps I owe *him* money.

I seem to be copying Isabel and her compulsive lists. Or is she copying me?

NOTES TO MYSELF

What's happening to Isabel in her new life?
Show, don't tell.
Use first person for immediacy.

THE MEETING

So there I was, sneaking around corners, for a tryst with my own housekeeper (former), Katie, who was meeting me with my mail and telephone messages.

How did I manage to do this to myself, and I and my two gladiators? Other wives remained in their own beds, while the husband moved out. They stayed in their own neighborhoods, answered their own phone. But my phone (former) went unanswered, or was answered by him, it was reported to me, with a triumphant: 'She's gone. The court ordered it. No, I don't think she'll be back. No, I don't know where she is,' – when I specifically left written instructions to forward my mail and telephone calls. People who called me right after the divorce, who perhaps wanted to offer me sympathy, friendship, money even, were told in no uncertain terms that Isabel didn't live there anymore.

It was strange, getting out of the bus at the familiar corner on Madison Avenue, walking past the familiar shops: the cleaner, the florist, trying to make myself invisible. One block away stood my old apartment house; I could visualize it, gray and grim, with the blind windows of my bedroom (former) facing Park Avenue. Katie was waiting a block away, just as we had arranged. She looked sad, in her woolen shawl, with her red-rimmed eyes. She shook her head when she saw me.

'You don't look so good, Mrs Webb. You got so thin, God bless you. When are you coming home?'

Katie, Katie, I'm never coming home, never again to lead the life I have led for so many years, and God knows what will become of me, Katie. God is far from blessing me, Katie, and if only you had been willing to testify about the time you saw her, Dorian, in my bed – but then, I probably would have stopped you the last minute.

All I said was: 'Hi, Katie, how are you?'

She was fine, she said. She was taking care of the doctor, bless him; he was working so hard to make ends meet, and he was so unhappy about the separation and all. Why did we do it, when we were such a nice couple, never raised our voices, never had a fight.

Maybe that's why, Katie, I wanted to say, but instead I asked for my mail and quickly looked through it. Hardly worth spending the bus fare to come across town: bills and bills, urgent, threatening – all those bills he was supposed to pay months ago, and a couple of ads. Nothing from the children? – Nothing. Not a word? – Not a word.

'Why don't you and the doctor make up, Mrs Webb?' Katie said. 'Why don't you make up and come back home?'

No way of explaining anything to anyone. Here we were, in Katie's eyes, two attractive and intelligent people, nice apartment, two beautiful, smart children, nothing missing – so why not make up and come home, Mrs ex-Webb?

People were passing by; I kept my coat collar up, face averted, a leper exiled and in my own land despised.

'You really should come home for the children's sake. Gregory is so sensitive, he looks so thin and pale – '

'He what? What do you mean? Is he here, is he home?'

She hesitated, looked uncomfortable. 'Well, yes, he is here, just for a few days on a holiday from school.'

'He's here?'

'He looks so thin, it breaks my heart. Why don't you and the doctor – '

'When did he come home? When did he arrive, Katie?'

'I don't know. I mean, I think just a couple of days ago. Thursday afternoon.'

'He's been here since Thursday? That's two – four – that's five

386

days that he's been here. And he never called me, he didn't even . . . Katie, does he know where I am? Does he have my telephone number?'

'Well, I know he has it because I gave it to him right after you told me to. I mean maybe he will. Maybe he just forgot. You know how young people are. He just forgot, so when I go back I'll tell him. I'll remind him.'

'Five days and nights here, in the apartment?'

'He forgot, I guess, or maybe he lost the slip of paper. The paper with your telephone on it. Maybe I can remind him. Maybe you will make up with the doctor and come home?'

'I can't, Katie, believe me, I can't. But you know where I'm staying, and you have my number – here it is again – on this envelope. Just ask Gregory if he has it – don't ask him to call me, just see that he has it. He may have called me when the line was busy, so don't ask him, just tell him . . . Katie, Katie, are you crying? You don't have to cry for me.'

'Make up with the doctor, Mrs Webb. Come home, I'll fix you my lamb stew you like so much, I'll take care of everything. Then you can talk to Gregory yourself.'

'How long is he staying, do you know?'

'The doctor said till Wednesday. I made him his favorite rhubarb pie but he hardly eats anything. Why don't you – '

'He and the doctor are having a nice visit?'

'Well, I guess so. Gregory just stays in his room a lot.'

'Studying?'

'Well, I don't know. He keeps the door closed. I just come in to make the bed. He shouldn't be alone so much.'

'His friends don't come? Isn't his father with him?'

'Well, you know the doctor. He's so busy and all.'

'On weekends?'

'Like now he's gone for skiing. He left Friday afternoon and he said he'll be back tonight. So he'll see Gregory then.'

'He left him alone in the apartment all this time? He isn't there even when . . . Never mind, Katie, just tell him that – no, don't say anything. Don't ever say anything to anyone about meeting me here today like this. Only – if there are any calls – '

'Well, you know, the doctor likes to answer the telephone himself.'

'I know, but in case you happen to talk to someone who wants my phone, give it to them, Katie. And keep my mail. I'm expecting a very important letter. Very important – so if anything comes in keep it for me and call me and we'll meet again – '

'Sure, Mrs Webb. Only – you know the doctor likes to see all the mail that comes in first.'

'But I'm speaking of *my* mail, Katie. Addressed to *me*!'

'Yes, ma'am.'

'He reads my mail too, Katie? Katie, you don't have to . . .'

'Oh, Mrs Webb, please make up, please come back.'

'Never mind, Katie, you don't have to cry. I'm fine – see, I'm really much better off. Soon you'll come and see my little apartment, I'm living in such a nice . . . Stop crying, Katie. It's really better this way. Are you giving Gregory a hot breakfast each morning?'

'He doesn't hardly eat, Mrs Webb. He just stays in his room with the door closed. Is there anything else I can bring you from the apartment? Anything you need?'

'No, I have everything. I could use my . . . No, it's all right. I'll call you – three rings and a stop, so you'll know it's me. I'll call you when he's in the office, and maybe if Gregory wants to – no, it's all right. I'm fine, really fine. Thank you, Katie, for everything.'

NOTES TO MYSELF

Trying in these scenes to shape Isabel's life after divorce. But she insists on dwelling on the pathos of her situation. What about my own, now that I've lost Max?

It's almost as if she's beginning to take over, to lead me. I think she wants to tell me how uprooted she is. Disoriented. Like waking up in a strange room, she can't understand where she is. Accustomed to seeing her own things in their right place, she feels lost. Remember how Jeremy, unhappy with his kindergarten teacher, refused to be transferred to another. 'I've got my hook, I've got my number,' he said wistfully: He knew where his little coat was hanging.

In contrast to all this suffering, should Isabel have a brighter scene?

Support of women friends: Write scene in which Martha brings Isabel two small cane chairs from her own home. She carries them into the subway, and — during rush hour — sits in the aisle on one of them. Another passenger sits down on the other. Subway passengers not surprised; they accept this without question as part of the unpredictable transit system.

No, this won't do. Isabel is in panic; unable to see humor in anything now.

[DIARY]

I'll put here, between these diary pages, this letter to Max I've been writing all morning, pouring out my liquid heart.

A while ago I went out to mail it, stopped at mailbox, lifted the lid – and – couldn't drop it in. I walked another two blocks, came to another mailbox, hesitated, waited – afraid of what?

I looked for signs: If the person in the taxi coming toward me is a woman, I'll drop it in; if it's a man, I won't. Two women sat in the taxi. But I couldn't drop the letter in. It seemed – irrevocable.

He may still come back to me; he always did. With money or without. He, too, must remember, in spite of his icy control, how it was with us.

I held the letter in my hand for a long time, waiting for courage to mail it. 'If the light turns green by the time I count to five . . .'

But what nonsense! I will simply – simply what? I will simply take it back. There is always time to send it.

Here, between these diary pages, no other eyes will read it.

Dear Max –

Dylan Thomas was wrong. After the first death there *is* another.

What happened to us is shattering. I waited for three months to see you, and you talked to me of Columbus.

I am neither angry nor bitter, only sad. Our parting was so abrupt, inconclusive, irrelevant.

I once said to you that love is the ultimate commitment; it risks pain. I took that risk. I gave myself with no subtlety or deviousness, and if I must suffer for it, it was worth it. I could have gone to my grave not knowing that I could love so deeply, that I could be so happy. I am indebted to you for much: for bringing my children to me. For making me laugh. For being the cause of my loving. I loved you not only for yourself, but for making me feel love.

Whatever you needed from me – assurance of manhood, a link to reality, a partner in a charade, or money (yes, that), I gave and gave freely. I said yes, even though the price was higher than most would be willing to pay.

You no longer let me bring light into your darkness. If you ever did. I thought I could be the bridge for you in your terrible struggle between fantasy and reality, between sacred and profane love, between joy and damnation. I thought that because I am I and you are you ('neither was born by hazard'), together we could make it.

We had it and we lost it. I don't know why. You gave me so much, but you withheld the most important gift: your real self. 'I could die for you!' you said, but you could not live with me. And you could not give me the one thing I deserved: truth.

'Only as I am can I love you as you are,' you said to me. But who were we? Whose fantasy were we inhabiting?

I am neither a princess nor a little girl-wife watching

391

you shave with wonder in my eyes. I am a grown woman with a need to be myself. And you are neither king nor magician — but a man, troubled, flawed, conflicted, perhaps a little mad, and in many ways wonderful. I say this with love.

I feel great sorrow. For me, for you, for all that never will be. Perhaps never was. But I think I will survive by loving, while you, poor Max, you must do the dragon's will, and you will continue to destroy those who dare to love you. Yet you can no more help it than you can help the color of your eyes.

We had it, and we lost it. I, too, am guilty. I pushed you away with one hand and pulled you toward me with the other. Once I wooed you back with letters, poems, pleas. And now I let you go. Had I fought for us again, had I wept — would you have stayed and loved me?

Our dreams have meshed, have crossed, have gone their separate ways. Yet in the few short months we were together we gave each other more than most have in a lifetime.

> I have nothing more to tell you. What has been said
> Cannot possibly be retracted now
> Without denial of the large universe.
>
> Some curse has fallen between us, a dead hand,
> An inclination of evil sucking up virtue,
> Which left us no recourse, unless we turned
>
> Improvident as at our first encounter,
> Deriding practical care of how and where;
> Your certitude must be my certitude —
>
> And the tranquil blaze of sky etherealizing
> The circle of rocks and our rain-wet faces —
> Was that not worth a lifetime of pure grief?
>
> Yes, Dear Max — yes, it was.

THE WALKING CRAZIES

There were hidden meanings everywhere, symbols, threats. Isabel would startle herself by a sudden outburst of anger at a bus driver, by uncontrollable tears at a song on the radio. A man pecking his wife on the cheek on the street, a limping dog crouching in a doorway – anything could set it off. Passing by a playground where she glimpsed the children with the Sunday Fathers of Divorce, she felt such a stab of anguish that she cried aloud: 'No!' No what? No to the music and laughter she had promised her children the day she told them about the Divorce? She saw the word 'Divorce' always in capitals, like Death.

She had become suspicious of everyone. Which of her friends was loyal? Who was seeing him on the sly? Why was that car driving so close to the curb where she was standing – was someone paid to follow her? The phone that rang late at night with no one there when she answered it, the window shade across the street not quite down, the letter which arrived with scotch tape on the envelope?

She collected indignities big and small and counted carefully the humiliations she suffered daily. Sometimes, when she least expected it, the horror would overwhelm her, the Black Death, she called it, for there was no word invented to describe it. People became unreal, walking about in their clothes in an alien world, while she remained in terror behind a sheet of unbreakable glass, forever lost.

Everything was too difficult, even the thought of killing herself. She gagged on pills, she feared heights, the sight of blood made her ill. She was afraid of being buried because of her claustrophobia. She was afraid of being cremated because she dreaded fire. Where, then, was a way out for her?

In her calmer moments she dwelled on the Divorce, over and over. How decent people, well-brought-up people, who had begun by wanting each other, nice, respectable, educated people turned into lock changers and detective hirers, mud-slingers and enemies unto death.

These were the walking crazies, and she was one of them.

[DIARY]

My hand is shaking so I can hardly hold my pen. I'm so furious, so outraged – At least here I can say it. I must, or else it will rise in my throat and choke me.

He left me nothing, not even my loving memories. Not even his silence.

I've just learned from Grace and Henry that they ran into Max quite by accident. He looked very distinguished, they said. Bronzed. At first he seemed embarrassed to see them; then stopped to chat, became quite expansive. He mentioned my name. He told them – but how despicable! – he said I had commissioned certain purchases he had gone out of his way to get me, to import for my apartment. He said he did many favors for me because I was alone and helpless, and because I had money problems. He even gave a party for me. But as soon as I began to want intimacy, he said, when I tried to involve him in a physical relationship, he dropped me. That's what he told them! He spoke of me with compassion. He said because I was a writer, I tended to fantasize. He went on to describe his recent holiday in the Bahamas, and he was as amusing, they said, as always.

For the first time I feel rage – violent rage – at him and at myself. While I've been sitting here waiting for him to call, composing tender letters, he has been spreading these malicious lies. While I was trying so hard to 'understand' him, he was having himself a holiday in the Bahamas. On my money.

'Sue the bastard,' Marge, who was with me at the time, said. I'm glad she called him bastard.

I'll sue him for my money. I'll expose him to the world. I'll call a lawyer. First, I'll call him. I'll show him he can't treat me like this. How dare he?

*

Later: Just dialed his number. The operator's electronic voice said: 'That number has now been changed to an unpublished number at the customer's request.'

So the customer is a coward too? To make sure, I dialed again. 'That number has now been changed . . .'

I called a live operator. I explained that I already had his unlisted number, so I was entitled to the new one. 'We cannot give it out,' she said, 'at the party's request.'

That's the party who used to spend hours on the telephone in a passion of poetry and love! I'm sick with shame for him.

And for myself — a middle-aged blonde prancing naked on a beach with a naked gray-haired man. How could I have believed him, a prizewinning photographer, that both of his cameras were broken? He must have kept all those photos — for what? Blackmail? No, this is the paranoia of separation I've been describing in my book. But at this very moment he may be laughing over those photos with someone. I keep confusing him with Edgar.

One reads about such cases in newspapers: a lonely, aging woman longing for romance falls prey to a charming, unscrupulous man who absconds with her life savings. Her name is legion.

Thank God I didn't mail him my letter.

NOTES TO MYSELF

This can't be all! The end is inconclusive. Severance in court can't be the climax of her life. It doesn't resolve anything. Something must happen beyond that – something of extreme importance.

If purpose of my book was only to show woman victim who tragically fumbled, lost her last chance – no, that's unfair to Isabel. She's a real person who must go on living.

Her divorce was but a dramatic incident in her life. As Max was in mine.

Question: What happens to her now? How does she pick up the pieces? And what's on that second raft?

THE BEEP

For weeks after her divorce, Isabel kept thinking she saw
Edgar – across the street, or just rounding a corner. She
recognized his back, the way he walked – only to realize it was
a stranger. She saw him getting out of a car – no, it was
someone else. Once she almost called out his name, but it was a
man who did not even resemble him.

She supposed it was her curiosity about him that produced
these street mirages. Her good friends casually dropped his
name into their conversation, and she would hold her breath:
this restaurant he was in, this theater – how did he look, what
did he say; above all – was he alone? With one of his
alphabetized, photostated women? A new one? Then he was a
couple again? Did he look unhappy? (She wished this fervent-
ly.) She became adept at ferreting out information about him.
The habit of spying had been a long one.

Once she phoned him, just to hear his voice. Strangely
enough, she had forgotten her own number and had to look it
up in the telephone book. She would hang up quickly when he
answered, she thought, comforted by the knowledge that he
was there, in the home where she had once lived. She was
frightened, as if the very sound of the telephone would betray
the caller. But she was shocked to hear an electronic voice. It
took her a few seconds to recognize it as his voice, which was
saying calmly, pleasantly, that he was out, and would the caller
please leave name, phone number, and a brief message. Brief
message? What brief message? She hung up quickly just
before the beep that was to receive her message. Perhaps just
one word: 'Help!' – Brief enough? She felt a twinge of satisfaction that he might be, for the moment, puzzled by the hang-up:
A crank? A crook? A patient? A former lover? An ex-wife,
perhaps? A brief message from an Ex, right after the beep. She
wondered if she might disguise her voice sufficiently to say
something devastating that would destroy him. Yet there was in

his voice something familiar, something that was not unkind. The way he said *Please, leave a . . .* She dialed the number again. Again, that voice: *please leave a . . .* Again she hung up just before the beep. What message could she possibly leave? Here I am, doing this idiotic thing, dialing your number to catch the sound of your voice. Here I am, breathing into the vacuum, knowing you will not know it is Isabel, your ex. For a terrified moment she thought he might be able to find it out by hooking up something to his machine that would register her number. Was that possible? She dialed again, hung up again. If the calls should worry him, so much the better, but that was not why she was doing it. She was trying to read a meaning in his inflection, to discover in his words a message for herself. And here it was, pleasantly asking her to wait for the beep. He was speaking into a vacuum – as she had done all those years, when she used to speak to him.

NOTES TO MYSELF

Does Isabel recognize in Edgar what I have denied him – his humanity? Is she ready now to understand *his* needs? 'Why can't you make me coffee in the morning, look glad to see me when I come home?' he had once asked.

She begins to be aware of his fears, inadequacies, his compensations: Because of his fear of heights, he became an accomplished skier. Because of his claustrophobia – an accomplished skin diver. Because of his inability to love –

No. Nice try, but doesn't work. My heart isn't in it.

Dear Nina —
Thank you for your letter of October 18, in which you
tell me I don't *have* to sing for my supper, woo people
with rhymes, be bright all the time. I'm beginning to see
that too. It's all right to say simply: 'Help, I'm hurting!' I
used to say it only in my diaries, where there was no one
except myself to hear.

There's more than pain; I can allow anger. Forgive me for
misdirecting it at you. Yes, I feel angry, outraged at his
betrayal of all we were to each other. I found out he has
been telling lies about me, shabby lies dishonoring our
love. And now he's run away; he has even changed his
telephone number.

Let him keep the money. He took from me something far
more important.

I had barely healed from my first divorce (this was a
divorce too; I felt more married to Max during the five
months we were together than in the quarter of a century
with Charles) when the blow came.

I can now feel grateful for your concern. You tried to
warn me about him; others did, too:

> 'His eyes are cold and shifty,'
>   They said. 'You'd better flee!'
> But I was six and fifty —
>   No use to talk to me.
> I thought I was in heaven;
>   My love was all I knew.
> But now I'm fifty-seven —
>   And oh, 'tis true, 'tis true!

No — that's unkind. Unkind and unworthy. I loved him,
and I alone know how greatly he could love and how
greatly he has failed.

Now I have a lot of thinking to do, about myself and about my book (the two have become interchangeable). I will write once more before you leave for New York.

But don't expect to enroll in my Workshop just like that! If you read the catalog carefully, you will note that acceptance is based on submission of a manuscript of at least twenty pages, subject to the instructor's approval. Have you written twenty pages?

Love,
Jess

MONDAY OCTOBER 23

As always in emergencies, went to my shrink. 'Lies, lies,' I kept saying. Couldn't stop weeping. I began to remember all my childhood disappointments, all the old betrayals.

The time they promised I could take the kitten home. I must have been four or five; in our dacha, near Kiev, at end of summer. We were standing on the railroad platform waiting for the train to take us back to the city. Mother said Petya, the caretaker's boy, was on his way, bringing the kitten to the train, the kitten I was in love with all summer, played with, slept with. But no sign of Petya. The train came, and only when mother picked me up and carried me into it I realized she had never intended for me to have the kitten; she had never told Petya to come. I wept in Schrank's office for that kitten and for that first unforgivable betrayal.

Lies. The time I was five and they took me to the doctor to have my tonsils taken out. In Kiev; my father still alive. They assured me it wouldn't hurt a bit, that it would be over in a second, that all little children had it done without ever crying. But that isn't how it was. A woman in white put me on her lap and held me very tightly, pinning my arms down, while the doctor asked me to open my mouth wide. When I did, he pushed a cold silver instrument into my mouth and began choking me with it and hurting me so much I couldn't believe it. I couldn't move; the woman held my arms at my sides. I couldn't scream. The doctor said if I closed my mouth my teeth would hurt his fingers, so I kept my mouth open and the pain went on and on, even when it was over and I walked home between Mother and Father, spitting blood on the sidewalk.

I wept now for that pain in my throat, and for all the

lies and betrayals I was remembering. No need to write them down here; I know them too well.

'How could he tell such lies about us?'

'I am not here to analyze him,' the shrink said, 'but I invite you to examine your own role with Max and with your husband in your marriage. Perhaps a pattern will emerge.'

'They're so utterly different!' I said. 'I've been rereading my diary of divorce because that's material for my book. But I can't bear to reread my current diary, it's so full of Max, from the first day I met him, I can't bear it . . .'

'I think you should, so that you can mourn for him.'

Obedient Jessica, like obedient Isabel, will reread this diary from beginning to end, though, like the coachman in the Russian song, she has no one left to mourn. He's gone, if he ever was, that Master Chef, Art Connoisseur, Photographer, World Traveler, Linguist, Translator, Wit, Importer, Exporter, Scholar, Superlover, and Fraud. And I? –

> Know me, have done – I am a proud spirit
> And you forever clay . . . Have done!

Not proud; I was the Perfect Pushover. He answered all I had been starved for: all my romantic yearnings, intellectual needs, sexual fantasies. He fed my dependence, my readiness for laughter and joy. He played on all my stops.

I didn't look beyond that. I saw him only from the angle where the crack didn't show.

He once said he couldn't imagine the days of his life before we met. Neither can I. Will we recognize each other in a year? we asked each other jokingly. What will become of us in five years? Ten? Overnight, can one stop caring? ('Must I stop praying for him?' Isabel's mother asked.)

If only he had left me an untarnished memory. Oh, Max, Max, you 'dug your grave in my breast,' and I must carry it until I die.

LIFELINE

The telephone was her lifeline; its wires – her umbilicus to the world outside. She sought comfort no longer from her married friends, nor from the bitter discards and sorry wrens, but from women who had survived a divorce well and had truly made a new life for themselves. If *they* did, perhaps she, too, might.

One woman, who had been a mere acquaintance dismissed with a casual: 'Let's have lunch one of these days,' had become her personal savior. What she said was based not on 'If I were you,' but on 'I *was* you.' She had known the pain and the panic. She had resolved the bitterness and the anger. She offered no platitudes or placebos. 'You will exchange one set of problems with which you can't cope for another with which you hope you can.' And she herself coped. She had a job she liked, a man she was interested in, an apartment she had fixed up from scraps rescued from the shipwreck of her marriage. It was her own. She could lie naked on the couch there, fuck anyone she liked there, read in the middle of the night, cook whatever she wished. She could spend money she earned on herself. She could think of the future with hope. Even if she had to spend it alone, it didn't frighten her. She had no fantasies or illusions. She knew who she was, and she liked it.

'I'm here for you if you need me,' she told Isabel. 'You can call me whenever you feel panicky.' She was just at the other end of the telephone wire; Isabel was not alone. 'Yes, I know,' the comforting voice would say. 'I know it's lousy. But I also know it will get better. You can't believe me now, but it will. In the meantime, put on your makeup, make coffee, go for a walk. If it gets too bad, you can always call me. Call me in half an hour and tell me you're up, okay?'

What unsung heroine was that, without a title, without a price, who had saved her?

NO ONE ON AT 5 A.M.

The telephone had been her lifeline; the TV was her life. Not the programs she used to watch occasionally when she was married, but soap operas only. She was absorbed in the characters on the little screen; she followed their conversations as avidly as she had eavesdropped on her husband's on the telephone extension. Godlike, she could manipulate them, make them vanish and reappear with a click of the dial. She could terminate a love scene, stop a murder in time. She was the one to give these people life or to annihilate them.

She would switch from channel to channel, from the moment of anguish of a mother whose baby had just been kidnapped from the hospital nursery – *click* – to the woman pleading with her lover to return the stolen money – *click* – to the doctor scrubbing up to operate on the girl who had been hit by his son's car – *click* – back to the woman whose lover was rushing out of the door – *click* – to the doctor, his face in his hands, having to scrub all over again since grief had unsterilized him.

Continuity was the thing. Life went on, day after day, weekdays only. Weekends she marked time, the screen preempted by sports and news and children's cartoons. On Mondays she reentered the lives of her only friends and neighbors.

When it grew dark, the serial dramas on the little screen gave place to other programs. Across the street, inside the rows of lit windows, people lived and talked and ate and fought and laughed, each in his own channel, unaware of the others. In windows next to each other, they pursued their lives, separate and apart.

She knew only the people on the screen. She envied them. Once a crisis was over, once it was made known and briefly mourned, it was seldom recalled. The past was swallowed up in a void. If some magic scalpel could excise the reels her memory kept unreeling, Isabel thought, she too could live on, episode after episode, ignorant of her past.

She wondered how her own life would look on that screen. Herself, the silent victim, the villain husband (of course, they would have to censor those scenes in his office), the lawyers (they, too, would have to be toned down), the children. How would the children be shown? What words could be written for them to say? What answers could be given to them?

The plots were strong on suspense, as her own life had been in the days when she pursued clues and photostated evidence, in the days when her own life was interesting. Accidents were frequent. Far away, on an icy road, a car would overturn and the faithless wife who was to drop out of the script would die. Illnesses were serious and prolonged; cures were sudden. Amnesia was common, and paralysis. Blindness occurred; a difficult operation was required, the outcome of which was uncertain. Bandages were kept on week after week until they came off and the patient saw, the patient realized . . . Leukemia struck; the woman wasted away through hope, despair, remission, while the husband repented and the children drew close. A nervous breakdown was frequent. The symptoms were recognizable to the viewer, though not to the loved ones: irrational jealousy, paranoid suspicions, nightmare terrors. This, like paralysis and blindness, was temporary. As was insanity. As was love.

Isabel sat in the darkened bedroom, sun or rain outside the drawn window drapes, sucked into the lives on the screen. At night she stayed awake, watching whatever was on, to prevent her thoughts from scratching like persistent mice inside her head. Sometimes she fell asleep to the sound of voices in her bedroom, but most of the time she stayed up watching the talk shows, mysteries, musicals, Westerns, comedies. She watched old movies at one, two, three, at four in the morning. How *young* everyone was once!

The panic of loneliness set in at five in the morning, when there was nothing, nothing at all on the gray and flickering screen. There was no one on at 5 a.m.

[DIARY]

Reading textbook on psychopathic personality Gilda lent me. Description of . . . Max? Almost made a slip of pen: it's of Edgar, too. Art antedates psychiatry.

My shrink wouldn't analyze Max, but here he is, stripped of poetry, stripped of passion:

> Disarming . . . persuasive . . . cultivated . . . often brilliant . . . appears candid and generous . . . cannot stand the mildest criticism . . . alternates between elation and depression . . .

Some of his traits — yes. But what do they prove?

> Lacks remorse or shame . . . emotional poverty leads him to promiscuity . . . attracts certain women who need to mother psychopaths . . .

But that's Edgar! The empty spade where feeling should be, it has a scientific name.

Edgar and Max. Both were angry men. Both were damaged men. Both betrayed the women who needed to mother psychopaths. Like me?

Odd — I'm writing of them in the past tense, like an obituary. As if *both* were real. Have to remind myself I made Edgar up. But surely, I didn't make up Max?

Psychopath — strong word. Edgar was not a psychopath. Merely a man, human and flawed, with his own strange hang-ups and needs. The threat of divorce threw him into a psychotic episode — as it did Isabel, too.

Poor Edgar. And poor Charles, so terrified of what divorce would do to him! All these years I was bound to him by my old, festering injuries. Max freed me. Now, for the first time in twelve years, I feel divorced from Charles.

But oh, my Max, how I did love you!

I no longer believe in miracles.

The fairy tale is over; now the real story begins.

['BOOK']

NOTES TO MYSELF

About loneliness – the human condition.

All reaching out to someone: the youngsters in their letters to Nina, the schizophrenic in his short-circuited signals, the prisoner in solitary. Each in his private wilderness, crying for love, etc.

Varya is never lonely: too busy living. Feet in patent-leather pumps planted firmly on ground. To her, loneliness is self-indulgence. Hard life, but knows how to squeeze pleasures from it. Whatever misfortune befalls her, she shrugs: 'Will heal before wedding.' For her it is simple: 'Sun rises, doesn't ask what time it is.'

But why Varya? She's not in my book – Isabel is.

Show how Isabel tries to cope with loneliness. (Remember Nina's description: greeting her plant, her view of bridge.)

Specific detail.

SELF-ACTUALIZATION

Isabel would walk into her small apartment, see the two chairs and piano stool awarded by the court and the gray wall outside her window, and she would stand still, struck by loneliness, the absolute loneliness of aloneness. Not even Clara, the cat, was alive and breathing in the same room. Isabel did not get custody of Clara.

Whenever Clara had been left alone too long, she would shred the toilet tissue in the bathroom. The amount of tissue shredded was the barometer of Clara's loneliness. Isabel's was her TV and her emergency telephone.

She tried to combat it. She went through phases that followed each other like well-timed scenes in a play: panic and self-exile. Going out with 'the girls.' Tentative dates with men – dry runs, to test herself. A fling at promiscuity. Sporadic job hunts.

She wrote résumés, filled applications, unable to answer the question: What am I good for?

She read articles on the art of macramé, the art of masturbation, the art of eye makeup; on how to choose a wine, lose weight, gain weight. She read books on divorce by women who had found happiness or the right man as soon as they were free. She studied their photographs on the book jackets and compared their faces with her own.

She looked in on courses and groups: *The Merry Midyears*, *Self-actualization, Problems, Inc., Singles Unlimited*. She was out of time, out of place, out of step. She was a slow learner; she needed to be young again, to catch up to the others. Who was she? She had been daughter, wife, mother. But now her fluctuating image in the mirror gave no hint.

She tried to fit herself into statistics: Fifteen million Americans, she read, had been divorced in the last decade. She was one of them. Had those fifteen million Americans been caught, too, under the wheels that had mangled them? Were they nice, decent people forced to trample on their feelings? Were the women like her, middle-aged adolescents alone in a frightening world? Had each gone through a private purgatory before the last memory grew dim, the last tear dried on the cheek?

Maybe age didn't matter so much to women who had more than their chronology to offer: the celebrities, the women in the news. They were at home everywhere. But she, even at eighteen unsure of herself, how could she now, with hair graying and eyes puffy from sleepless nights, step forward and proclaim herself in the arena as a contestant?

She tried the resorts of the singles, with their structured entertainments, categorized by age, by money, and by degree of desperation. Here she found the same sad wrens huddled on the telegraph pole, dressed in finer feathers, flapping their frantic wings in the cold.

She discovered, discreetly tucked away in the back of a magazine, the ads of the lonely hawking their wares. None was for her. She called old lovers, who weren't there. She studied the zodiac for a sign. One day she caught herself about to bend down to pick a pigeon feather from the ground.

MATURE, CULTURED SAGITTARIUS

Mature, cultured Sagittarius seeks young woman for sensual ties, possible permanence.

Loosely separated gentleman, sexually oriented, financially secure, seeks female 25–35 to share interest in art, literature, and dining out.

Submissive male seeks dominant dark-haired female, must be over 6 ft.

Attractive couple, physical and daring, seek young woman for ménage of interest.

Isabel studied the ads of these seekers of women, all crying *Help! Find me!* – but she saw no way she could suit any of their requirements. She herself was walking around, loosely separated, seeking survival.

Perhaps she might insert an ad of her own?

Immature, unliberated middle-aged woman, frightened and financially insecure, seeks someone to love her.

Why hadn't anyone told her divorce did not end a marriage? She was still writing her lawyers that she wasn't getting her checks, her 'weakly alimony,' she had misspelled it, her severance pay. They, in turn, were threatening her because they had not yet been paid by her husband. Her ex. The old bills from the department stores kept coming, readdressed to her. She was interviewed for a job in a real estate firm (experience unnecessary) by a man younger than her son; she did not get it.

Help! she, too, was crying, but no one heard her. She was a mute in the country of the deaf.

This last sentence (Max's) – too 'literary' here? Does it distract from pathos of those ads?

Should her cry, perhaps, be a personal one, to actual people?

HELLO, OLD LOVERS

Each evening she crossed out on her calendar the day she had survived with a thick black marker, obliterating it totally.

She tried to find small pleasures in her life. A cup of hot chocolate in front of the TV that drew her into its flickering screen. Clean sheets, cool and taut, with neat hospital corners her husband once, long ago, had taught her to make. A soft pillow. One pillow. For one person. 'Madame is alone?' Yes, Captain, Madame is certainly alone.

Mornings, she forced herself to get up, put on clothes, brush the hair. People who do not have a strong self-image, said the good Dr Kellerman, don't say: '*My* hair, *my* breasts,' but '*the* hair' . . . Right you are, Doctor. And then? She could go for a walk. Where would she walk? Anywhere. Around the block. Around two blocks. Shoe-maker, cleaner, butcher, grocer. You could skip rope to that.

Telephone the children? But she knew the pain of their cold, indifferent voices. Edgar did a good job of turning them against their ex-mother. Call a woman friend, her savior? Unwise to use up credit; save for a rainy day. Old lovers? Men who once – ? She had tried it one awful day when she was drowning, clutching at every straw in the swirling waters; she had called them, one by one. 'Hello, old lovers, how do you do?' Except that she didn't sing it. All she said – it wouldn't do to scare them off – was: 'Hi, there! Remember me?' All she asked was: 'Are you busy tonight? They were busy. They were very busy. Too busy for her now that she was no longer busy. 'Oh, yes, how nice,' they said. 'Loved hearing from you. Take care now, you hear?' I hear. How well I hear. Goodbye, old lovers, wherever you are . . .

NOTES TO MYSELF

Where is Isabel taking me? Is there nothing, then, but despair?

THE WATCH-WINDING

The thing to do was to keep busy. 'You've got to fill up the hours of the day,' Helene told Isabel. Helene was the envy of her friends: she had no money problems. Her husband had left her for a young man, but she remained in their luxurious Sutton Place apartment, well provided for. She was in her middle sixties, immaculately groomed, leading a life of pleasant leisure.

'You've got to have a routine,' she said. 'Look at me: Thursdays I volunteer for the Center for the Blind. Friday mornings – hair, pedicure, massage. That takes a good three hours, three and a half, if I'm lucky. On Tuesday – that's today – the watch winding.'

'The what?'

'At my bank. You can't let them run down, you know.'

'You're talking about – ?'

'My watches. I keep them in my strongbox, in the bank vault. I hand the key to the attendant, he takes my box out, I bring it to the small cubicle, sit down, take them out one by one, and wind them up. So that they will keep going.'

'Your watches?'

'All of them. The platinum with the diamond chips, the gold bracelet watch, the emerald-face Piaget, the sports watch, the ring watch, the summer enamel one, the square silver with the checkered face, the antique gold watch my father wore in his vest pocket. All ticking away time.'

'You do this each week?'

'Each Tuesday, rain or shine. They know I'm coming. Then I return the strongbox to the attendant, look carefully to make sure he places it in the right niche, take my key, and walk home: mission accomplished. The watch winding takes a good thirty, thirty-five minutes. With walking there and back in good weather, that's almost an hour.'

'I see.'

'I don't think you do. The important thing is – you're expected. Someone is thinking of you. Like *The New York Times.*'
　'The *Times*?'
　'I used to buy it at the newsstand, but now I have it delivered
to my apartment, so that every morning, except for legal
holidays, I open the front door as soon as I get out of bed, before
I have my juice and Ry-Krisp, and there it is, waiting for me. I
know someone was thinking of me: the delivery boy, the
elevator man, the clerk in some office who receives my checks
for it. It shows someone out there is aware I'm *here.*'
　'I see what you mean.'
　'On Sundays, the paper is so heavy, it's not easy to pick it up;
my back has been acting up lately, but it's a great comfort to
me. Besides, if I should die – don't think me morbid; it's a
practical precaution – the papers accumulating outside my
door would let them know.'
　'Come on, Helene, what a way to – '
　'Get the paper delivered to your door. It's worth the extra
money. I'm giving you good advice. I *know.*'

NOTES TO MYSELF

Becoming impatient with Isabel. Isn't it time for her to
shed old injuries, get moving, do something about her
life?

What is she doing, naked, in front of that full-length
mirror? Examining a lifetime of scars: knee infection
when she fell off bike. Appendectomy. Cut with bread
knife never properly healed. Keloid from removed mole.
Nicks, cuts, scrapes, bruises, abrasions. Accidents,
surgeries – indelible reminders, hieroglyphics of pain.

[DIARY]

I've been adding and subtracting: Feb. – Mar. – Apr. – May – June. Good days with Max = 106. Bad days with Max = 22. 106/22 is about 5 to 1; not a bad ratio. July to October = 101 bad days with Max. That is, without Max. More bad days than good. But if I count only the five months before he went away –

What nonsense! Like trying to add up his expenses to make up for my loss. No wonder Isabel is a compulsive list maker: look who created her! I'm examining feeling here, and in the balance, my love for Max, my gratitude for all the joy he gave me cancels out the pain. Or almost.

As Schrank suggested, I've been rereading this diary, from my first entry on February first until yesterday's, when I tried to pin on Max and Edgar/Charles a clinical label. But people, in fiction, as in life are more complex. Insight is no sudden light bulb in a balloon over one's head.

Why compare Max, with his grand gestures and largess of spirit, to mean-minded, tight-lipped Charles, who wouldn't even give me the time of day?

Yet, when I met Charles, he was a better man. There *were* good days in our marriage. At least, in the beginning.

Was Laura the only reason I couldn't forgive him? Was it because of his one affair (is one less painful than a dozen?) – or because she was no younger than I, less attractive than I? Is that why I made Dorian young and flashy?

Do I still need to hate Charles?

I remember, as a child, the startling moment when I realized that another child, who was crying, had feelings too. Feelings like mine. It was a revelation then. It still is.

And Max? His tears for humanity – were they real

416

tears, with salt in them? His treatment of the beggar –
principle or cruelty? His ear-nibblers and telephone cords
– protectiveness or paranoia? His love for me – No! I
can't believe it was all a pretense.

How ready I was for a Max! After years of deprivation,
there I was, with all my needs spread out before him like
hungry mouths to be fed. My need for self-sacrifice. For
admiration. For words, for poetry, for romance. My
insatiable need for love.

Rereading these diary pages, I realize how frightened I
was of awakening. I see recurring words: *incredible,
fantastic, unreal, fabulous, dream come true, fairy tale,
miracle* – and I understand how terrifying it must have
been for Max as well.

I must mourn for him, said the shrink.

Poor Max, I can cry for him now. I have already cried
for myself.

ALIVE IN THE WORLD

There were moments when the pain lifted. She did not know why. Suddenly, for no apparent reason, she would feel light-hearted. She might be walking on the street, on her way to the grocer's, when the air, the dappled sun on the sidewalk, the motes of mica silvering the asphalt, the people hurrying by, made her feel alive in the world. It was a feeling she kept remembering during the bad times. It was hope.

Even her children, she thought, would one day understand.

When she thought of Edgar, it was with something like detachment. She had no need now to hate him. He was what he was; he could not help it, and now he was her past. She could even feel a measure of compassion for him. Trapped into marriage he wasn't ready for, he did accept his responsibility that day on the steps of City Hall, when she offered him a last chance at freedom. How scared he must have been – a young student, poor all his life, with long medical training ahead, suddenly burdened with a wife . . . She had been concerned only with herself, she could not see his courage, his niceness. Now she remembers: As they part at the subway entrance, he puts his arms around her reassuringly, smiles weakly, and says: 'It'll work out, you'll see.'

And their marriage – it was not all unhappy, not at the beginning. She was able to recall the good days they had. There were not many, but they added up. When it got bad, he had escaped. She could see that now; he had fled from a contemptuous wife and indifferent children to women who gave him the admiration he craved. She saw that with sadness rather than with guilt.

Guilt was her mother's province; guilt was omnipotence. It took credit for what happened. It proclaimed self-importance; it assumed every action was noted, had effect.

As God's representative, her mother was connected to

418

Jesus. It probably kept her loneliness away. Isabel wished she had understood it sooner.

She wished she had understood her brother, who – unable to make contact with his wife – made it with authors long dead. How good it was of him to speak to Gregory on the phone that awful evening of the tabloid . . .

And Molly – trying so hard to become the woman she coveted.

All searching for contact with someone.

She too.

NOTES TO MYSELF

Brava, Isabel!

But to continue to feel alive, what will she do?

A man. She needs a man. There must be good men, loving men someplace, but Isabel wants to show me – what?

An ironic scene, in which she is 'the other woman' in someone else's triangle?

Or a date with a man who is in process of divorce, a man like her husband, whose unknown wife is at that moment, perhaps, wondering where he is, tracing his calls, searching through his desk?

This crazy-chain, daisy-chain of wounded women . . .

DRY RUN

She had dressed carefully, anxiously, the way she used to as a young girl before a date, but she was even less sure of herself now, more fearful of rejection. This was an important evening, a test for the future.

'Hi!' – he was properly casual, the gentleman caller, the potential lover, the possible Mr Right.

'Do come in, I'm glad to see you.' Her manners, polished by years of being wife and hostess, were automatic. 'What are you drinking?'

Perhaps for him, too, it was a significant date, a chance to reestablish himself as a desirable man. As he talked, she found herself playing the warm, sympathetic woman who knew better than anyone how traumatic the process of divorce was.

'And would you believe,' he was saying, 'she had the gall to make a fuss about some cockamamy coffee set she wanted?'

'No!' she shook her head incredulously, crossing her legs in the new black satin pants.

'She claims it was a wedding present for *her*, not me! She says she wants to sell it. Ever hear of such an act?'

'I know,' she nodded. 'It must be rough on you.'

'She's out to skin me alive, so I would have nothing left for myself or for anyone else.'

'For anyone else,' she echoed, faint hope stirring. Perhaps this may turn out to be the man for her, his problems like her own, except that they seemed to be in reverse.

'All she wants is to break me!' His voice was beginning to sound a bit like her husband's. 'She had me slaving for her all these years, never lifted a finger, never tried to understand my problems.'

As I am understanding them, her face was saying to him. She crossed her satin legs again. She wished he would get off the subject.

'After all I've done for her, seen her through her bladder and all. She's sucking me dry, she and her fucking lawyers. You know how much those fucking lawyers, excuse me, cost me?'

'I think I do. I myself – '

'Jealous,' he was saying, 'you wouldn't believe. Always snooping in my desk!'

'I know,' she kept nodding like a metronome. 'Some women are like that. But I think you'll find – '

'She thinks money grows on trees. She has no idea how hard I work for a buck.'

She made a sympathetic sound with her tongue. 'Can I freshen your drink?'

But he was tearing through the old terrain of his grievances. She might as well not have been there in her satin pants.

'The scenes she makes in front of the children, filling their ears with how rotten I am. Would you believe, she even tried a phony suicide? Blackmail is what. Well, she isn't getting away with it now, she's going to pay for all the – ' He stopped, suddenly aware of her sitting beside him, sympathetic in her black satin. 'Say,' he grinned boyishly, 'I must be boring you with all this.'

'Not at all,' she said. Where were the bright phrases she had rehearsed the night before? She had imagined their cozy conversation, the little candlelit restaurant, two lonely and attractive people about to form a meaningful –

'You don't mind if I make a phone call?' he asked. 'I think I have this dinner date, but I'm not sure. I certainly enjoyed our meeting again, the drinks and all.'

She supposed his first cautious step was to see how the drinking time went. If she passed the test, he would buy her dinner, take her to bed (just in case, she had that morning put her best lavender floral sheets on her bed), and eventually, they might even –

'I'm sorry,' he said as he returned from the telephone in the bedroom. 'I hoped we might dine together tonight, but I had this previous . . . Perhaps another time? Thanks a lot for the drinks, and for listening.'

'It's all right,' she murmured. *That's what we're here for*, rang crazily through her head. She had flunked the test. She couldn't make it even with this self-involved bore. He was going off to be with someone young and untraumatized by divorce, while she was left to wash the glasses and put away the wilting canapés she had so carefully prepared only an hour before.

'If there were more women like you, there would be less divorces in the world,' he said, pecking her on the cheek and reaching for his coat.

Fewer, you illiterate boor, fewer, not less! she thought with venom, but aloud she said: 'So nice to see you again; such a relief from all the running around just to sit and talk like this.'

'I'll call you,' he said. 'I'll call you real soon. Right now I'm up to my ears in litigation. I think she's gone off her rocker. She's not getting another penny out of me, the ungrateful bitch, excuse me. I shouldn't burden you with this. Well, be seeing you.' And he was gone.

What will I do with the bed sheets? she thought bleakly.

NOTES TO MYSELF

She's trying. God knows, it isn't easy, but she's trying.

Tries aids to youthifying. Aging — as irreversible as falling out of love.

Learns party tricks: To catch names when introduced — who married, who not. To leave early, to avoid: 'Would-you-mind-dropping-her-off-it's-on-your-way?' To answer, when asked if she's married: 'Currently not.' Was, will be, but just now, temporarily, not.

Tries bed-hopping. Use some of the men Nina mentioned in letter: the laugher, the washer, the man divorced from her namesake. Embroider them, invent others. Nina's *tout compris*, which these men expect.

Rearrange reality to find something that is true.

['BOOK']

I FUCK, THEREFORE I AM

After the shell shock, after the panic, after the period of lethargy, killing the enemy, time with TV soap operas, Isabel entered a new phase: obsessive pursuit of happiness. She spent a few helpless months compulsively bed-hopping. Or rather, it was the men who were hopping in and out of her bed. In swift succession on the pillow next to her (empty now) lay their heads: the bald, the blond, the tousled, the gray, yet none had left a mark. None of the bodies, sweet or cruel, had left a dent in her bed. To reassure herself that they had been, she made a list, one of many she kept, untitled, so that if she should die, she would betray no one. She listed only first names.

Lennie. Tall, fair, with his faint smile and faint eyes, he had called her 'utterly lovely.' Because of that (she was easily bought) she invited him for a drink. He told her a little about himself: a bad divorce, after a bad marriage. The wife's name, by a strange coincidence, was also Isabel, although she spelled it *Isabelle*. He avoided the name by calling Isabel 'Look,' or a slightly condescending 'My dear.' He put his drink down, put his arm around her, and kissed her. She was wearing her green blouse, her nipples outlined against the silk. (She had begun going braless.) Wordlessly they got up from her couch and walked slowly to her bedroom, slowly undressed, slowly got into bed. There was no hurry. He was white and lean and hairless as a statue as he lay still, waiting for her. But nothing. No matter how she tried, how she kissed and cooed and urged and sucked and rubbed and whispered and caressed – nothing happened. He lay like a cold white statue, like a drowned man, motionless and sexless. After a while he said: 'It's no use; I guess I'm tired tonight,' though they both knew that wasn't it, not it at all. He got up and dressed. As he left, he kissed her gently. 'I'm sorry,' he said, 'maybe another time,' but they both knew there would be no other time, ever.

She sometimes wondered if it was the other Isabelle who lay between them that night.

423

Chuck. With him, too, she had been in bed only once. He was quick and bright and funny, and he made her laugh. Better still, she made him laugh. Each set the other off; each was a bit wittier with the other, and therefore grateful to the other. They were so good together, making an island of gay quips at parties, having a jocular exchange after a bad movie, enjoying each other's cleverness across a restaurant table, that it was understood they would eventually find themselves in bed. Which they did. They were so amusing, there was such wit in bed, that sex disappeared. Evaporated. It was ridiculous to make love; they were quick to see the absurdity. It was impossible to make love. If only they could, they told each other, how fabulous it would have been. Well, sex wasn't everything, and their friendship was more valuable than any roll in the hay, wasn't it? Except that she never saw him again. The few times she called he was charming and amusing on the phone, but busy – involved at the office, or leaving on a trip. After a while she did not miss him; she even forgot his last name.

Pedro. For a short time the pillow next to her lay under the dark, bushy head of this ragged poet who had followed her, literally, from a party one evening, insisted on going upstairs with her, made instant and violent love to her, and dropped off to sleep as suddenly and soundly as an infant, while she stayed awake, puzzled and exhausted. After a while he awoke and went at her again, as eager as the first time, and again, and toward morning twice more. He smelled of rancid oil, garlic, and stale tobacco, he never took *no* for an answer, and there he was, night after night in her bed, fucking away. Her barefoot poet, she used to call him: he wore old sneakers with holes in them and no socks, no matter what the weather. Instead of a belt, a rope held up his trousers. He drove a Mercedes and wore a diamond ring. He had a distinguished black-and-white beard and the bluest, most ingenuous eyes. What poetry he wrote she never knew; he said it was too private for publication. He never talked of anything but their 'love bed,' he called it. After a while, bored and no longer grateful that he chose her, she told him a man she used to be in love with was moving in

424

with her. Pedro did not call again, although he did say, ruefully, that they had been the greatest in their love bed.

Fred. He used to preempt the pillow on his business visits to New York. She was pleased to see him, pleased when he left. They wrote letters to each other which sounded like book reviews. When he wrote that he was getting married, she felt but a fleeting pang. Now she would never have him in her bed, she thought. Which proved to be wrong, for he was as eager as ever, although his marriage was happy, to see her on his trips to New York.

In between there was Julian, who came regularly, every two weeks, like someone to service the grandfather clock running down. He wound her up and left until next time. She suspected that he rotated himself among some dozen ladies, offering each a night in turn. The two extra nights, perhaps, were for himself, to recuperate, or to masturbate, she thought uncharitably, and was ashamed. Julian was very nice, very clean. Just before sex, he would go to the bathroom, stark naked, leaving the door open. From her bed she could not help seeing him, totally unselfconscious and amiable as he conducted a conversation with her, standing at the sink, carefully washing his genitals before climbing into her bed. His ablutions were as efficient and unromantic as his punctual arrivals and departures. She rather liked him, and was sorry when he left for good. Left to live with someone in Florida. He sent her a Christmas card. 'Hi,' it said, 'Have a merry.'

Well, she didn't exactly have a merry. Not with him, nor with any of them, each with his own needs, his quirks, his pleasures. As a matter of principle, she would not go to bed with husbands of women she knew, but if they were divorced, she found that she learned a great deal more than she wanted to about their ex-wives. 'So that's what Helen likes!' she would think, or 'Poor Selma – no wonder she's so strident!'

She learned another thing: These ships that passed in the night, or rather, docked in her bed for the night, owed her nothing. On rare occasions she would receive flowers the next day, or a phone call. More often than not – nothing. They did expect, however, a good night's lodging in a comfortable bed, breakfast included. She provided them with her sheets, her orange juice, her cheek for the kiss at the door. And she accommodated each. It never occurred to her to have her own needs met; by this time she no longer even knew what they were. With each man she erased herself as neatly as she had always done with her husband. With each, she tried to learn his fantasy and step into it. She could be an innocent flower deflowered by a brute, an Amazon riding a man to frenzy, a poet, a mother, a whore. But through all the murmurs and gyrations, she felt empty, vacant. Only after the man left, for the day or for life, was she able to become herself again.

Yet it was good, after the divorce, to re-emerge, like a snapshot from the developing fluid, and to see herself through the eyes of a man who found her, for a while, desirable. It was her proof that she *was*, that at such a time for such a man she existed. The words remained; the mouths that had said them were forgotten.

She had never exercised her own choice, never pointed and said: 'It's you I want!' But when a man said that to her, she was grateful.

Afraid to lose him, she became anxious, subservient, a pale shadow of him, crushed by a frown, so that his own tensions grew, and with them his anger, and with it, his guilt and his restlessness. The more she tried to please him, the more he withdrew, until one day, with no warning, it seemed, she was alone once more. Until the next man chose her, and made her feel, for a while, alive.

NOTES TO MYSELF

Something not right in last paragraph. Isabel pulling against this scene. I intended her to be casual, obliging bed partner, but she has suddenly turned into frightened, emotional, insecure woman, clinging desperately to her man.

Keep me and Max out of it!

426

Dear Nina –

I haven't written to you all week because I was busy writing scenes for Isabel. Or rather, she's been telling me what to write.

Something strange has been happening to my book! I thought working on it would blot out my pain, but instead, it's transforming it. Whatever is going on (and I'm a part of it) is a mystery of the creative process, in which fictional characters take on a life of their own and lead the author to their own truth. This is what Isabel has been doing for me. I think I'm on the verge of some important revelations; important not just for the characters in my book.

I seem to be living the tenets of my Fiction Workshop. Remember, I used to say in writing, as in love, one mustn't fear to take risks? I've taken a few in both – with surprising results. I used to say fiction should shed new light on something known. This has been my insight into myself: I recognize things I must have known all along, but could not face.

I have been balancing between my life and Isabel's, simultaneously loving Max and hating Edgar; but I couldn't write the truth about her divorce until I had achieved my own. It was Max who helped me to divorce Charles. In rereading my diary of Max, I find so much joy in it, in the early happy pages, that I wonder how I could have forgotten the good days with Charles, at least, in the beginning. The madness of divorce has quite obliterated them.

When I allowed spite, what Varya calls *zloba*, to melt, the large space it had occupied could admit compassion. For Charles, who could not love, for Max, who tried so hard to love, and for myself. I could at last forgive myself, deny myself the guilt, my mother's scourge. I am no longer responsible. Like those newspaper notices by husbands separated from their wives, I am no longer responsible for the problems of others, or for the weather. That's quite a step, and Isabel has helped me make it.

Dear Nina, bear with me. This letter is full of *me*; I've been so self-involved because I'm excited about what's happening. I see the gradual changes in my book. What started as satire has somehow become sympathy. What started as anger has become understanding, awareness of the dragons that beset us all.

I speak of dragons and I think of Max. Who was it who said: 'If no one had learned to read, no one would fall in love'? I sure have learned to read! For all the pain, I'm glad of it.

Varya quotes a proverb: 'Paper is still; only pen moves.' Something is moving my pen, or my typewriter fingers; it's puzzling – and it's fascinating. I watch Isabel act out my fantasies and revenges, I see her trying to change, and I wonder what will become of her.

> Because non quo
> Has been her status,
> It's hard to know
> Just what her fate is!

But I'm betting on her. I hope you are, too.

Much love,
Jess

['BOOK']

NOTES TO MYSELF

How memory distorts: villains not as villainous, saints not as saintly.

Feelings changing.

Contempt I felt for Edgar I no longer feel for lonely little boy abandoned by his parents, brought up by rigid aunt, caught in game of 'dirty doctor' with little girl next door by her chastising mother. Little wonder. His need for furtive sex. Thrill of danger: being discovered. Taking chances with patients in office, scattering clues, exposing himself to detectives. His very choice of women. No goddess took him to her bed, so he had to settle for Rhoda and Janet and Dorian —

Understanding Edgar helps me see Charles differently. How could I have forgotten (refused to remember?) it was *I* who often turned my back to Charles in bed? Forgotten, too, our picnics in the country, New Year's party, Parents' Day in camp . . .

New thought: Maybe Charles really loved Laura? Maybe he loved young man with comb? Will never know.

Has he changed in last twelve years? Is he a different man — with a different woman?

Perhaps any woman can make of any man a monster or a saint.

If so — book on wrong track! Motivation wrong: Need for vengeance. Need for victimization. Characters distorted. Isabel, with her ostentatious sunglasses at dinner, her tyrannical suffering. Edgar . . .

Then what? Give up book? Abdicate now, two months before it's due?

No! I won't! Much that is good in it — but I need to find new truths in old scenes.

Whose truths?

429

[DIARY]

Is it possible it's only four months since his fabulous (there goes that word again!) surprise party?

In this diary, all my clinical observations and lists and figures and additions and subtractions mean less than a single page of pure feeling for Max. At such a time, on such a page, I was the happiest of women. It's recorded here, and nothing can erase it – not loss, not grief, which came later. Those pages remain Max's greatest gift to me.

During these last nine months – five with Max, four without him – there should have been some growth, if not a birth. In fiction, this can be a sudden, dramatic revelation. Only in fiction.

My own insights have been gradual, uncertain. There's much I still don't clearly see. Some things I must have known: that in my divorce from Charles I was my own victim. I didn't realize I was the victimizer, too. Max's 'the victim strikes again' – I understand it now. My self-effacement was as demanding as Teresca's narcissism. My role – as crucial as my husband's.

The characters in my book are beginning to show me where I have erred. I've got to listen to my characters.

May even have to start afresh at this eleventh hour. But that means there's a whole hour left, there is time.

To be alone again is not bad. It's cozy to feel the rug under my bare feet, to see Cat sitting stern as a statue on my messy desk, watching me as I write this. And in a couple of weeks Nina is coming, my good friend.

It's Friday, 10:15 in the evening, and I remember that I loved him.

NOTES FOR A SCENE

Having lost everything, Isabel is beginning to find herself.

Sees she had choices. Wrong choices were her own: wrong husband, wrong analyst, wrong lawyers. Even as a young girl, she fixed only on the frightened boy who had to be forced into marriage.

Is she ready now to make right decisions? To speak up for herself?

I sense some kind of dissatisfaction in her. She seems to be angry with me, accusing me of something. What does she want to tell me? If I could hear her –

ISABEL: You used me!

– *Of course I did. I'm a writer.*

ISABEL: You used me to mask the truth from yourself. The truth about yourself.

– *I was looking for your truth.*

ISABEL: You claim the wrong choices were mine. They were yours. You made me act out all the terrible things you wanted to do to your husband, and you made me suffer for it. How you made me suffer! Why didn't you let me have one normal, happy relationship with a man?

– *I was trying to show your distortions, your guilts and panics.*

ISABEL: I'm not the only one. Look what you did to Edgar!

EDGAR: You used me!

— What's this — a rebellion?

EDGAR: You made of me an unmitigated villain to justify yourself. To avenge yourself on Charles. No, don't say anything. You've said enough. Pages and pages. Now you just listen. I heard Isabel on the extension complain to one of her friends, when she was locked up in the bedroom, that I was having a ball. A ball? She had no idea what I was going through — because you didn't. Did you ever try to understand me?

— Yes, I did — about your childhood —

EDGAR: How do you suppose I felt when those detectives burst in on us, naked in bed? How do you suppose I felt being locked out of my own bedroom?

— She was in terror.

EDGAR: She was too full of self-pity to see *my* terrors. Terror of poverty. Terror of loneliness. She was interested only in my money. She cared nothing about my needs, my feelings, the demands of my profession. Don't interrupt. Shall I tell you what I hated most about her? Her unhappy face across the table.

— I'm not writing a book about happy marriages and healthy relationships. I'm describing one woman's experience during —

EDGAR: And you — you're no better! Because Charles called you extravagant, you made me a pathological miser! You blew up his one affair into a whole bunch of mine. His one letter from Laura into dozens in my desk that you photostated and stuffed into

432

those two bloody valises! And because you rejected Charles, you even made me impotent! Can you understand how a man feels about that?

— I was beginning to. If I didn't, you couldn't be saying this to me.

EDGAR: Trying to make me into a case history! I'm not a case history. I'm *me* — a human being.

MARCUS: You used us!

— Who else is here?

MARCUS: Me and Samuels. We represent the other attorneys.

— What are you accusing me of?

MARCUS: You got Isabel to choose the worst in our profession. And you yourself saw how she tied our hands: she hired us, fired us, changed her mind every other day, didn't let us proceed as we saw fit. She was one lousy client. Impossible woman!

DR KELLERMAN: A neurotic.

— You're here too? So you can talk?

DR K.: When necessary. I'm also speaking in defense of my profession. Your husband was a psychiatrist, so you were striking out at all of us, trying to be clever at our expense with those rhymes and fables. Your understanding was faulty. My reason for not seeing Isabel that time had to do with her therapy and not my fourteen dinner guests. That was the reason for my silence too. She was trying to force me, by her apparent

433

helplessness, by her intense suffering, to make her decisions for her.

— *She only wanted to be free of him.*

DR K.: You don't divorce a neurosis by divorcing a man. You know that about yourself.

— *I'm not on your couch! Besides, this isn't the way I wrote you.*

DR K.: This is the way I am. Did you understand *any* of the men in your book? Is there one good, decent man in it?

— *Well — let's see. The locksmith? The process server? Jim?*

JIM: What kind of role did you give me?

— *Everybody's getting into the act!*

JIM: You brought me in only to identify the snapshot and for Isabel to lean on me in court. What dimension did you give me?

— *You weren't a major character.*

JIM: That's not the point.

— *Are you all trying to rewrite my book for me?*

DR K.: What about the men you put in Isabel's bed?

PEDRO: She gave me the gate! I let her have the greatest time in our love bed, and she gave me the gate!

— *I was merely showing —*

FRED: Our letters were *not* like book reviews! We had an interesting literary correspondence. And what about all the good talks we had in bed, all the pleasures?

434

— You did get married, you know.

FRED: It could have been Isabel I married. I was ready for marriage. But she didn't *see* me. She just didn't *see* me.

LENNIE: No, she was nice. Only her name turned me off.

CHUCK: She tried too hard to be clever. To outdo me.

JULIAN: She didn't care for cleanliness.

— The purpose of that chapter —

DR K.: Think of the men in other chapters.

IRV: She kept me up half the night carrying on about a fire down the street!

DIVORCED MAN: A nice, sympathetic woman, but not my type.

JULIAN: You saw us only as fools, or worse.

FRED: You never saw us!

JULIAN: Made fun of us!

PEDRO: Dismissed us!

EDGAR: Made us monsters!

— Is this a mutiny? A mass protest?

FRED: You never gave us a chance!

— You're talking about Isabel. You're confusing me with Isabel!

MARCUS: You're passing the buck. It's *your* problem.

— That's Adams' line. He didn't even show? Nor Gross? No wonder.

DR K.: If that's your attitude toward men, how did
you expect Isabel to be loved? Look at your
own track record: romantic figures or clob-
berers. Or both.

— I'm *not in the book* — you *are.*

DR K.: You *are* the book.

— *I've been hearing a lot of gripes from the men here.
Anyone else?*

ISABEL: My mother.

— *Yes, what's* your *complaint?*

MOTHER: She so seldom came to see me.

— *She couldn't bear to see you in that shabby room.*

MOTHER: It was your influence. If not for you, she
would have. You made her mock my
faith. My belief in God. She didn't know
the miracles that came to pass. She
didn't know how much I loved her.

— *She must have known, because I do.*

ISABEL: Because I loved my own children.

— *The children! Let them speak.*

ISABEL: No, please! Keep them out of this.
They've been hurt enough.

— *IT'S ONLY A STORY!*

DR K.: Look at all the pain you handed out.

— *I don't have to listen to this from a paper
psychiatrist I invented!*

DR K.: Precisely. These insights are yours. It's you
we're talking about. We're in a book, but
you're out there, living. Will writing Isabel
change you? Then it makes sense, then it's
worth it.

— Let's go back to you and me, Isabel. What is it you want?

ISABEL: You made me into a puking, weeping, sniveling creature with no wit, no spunk. You condemned me to being a constant victim. Rejected by my own children. Humiliated at Dorian's. Skinned in court. The only thing you ever gave me was the 'Worm Turns' scene, and you even took that away from me!

— All right, Isabel. What are you asking me for?

ISABEL: You yourself admitted I'm trying.

— It takes time to change. It took me twelve years and a Max. All you can do now is show that you're on your way. How would you like to do it? What scene would you like to play?

THE SCENE

One evening, a man who had brought Isabel home from a party insisted on going up to her apartment with her. She was tired; she wanted to be alone.

'No,' she said, 'I'm sorry.'

'Why not?' he asked. 'You some kind of prude? What's the harm?'

She shook her head.

'What are you afraid of?' he persisted. 'Just for a nightcap. Come on, what do you say?'

'I say' – she hesitated – 'Boo!' she said, and again, 'I say Boo!'

At his bewildered face she burst into laughter, free, purging, bubbling laughter. It was contagious; he began to laugh too.

'You win,' he said. 'I'll call you tomorrow.'

'Yes, I win,' she repeated. 'I win.'

WEDNESDAY NOVEMBER I

It was inevitable that I should run into him. I was crossing the street near Bloomingdale's when suddenly I saw Max crossing, coming toward me. Too late to turn back. No place to duck, to hide: the lights were with us. We continued to walk toward each other. For the briefest moment we glanced at each other. He pretended not to recognize me; I too – and we walked on, split-second strangers.

He looked thinner. Suntanned, grim. Once we passed each other, I had to fight the temptation to turn around. I walked stiffly to the corner, turned it, like a wound-up mechanical toy, and only then, as I passed a store window, stopped to see my reflection in it. Why hadn't I worn my better coat? Why hadn't I fixed my hair before I left the house?

When I got back I couldn't work. I kept thinking of all the things I might have said to him, in passing. But why, what for? He chose not to recognize me – let it be.

I remembered the woman he crossed the street to avoid when we were walking together. 'Hell hath no fury like a woman scorned,' I think he said. Not I; I feel only vast sadness. I am now 'the other woman' in his history.

It's truly over. We will never be together again.
Requiescat.

LATER: This evening Varya dropped in.

'I saw Max today,' I said. 'We didn't recognize each other.'

'Akh,' she waved him away. 'Is Rrawshian saying, Lapochka: "Goat on hill look taller than cow in meadow."'

I burst out laughing. 'That's *funny*!'

Varya looked puzzled, but she laughed too, pleased to see me happy.

'All this time,' I said, 'while Mr Right has been grazing in the meadow, all the pinecones kept falling on my head?'

'*Da, da, shishki,*' she agreed, laughing companionably.

'In other words, I've been sitting down in a galosha?'

'Galosha,' she nodded.

'That's funny!' I laughed so hard, tears rolled down my cheeks. 'That's really funny!'

A great release, that laughter. It helped me do some serious thinking when Varya left.

Nine months since I began to write in this diary. Nine months of Max. Before that – blank pages.

The joyful days remain. As for the rest – 'Your pain shall be a music to your string.' And that shall be my book.

['BOOK']

THE DIPLOMA

Each day became more possible than the previous one; each brought its small comforts, small triumphs. She could unscrew tops of jars by herself, reach the highest shelf in her closet, exercise her own taste, make decisions. She discovered an anagram for her name: 'Isabel is able.' Isabel was also witty and nice.

She had a job in a neighborhood bookshop, and she was enrolled in an evening course on book marketing at the New School. She barely managed, but she paid the rent.

She worried about money, she worried about her children, but she was calmer than she had been for a long time. When friends contemplating divorce talked to her, she listened. She listened patiently to their ambivalences and rationalizations; she listened to their expectations and fantasies:

'I'd like to meet an interesting man now, it would make the divorce easier. Maybe I'll live in Europe for a year; I've always wanted to travel. Or open a little boutique on Madison Avenue. Or go back to my painting. My husband will take care of everything. He'll come to dinner. He'll be a better father. My lawyer promised me two thirds of his salary. At last, I'll *begin* to live!'

Isabel listened.

She no longer had to seek love, plead for love, buy love with pain and guilt. She was able to *feel* it.

Sometimes she found herself on the other end of the telephone, hers the voice of comfort in the void. She was the unsung savior to a newly-divorced, panic-stricken friend. 'I know,' she would say, 'it's lousy, I know, but it will get better. You can't believe me now, but it will. I'm here, you're not alone.'

She had retrieved from her lawyers her two valises heavy with evidence and burned the now needless papers in the building incinerator. There was a faint whiff of smoke, but the valises were in good condition – and useful.

Edgar had receded. Still the compulsive list maker, she added up, one day, the number of days and nights of their marriage. Twenty-nine years = 10,585 days and nights. That was a lot of days and nights to be married. Yet now she found it difficult to remember his face. She had thrown out all the snapshots of him except those when he was young, with the children as babies. Surely, she should be able to recall what a man looked like with whom she had spent 10,585 days and nights. More, if you counted the days and nights (nights mostly) before their City Hall wedding.

But when she saw him, she did not, at first, recognize him. She caught an unexpected glimpse of him as he was leaving Bloomingdale's. He nodded curtly, and hurried on.

Why is he so old? she thought in dismay.

In the mail the next day she received her divorce papers. They ordered, adjudged, and decreed that the marriage heretofore existing between the parties was dissolved. 'Final Judgment of Divorce,' it was called. 'My diploma,' she said to herself. The circle was complete.

Dear Nina —
I've been conducting a curious internal dialogue with my
characters. I think I have to rewrite some of them and
apportion the blame more justly. I seem to have got my
villains and my victims mixed.

Of course it's not the characters who are changing. I still
have doubts, angers, regrets; there's still pain, but it's a
distant pain, like someone else's, read in a book. Remember, I once wrote you about the road not taken? But it
means a road *was* taken; I'm on it; I'm here. Truth is
what I'm after. I've reversed Varya's proverb to read:
'Happiness is good, but truth is better.'

Why can't we have both?

Varya is beside herself at the prospect of meeting you.
She's already cooking up a Russian storm that's waiting
for you in her freezer. Your arrival and her daughter's
pregnancy (yes, Nancy-Anastasia went and followed
Varya's prediction!) are the two most talked about events
currently in her life.

She has bought a copy of *The Sad Merry-Go-Round* for
you to autograph. Although she says she has never
learned to read English, she loves your book.

Me, I'm dusting the extra chair in my Fiction Workshop,
in the hope that you'll visit – and maybe address the class.
My students want to touch you, to have it come off on
them, like the powder of success you once mentioned. A
few have been working hard; occasionally I come across a
paper I find exciting and rewarding. I say so in my
comments. Why haven't I mentioned this to you before? I
suppose praise doesn't make good copy. Satiric thrusts
are more interesting, though less just.

Yet *your* humor, dear Nina, is the best there is! You

know how to laugh at yourself, which is what I'm learning to do. I can laugh now even at things that used to be full of pain. In my diary of divorce, my shorthand of anguish, I noticed an entry: 'anal fun.' What kind of sexual frolic was that? I wondered, until I realized it was an abbreviation for 'analyst's funeral.'

As you see, I'm healing.

I've been doing a lot of thinking and a lot of feeling lately. Walpole may be right, but I go along with Varya: 'A life to live is not a field to cross.' Good proverb, clear, specific. A life to live is very hard to do. Yet I've done it, I've lived it, the good days and the bad. All the uneven, disparate, fragmentary experiences of my life *are* my life, just as those bits of scenes make your film, just as the sketches in my manuscript are my novel.

In the ultimate column, my Credits outweigh my Debits. It's Varya's loud *Yes* against my mother's *No*, and Varya wins.

I've learned from my book and from my life. I know that I'm not a statistic, that I'm no one's catspaw, that there are no miracles, that laughter is better than tears, that morning is wiser than evening, and that love is as strong as hate. Stronger.

I've learned that most suffering is unnecessary and most endings are irrelevant; that XYZ is the last confidence; and that man is the measure of his own cross.

I know that my love for Max was as real as any fantasy, and that fiction can certainly be truer than life.
And I know that you were right when you said that to love is more important than to be loved. I was my best with Max, so now I know my value.

I tried to explain it to Gilda.

'Why?' she asked.
'Because I loved him.'

444

'That con man? That crook, that cheat, that hypocrite, that liar? That swindler and that shark?'

'Doesn't matter.'

'But *he* didn't love you!'

'He made me feel he did, and when he left, the feeling remained.'

'Is that enough?'

'Much more important is that *I* loved *him*.'

'That crook, that cheat, that con man?'

'Whoever he was, whatever he was, he made me feel love.'

'What's so important about that?'

'I love, therefore I am.'

I don't think Gilda understood; I'm sure you do.

Look at that – in my book I began to write about hate, and here I ended up writing about love!

A couple of days ago I saw Max. He crossed the street, stepped into my past, and became part of my history.

What I'm saying, dear Nina, is that you needn't worry about me. I have survived my divorce twelve years ago; I have survived another now – a simpler severance, rounder, cleaner, because I like myself better.

And this morning in the mail came an invitation to a dinner party, undoubtedly to meet a man who is 'not so tall but a widower,' or his reasonable facsimile. And I will say yes. And if I sense a killer, I will run.

I won't be writing to you again; this is my last letter to San Francisco. Soon we'll be together. Dear Nina – there's so much for us to say. You don't suppose we've talked ourselves out in our letters?

In the meantime, my book is waiting. I don't know if I'll be able to revise it, but I feel hopeful.

All I need is to look at my characters and myself with new eyes.

For me and for my book, dear friend,
It's the beginning, not the end.
I'll speak the truth . . . Well, more or less.
So – till we meet –

Your loving
Jess